JOSIAH DEKANU

INEVITABLE
COINCIDENCE

INNERLACE PUBLICATIONS
Copyright © 2017 by Josiah Dekanu
InnerLace Publications LLC
Syracuse, New York 13207

ISBN: 978-1-7326716-0-7

Published in the United States by InnerLace Publications, Syracuse New York.

InnerLace is a registered trademark.

Front cover illustration by Yael Abraham

For information regarding special discounts for bulk purchases, please contact
sales@innerlace.com

We want to hear from you –
ICLondon_feedback@innerlace.com

To my manager, editor and the
love of my life,
Daelene
Rebecca, *my inspiration*
Miryah, *my joyful healing*
Joelle, *my motivation*
Seth, *my pride*
Nethaniel, *my purview*
Mykal, *my hope*
and my soul resides with **Micaiah**

Chapter 0 ~ *Four days later*

CHIEF SUPERINTENDENT PHILIPS OF Scotland Yard made his way quietly through the vacant corridors of city hall. The building, suspiciously empty, showed no signs of the usual hustle and bustle he had come to expect when gracing London's central nervous system. Only the monotonous drone of a distant copy machine permeated the silence.

Approaching the only cracked door in the corridor, "Mr. Mayor?" he called out. The lights off— apparently the heater as well, "Mr. Mayor?"

"Yes, Chief, come in," the mayor answered from an inner office.

Philips glanced at the vacant reception desk as he made his way across the room. "Where's Greta?"

"It's Saturday, Chief."

"Is it?" Having had no sleep the night prior, it was little surprise the chief's internal clock hadn't registered the day yet. "So, none of your deputies will be present then?"

The mayor looked up from a newspaper, a grimace set on his face. He sternly motioned to the seat across from him. Philips obediently sat and shifted uncomfortably in the chair unprepared for an open ass-chewing. He knew all too well that this mayor— though always the politician— would have no problem speaking his mind in private.

"I assure you, Philips, there will be plenty of time later to meet with the mayoral deputy staff, I am certain the Yard's attentions will be required far beyond the reach of this office in the coming days." The mayor's expression was tense.

"I suspect you're right, Mr. Mayor."

The mayor folded his arms and pushed back in his chair, his exasperation apparent. "Another terrorist attack in London this year is bad enough, Philips, but come now! What happened last night? We agreed to contain this."

"Yes, sir, we did… and great efforts were made— are still being made…" the chief considered how to best appraise yet appease him.

The mayor frowned, "The media is breathing down my neck on this one, Chief! I certainly would not have called you here before 8 AM on a Saturday if it were otherwise, would I have? And that tyrant from the Register Guard? What the hell happened there?!"

"I must have missed the morning paper, sir."

"Yes, yes, I suspect you did!" The mayor snatched the paper off his desk and waved it fervently in the man's face. "And the evening news? I assume you missed that as well because you were TOO BUSY MAKING IT!"

"Yes… right, right," Philips sat straight in his seat, "you're referring to the Guard exclusive. We have our men on that now, sir. We are very aware the press had the up on us with the investigation."

"Media fallout is expected, but damn all! I thought we caught the terrorists?!"

The chief hesitated, "Yes, they were all subdued, sir… but problem is, we didn't take them down."

Perplexed, "What do you mean, WE didn't take them down? Who did?"

"It appears we have a vigilante on our hands."

Momentarily dumbfounded, the mayor stared at the chief superintendent. "Please tell me you have him in custody?" He feared he already knew the answer.

"Afraid not, Mayor," the chief answered with regret, "he disappeared in the crowd. But we are collaborating with MI6 and the Prime Minister's office. In fact, I just left SIS at the crime lab."

The mayor took a deep breath, "Are you telling me that some unknown person took down the terrorists by himself and then just vanished?"

Philips stared back blankly.

"Who the hell is this guy, Philips?"

Chief Philips glanced to the floor. "That certainly is the question, isn't it, sir?"

ACT I

CRAWL

Chapter 1

"EXCUSE ME, MADAM...? Madam?" The flight attendant reached across the gentlemen in the aisle seat to tap the shoulder of the woman seated next to him.

Turning slowly, the woman could see the attendant's mouth moving. She removed her earpiece as the flight attendant repeated, "You will need to shut off your phone for takeoff, please."

With an audacious smile, the woman in 21F lifted the armrest between her and the aisle seat and leaned across the man seated next to her. Stretching, she braced herself with a hand upon his knee and extended her iPhone within inches of the other woman's face. "See? My phone's in airplane mode."

The flight attendant stepped back and stood upright in the aisle. She smiled almost pleasantly, then proceeded to address the now presumed couple, "Thank you, I see that. But as the captain has just announced, all phones must be completely off during both takeoff and landing— and while in Israeli airspace." The man in seat 21G remained wide-eyed and motionless, pushing himself back in his upright seat. "Please shut down your phone now," the attendant continued, "and the captain will let passengers know when it's all right to turn them back on."

"Fine." The woman reluctantly turned her phone away and began to slowly run through more than a dozen open applications, dramatically shutting each one down individually. She absently returned to a seated position situating herself comfortably with one leg bent beneath her, her foot tucked between the seats and slightly under the man's thigh. Her phone, still inches above his lap, had finally shut off. Then with a whip, she tucked it neatly into the magazine pouch, glanced toward the window, and returned the headphones to her ears showing no apparent interest in the resident of 21G.

The man sighed, closing his eyes in a futile attempt to sleep. He tried to focus on the feel of the plane, on the purr of the engines.

Having just settled his thoughts, his attention was drawn to a commotion a few rows ahead in the first-class section; a passenger had abruptly risen from her seat and opened the overhead compartment. She was attempting to pull something from her luggage.

A man in an airline uniform unbuckled and rushed to the woman's aid, "Please take your seat, madam, we can't taxi until you do."

"Leave me alone," she protested flustered, "you don't understand!" She frantically began to fuss with her carry-on.

As calmly as the attendant could manage without sounding patronizing, he quietly pleaded with the irrational woman, "Ms. Adams, if you can't take your seat, we'll be obliged to remove you from the plane."

Immediately slamming the bin above her head, "You can't make me leave!" she snapped. "Don't tell me what to do!"

The woman was clearly distraught, but it was the contradictions in her actions that caught 21G's attention. She was an attractive woman, meticulously dressed; her voice potentially pleasing, her posture exuding a measure of poise. Yet her demeanor was frazzled and confused, the behavior clearly out of character for this woman— especially this woman. The man knew her, recognized her. In fact, everyone did.

The flight staff, half star-struck themselves, scurried to join the attendant in trying to get the delicate situation under control. Voices undiscernible in the hushed commotion revealed little more than the celebrity's stubborn reluctance to be assisted and her refusal to be calmed. Defiantly turning away from the flocking attendants, the woman caught eyes with the man in 21G.

At first glance, she appeared strangely captivated. Whatever her situation was, it seemed to instantly change. Becoming completely still, she stared as if she knew him. Frozen in the moment, there was a mysterious silence followed by an indisputable expression in her eyes— not one of pleasure, but rather as if he were someone she didn't want to see; or more likely, someone she didn't want to be seen by.

The apparent recognition made the resident of 21G uneasy. After an uncomfortable amount of time he was able to shift his eyes away. But out the corner he continued to watch Ms. Adams. She unexpectedly conceded to the flight staff's barrage of assurances and took her seat as if nothing had happened.

21G sat there brooding, his brow furrowed. He didn't want to make more of the exchange than it most likely had been. *It's nothing… nothing to do with you,* he told himself. *She's a famous actress, she doesn't know you. And you have nothing to do with her situation. Besides, there are PLENTY of people already involved. How many first-class flight attendants are there anyway?* The man tentatively leaned back, unconsciously counting the number of uniforms.

He must have finally drifted off because after what had seemed like only moments, he found himself rubbing his eyes as the dinner cart made its way to the front of the plane. He briefly pondered how he'd missed take-off and the first round of beverages.

"Was this your first visit to Israel?" The man was summoned by passenger 21F.

"Excuse me?"

"Was this your first visit to Israel?" she repeated.

"No, it wasn't, I…"

"It was mine. My first time, that is," she announced. "It was actually my first visit to Asia. Did you know Israel's in Asia? The Middle East is in Asia."

The man nodded.

"You know, I almost didn't come. EVERYONE said it was too dangerous, but I came anyway," she boasted.

"Everyone? Really?" He smiled pleasantly. "You must be very brave."

"Oh, it was nothing, really. In fact, it was almost disappointing. I thought I would at least see a tank or a missile or a riot— something."

"Well, there are some very nice points of interest. Military memorials. No riots, though… unless you call hundreds of exuberant tourists on a time schedule a riot. But there are places where you can catch a glimpse of a tank or two, even sit on one."

"Yes, yes, I know. I went. But it's not the same," she pouted. "My name is Casey, by the way."

The man nodded and tipped an imaginary hat, "I'm Micah."

The young, blond-haired woman smiled and stretched out a well-manicured hand. Biting the inside of his lip, the man offered his hand in return. But instead of the anticipated shake, his hand was quickly snatched palm side up and held tightly by the overly-comfortable young woman.

After an awkward inspection, "This is weird," she commented, staring intently at the man's upturned hand. "How old are you?"

"Excuse me?" Micah was getting the impression he'd be saying that a lot if he embarked on conversation with Casey.

Casey studied his youthful face; bright blue eyes framed by dark brown hair with salt and pepper highlights. His boyish features showed signs of experience etched around his eyes and corners of his mouth. He was a handsome man she was certain couldn't be forty. She frowned. "This is strange," she said. "According to your palm, you've already died— twice." She held him with an accusatory stare less than five inches from his face. Personal space seemed to be a foreign concept to Casey.

Micah almost chuckled until he realized the seriousness in her expression. He quickly altered his emerging grin into a puzzled look of interest.

Opening his mouth to reply, he closed it again upon hearing raised voices from behind the curtain near the first-class restroom. Although the bulkhead curtain was now drawn closed, being seated in the first row of the economy cabin, he was able to stretch his leg forward and move aside the heavy blue fabric. With just a peak, he spotted a disproportionately frustrated Ms. Adams having to explain her need to use the restroom to an entourage of flight attendants. The escalating conversation wafted down the aisle.

"The fasten seatbelt sign is on, Ms. Adams, we need you to take your seat. Are you alright? You seem extremely distraught..."

"I'm FINE!" she yelled. Micah jarred in his seat with the simultaneous burst of turbulence that seemed to extenuate the adamancy of her claim.

Ms. Adams proceeded to aggressively push past the attendants, the plane violently shook in emphasis to her movements. The lights flickered and the engine raced. Eyes wide, *Is she doing that?* Micah thought. He squinted to see the woman more clearly. Immediately another bump of turbulence hit accompanied by an unmerited sense of terror in his gut. A brief sense of nausea caused Micah to close his eyes.

The plane suddenly surged forward and roughly jutted back. The craft bumped with a staggering dip; a high-pitched whine squealed throughout the cabin. A drastic dive accompanied the noise.

Losing altitude quickly, Micah white-knuckled the armrest. His foot braced the bulkhead partition. It required all his strength to maintain an upright seated position; the sudden g-force caused his teeth to clinch. Short exhale bursts only, it felt as if oxygen had fled the cabin. He became light head fearing he would soon fall unconsciousness.

"Are you alright?" Casey tapped him on the shoulder.

The normality of Casey's question and the reality of her touch was bewildering, slowly pulling him from his heightened state. Straightening his back he opened his eyes. "Excuse me?"

"Are you alright?" she repeated. She sat precociously upon one knee, engaging. Still holding his hand she impatiently awaited his attention, poised to read his past and future.

Micah discreetly glanced about the economy cabin; the lights were stable, the passengers undisturbed. "Ah, it was nothing," he said, clearing his throat. "Just a bit nauseous."

"Airsick?" Readjusting his hand with a well-timed, sensual caress, "or was it possibly my influence?"

The man raised a brow, "Your influence?"

She smiled coyly, "Well, I've been known to be…" pausing to consider the fitting word, "I wouldn't go so far as to say 'psychic', but I would say 'extremely perceptive'. It can effect some people differently."

"Hmm, interesting." Micah forced an intrigued smile. "So, you believe in such things?"

"Oh, yes!" she proclaimed with enthusiasm. "There are other-worldly things happening around us all the time!"

The man's eyes narrowed slightly causing Casey to laugh. "You'd be surprised!" she said. "I'm just in-tune with such frequencies more than most." But unable to decipher his expression she casually released his hand. "Why? You don't believe?"

He attempted to stifle a chuckle, "Undecided, I'd say." If not for the strange, potentially serious situation developing in the forward cabin, Micah would have laughed at the irony. Casey (a self-proclaimed, palm-reading psychic) was completely oblivious to the fact that the man she was seductively attempting to impress was at that moment contemplating a very real 'other-worldly' storm brewing a few rows ahead— one that was obnoxiously taunting to take down the plane. Or so it seemed.

Micah's eyes shifted toward the disturbing commotion in first-class. He tried to reason away the chill in the air and the strange turbulence that had accompanied the actress's movements— the frightful illusion which had become shockingly real. But in spite of himself, he couldn't dismiss his own unease nor the hair standing up on the back of his neck.

Ms. Adams was both angry and clearly afraid, the volume of her hysterics rising way above normal. With the aircraft's white noise it shouldn't even have been physically possible for him to hear her rantings much less the muted words of comfort from the flight staff. The anxiety apparent in Ms. Adam's manner was genuine; she was terrified of something. Something dangerous. Something real. And whether physical or metaphysical, whatever it was, the outcome could likely be the same— real. *There's obviously more to Ms. Adams than the tabloids suggest.*

"I'm retired," Micah muttered, his reluctance turning to annoyance. Still shaking with adrenaline, he ran his hands through his hair stretching the skin tight across his skull.

This was not unfamiliar territory. On the contrary. His mundane life of solitude was intentionally well-crafted to avoid such 'annoyances'. But now, if there was even a chance that this woman's fears could physically manifest and pose a threat to the plane or its passengers, he could no longer remain a mere spectator. With a heavy sigh, he politely addressed Casey, "Will you please excuse me?"

Unbuckling his seatbelt, he rose to his feet and moved forward through the curtain.

∗   ∗   ∗   ∗   ∗

Fighting her way to the restroom, Ms. Adams braced herself on passing seats. The sound of crashing metal against the shell of the aircraft as if it were being ripped apart heightened her panic. She watched in terror as the outer windows appeared to crack one by one, ice instantly forming on the inner glass. *This isn't real, it isn't real... I know this isn't real!* She failed to convince herself.

The passengers' faces flashed in the strobing cabin lights; their expressions horrified and screaming in the dark, returning to calm and silent in the light. The images were warped and changing. "Just let me get to the bathroom!" she pleaded close to tears.

The desperation in Ms. Adams' voice seemed to jolt the plane with a dramatic drop. A nearby flight attendant's eyes widen in horror grabbing a seat to steady herself— a reaction the actress could not reconcile. *Oh, my god, we ARE going to crash!*

Ms. Adams senselessly pushed forward singularly focused on the restroom stall. She was determined to lock herself in it and wait for either her demise or (more believably) to awake sedated in a rubber room.

∗   ∗   ∗   ∗   ∗

Once again engulfed in the chaotic storm, Micah fought to keep his balance— the floor shimmied, the sound of stressed steel echoed. He calculated his last steps to the restroom door, looking away so as to time his hand reaching the handle seconds before the woman's would.

Although Micah couldn't get passed the real sense of danger that kept his feet moving forward, still he hesitated. Before changing his mind, a violent burst of turbulence struck and caused the petite actress to lunge into him. He grabbed the door handle to catch himself.

The moment they touched, the shrilling wind outside silenced, the plane settled. Ms. Adams watched as the dimmed lights returned to full strength and heard the cabin bell tone indicating the captain had turned off the fasten seatbelt light. Attendants were handing out dinner trays.

Fervently grasping the man's arm, the woman frantically darted her eyes about the plane. Heart racing, it took her a moment to catch her breath. She blinked hard trying to clear her head— but the problem was, she was already focused.

Although unusually vivid, this was far from the first time one of her episodes had brought her to such a panicked state. The difference this time was the way it had ended. The storm was over, completely over. She, and everything around her, at peace. No winding down, no meditating solitude, just over. Not only did the mundane behavior of patrons and staff indicate as much, but the temperature of the cabin had warmed. And more obviously, her oppression had lifted and she could breathe normally. Slowly composing herself, the drastic change made Ms. Adams question what was real even more.

Still holding the man's arm, she was left in an awkward situation. She reconciled it was at first to catch her balance, then possibly to use it to push him aside so she could barricade herself in the stall. But neither explained why she hadn't released him. That, she didn't know, either. She was certain she was obliged to apologize or at least make a friendly gesture, but the stranger just stood there. He was neither angered nor pleasant. Unlike the British Airline staff who had been attempting to humor and calm her, this man was just there, neither eager to use the restroom nor to relinquish it.

Through the weight of her thoughts Micah spoke. "Can you hear that?" he asked quietly.

She gave him an odd look. Not knowing what to say, she tried listening. There was nothing to hear. "Hear what?" she finally asked.

"Nothing."

She returned a blank stare.

"Nothing," he repeated. "It's the hum of the engine, the sound of the wind. It's like deafening silence. Some people can't stand it, but I sing out loud on a plane and no one beyond five feet can hear me. Two hundred people within a hundred feet and no one can hear me." Micah managed a smile, "And I don't have to hear anything I don't want to hear, either."

She listened again in spite of herself. Why was she entertaining this nonsense after all she had just been through? Maybe it was a civil acknowledgement that she had forcibly bumped into him? Maybe a subconscious excuse for why she still hadn't relinquished his arm? She honestly didn't know why. So she continued to listen— and the roar of nothing over-took her.

Her eyelids felt heavy. *Sleep,* she thought. Ms. Adams hadn't slept in so long; uninterrupted, restful sleep. She closed her eyes and began to instantly drift, teetering a bit toward the man.

Surprised, she shook it off with a hard blink and gave him a bewildered stare; the difference between right then and only moments before was so drastic her eyes began to water. It was like a headache gone that she hadn't even known she'd had until it lifted.

She couldn't take her eyes off the stranger. His piercing blues showed neither compassion nor pity, they were near emotionless. He looked right through her as if she were a book to be read— or, more likely, had already been.

Instant feelings of guilt and self-consciousness rose up inside her then fled just as quickly. Contempt turned to contentment; her embarrassment, strangely into a sense of confidence. Not the confidence of her position nor her accomplishments nor her beauty that that earned; that didn't seem to matter and those eyes didn't care. There was something growing inside her; something she couldn't put her finger on nor from where it was coming.

Hand still gripping the man's forearm, "Who are you?" she asked quietly with profound sincerity.

He answered with equal sincerity, "I was just thinking the same about you."

"Me?"

Micah smiled and merely opened the restroom door, motioning for her to proceed. "I can wait," he said.

Ms. Adams suspiciously narrowed her eyes but obediently entered the restroom.

∗ ∗ ∗ ∗ ∗

Locking the door, the woman was hesitant to look in the mirror next to her, she hadn't liked what she'd seen in it of late. But turning slowly she found her eyes surprised. Maybe it was the lighting, maybe she was just tired— but looking back at her was the child she had once known, someone she hadn't seen in a very long time. Her mascara run slightly, her makeup streaked; but underneath, a face she recognized— a hopeful youth with endless possibilities.

She tucked her thick chestnut hair behind her ears and moistened a towel. She wiped off one strip of makeup at a time. Like a wet washcloth on a steamed mirror, she revealed herself inch by inch. A few softened wrinkles were visible and she smiled; for the first time she saw her gentle aging as a relief from the façade that took so much effort to uphold. She saw them as battles of youth won instead of lost. She admired the maturity they revealed. The war was over and she had gotten to the other side unscathed, natural, real.

She wasn't old, barely forty. But in an industry where remaining twenty-five forever dictated career survival, forty (for a woman, especially) was ancient. Her best years were behind her having made her claim to fame twenty years before and been able to ride the coattails for a decade. The upside was that once you'd made a name for yourself, most people didn't even notice when you fell out of the limelight. As long as your picture hit the tabloids on occasion, you were still a celebrity. Her unconventional, on-again-off-again marriage to a man over thirty years her senior, guaranteed that.

The industry, however, was improving for mature actresses, but the option to transition from romantic lead to a more maternal or matronly role was beyond her consideration. *Victoria Adams, a mother?* She gave the reflection a wry smile. Having had no experience with it herself, she couldn't fathom it… or at least had never thought to try.

But at that moment it did cause her to remember her own mother; her mother's sacrifice for her and her siblings. Her eyes widened. What Victoria had once abhorred as weakness (forsaken talent and potential given to a relentless man who worshiped his children at the expense of his wife), she now strangely saw as purpose, a gift, a well-lived life. And the one thing she lacked.

Where is all this coming from? She looked to the ceiling, the four small walls, the mirror. *Is this some magical chamber?* She listened to the deafening sound of the engines, the wind, the loud silence the stranger had mentioned.

She had always hated planes; the dehydration, the crowded surroundings. Claustrophobic prisons— a death trap. Now somehow the imprisonment— the no-where-to-go, out of control, disconnected world without phone or internet— was a fortress of solitude. *For the next four hours there is nothing I can do. My problems are unresolvable, unsolvable and unavailable. I'm unavailable,* she realized. *If this plane did go down…* the thought surprisingly made her giddy not fearful, *my problems would no longer exist!*

"Who the hell was that guy?" she asked aloud. "What did he do, hypnotize me?" She tried to remember, "Nothing? NOTHING. Something about not being able to hear or not needing to hear?"

She took a deep breath, "He's probably just crazy. That's got to be it." Beginning to rave, "Or maybe he's a psycho— a stalker?! Yeah, that would just figure. Or, hell, maybe he's a demon… or an angel! We just left the Holy Land so why not?!" her voice bitter and sarcastic, rising in volume.

Victoria heard herself ranting and realized she'd been speaking quite loudly—to no one. In a moment of self-consciousness she panicked, grabbing the counter edge to stop herself from shaking or succumbing to the anger. She closed her eyes and exhaled, "God, I'M the one who's crazy."

She shook off the moment painfully and her eyes began to burn with unshed tears. She lowered her head, "What I've put my family through."

∗   ∗   ∗   ∗   ∗

"Sir, are you seated in first-class?"

Micah shook his head.

"You need to use the restrooms in your assigned area," the attendant insisted. "Please return to your cabin."

Micah nodded and returned to 21G.

Stepping up to his row he found the contents of Casey's purse strewn across his seat. He looked down the aisle (now blocked by the food cart) and saw no chance of retreat to the econo-class restrooms.

"I got you the chicken, I assumed you were a carnivore," Casey invited.

This is going to be a long flight, he thought. Smiling politely he answered, "Thank you."

Scooping up her bag so that Micah could take his seat, she asked, "Are you staying in London?"

"I'm in Britain for the week but no plans to visit London this trip."

"Oh, you should always carve off some time for London! London is a party town."

"One of my favorites," he chuckled.

"My name is..."

"Casey," Micah finished.

"Right. And you're Michael."

"Sure."

Gathering up the rest of her belongings, she stopped at the last item. She looked directly at Micah meeting his eyes, "Can I have a sip of your water?" she asked. "I've already finished all of mine and forgot to take my pill." She proceeded to open a small pink compact. "What day is it today?"

Micah glanced at the compact. *Seriously?* He blurted a comical exhale then raised his eyes as if to find the answer in the luggage compartment, "Uh… um, Tuesday, I believe."

"Tuesday." She rotated the compact with a single click and popped out the next tiny blue pill. "All accounted for," she grinned with a bat of her eyes.

Micah handed Casey his unopened water. "That's always a relief, I suppose."

"Oh, you have no idea."

"Every day's a bit like either Christmas morning or a Halloween haunted house?"

"Exactly!"

Leaving Casey to her duty, Micah turned toward the aisle. He noticed a man on the flight staff peek through the first class curtain. The attendant quickly scanned up and down the rows then across, finally spotting Micah seated in the first seat. He glanced at Micah's row number and disappeared behind the curtain.

"That was strange," Micah commented. He chuckled, "Pay no attention to the man behind the curtain."

"What?" Casey asked.

"Pay no attention to the man behind the curtain…?" he repeated. "Things are seldom as they seem…?"

Still nothing.

Micah had always loved that line, it was interesting how often he'd had opportunity to use it. He leaned in toward Casey and whispered, "Do you ever feel like the world is in cahoots and there's an elaborate conspiracy against you?"

"Never." She smirked with a cat-like gesture, "You think I ever get less than exactly what I want?" Conspicuously perched upon her seat, Casey stretched out her leg to senselessly push her purse further against the bulkhead wall.

"Hmm," Micah nodded, now noticing the curly-q tattoo writhing up her lower abdomen in the widening gap between her snug cashmere sweater and tight hip-hugger stretch pants, "I suspect you don't."

"Mr. Graff," a voice spoke from behind him. Micah turned toward the aisle to see a man in uniform standing over him. "May I speak with you for a moment, sir?"

"Sure." Micah stood, the man motioning toward the galley.

"I believe one of our private guests bumped into you at the restroom earlier?" the attendant continued.

"Yes."

"Well, she regrets the collision and her lack of an apology— obviously thrown off by the turbulence…" stammering, "so in a gesture of goodwill, she would like to invite you to spend the rest of your flight in the forward cabin."

Micah shook his head, "Really, that's very nice of her but not necessary. It was an accident caused by the turbulence. No harm, no foul. Please tell her thank you for the generosity, however, between you and me, I think it would be a bit awkward to accept."

"I understand, sir," the man nodded.

The flight attendant motioned to leave but stopped in mid-stride. He took a deep breath and sighed with resignation. He turned back to Micah, "Listen, Mr. Graff, Ms. Adams has REQUESTED that you take the seat next to her."

"I see," Micah replied.

The man began pleading, "I don't think you do, sir! She is one of British Airlines most private guests and this is a rather extraordinary request coming from her!" The attendant paused, took another deep breath and briefly glanced at his shoes. "Ms. Adams has been less than 'satisfied' with the service this trip," he confessed.

"Yes, I noticed."

"Then you should also know, Mr. Graff, the airlines will not be taking compensation for your upgrade— if that makes you any more comfortable? After all, you are one of our Emerald Gold Members and not unfamiliar with our upper-class cabin. You might just think of it as a fellow passenger merely asking me to invite you to her table, so to speak?"

Micah tried to laugh, more concerned about meeting Ms. Adams than he was willing to let on. "That's pretty funny. A famous celebrity asks you to invite me to 'her table' and you think I might be more comfortable because I'm enrolled in your frequent flyer program? This day keeps getting weirder and weirder."

Chapter 2

THE SEATS IN CLUB WORLD fully reclined and were split in pairs.
Window seat K faced the rear (or stern.) It was a private window cubical with no
visible access to other passengers. Its pair was J, an aisle seat that faced to the
bow (or front of the plane.) Each pair had a frosted glass partition between them
so if both seats were in an upright position with the partition down, the paired
passengers faced each other like sitting in recliners attached at the hip.

Although neither seat was reclined, the partition was closed when Micah took
his new place in Club World seat 10J. Through the fogged glass he barely made
out the faint silhouette of Ms. Adams facing the window. He sighed.

A flight attendant swiftly brought a glass of orange juice and a menu, "Will
you be eating today, sir?"

Micah hadn't gotten to his chicken back in coach and was actually hungry but
declined the offer just the same, "No… no thank you."

The flight attendant scurried away leaving quiet to engulf the next five
minutes. Glancing back and forth from the closed partition to the embedded
video screen in front of him, Micah began to wonder if he should just start
watching a movie. *What am I doing here?* Leaning into the aisle he could see
Casey making her way to the restroom followed closely by the man from 21D.
Yeah, they're going to be a while, he thought, *I probably could have gotten some sleep
back there.*

"You're more fidgety sitting in a seat than standing by the restroom in the
middle of a turbulence storm," a voice commented from behind the frosty
partition.

Micah quickly sat up straight, hands in his lap as if the teacher had caught him
daydreaming. "I suppose."

"What do you do, Mr. Graff?"

"Mr. Graff?" he questioned, "You must see me far better than I see you."

"Funny you say that, I was thinking the same about you."

"Hmm. I do appreciate your generosity, Ms. Adams, however it really wasn't necessary. I was quite comfortable in coach. Matter of fact, the seat right next to mine just opened up."

Now it was Victoria's turn to fidget. Without thinking, she clenched her fists to calm her nerves, a habit she'd acquired much too long ago. The stranger was clearly reluctant to be there—not the most common response from a man of comparable age to THE Victoria Adams.

She had a brief second-thought about her presumptuous invitation, but she needed to know. *Was meeting this man a mere coincidence or did he somehow witness or even participate in my paranoia?* The timing at the restroom coinciding with the instant cessation of her most recent and vivid delusion was something she couldn't ignore. Normally, she would have excused the whole incident as the uncontrollable behavior of a pampered Hollywood celebrity (her mode of survival over the past few years). But there was something shockingly different this time and she couldn't dismiss it. This time she felt completely sane.

Unfortunately, the problem with insanity was that normal behavior felt the most insane of all. It was a catch 22. Any chance of healing required self-forgiveness— even forgetfulness and the confidence to move on. But any considerate person would be unable to excuse their irrational outbursts, and confidence was always followed by the guilt of not taking responsibility for her actions. It was a far too familiar cycle. But at that moment, none of that was present. And that, too, was too overwhelming to ignore. She not only DIDN'T feel delusional or guilty, she felt GOOD and clear-headed for the first time in years. *How is that not insane?*

She lowered the partition. "Are you staying in London, Mr. Graff, or just passing through?"

"Just outside of London," he answered. "I travel to the UK quite a bit. Frequently… on business."

"My father used to travel a lot for business."

"Really? I know that's not always easy on a family."

"Oh, it wasn't so bad," she answered. "As a child, lots of trinkets and souvenirs from lots of countries and places were always nice to look forward to.

In fact, my mother had the most amazing collection of refrigerator magnets… I don't think I could honestly tell you what color our refrigerator was."

Micah couldn't help but smile, "That's funny."

"How so?"

"I think I have the same refrigerator at home."

"I doubt it," she grinned, "it would be VERY old!"

"Ah…" Micah laughed in spite of himself, a twinkle in his eye, "you confessing your age is quite becoming, Ms. Adams."

Victoria surprisingly blushed. Everyone called her beautiful, but what this man found attractive was her moment of honesty. "Careful, Mr. Graff, flattery has diverse effects on a woman."

"I would think you would be used to it."

"But are you?" she teased. Given the moment of levity and easy of the conversation, she dared to pursue, "So, what was it again that you said at the restroom, Mr. Graff?"

Micah kept his expression light and neutral. He knew her real interest but had no desire to participate. "Didn't they give you my first name when you cleverly discovered my identity?"

Victoria smiled, he was clearly avoiding the topic. His evasion spoke volumes. If he had simply been a coincidental bystander and the entire plane incident had been nothing more than her imagination, there would have been no reason for him to skirt the topic. *He's far too cordial and personable for such blatant avoidance. Somehow he knows,* she thought. She grinned, "So we're moving to a first name basis now, Mr. Graff?"

"I suppose that'd be fair since everyone already knows your first name. Please, call me Micah…" pausing for effect, "*Ms. Adams.*"

Victoria seemed pleased, "*Micah,*" she smiled. "Actually, the flight manifest only listed you as M. Graff."

"Ah, yes, I suppose that's airline policy, *Ms. Adams.*"

"You know, *Micah,* I may have possibly guessed 'Michael' had I thought about it."

"If you had, it wouldn't have been the first time, *Ms. Adams.*"

Victoria giggled, "You think I haven't notice, *Micah*… I just haven't decided what I want you to call me. Strangely, I would let you call me *Ms. Adams.*

That's actually what they call me on the set and it does annoy me, but the way you say it, there's something to it. You say it like the farm boy telling Buttercup, 'as you wish'. But it does sound a bit too formal."

"Can I help?" Micah eagerly offered, "Vic? Vicky? Tory?"

She laughed. "Do you have any nicknames, Mr. Graff?"

"Ooh, first name basis is suddenly back off the table?"

The ease of the mood was pleasantly surprising. Victoria had her answer; their meeting was no coincidence. Yet it still intrigued her— and so did this man. And as for Micah, Ms. Adams was not who he had expected. He chuckled.

"What are you laughing at now?"

"Just the way you went back to *Mr. Graff*, which means you haven't decided whether I can call you Victoria or not. But to answer your question… no. I mean, I've had a few nicknames but nothing stuck. My daughter, on the other hand, is a nickname magnet. Everything sticks to her."

Victoria smiled picturing him as a father, "Is she beautiful?"

"Oh, yeah— owns every room."

She paused, looking at the ring upon his right hand. There was no ring on his left but experience had told her that meant nothing. "What does your wife call you, Micah?

Micah's eyes lowered solemnly but he spoke with unbridled affection, "She called me Kai."

He didn't need to say any more. "I'm sorry," Victoria said softly.

Micah looked in her eyes and returned with sincerity, "I see that."

The response caught Victoria's attention. Even his casual conversation was unusually colored with insight. Maybe she was looking for something that wasn't really there, but although it was subtle, it was as if he ignored the words in her questions and rather answered the intent and emotion behind them. It was like a blind man with a heightened sense of smell and hearing pretending to see—indicators in his speech would still inadvertently give him away by the mention of sounds and smells around him.

"The way you speak," Victoria said, "what is that?"

Taken by her gaze, he responded without thinking. "Atonement."

She smiled with curiosity, "Who uses words like 'atonement?' she asked.

"Regretful."

"What?"

"Regretful people use words like atonement."

She gently nodded, "You can call me Victoria, Micah."

Back and forth the conversation continued for more than an hour, Victoria interviewing him like a late night talk show host. Micah was direct, engaging, even funny. She knew he could hold his own in any crowd or conversation though he seemed to have no interest. He was no priest, he avoided the soap box; but the careful selection of his words and the occasional slip— like the use of the word atonement— she couldn't tell if it was accidental or Freudian. None the less, she felt sure he was hiding something. *Maybe he never recovered from the loss of his wife.* But pursuing him now somehow aided in her proposed deliverance.

Considering his vulnerability, she suddenly realized how tired she was. Sleep had become something she feared, often plagued with night terrors or the fear they might come. She lived with insomnia. But right now, that too, was different— she wasn't afraid to sleep. "I'm so tired," she sighed.

"I can see that," Micah answered.

"I haven't slept in such a long time."

"Why don't you try to sleep now? I'll wake you before we arrive in London."

Micah slowly began to roll up the partition but Victoria gently stopped him, rolling it back down. She smiled. She leaned back in her seat, turned on her side and fell instantly asleep.

Chapter 3

THE AROMA OF SWISS MOCHA coffee filled the car as it headed down from Leontica to Bellinzona, Switzerland. On a secluded mountain road just past Corzoneso, Dr. Heimlich Phelps handled the ice-packed switchback corners with ease in his Volvo XC90. The early spring thaw hadn't yet reached the base of the Alps.

Coming out of the corner increasing in speed, the dark silhouette of a man suddenly stood in the middle of the isolated road. Phelps had two choices; swerve right into the sharp jagged edge of the mountain, or veer left off the embankment to a thousand foot drop.

Without warning the silhouette darted right, eliminating Phelps' options. Locking his brakes in a near impossible maneuver, the doctor sent the car into a 180 degree spin, clipping the stranger with the backend of his car then snowplowing the passenger-side against the 4-foot ice-packed embankment, narrowly avoiding the steep cliff face.

Now facing back up the mountain, with the incline and scraping of the snow barrier against its side, the Volvo slowed to a screeching stop. Dr. Phelps sat behind the wheel, heart racing, collecting his nerves, certain the man in the road was dead or critically injured at the least.

The tires spun in the loosened snow, but with some back and forth coaxing, the all-wheel drive eventually reversed and he spun around to head back down the hill to where the stranger lay.

Dr. Phelps, a man of science not medicine, rushed to the unconscious stranger. The man was alive, breathing. But with no bars on his cellular and knowing the road as he did, Phelps feared waiting for help might last until dawn— whereas he was not at all certain the stranger would; moving him could prove to be fatal but in good conscience, he couldn't risk the wait. He struggled to place the large man into the backseat of his car.

Not ten minutes down the mountain pass, a shadow in the rearview mirror reflected from the backseat of the car. The movement prompted a sigh of relief, "Thank God, you're conscious. Stay still and calm, you've been in an accident. I'm taking you to the hospital."

"You'll never make it to Milan," the stranger told him as he pulled himself to a seated position.

"I know this road well, there's a hospital only forty minutes away," Heimlich consoled, "just hold on."

The stranger pulled a pack of cigarettes from his jacket pocket and lit one. He deeply inhaled, burning through nearly half the cigarette in a single drag.

"How are you moving?" the doctor asked, glancing in his rearview mirror. "Your neck appeared broken, you must stay still. You're in shock… do you know where you are?" Suddenly, the doctor's own question caused the stranger's words to register, "Wait… how did you know I was going to Milan?"

"As I said, Dr. Phelps, you will NOT make it to Milan."

Shocked, Phelps stared into the mirror. He hadn't initially had the presence of mind to consider what someone might be doing on the road at that hour. Now, not believing his eyes, he watched the man straighten his neck with contorting force. Terror struck the doctor's face.

Once fearful for his passenger, Dr. Heimlich Phelps suddenly feared for himself, "How did you find me?" he exclaimed in astonishment. "I was going to take the offer, I never said no… I can play along! You need me!"

"Dr. Phelps, you overestimate your importance— and underestimate mine."

Seeing the upcoming switchback, Phelps' hands began to shake; he needed to slow way down to make the turn, but in that instant his legs seemed paralyzed, his foot pressed on the accelerator.

"It was never a choice," the dark man declared.

Phelps screamed, "What are you doing to me?! We will both surely die!"

Sinister laughter came from the backseat, "Don't you see, doctor? With your demise, no other will refuse."

"How are you doing this?!" Heimlich struggled, unable to move his hands nor lift his foot from the gas.

Reaching the hairpin curve, the mysterious man mockingly reconsidered, "Perhaps you're right, doctor. You choose."

Phelps' body was instantly released. He jerked the wheel locking up the brakes just seconds too late, launching into a power-slide off the embankment. Crashing a hundred yards below, the car barrel-rolled across the road and through the next guard rail, plummeting to its final resting place on a switchback far below. The vehicle came to a violent stop wrapped around a street post.

The car horn blared stuck screaming within the confines of the steel coffin. Rain fell upon the cracked windshield; the wipers feebly grinding the window like nails on a chalkboard, the pace matching the driver's fading breaths. Eyes glazed and still, death's darkness had already swallowed Dr. Phelps' sight; a streetlamp lying broken on the hood failed to even reflect in his eyes. Sounds echoed tirelessly through what little consciousness he had left causing his teeth to clench to the rhythm of the metal and glass shards scratching as they were disturbed by the wipers' movement.

The sinister silhouette sat motionless in the backseat waiting patiently for the doctor's final exhale. When it came, the darkened figure deeply drew in its own breath symbolically extracting the man's essence from the cool, metallic air.

After a deathly moment of silence, the torqued, bending sound of flexing metal echoed the mountainside as if being pried by the Jaws of Life. The backseat passenger door opened easily and the silhouette emerged the wreckage unscathed.

The stranger stood there briefly in the fading night. He inhaled the cool mountain air, twisting a gold signature ring round his right-hand middle finger, a contemplative gaze on his face. He turned up the collar on his long black coat and walked away. A concerned Samaritan, having stopped on the highway below, ran past the darkened man as if he were unseen.

Chapter 4

AS THE PLANE BEGAN to descend, the fasten seatbelt light flared on. "We're beginning our approach into London Heathrow International Airport. The captain has put on the fasten seatbelt sign. Please return to your seats and stow your luggage in either the overhead bin or the space in front of you. Tray tables should be stowed and your seat in the upright position. Fasten your seatbelts."

Victoria remained sleeping so soundly, Micah almost didn't have the heart to wake her. "Ms. Adams? Victoria? We're preparing to land now."

Victoria's lashes fluttered. She rolled over to face Micah, smoothing her hair and rubbing her eyes as the seat slowly moved to an upright position. She looked at him and smiled. "Hi."

"Hi," Micah smiled back. "We're preparing to land."

She laughed. "Wow, I was out," she said. "Was I snoring?"

"Another benefit of loud engines."

"Ha, ha, very funny. How do I look?"

"Rested," he answered. It was strange she'd asked because, although Micah had only just met her, she appeared noticeably younger, more vibrant— relaxed. Her smile was genuine, not staged.

* * * * *

The city, the food, the weather. Victoria and Micah were chatting comfortably, winding their way towards passport control when Micah's phone dinged as Heathrow Internet engaged. He pulled it from his pocket to briefly check for urgency.

"Is that the new iPhone?" Victoria questioned.

"It is," Micah replied.

"May I see it?"

"Sure." There was no message of importance waiting. He handed her the phone.

Turning it over a few times, Victoria nodded, "Uh-huh… nice weight," she flipped it again, "and the screen is good-sized, too." She looked closer, "Hey, you're on WhatsApp."

Micah grinned, "Isn't everyone?"

Eventually slowing just prior to the booths, Victoria returned Micah's phone and pointed across the open hall, "I have dual citizenship, so I guess I'm over there." She motioned towards a quickly moving line.

"Foreigner status for me," he shrugged, shoving his phone in his pocket. He sighed at the extremely long foreign passport line.

They stopped and Micah faced her. "Well, Ms. Adams…"

"Victoria," she corrected.

He grinned, "Victoria. It was truly a pleasure meeting you." He gave her a gentlemanly nod, "I hope you get some rest."

Flashing a charming smile of her own, "I will," she replied.

Adjusting her coat and hand bag, with no more than that, Victoria gracefully turned to go. Micah watched as she quickly disappeared into the flowing tide of immigrating passengers. It felt strange to see her leave, and so quickly.

He was still just standing there when it suddenly dawned on him— *No one will ever believe me! No one will believe I spent an entire flight with THE Victoria Adams! That's just great.* He hung his head, shaking it back and forth.

Catching himself after a moment, he had to chuckle at the ridiculous thought; he was surprised to sound like any other admirer. He really wasn't. True, there had been something special— attractive— about Victoria; something deeper than her physical beauty and beyond her celebrity status. But Micah had long ago made a reputation for himself as someone who wasn't a respecter of persons; meaning he naturally treated all people according to who they were as opposed to who they seemed to be or their social status. Prince or pauper, both initially had his respect and graciousness until proven otherwise undeserved. This was something easier to boast than to actually execute, but for Micah, it was genuine. Little intimidated him and even less made him feel superior. On the plane, he hadn't approached THE Victoria Adams out of some manufactured adulation; he had truly been moved to comfort a troubled human being. However, by the time they parted (under any circumstance) he was sure it wouldn't have been cool to have asked for a photo.

I should have just taken a picture while she was sleeping. "No one's going to believe me," he muttered in spite of himself as he begrudgingly strolled into the stagnant sea of non-residents and tourists. He saw no hope of possibly bumping into the captivating Ms. Adams at baggage claim.

Chapter 5

AS MICAH FINALLY REACHED the front of what had seemed to have been an endless line, he happened to eye a security guard with an entourage of Asian tourists (all with matching hats) making their way down a connecting hallway in his direction.

Micah's eyes grew wide. He briefly glanced away from the group to check out the immigration officer in front of him— the officer who was only moments away from helping him. To his dismay, he noticed that she, too, was Asian, maybe Chinese. Micah had traveled enough to know what this might possibly mean. *No… it couldn't be, could it?*

It was. The Chinese tour group of more than thirty people didn't speak English. As an airport courtesy, a security guard had been assigned to escort them to the one Heathrow passport control officer who also spoke Chinese.

Come on, c'mon, c'mon, Micah coaxed in his mind, praying that the woman at his window would finish with the gentleman in front of him and call him forward before the group managed to traverse the immigration hall. Micah knew all too well that for whatever reason, security-escorted people were always brought to the front of the line.

At the booth, the gentleman was finally done being processed and was handed back his passport. The Chinese-speaking immigration officer started to wave Micah forward when suddenly the gentleman turned back to the window remembering an unasked question. The officer offhandedly motioned Micah to remain behind the red line and returned her attention to the other man.

A few moments more, the gentleman nodded and thought to step away… but once again a question, a clarification, had him turn back. Once, twice, three times the gentleman reneged on the promise to leave before he eventually moved on.

"Thank God," Micah whispered under his breath when the immigration officer finally waved him to her booth.

Before he could take a step forward, a large hand from slightly behind met him in the chest. "Sir? Excuse me. Just one moment, please."

Micah didn't need to look to know it was the security officer and the Chinese entourage.

"Of course," Micah conceded without raising his head.

It appeared that none of the tourists from China had the appropriate visa. Although it was obviously a group oversight, the passport control agent determined it was still relevant to discover this oversight on a case by case basis— one tourist at a time and after a considerable interview with each individual.

What Micah found most frustrating was how much time the process wasted. He seriously couldn't imagine a slower way to do it. Not only was immigration determined to discover individually whether a visa had been issued or not, once it was determined that the proper visa was in fact, missing, each person was singly directed to the visa application department; having to first wait for an available security officer to escort them there. One by one they were being called forward, scanned, denied, interviewed, made to wait, and then finally escorted to the visa department with security— the process repeated again and again for each tourist. All of it, just to return to passport control and start over with a shiny new visa.

Micah couldn't hold his tongue any longer. He spoke loudly and to no one in particular, "Might it be more efficient to ask everyone in unison?" He turned to face the greater portion of the group (the ones who had yet to be shuffled through the process.) He called out, "Is there anybody here who actually has their UK visa?" The tourists had no idea what he was saying but the Chinese-speaking officer gave him a stern glare.

Micah reluctantly stepped back, settling in for what would no doubt be a considerable wait.

* * * * *

After the better part of an hour had passed, Micah was saying goodbye and shaking hands with the last of the Chinese tour group, "Enjoy your stay in the UK, Renshu… remember what I said about the gardens." It was amazing how much could be communicated despite a language barrier if one only took the time. Renshu smiled, waving at Micah as he followed an exhausted security escort to the visa application department.

The immigration officer was surprisingly chipper after having just interpreted for over thirty foreign nationals. She finally called Micah forward and Micah happily proceeded to her window, waving back to Renshu as he did.

The woman took Micah's passport and unsuccessfully attempted to scan it into the system. She straightened the edges and tried again. "It looks like your passport is not scanning," she said when the second attempt failed as well. "Wait here for a moment and an officer will escort you to the waiting area. It might take a bit to enter your information manually."

A few minutes later, she gave Micah's passport to another officer who motioned Micah to follow.

The two men walked silently, side by side, arriving at the secondary location only to find the booth empty. The officer reached inside the window and placed Micah's passport on top of a sizable stack of waiting passports and documents. He then pointed off to the left to a seating area which held all the other unfortunate owners of unscannable documents; the majority of them African immigrants— refugees from Sudan and Chad— with all their worldly possessions in tow. "Wait there," the officer said.

There seemed to be no official line, so seeing his passport on the top of the stack, Micah strategically decided to wait at the counter instead, hopeful to be the first assisted when the attendant returned.

After several minutes, a heavyset woman entered the small booth. She placed a security badge on the counter and sat down in the high swivel stool. To Micah's dismay, while rotating her chair to face the computer, she inadvertently knocked all the passports and documents onto the floor.

Micah's head dropped to the counter with a sigh of disbelief. "This is turning into a very long day," he mumbled to the smooth surface beneath his forehead.

Gathering the pile from the floor, the woman clearly remained unrattled. "Please take a seat, sir. I'll call you when I'm ready for you."

Resigned, Micah lifted his head from the ledge and took his place in the small waiting room. Leaning against the wall, he silently began coaching himself, *Smile through your eyes, buddy.* He'd found that forcibly smiling (not necessarily with his mouth but with his eyes) actually put the world in a different light. After all, the people surrounding him were pleased to be there— vacation, holiday, a change of scenery. And those beginning an entirely new life? Their joy was almost overwhelming. He could remain miserable or join in the celebration. He decided to choose the latter.

There were seven, maybe eight African families seeking refuge in the United Kingdom. Micah discovered that most were from Sudan and that several groups were related, he just wasn't sure what the makeup of each family was. There were about a dozen small children included with the families, sitting on the floor playing a game with polished stones and carved sticks— treasures they'd managed to salvage from home. Micah had to marvel at how well-behaved they were. But as the waiting endlessly continued, even the best of the children began to get restless and the game began to wane.

Squatting, Micah joined them on the floor, upping the ante with a box of mixed chocolates he'd been carrying as a gift. The laughter of the children seeing the purse, was a delight. Their enthusiasm to teach him their game (periodically adding new rules to help win them chocolates) was heightened by the incentive. Though Micah didn't speak their language, it wasn't hard for him to call out a questionable move by giving a look of suspicion, or teasingly distract them in order to move an extra chocolate in front of the tiny girl to his left. Her pile was surprisingly the largest.

The room filled with the sound of laughing children. There were many, "Oh, oh, oh!"s, and, "No, no, no!"s and other words that could only mean, "You can't do that!" Micah even noticed one player sneaking his hard-earned chocolate to his mother sitting behind him.

The woman in the booth, having taken a break from her data entry to watch the game, decidedly began to thumb through the many passports; she suddenly felt moved to rush Micah to the front. She reasoned it was only partly because she appreciated his entertaining the children but mostly because her boss had complained about the noise.

"Micah Graff?" She called him to her window.

Before Micah moved to stand, he turned to face the circle. Pointing first to his pile of chocolates and then around the circle at the children, he slowly gave them the evil eye. "These had better all be here when I get back." He aimed an accusing finger at each child.

Giggles (and attempts to stifle them) made their way around the circle, each child trying to hold their laughter for fear of the evil eye. But by the time Micah had risen to his feet, little hands from every direction had flown across the circle and grabbed up all his chocolates.

Smiling, he pulled a second box of candy from his bag and handed it to the mother sitting behind her son before turning back to the children. Feigning a look of surprise at seeing all of his chocolates missing, Micah gave them a suspicious glare. The entire area immediately filled with their laughter; they even burst into their own rendition of the 'Neener, neener, neener' song. It seemed to be universal; Micah had heard the song many times before in many different languages— usually for the price of a box of chocolates.

"Thank you for your patience, Mr. Graff," the woman at the booth greeted, smiling sincerely.

After matching his face to his picture, she attempted to scan the passport. Once again, it failed. She sighed and resigned to log the document manually, eventually entering the last of Micah's information and pushing 'submit'.

While Micah stood patiently watching the Microsoft hourglass spin relentlessly as it waited for the database to accept the entry and refresh itself, the woman in the booth noticed the children had ventured into her area. Whispering and giggling amongst themselves, the group appeared to be planning a rear assault on the candy man— the man who happened to be standing at her counter.

Deciding to give the children no opportunity to maneuver, the woman hurriedly hit the blotter and stamped Micah's passport. "Enjoy your stay in the UK," she said as she hastily returned his passport. Then, having nowhere near the candy man's patience, over his shoulder, the woman gave the children her own version of the evil eye— completely missing the online page timing-out.

✳   ✳   ✳   ✳   ✳

Hours later at baggage claim, Micah wasn't the least surprised that Victoria Adams was nowhere to be seen.

Chapter 6

ANNOYED, IRRATATED, AND PONDERING her life's career choice, Sara held Henry's backup coffee, reading glasses and secondary napkin over her lap in the passenger seat of the Register Guard News van. Henry's primary napkin was tucked in his collar to prevent any possible grease or mustard from staining his musky, tweed jacket or decade-old shirt and tie. Using her free thumb at the pace of Henry's vulgar open-mouthed chomping while rehearsing his news report, Sara scrolled through the Reuter's newsfeed on her phone, searching for up-to-the-minute, worldwide, breaking news.

A headline finally caught her attention. "Weren't you saying something earlier about the upcoming ecological summit being a hoax?" she asked of Henry.

"I'm not certain what you are talking about," Henry muttered, his mouth filled with sandwich.

"Come now, Henry. Seriously. The other night you wouldn't give it up."

"I was drunk."

"No, you weren't," Sara argued.

"YOU were drunk."

"I don't drink, Henry."

"Hmm, I knew there was something I didn't... uh, something wrong with you."

"You were going to say that you knew there was something you didn't LIKE about me, weren't you?"

"Are you certain you're not a reporter?" Henry mocked. "I don't trust anyone who doesn't drink."

"You don't trust anyone, period."

"That's not true."

"Name one."

Henry thought about it, "Well... there's me."

"Lovely, Henry. Might have been a good time to say you trusted ME."

"I'm a journalist— integrity and all. I start compromising the truth..."

"QUITE lovely, Henry," Sara scoffed. "So, 'Mr. Integrity', what were you saying about the summit?"

"Nothing. It's a farce."

"Why would you say that?"

"Think about it; the only member of the committee with any environmental credentials is the Chair. Everyone else on the committee is part of the 'who's-who' of pro-nuclear proliferation activism and certainly have nothing to do with global warming."

Sara looked at Henry suspiciously, "Since when do you follow environmental issues or anti-nuclear rallies? I know you don't read."

"I read," Henry defended.

"Other than your own articles?"

"That's reading."

Sara frowned, "I doubt even that. I've seen you write entire pieces without looking back at a single line."

"I'm gifted that way," he retorted smugly.

"Oh, yes I see, 'Mr. Dickens'."

"Come now… if you have to compare me to a literary genius of the nineteenth century, I prefer Carroll. Then of course, while we're on the subject, Swift is a much better fit with the current absurdities of Her Majesty's country and all."

"Did you say 'genius'?" Sara dawned a newfound look of bewilderment.

"I did."

"Henry Wilkens, you leave me speechless. Fine. Then, I suggest you finish your Egg McMuffin so we can get on with reporting the Great London Sewer Crisis of the TWENTY-FIRST century," her tone, sarcastic.

Henry took a bite of his muffin, "There's nothing small about sewer management in a city of nine million people, Sara. Besides, this is sure to be a political conspiracy leading all the way to the upper echelons of Parliament— possibly higher!"

Sara could barely keep a straight face, "Yeah, right, Henry." The only joy in her job as of late was trying to get under Henry's skin, "I believe you. Which brings me back to my initial question; didn't you say the environmental summit was a government conspiracy? If so, are they possibly connected?" Sara ominously lifted her eyebrows up and down.

Henry narrowed his eyes and pursed his lips, "Though I sense a MINOR tone of sarcasm… considering we have to work closely… I choose to overlook it." He took another bite of sandwich.

Swallowing and wiping his mouth on his sleeve, Henry continued, "No, Sara, the sewer crisis and the environmental summit conspiracy are not…" considering for a brief second, "*likely* connected. The sewer crisis is a UK travesty whereas the environmental summit is made up of nine member-states and their representatives. And just so you know, the idea of conspiracy is not my summation; the chairman, Dr. Heimlich Phelps, was the first to declare the summit a ruse. He filed complaints about the chosen members— actually got quite a few nickers in a twist. The sorry doctor even eventually sent out letters with grave concerns for his life." Henry shrugged, "After that, he seemed to fall off the grid. Likely hiding in his Swiss estate until the summit, I imagine."

"Oh, my God, Henry! How do you know this?"

Henry stammered, "Well, um… he sent letters to the Guard."

"What?! Addressed to you?"

"Let's just say they were not, NOT addressed to me."

"Henry, Dr. Phelps died in a car wreck near Bellinzona, Switzerland this morning!"

Henry's eyes got big then narrowed with suspicious inquiry, "How?" he interrogated seriously.

"Strange car wreck. He drove through two barriers and plummeted hundreds of feet to his death." Sara stared at Henry, waiting for his take on the situation.

"Hmm. Interesting. That was his home town, I'd think he would have known the roads better than that." Henry became unusually quiet.

"What are you thinking, Henry?"

"Nothing." He shook it off and quickly opened the door, preparing to climb out of the van, "You coming?"

"Where?"

"To interview the sewer magistrate?"

"Hold up! You've got something here, Henry. You can't stay quiet on this one."

"They'd never let me publish, Sara."

"Are you certain? I've watched you uncover these things— you can actually be quite brilliant when you're not being a complete arse; but then you always turn away, you refuse to react. You talk about the glory days… don't you ever want to be back on top?"

Henry paused to think about it. As a veteran reporter he had taken more than his share of lumps from political fallout. With sincere regret, he eventually confessed, "You've got to choose your battles, Sara, and this is not one."

Sara Jennings, the newest producer for the Register Guard, could still recognize the obvious journalistic war wounds of more than twenty years upon him, "You've got to take a risk sometime, Henry."

Henry balked, "Come on," he said jumping out of the vehicle and slamming the Guard van door behind him.

Chapter 7

AS MICAH APPROACHED THE rental car counter, a tall thin man in an Avis jacket abruptly pushed past him and slapped a set of keys down on the counter. "How's my baby doing?" he flirted, addressing the girl working behind the counter.

"Boy, I will whoop your ass right where you stand," Denise snapped, lovingly holding her stomach. "This ain't your baby, Leonard. I told you never to say that again."

"Oh, don't do me like that," Leonard whined.

"Do you know how embarrassed you'd be, being beaten by an 8-month pregnant woman right here at your place of employment?"

Turning his head to the side, "They get so testy in their third trimester," he commented in Micah's direction.

Denise rolled her eyes, "What are these keys for, Leonard?"

"That's the Civic for decommission."

"I don't have time for this crap, can't you see there's a line?"

Leonard looked behind him to see only Micah waiting there.

"You need to follow procedure," Denise continued.

"THIS is my procedure, baby…"

"Boy…! You better get your sorry ass out of my sight right now!"

"Woo-hoo, she's warming up now!" Leonard looked at Micah, raising his eyebrows up and down. Then winking at Denise, he sauntered away from the Avis Preferred booth.

Denise turned back to the Micah. Pointing to her stomach she adamantly reiterated, "This is NOT that boy's baby."

"Uh… good?" Micah replied.

"Hell, yes, it's good! Could you imagine what that boy's child would look like?" She adjusted the computer monitor in front of her. "So? What do you want?"

"Uh, my name is Micah Graff, I'm a Preferred member. I reserved a car but my name isn't on the board…?"

"Did you order your car for Terminal 5 pickup?"

"Always do."

"Hmm." Denise looked back to her computer and started typing. "License and credit card?" Micah gave them to her.

Denise entered the first set of numbers and suddenly stopped. She squinted at the screen. She leaned her face into the monitor and jabbed at a few keys.

Sitting up straight, she folded her arms across her chest, "Hold on, my computer froze."

"That's okay," Micah offered, "I have a printout of my reservation if you need it." He handed her the paper.

Denise hesitated. She took a deep breath, "Listen. We're all out of cars due to some political summit in town this week. If your name ain't on the board, your reservation might have slipped through the cracks."

"Ugh," Micah sighed.

"But hold on, hold on… let me see if they have a car for you at Terminal 1." Denise picked up the phone and pressed speed-dial. "Hey, this is Denise, do you have a car over there for a Michael Graff?"

"Micah."

"Excuse me?"

"My name is Micah."

She put her hand over the receiver, "Whatever. They go by last name. Hold on." She spoke into the phone, "No Graff? I have a reservation number right here." She began to grow irritated, "I'm holding it in my hand right now… no, he's standing right here."

There was a pause. "Well, what am I supposed to tell him? Uh-huh… uh-huh… I see. I'm not telling him that. He's a PREferred member— you tell him. I don't care, tell Janine." A longer pause. She turned back to Micah, smiling and nodding, "Just one minute, sir, they're finding your car. I'm getting the manager to talk to you right now."

"You go girl," Micah said with a wink.

Denise grinned with mock surprise and coyly raised her eyebrows. Leaning in, she whispered to Micah, "Hold on there, honey, D'neece gonna take care of you... sshh, she's coming back now." She returned her attention to the call.

"No, no, uh-uh. I'm not telling him that! This fine looking gentleman has been standing here for— two hours!" Denise gave Micah a wink. "No, no, no— put Janine on the phone. I said no. Listen, I'm done talking to you, girl, this ain't going nowhere." Again to Micah she said, "I think we got something for you, honey. You just hold on one minute."

The charade was charming, but Micah felt it was time to say something. "You do realize I'm standing right here and can hear every word both you and Beth are saying, don't you?"

"Sshh," Denise motioned, pointing at the phone, "I can't hear you, I'm on the phone." She turned her back to Micah.

Someone had returned to the line, Denise was not happy. "Nuh-uh! What are you doing back on the phone, Beth? They didn't send my fine self all the way here from Detroit to deal with your lazy ass. Girl, get that milkshake out of your mouth, you got brain freeze. And get yourself on a diet, no one's gonna touch that thing the way it is now."

Another pause. Denise started nodding. "Okay... okay... I understand. You just do that... I look forward to it. Yes, both me and my baby will take care of ALL your problems in the parking lot, you can believe that! Yeah, yeah... you have yourself a Merry Christmas, too!" It was the first week of April.

Denise hung up. "Girl's so stupid she probably thinks I meant the Merry Christmas thing."

Micah nodded his head in agreement.

Denise turned back to Micah, "Listen, I got this older Civic I can give you. Matter of fact, it's complimentary... just make sure you bring it back here to this booth and give the keys to me or Leonard personally."

"That's perfect," Micah said.

"Now if we're not here, drop the key in the dropbox... don't be giving it to none of them British people."

"I completely understand."

"They don't know what the hell they're doing," she shook her head back and forth. "Fine looking man like yourself expects a certain level of service. I swear when I go on maternity leave… you try Karen at Hertz, don't you come back here for at least six months."

"Honey, you are a peach," Micah teased.

"Don't you be calling me 'honey'! What? Am I putting out vibes? You better get your snarky ass out of my sight."

Micah smiled.

"I ain't kidding, neither. Take your key and get out of here."

Still smiling, Micah bowed and slowly backed away.

"Go on, go on now. Leonard will show you where the car is."

Shaking her head and rubbing her stomach, Denise looked down at her belly, "Damn baby, what are you doing to mama? …got men hitting on me all day long!"

Chapter 8

SAINT ANNE'S MANOR WAS a lovely establishment; both historic and modern, tastefully combined.

"We have you for four nights, Mr. Graff?"

"That's correct." He handed his passport and credit card to the pleasant receptionist.

"Your room has been upgraded, sir… thank you for being a Hilton Honors member. Would you like a hot biscuit?"

"The primary reason for my loyalty," smiled Micah.

"Well then, take two," she replied, returning the smile. "Will you need help with your luggage today?"

"No, I think I have it, thank you." Micah gratefully took the key card and the cookies and headed to his room. It had been a very long morning and an even longer afternoon.

*   *   *   *   *

Lying face down on the stone prison floor, Micah's hands stretched behind him chained to a wall. In the dark, he faced away from the door toward an even darker corner.

As a child, he was afraid of the dark and always faced toward the door in fear of an intruder, needing only to open his eyes if the doorknob turned. Sleeping that way added to his reaction time, but more importantly, turning over suddenly at the sound of every subtle creek of the old house where he grew up was painfully frustrating— the frightful jump of panic was always far worse than any crackling tree branch scrapping across the siding outside his window.

Strangely, Micah now found peace chained to a wall in the solitude of the dark. He realized there was no reason to react, nothing he could do. Facing toward the wall actually relieved him of any unwarranted fear. The stone cold floor contoured to his body as if perfectly designed for his rest; slightly elevated head, left knee and torso. Even the chill of the room— he received comfort from drawing warmth from the inner core of his own body. Concentrating on that warmth and willing it to flow to his extremities became a form of meditation.

A familiar outline began taking shape… *Is it a map? A diagram?* Micah realized it was a spreadsheet. *I used to know what went in the third column… did I save pictures, jpegs there? How do they appear in an Excel spreadsheet, as just icons or the whole picture?* Micah hated how large images distorted the organized structure of a nicely spaced spreadsheet.

Running down a spiral staircase and through the kitchen entrance of a Chinese restaurant, Micah was stopped at the bottom of the stairs. "Hold these for me, I can't stay," his wife said, pulling something from her purse.

Micah looked down at his hands to see a sword in his right hand and a balm in his left. A baby sat crying on the floor. "How will I hold the baby?" he asked, but she was gone.

Micah pushed open the restaurant door and stepped into the street. Through the fog, he saw the tall dark figure of a man staggering along the wet pavement toward him. *Is that him?* The figure limped on its right leg, veering slightly right with each step.

A bus swiftly traveled down the road behind them, its horn blaring. *He must hear the bus coming?* Micah's anxiety building; it was a perfectly staged collision course, the man's stagger having moved him near the center of the street.

Again the bus sounded warning, this time ringing like a child's bicycle horn. The melodic chime repeated. *Where's that coming from?* Micah opened his eyes and saw his phone lying next to him on the comfortable hotel bed.

> Dinner at 6:30 – Chi'Yangs hope you like Asian Fusion. ~Victoria   **16:29**

Chapter 9

EXTREMELY UPSCALE FOR AN Asian-fusion establishment, Micah entered the restaurant feeling underdressed. It was possibly the finest restaurant in its category that he'd ever visited. Not that he wasn't accustomed to high-end dining during his travels, but typically Asian restaurants were three, maybe four stars, whereas this restaurant was in a league of its own. He regretted not checking online before coming or at least inquiring about a dress code at the concierge desk before leaving the hotel. He intended to walk in cool, calm, collected; mildly interested. He'd already made his first mistake. When planning to walk into this level of an establishment in jeans and a sports jacket, he knew you'd better have a recognizable face.

Fortunately for Micah, he also knew that both millionaires and working stiffs wore jeans with a polo; the only distinction was the watch, the belt and the shoes— and his were all five stars. He wore Italian leather boots and matching belt with an upper mid-range Omega strapped to his wrist. For Micah, the only difference was that he had just one fine watch (a lifetime achievement gift from his wife) while he was sure the patrons of this establishment likely had one for each day of the week.

In the foyer the maître d' briefly looked Micah over before returning his attention to the reservation book. Rudely studying the evening's entries, he refused Micah a second glance. Micah patiently stood there.

With reluctance, the man eventually greeted him without looking up, eyes glued to the pages. "Do have you a reservation, sir?" His doubt was clearly apparent in the question.

"I'm meeting my party at 6:30. I suspect the reservation was made in their name."

"Name?"

"Adams."

Without checking the list nor raising his gaze, the maître d' was short with his response, "We have no reservation for Adams here tonight."

"How about Victoria?"

"No, sir," the maître d' quickly responded. "Are you certain you were to meet your party at THE Chi'Yangs?" He lifted his eyes and met Micah's with impatience. "There is a Chi-NESE restaurant in the mall across the motorway; your party is possibly meeting there?"

Almost smiling, Micah couldn't help but to like this guy. The man was entertaining like a dinner-theater player and Micah was looking forward to the finale. Chi'Yangs was crying out for the likes of Tyler Durden as a waiter— he could see Brad Pitt as Tyler Durden from Fight Club taking a job there just to pee in the soup. *Stay away from tonight's soup special,* Micah thought, amusing himself. The fall of this type of place was always a pleasure to read about in the tabloids of London.

"All right, then," Micah said politely as he attempted to glance at the reservation book. The maître d' abruptly slammed the book shut on Micah's proverbial hand.

Micah stepped back and took a few deep breaths deciding to get into character. When he next spoke, out came an obnoxious, backwoods southern drawl, "This may be a long shot, mister… but how's about Graff?"

"Take a left out the parking lot, a right at the bridge. Can't miss the mall, two miles down."

Unable to contain his pleasure, Micah continued, "T'wut's the likelihood that I might take a gander 'round before I mosey off?" Micah tried to think of unreasonable requests just to further annoy the man, "Do you sull Chicklets…? I've got this here nasty taste in my mouth." The maître d' was now on the other side of the desk opening the door for him.

Micah exited the building with a chuckle.

"Who was that?" The Executive Chef had just stepped up to the front desk.

"Oh, some SOD American without a reservation. Said he had a reservation under the name Adams."

"Victoria Adams?"

"Victoria Adams?" The maître d' went pale. "Bloody hell! Him…?" He wiped a dab of sweat from his brow. "The man said 'Adams' then 'Victoria'… he didn't put the two together!"

"You bloody idiot! She's in the Thames waiting."

"I know, I know. I'm…" He was at a loss.

"She's been there for some time. Go get him back."

Obediently the maître d' ran into the parking lot. "Sir! Sir!" he called across the lot. "Please wait a moment, sir!"

Micah wiped a smug grin off his face but continued walking toward his car torturing the man and causing him to run faster. "Sir, please stop," the maître d' panted.

Micah did stop, but without turning around. He put one hand on his hip and used the other to scratch his head, "Now, is it a left out of this here parking lot…? Cross that bridge down yonder?" He looked behind him to address the maître d', "Do you know if they have a Dollar Tree at that there mall?"

"Sir, did you say a reservation for Ms. Victoria Adams?"

"Why, yes I did." Micah enjoyed watching the man squirm.

"I made a terrible mistake, sir, will you please follow me…?"

"Well, how 'bout that! She's here after all?"

"Yes, sir. She is waiting for you."

Mercifully, Micah dropped the act and followed the relieved maître d' back into the restaurant. Once inside, the man regained his composure.

"Mrs. Rexroth," he told Micah, gesturing with air-quotes, "is in the Thames Suite… straight up the stairs to the left at the end. Private door on the right."

"Rexroth, huh?" Micah discretely chuckled recognizing the movie reference. *I like it.* "Thank you, sir."

"May I take your coat?"

Is he talking to me? The sudden shift took Micah off guard, "Sure… uh… absolute… that would be nice." The man assisted Micah in removing his coat before walking him to the stairs.

"To the left, all the way back. The door reads, 'Thames Suite'. Will you be requiring anything further?"

"I don't believe so, thank you."

Having only taken the first few stairs, Micah did have a thought that turned him around. The maître d' was still there, watching his ascent. "On second thought, what is the lady drinking?" Micah asked.

"She's having wine, sir."

"Bottle or glass?"

"Bottle, sir."

"We'll need a second glass then."

"It awaits you upstairs."

"Great. Thank you."

Micah resumed the climb but turned back again, this time snapping his fingers. "Tag," he said, "…will I need a ticket for my coat?"

"Of course not, sir, I will tend to it myself."

"Wonderful."

The maître d' nodded with respect. It was an extraordinary change in attitude.

*　*　*　*　*

Victoria's face lit up as Micah entered the room. "Nice, isn't it?" she said. "I love this place, it's wonderful."

"Oh, it surely is… I reckon the food is mighty fine, too!" Micah had fallen back into his southern drawl.

Victoria laughed, "What's that accent you're doing?"

"I am dreadfully sorry, Ms. Adams, but you may be stuck with it for the rest of the ev'ning… or at least 'til we leave this here fine establishment."

"Okay, that's interesting," she giggled, "there's got to be a story. Do tell."

"I assure you it is far less entertaining than it sounds."

"Well, it appears to have put you in a good mood."

"Real good mood," Micah smiled from ear to ear. "It takes a real special kind of event to put me in this here type of mood."

"Really?" she teased, "What's her name…?" Victoria drew out the question with a raised brow.

Micah shook his finger at her, laughing, "Well, I didn't catch HIS name, but if I were to guess, it would have to be something like, Jean-Luke or Jean-Michel."

Victoria burst into laughter almost spitting her wine, "And you say it's not an interesting story?" Delighted, Victoria seamlessly joined in as the innocent southern belle. Leaning halfway across the table, she delicately rested her chin upon her hand and batted her eyes playfully, "Why, Mister Graff, I do declare… I have most unfortunately misread you. I honestly didn't think you swung that way."

"Oh, Lady Adams, I assure you, I am full of surprises. You have only begun to unwrap this here mystery box." Micah straighten in his chair, continuing, "However, ma'am, I must admit… of all of my proclivities, the likes of Jean-Luke-Michel is not one."

"Well, that is good news to me, sir!"

Micah's eyes widened, "Why Ms. Adams! You can cause a poor boy to blush."

"Oh, of that, I assure you." She winked and picked up the menu. "Shall we order?"

"Please! I can maintain this here accent no longer."

Victoria had been truly surprised by his wit and charm. It wasn't common for her to spend unscripted one-on-one time with anyone. People in general either treated her like a goddess in delusional admiration, or completely the opposite in an attempt to seem above being affected by her celebrity status. She had very few friends. Of those, most were in her profession; a profession (unfortunately) full of narcissists, egotists and fewer real people. It was the curse of stardom.

Micah was an enigma to her. Far more than his confidence, he wasn't afraid to be humble; his self-deprecating humor, refreshing. "You're very funny," she said, "you should be an actor."

Micah smiled, "Ah, well… there may have been a little amateur theater somewhere… some comedy and music in my youth."

"It shows. I think you could do a lot more. Are you a musician?"

"I'm a wannabe musician."

"I love music."

"So do I. It's soul food."

"Did you ever pursue music... professionally, I mean?"

Micah paused, thoughtful. He finally responded, "It's not that I didn't considerate it. It was that... fate... had other intentions for me."

Victoria grew silent and looked closely at Micah, studying him. Finishing her assessment, she sat back and finally spoke. "There it is," she said, a matter of fact.

"There's what?"

"That— I don't know. But I saw it on the plane. As an actress, you constantly look for inspiration, watch people to help you build characters." She crossed her arms and brought a finger to her lips, "You have a secret, Mr. Graff. I haven't come up with it yet, but you wear it on your sleeve. Certain questions cause you an out-of-place look... something distant in your eyes. I've seen you bite your lip... and the way you pause before you speak.

"Sometimes it's like I can see a deep look of sadness; sometimes, it's a joyous twinkle. Either way, it's addictive. The twinkle is overwhelming like a hidden passion on the verge of exploding! But the sadness is equally enthralling like a pain I can't help but want to see healed. What IS that, Mr. Graff? What exactly are you?"

Micah shrugged, "I sell hardcopy encyclopedias in the Wikipedia age."

"Well, good luck with that."

"Thank you, business has been a bit slow lately."

"I bet," Victoria smirked. "May I order for us?"

"Of course."

Victoria felt light, overwhelmed with a peacefulness that, if she had ever known it before, she'd forgotten long ago. There was no effort, no hidden agenda; she fell naturally into relaxed and comfortable conversation with this man she barely knew yet felt she'd known her whole life.

"I'd like to try the Chef's Special— if it's all right with you?" Victoria suggested, getting back to the menu. "It may take a while, though."

"Then, we can wait," Micah announced, smiling. "The company is appetizer enough for me."

Chapter 10

HOURS LATER IN THE restaurant parking lot, having had the most satisfying evening of extraordinary food and delightful conversation, it was time to say goodnight. "I had a lot of fun, Mr. Graff," Victoria said. "An evening out with you is like dinner and a show… and I got to pick my role."

"I would love to take all the credit, but surely you must know that it is YOU who incites theatrics in the company you keep."

"Well, if that's true, then you are a far better actor than I."

Micah had been able to be someone else— someone less serious, for a night. Someone he had forgotten. And in turn, Victoria was able to be herself for the first time in many years; someone who had long been buried beneath the image, the brand, the icon; the depreciating global sensation that was Victoria Adams— the unobtainable, provocative, youthful Jennifer from the block-buster that made her famous. Completely unsustainable. A glorious effigy slowly dying with every unflattering camera angle, every wrinkle, every pound gained; dragging shreds of her psyche along with it. Not her manager, her agent, her mother nor psychiatrist could possibly understand the robbed sense of worth, perpetually pressed to uphold an image no one could actually attain. An illusion made of makeup, retakes and words from a script she could never have written, much less ever lived.

But to even mention the pressure gave way to feelings of guilt or led to accusations of being too self-absorbed. Either way, both added to the deprivation of the Victoria Adams Industry (property of nineteen major motion pictures, three studios, two agencies, the Actors Guild, the Oscars, Valium, Librium and occasionally Xanax.) It was something no one could understand.

Of course, that wasn't exactly true. Every few years or so, someone in the 'biz' would attempt to initiate an exclusive support group. A dozen or more entertainers coming together to share their narcissistic insecurities and manic depressive episodes with their fellow ego maniacs; boasts of fabricated roles in the works or the occasional weep-fest while reminiscing the glory days, always ending within the first couple of weeks due to violated nondisclosure agreements or the threat of a liable lawsuit. The end result being— just bottle it up. Live luxuriously and hope to die before it caught up with you.

Victoria sighed and focused on Micah's handsome face. He looked relaxed, comfortable in the silence. *I've met a thousand men and women— both civilians AND veterans of the celebrity trenches. How can he be so different from ANYONE I've ever met? It's like this strange disconnected man is completely oblivious without being ignorant.*

But tonight, none of that mattered. She was young again and on a first date— or something. And she was herself, not the Victoria Adams Corporation.

She shook her head and sighed, once again letting a smile almost touch her lips. *It has to be me, just right now at this moment. That must be it. The stars are aligned in my head and I noticed him. End of story. We collided, that's all. Just an inevitable coincidence.*

Victoria hugged Micah. When she finally released him, she realized she might have held him just a bit too tight considering they had known each other for less than a day. She casually dismissed the worry. *I'm sure he didn't even notice. He's not familiar with 'Hollywood' protocol, chalk it up to that. In fact, he's probably grateful I didn't give him an air-kiss on each cheek!* She chuckled to herself at the thought.

As Micah started to walk away heading toward his car, it dawned on Victoria that Micah wasn't the only one who might not be aware of certain protocols. She wasn't familiar with HIS protocol— 'normal people' protocol. *What if I want to call him?* she thought. How soon did proper etiquette dictate before she could call— if she could call him at all?

Although not wanting to appear too forward or aggressive, she still wished she had just asked. Problem was, 'Victoria Adams' could call whomever she pleased whenever she pleased. But not wanting to ruin him with 'Victoria Adams', she found herself in unchartered waters feeling like a school girl who had forgotten to ask the boy for his phone number.

With every passing moment Micah grew further and further away, crossing the vast expanse of the parking area. *Well, if it wasn't cool to ask him face to face before he walked away, it's probably ridiculous to yell to him across the parking lot.* She scoffed at herself. *Now, THIS is what's really ridiculous. The longer I wait, the worse it's getting.*

Biting her fingernail she finally blurted, "Hey, Micah!" her voice echoing in the quiet evening. She rolled her eyes. *Nice. Way to go Vic, that was cool... the way you screamed at him? What, are you, twelve?* If she had been a tad too aggressive, hopefully it had been disguised by the growing distance between them.

Micah quickly turned around. *Well that's a good sign,* she thought. "Be cool... you are cool," she told herself. Calmly and overly nonchalant, Victoria casually called out to him with a flip of her wrist, "Can I call you... sometime?" *Yeah, that was okay,* she thought, *maybe a little flamboyant with the hand thing, but whatever.*

"What?" Micah yelled, cupping his hand to his ear.

Victoria sank. *Oh, God, this IS junior high all over again! I can literally feel pimples growing on my nose.* She cleared her throat, "Uh... I'll call you sometime... okay?"

It took everything she had to keep her head up smiling instead of throwing it to her chest in embarrassment. She was completely mortified by the words that had just come out of her mouth. *Yesterday I was a famous actress, now I'm a twelve year old little girl. Great, I can get braces again.*

"I look forward to it," Micah called back, giving her a thumbs up.

Did he just give me a thumbs up? She wasn't quite sure how to interpret that.

Victoria continued to watch Micah as he resumed the trek to his car at the opposite end of the lot. She did, however, notice a sudden pickup in his step. Watching him, she asked herself aloud, "Is he dancing?" Squinting her eyes, *If he splashes in that big puddle...* she waited in anticipation.

"Both feet! YES!" she raised her hands in the air. "He's singing in the rain!" Smiling from ear to ear, she spun on one foot, stopping to take a last look at the mud-splashed Micah now dripping in mud-puddle-crotch pants.

"Ugh, that's gonna leave a stain." Victoria scrunched her face. The adult voice in her head added, *Well done, Vicki, now you can go home and write his name all over your PeeChee.*

"What the hell is wrong with me?" she asked herself when she couldn't take her eyes off of him. "Sleep deprivation maybe? I don't know. What is it about this man?" Ignoring the fact she was now talking to herself, she continued to ponder. "I mean he's mildly attractive, I admit, but he's… what? Truly down to earth?"

She groaned but proceeded to make a sincere list. "He's kind, he's generous…" she laughed then smiled, "and funny. He's serious, he's hurt… he's broken." *That's okay, so are you.* "What, though? What is the big one; what's the DEFINING thing? I know it's right there, I can see it." She stopped and thought. "Is there a word for it? There has to be. It's… it's a…" then shaking her head, "I can't come up with a word for it."

She giggled, turning toward her car parked at the far side of the lot. From there she could see the freeway stretching away from the restaurant; a parade of red lights like an army of ants streaming toward the faint glow of a mall in the distance.

Victoria began to consider the freeway and the two-plus hour drive ahead when suddenly the parking lot lights went out. She looked up at the nearest lamppost as the last flicker died and the pitch darkness closed in around her. A sensation shot through her— her gloom began to resurface with each step further into the darkness. "I can make it, I can make it… get to the cabin," she reassured herself.

*   *   *   *   *

Micah wiped off his puddle-soaked pants as he made his way to his car. *Great, this is going to stain,* he thought as a cold chill went through him; not from the wind or his recently doused slacks, but like hitting a cold spot in a lake. He fastened his coat tighter to no avail. He then realized the cold came from within.

He stopped. Everything was deathly quiet; he didn't remember it having been so quiet before. There was no wind— none. "Too silent," he thought out loud.

Then Micah saw two trees rustle from a sudden forceful gust at the edge of the parking lot. All the other trees still stood motionless as if the wind passed only between those two. Leaves blew and settled in its path as a single current headed across the parking lot.

As it passed the first street lamp, the light bulb exploded. A second went out, then a third. As the gust passed in front of Micah it seemed to take form— a fierce force. He heard its howl, its growl. What was one then split and became three distinct forces deviating from the leaf-swept course, seeking a destination. They were not heading for him.

Micah turned in the direction of their target to see Victoria walking to her car. Calculating her stride, she wouldn't make it there before the solid wind would sweep through her path.

He noticed an anomaly in the shadows on the ground; they seemed strangely too pronounced. There was something very wrong. At first he wasn't even sure why his attention was drawn to them at all, but then he realized the shadows were facing toward the light, not away. No source cast the shadow, neither did light explain their movement as they stretched like hands toward Victoria.

Suddenly all the lights went out and the parking lot was dark. The shadows did not disappear in the darkness nor grow and dissipate, but rather shrunk in size; became denser, more profound, more solid. No longer lying on the earth but animated, standing, moving in wait.

"Just get to your car... just get to your car," Micah urged under his breath watching Victoria. Her head, which had been held high throughout the night, now began to sink into her shoulders.

∗　∗　∗　∗　∗

Victoria had been sleep deprived for years, and other than a couple of hours on the plane much earlier that day, she hadn't slept since she couldn't remember when. Driving on the road for any amount of time would be a huge challenge. Fear crept in that her anxiety might return and the debilitating panic that accompanied it, though at the moment, there were none of the other symptoms indicating such, just the fear that it might. *Don't panic, don't panic, you're fine,* she tried to calm herself.

With a heavy exhale she spoke under her breath attempting to chase away the aloneness carried by the dark, "Okay. You're okay... nothing is really happening. You're just stressed about the drive, that's all. You are OKAY.

You've lived on adrenaline much of your career, this is nothing—a two, maybe three-hour drive."

Her eyes got wide, "A three-hour drive on adrenaline? Adrenaline feeds my anxiety!" It was a catch 22. "Either I make the long drive fueled by torture or I fall asleep at the wheel and end up in a ditch!"

A haunting wind blew her coat open, chilling her. The rain began to pour as she nearly approached the car. A physical shiver shook her adding to her mounting anxiety and the thought that she was truly alone. Her steps quickened, her keys fumbled in her hand. As she hurried to the car door scrambling to open it, panic overtook her like the fear of being chased. The sensation of fleeing a mysterious assailant mounted with each second delayed.

Finally with rushed, clumsy movements, Victoria was able to throw open the door, tumble into the car and slam the door shut. She found herself soaking wet sitting in the passenger seat having forgotten the driver's seat in the UK was on the right side of the car.

Cold and damp, the thought of getting out of the car to walk around to the other side horrified her. But likewise, sitting in the passenger seat and not being able to drive away quickly (or even turn over the ignition) added to the oppressing anxiety pushing down upon her.

* * * * *

Micah saw the left wind catch Victoria, encircling her as prey. "It's only wind," he rationalized, heading toward her at a quicker pace. But as his walk became a run, the shadow ahead took form. Like a reaper cloaked in darkness, the first shadow crept toward her; its shape stretching, reaching to grasp her.

The rain began to pour, pounding down as the second and third fierce winds circled back and knocked Micah off his feet. Attempting to rise, he was thrown forward upon his knees. The rushing gale and violent rain made it impossible for him to see. Fighting the impenetrable storm, he finally got to his feet and raced three steps forward only to be drug two steps backward. Yet he stayed determined and fixated on the first shadowed beast ominously encircling Victoria's car.

The reaper shadow, now pressed against Victoria's window, slowly began reaching through the glass. Desperately, Micah shouted at the creature,

"Tenebris et umbra mortis!" but his words were viciously swallowed by the howl of the second wind as it thrust itself deep into his throat and lungs, drowning him with air and forcing him back to his knees.

The third threw Micah flat on his back— a force without surface to repel; dirt, gravel, water and air swirled in a raging whirlwind intended for Micah's demise. He couldn't breathe. His lungs ached to bursting, his eyes, pelted shut. Choking on debris, Micah began to suffocate.

His mind spun, drifting. The headiness of unconsciousness weighed down on him; he couldn't remember where, when or who he was. Grasping for anything— any one thought that might settle the spin— only a single ancient phrase echoed beyond his mind. He couldn't remember what it meant, but the provocation grew until it screamed out in his thoughts, *B'alma di b'ra yamlekh!*

*   *   *   *   *

The violent storm of pounding rain mixed with rushing wind howled loudly around the car like the sound of an encroaching beast and caused her hair to stand on end. Victoria threw her purse on the floor and quickly crawled over the gearshift into the driver's seat. By more reflex than reason, she shoved the keys into the ignition— her hands shaking so badly it shouldn't have been possible.

Desperately gripping the wheel in an attempt to calm herself, the contoured leather provided a source of stability for her shaking hands. She sat there a moment immobilized in the silence.

Drawing a deep breath, she attempted to turn over the ignition. Her trembling fingers brushed the dangling keys causing them to rattle. Unnerving her so deeply, her hand recoiled, once again seeking the sureness of the steering wheel. Unsuccessfully the ritual was repeated again and again, Victoria reaching for the keys only to return to the security of the leather-bound steering column. Her failure brought her to a place of hopelessness. "I'm never going to make it to Swansea," she said, choking back a sob.

Her breath weighted, she searched her mind for a shred of strength to move forward. "I can just stay in a hotel... yes, a hotel," she conceded. "Okay, okay. Wait... oh, God! I don't even rent my own hotel rooms!" She threw back her head in dismay.

* * * * *

Micah awoke flat on his back, the wind had subsided but the rain still poured. Fifty yards to go; the predator's darkness whirled around Victoria's car manifesting faces of horror and dread, seeking to creep into any crevice of the vehicle.

As Micah ran impeded by the rain, every darkened shadow rose like hands, scourging his flesh and passing through him leaving an unnatural ache and chill where their fingers had struck. It was terrifying to navigate. He veered his steps towards only the dimmest of light thinking to avoid the deeper dark… but where there was light, the form of the shadow was more profound.

Flinching desperately, attempting to ignore the ghostly images and chilling strikes, Micah failed to see the two near-solid entities formed on either side of him. Their strike was not mere chill but impaled him like jagged shards of broken glass. With the speed of the wind, they wrapped him in darkness and began gnawing on his side like two blackened-fanged panthers, snarling and ripping at their prey as they dragged him across the asphalt.

Micah broke free and rolled huddled into a ball; not a position of submission nor defense, nor fetal, but of preparation. "Now I'm angry," he said in growing authority, drawing all his force from inside into focus like a tiger readying to strike.

The creatures continued to rip at him like savage dogs as Micah spoke, "Edim kamu ale'yanu bik'shu naf'shenu… if you can touch me, then I can tear you limb from limb!" In a single movement Micah struck, confirmed by the frightening howl of the wind.

* * * * *

The reflection of headlights in her rearview mirror indicated a car pulling out of the parking lot. It drove steadily away leaving her completely alone. Victoria began to cry; she let her head fall against the steering wheel accidentally honking the horn and startling her. She exhaled. *Who was I kidding? Who AM I kidding? A couple hours of rest and I think I'm suddenly Jennifer in some fairytale life?* She now felt more irreparable than before. *This wasn't salvation, this was the calm before the storm. False hope is far worse… it's raining hopelessness and helplessness absolute. Maybe I'd be better off in a ditch.*

For a moment she was angry at Micah. HE gave her the hope; the thought that she could be normal, pleasant and happy. All hope had done was take away her only ability to cope. It took away her anger, her self-defensive arrogance; things that may have appeared to be bad on the outside but were the only mechanisms she had to survive. Victoria wept.

✳　✳　✳　✳　✳

Battered and bleeding, Micah slowly approached the car. He could see Victoria slumped over the steering wheel. *Who is this person who warrants the keeping of such powerful tormentors?* he questioned. *Creatures such as these are on reserve. Who is she and why have I been brought to her?*

Seeing the horrid dread manifesting many faces beside Victoria in her car, Micah whispered to the entity, "Umbra tenebrosus invasit."

The dark reaper— the shadow of dark dread— circled the interior of the car then slowly bled out from every crack to form a cloud of blackness around Micah. It swirled round him with shrill shrieks of near paralyzing pain, pulsating with the beat of his heart and the sense of running head-on into horror. Images of an ambulance and the sound of sirens drawing closer on his darkest day— the day his wife died— screamed through his mind.

Micah lowered his head as the monstrous beast recoiled and reformed into a single entity before him. In the shrill sound of a violent storm like fingernails on a chalkboard, the darkness snidely chided, "Is that Latin you speak? I don't understand a word you are saying."

Slowly raising his eyes Micah sneered, "I thought that would catch your attention… Tzal'ma'et hishek - marae'det shahat!"

✳　✳　✳　✳　✳

Victoria blew out her cheeks quietly. Solemnly, she finally conceded to the inevitable. Her hands shook, her lips quivered; a faint twitch reached her eye. She let her head sink into her shoulders, "I'm home," she said sorrowfully, "THIS is my home." She succumbed to the cold, terrifying solitude of the car, waiting for fear to overtake her.

She had grown so accustom to panic it was actually her quiet place, her fortress of solitude. It was her own. "This is where I belong, I'm home," she repeated, tears flowing down her face.

A tap on the window startled her. It was Micah. Victoria stifled a cry and attempted to still herself, sucking up the sniffles.

Wiping her eyes, she immediately reached to roll down the window. The window didn't move; she had forgotten the car was not running. Briefly feeling panic begin to rise, she saw Micah smile and motion, questioning whether or not he could jump into the passenger seat. She eagerly nodded.

He ran around the car and opened the door. Shaking the rain and mud off his coat before climbing in, he shut the door behind him, "Brrr! Cold, huh?" Victoria stared silently out the front windshield, a white-knuckled grip on the steering wheel.

Micah was quiet for a moment, interpreting and absorbing all she had gone through. When he broke the silence he spoke slowly and calmly right at her— right into her. "These European rental cars... they tell you the code once and you're expected to remember it forever."

Victoria heaved a stuttered breath; not unburdened, but willing to hear.

"The stick-shift, a different clutch, sensitivity of the brakes... and their cars are geared higher."

She listened.

"Even a European Ford FOCUS, Victoria..."

Focus Victoria' echoed in her mind.

"...is geared higher," Micah continued. "It's hard to keep it under a hundred. You know what I mean?" Micah waited for a nod.

Still gripping the wheel, Victoria nodded.

"You look down, you find you're driving too fast. It can be unnerving." With a slight chuckle, Micah sat back in the seat and went on, "And here in the UK, on top of everything else, you're driving on the wrong side of the car... on the wrong side of the road." He watched for her receptiveness.

"And the roundabouts? You never slow down, you never get a chance to stop. Traffic moves so fast. First couple of days I just want to hit the freeway and turn on the cruise control... drive straight. No lights, no shifting... stay in the slow lane until I get the feel of the car— the road. You know?"

Victoria sniffed, nodding.

"I never thought I'd be so grateful to hit a stoplight red until I drove in London." He paused, thoughtfully, "You just need to stop occasionally and adjust to the traffic."

Just need to stop... adjust. Victoria continued to stare out the window, but now she occasionally closed her eyes in rhythm to sighs of progressive relief— as if stepping down a ladder from a frightful height one step at a time.

Micah continued, "It takes a while to get used to new surroundings... like sleeping in a foreign bed. You get one good night's sleep, forget where you are; but by the second night, the realization that you're NOT HOME anymore begins to settle in."

You're NOT HOME anymore... Victoria thought. *Will I ever be home again?* She sighed. *What is home? Would I even recognize it if I found it?*

Micah quieted for a moment and then went on, slightly increasing his enthusiasm, "But then I give it a few days, and by day three, I find it's actually fun driving on the left side of the road. I realize I'd forgotten how much I enjoyed driving a stick-shift! Shifting down, hitting a round-about— even missing your exit... just keep circling until you find where you need to go. It's exhilarating! Makes me feel like a racecar driver. And driving on the wrong side of the road...? It's naughty!" Micah laughed, "It's like I'm breaking the rules. The same rules don't apply to me here. Speed limit? Out the window! Let's go drive the Autobahn! Hit the Tunnel in two hours... go anywhere, you know?"

Go ANYWHERE... Victoria nodded. "Anywhere..."

Micah smiled, "Within a week, I'm wishing I lived here all the time. I feel right at HOME."

A small grin found its way across Victoria's lips. She put her face in her arms. Quietly laughing, she whispered, "The magic man." Lifting her head slightly, she gave him a sideways squint, "Where to, Mr. Graff?"

"Well, I'm so glad you asked," Micah said, his tone light, "saved me from an extraordinarily improper first... dinner request."

She gave him a playful glare.

"I forgot the code. Forgot the code or couldn't start my car... something like that."

"Uh-huh. Of course. The code."

Micah looked to the ceiling for words, "Now please understand that I mean this in the most platonic of ways…"

Victoria raised a suspicious brow, "Yes?"

"Any chance you can drop me at my hotel?"

She exhaled and nodded with a grin, "Well, fortunately for you, I was just considering my two-hour drive and thought I might also take a room for the night."

"Perfect," Micah said, rubbing his hands together to warm them, "you'll love the Saint Anne's. This is serendipitous."

"I don't know if I believe in fate."

"Ah, well… then call it an inevitable coincidence."

For some reason Micah's phrasing didn't even surprise Victoria. Instead she considered it with curiosity. "I think I already have," she decided.

"So, there you go," Micah stated. "Shall we?"

Chapter 11

"VERY NICE, AND ADJOINING rooms, no less. Need I lock my door?"

"Need you ask?" Micah grinned.

"The room is old, yet luxurious. I like how they've kept the original motif."

"It's probably five-hundred years old or better."

"And the furniture is beautiful. I actually own a number of antiques myself, but to be quite honest, they kind of give me the creeps." Victoria wrapped her arms around herself and shivered, "It is cold in here, though."

"Yes, these rooms have old-fashioned water radiators. Take forever to heat up." Micah knelt down beside the radiator to adjust it.

Victoria sat back on the sofa, sunk in, and truly relaxed. Her mind drifted to the night's (and day's) events. She thought about how drastically her life had changed in less than twenty-four hours. She had started the day three-thousand miles away— mentally, emotionally and literally; now she was strangely in a hotel room with a man she had only just met, neither of them having any licentious intentions.

She would never have believed she would wind up in a hotel room with a strange man, much less be prepared to ask him to unlock the adjoining door—EVER. Even with the reality of it staring her in the face, she'd still never consider advising it to another. Despite the ramblings of the tabloids, Victoria couldn't even remember the last time she'd been alone with a man under such promiscuous circumstances. She knew it had been years.

"Okay, it looks like your heater's working now, ma'am," Micah fell into his hillbilly twang. "Anything else ya need before I let ya wander off to bed?"

Hand on her chin, staring intently at him, "How did you know?" she asked.

Micah knew what she was referring to but refrained from responding. He knew she wasn't ready to hear— and he was less willing to tell. He glanced up from the old radiator, "Know?" he questioned innocently. He hoped she might retract the question.

She nearly did, remaining quiet for a moment. But in the end, she couldn't. "In the car, how did you know? What I was going through, I mean. Or are we going to continue with the charade that driving in England profoundly challenges you?"

Micah thought how to respond. Before he could answer, Victoria noticed his pants were ripped at the knees. She was suddenly alarmed. "How did this happen? Are you bleeding?" she asked. "Come here, sit down... sit down."

Micah sat down on the ottoman. When Victoria knelt in front of him, she saw the side of his dress shirt was also ripped and covered in mud. A look of concern crossed her face.

"I slipped in the parking lot," he answered.

"Both knees? ...and your side?" At closer look, the gash across one knee looked like it could use stitches. Red stains were mixed with the dirt soiling his shirt. "What did you fall on, a grizzly bear?"

Micah remained reluctant. She could tell there was more than he wanted to share.

"That knee needs to be cleaned off, Micah... and I'm betting your side is worse than it looks. Change into something... or just let me tear your slacks off at the knees, they're ruined anyway. I'll get a washcloth from the bathroom. Oh, and take off your shirt."

"Excuse me?"

"I'll bring you a robe," she said with a smirk.

"Don't forget this is Europe," Micah called out after her, "they don't have washcloths in hotel bathrooms."

"Well, so much for their hand towel then," she retorted. Holding the partially opened door, Victoria tossed Micah a hand towel, "Here, cover up with this."

"Very funny."

Reentering the living room area of the suite, she gave Micah the courtesy robe. "Sit back down," she reprimanded.

"Yes mother." He rolled his eyes.

Victoria knelt at his feet, wiping blood and dirt from his knees. She imagined a fight, violent images running through her head. "What happened in the parking lot?" she asked again.

"I fell."

Moving the wet towel toward his exposed side, Victoria was hesitant to touch the abrasions striped across his ribs. *If it wasn't a grizzly bear, it sure was close,* she thought, noticing how much the injury resembled claw marks. Her mind flashed back to the car and the storm's roar, the beastly sounds echoing in the cold frightening night.

She shivered and dabbed at the wound. Micah flinched. "You should wash this out in the shower," she said absently, preoccupied with her thoughts. After a moment, "What made you turn back?" she asked quietly.

"I never left."

"You never left? That doesn't make sense. I was in the car fifteen, twenty minutes— maybe longer before you came to my window." She frowned, "It took you that long to realize you forgot the code?" Victoria kept her eyes fixed on the wound, fearing to look up lest Micah's eyes revealed more of the story than she wanted.

Micah appreciated the reluctance to ask, and he could tell she was even more reluctant to know. "I got a little distracted on the way to my car."

She nodded and pursed her lips. Her breathing slowed. "Did it have to do with me?"

"You are no distraction, Victoria."

She dismissed the comment, continuing slow and quiet, "I have nightmares, Micah," it was hard to confess. "I think I see monsters. I haven't slept in a long time. I've been told my sleep deprivation causes delusions."

"I know."

"Don't you see I'm cursed? I see ugly things." She looked down at the floor, "Sometimes they even come true... sometimes they make me think— things."

"Like what?"

"Like I bring bad things upon good people... and bad people bring bad things upon me."

"I know."

Victoria looked up and stared him straight in the eyes, challenging. "HOW do you know, Micah? You met me this morning— Micah." She pushed back from the ottoman with intensity. "Why did you come, back? Why did you lie about your car not starting, MICAH?" She paused and exhaled loudly, her voice dropping to almost a whisper, "Why did you stand up on the plane, Micah?"

Micah returned her directness with his own. He did not answer compassionately. He did not console with pity. He spoke to her with authority, "Give me your hands."

Victoria was unable to deny his request. Not that she wanted to, but she was very aware it wasn't a choice. Kneeling on the floor in front of the ottoman, she placed her hands face down upon his. He gripped them tight, wrapping his fingers around her wrists. The pressure made her gasp and she felt her shoulders immediately relax. Her head began to swim and her eyelids grew heavy. She suddenly felt lightheaded in a giddy sort of way.

She felt her lungs fill and heard her heartbeat with each breath. It was like being inside and outside of her body at the same time in surround sound; feeling the blood rush though her veins, seeing her heart beat in her mind's eye with eyes wide-open. The control of subconscious things almost within grasp— synapsis firing, nerve endings sensitized; feeling the cool air in her lungs refresh her body and warm it like a shot of fine whiskey. Lastly, she became aware of a hole in the center of her being that became the primary focus—more than something physical ached to be filled. From this place she was lifted outside of her body letting all the rest go. It was exhilarating, frightening— and too easily denied.

"Can you feel that?" Micah asked.

"I don't know," she timidly responded.

"Really?" Micah was put off, "You don't know?" The blatant denial was so typical. *People and their ignorant one-sided ideologies.* "Well," sternly, "if you are brave enough to believe in monsters, then believe this…"

Suddenly Micah's palms grew intensely warm, near burning. When Victoria looked down, a faint shimmering blue light— blue, like the hottest part of a flame, radiated from his hands to hers. As she watched, heat rose up her arms invading her chest and abdomen so intensely, the sensation nearly frightened her. She wanted to pull away but his grip was either too strong or her will was too weak. She looked up helplessly and saw the faint blue shimmer had encapsulated his entire body.

The moment Victoria met his eyes, she saw his strength; his heart. His willingness to fight for her overwhelmed and shook her. She saw the battle that had ensued to protect her; the fear, the pain, the beasts—the creatures he had slain to save her— played out in her mind's eye. A sob caught in the back of her throat as the heat slammed full force into her chest, opening her heart wide and receptive.

It was power; hot, dangerous and thrilling. Somehow Victoria understood she was more than a receptor in the circuit— with or without Micah's touch, the heat would find her. Yet he remained a part of it, holding her unflinching.

Like lightening, it shot through her shoulders; like scalding water it streamed down her back and caused her to arch fully extended, her head thrown back and eyes to the ceiling. Her mouth opened almost caught in a scream. The wind knocked from her with no time to breathe. She exhaled all she had left as if exercising something deep from within.

The electric force rounded the curve of her lower back leaving a deep, aching hollowness in its caressing wake. Moving forcibly downward across her buttocks, the tingling heat spread into her thighs and threatened to ravage her entire body outward and upward. She feared (and yearned) what exposure to such a force against her pelvis might bring.

Somehow, she held the force back at the furthest reach of her thighs, fighting the tremor of power teasing at her core; not because she perceived it as an intruding force, but on the contrary— fearing how receptive she might become.

Pressure building underneath and between her legs; every muscle within her body tense and quivering from a long and emotional day that seemed to have spanned years. She held off the advancing invasion until there was no more strength— neither body, soul nor mind. The fiery force peaked below her where she thought her ground was most feebly held. Her eyes fluttered and her breath caught as she surrendered to be devoured, laying back and accepting it all. She fell instantly into a heap upon the floor, asleep.

Drifting out of consciousness, "It's time to put this away. You need your rest," faded in her ears. Micah gently released her hands; his body quaking, energy still surging through him.

Looking down at Victoria lying peacefully upon the floor was not what Micah had expected. He found himself questioning once again, *Who is this woman?* He had seen many things far harder to explain, but he knew this level of receptiveness was not earned or learned. It was not by will nor might. There was something at play here— more than even he was willing to consider.

Micah had lived with the same torment as Victoria his whole life. As a child he would cringe in fear, facing the things of nightmares. He remembered cowering in corners or under the bedcovers praying that the aliveness in the dark— not only seen and heard but felt in the center of his being— would just go away and leave him be.

But it was relentless— THEY were relentless.

Fear led to panic; panic to anger... and anger finally on to annoyance. The more he had fought for peace and sanity, the more he had realized his power over it— over them. And in turn, he'd discovered their fear of him. It was a gift, a sense; an ability he was born with. It was not something to question but a power developed over the years. It had become a means he counted on in faith to remain sane— and to live as close to a normal life as the world's unseen occupants would allow.

Micah couldn't deny the power or the many unexplainable things that came with it. And, although never able to fully comprehend or control it, he used it to survive; he had learned that even trying to avoid or ignore it (and them) only led from one inevitable coincidence to another that still eventually brought them into his path... or him, into theirs.

Chapter 12

IN A DENSE FOREST near the Moldova border south of Iasi, Romania, a Range Rover approached a secluded, single-cabin estate. A large man exited the vehicle. He breathed in the fresh mountain air and gazed reminiscently at the timeless surroundings. Cherrying his cigarette, he crushed the remains between his thumb and the backside of a large gold ring he wore upon his right hand. He palmed the filter and headed for the door.

A doorman standing outside on the wraparound porch made way the man's entry, opening the door and maintaining a respectful distance, neither raising his eyes nor making any other gesture of notice. Guards and servicemen shared many of this doorman's qualities— discipline, honor in servitude, respect— and although strength was also most often found in men such as these, this doorman conveyed none. He would dare not presume his presence of mind or body compared to the strength of those he served. Self-sacrifice was value enough.

With the exception of the broad front door made of 5-inch thick, single-slat oak, the cabin was entirely domestic stone. Its enclaves gave the illusion of window bays but no windows were visible. Polished stone filled the faux framework appearing at first glance to be darkened glass, offsetting the structure and adding to the illusion. Light could neither enter nor exit the edifice. Once inside, only sparse oil lamps embedded in the slate floor made it possible to see, yet still secured the identities of those present.

In the center of the exceedingly large room, a cavernous, perfectly circular pit was nearly invisible from the doorway. Many ancient tribes had similar; what the mysterious Anasazi natives called a kiva. Its origins were unknown, though the perfectly circular dimensions likely indicated a tribal gathering place for a council giving members an equal seat.

Steep stone stairs headed downward more than twelve feet from the edges of the circle. The last step, wider than the rest, provided seating. Unusually deep impressions worn into the stone suggested that men had sat in council in the kiva for hundreds (if not thousands) of years.

In the center of the pit was an immense round slab serving as a table, situated close and low to the bottom step leaving little room to navigate anywhere but up and out of the pit. The slab appeared to have been there long before the cabin and, more likely, had been unearthed to form this unique place of gathering.

In the center of the stone table, a natural trough held burning coals giving little warmth and less light. Ring Finger made his way down the kiva. He tossed his cigarette filter into the coals where it instantly burst into flames and provided a matchstick's worth of light to the annoyance of the other attendees.

There was no hierarchy in the round, every voice heard carried equal weight. The darkness was not for anonymity— it represented equality in voice. No statement was to be judged according to the speaker; all were to speak as a collective, to the Collective; to be of one mind. Dismissing one was dismissing all.

In blatant disregard for the council's latest arrival, the youngest seated at the table directed his complaint toward the other council members. With a British accent he questioned, "Why do we insist on meeting in this relic?"

Ring Finger responded coolly, taking his position in the round, "It's a matter of respect." He maintained the discipline of a collective voice and did not correct UK but rather spoke to the table, "Is there schism in the Collective?"

"Respect for what? Hiding in the shadows? Dust and stone? With all we have so easily accomplished? Don't feed us rhetoric of humble beginnings," UK scoffed.

From the other end of the large table, a thick cigar cherry brightened, illuminating the billow of smoke that followed. An eastern European accent came from behind it, diverting the discussion in correction of UK's defiance, "Why are we here?"

"He's resurfaced," one announced.

"Who?"

No one responded. Europe turned suspiciously to see Ring Finger's expression— his face had dawned a smug grin.

"That can't be. He's dead," a voice with Asia diction declared, breaking the silence.

"Our sources believe it's him."

"He died in Tokyo seven years ago."

"Did we see the body, compañero?"

"We saw a body," Asia responded, "they buried him. He's not coming back."

"Why would we be concerned with him in the first place," UK scoffed. "Alive, dead; what did he ever do? If he's alive, he hasn't done anything for seven years. Seven years off the grid."

"It's not him."

"What does it matter if it is?"

"He seems to have the habit of being in the wrong place at the wrong time," another answered. "And this is not the time for unpredictability."

"We make too much of him," UK went on, "consider him, don't consider him. What is he? He's got to be almost fifty... tired, retired. This can't be the only reason we were summoned to this forsaken shithole."

"Of course not— and watch your tongue," Europe corrected. "There's no animosity here, we're above that. Keep it civil."

Ring Finger rose from his seat. His voice was cold, collected, confident as he broke tradition and cautioned, "I warned you all seven years ago; I told you he wasn't dead. I told you he couldn't be killed by thugs, by... what do they call them? Gang-bangers? He won't die a senseless death. And no offense to our friend from Japan, but the man certainly won't meet his demise in Tokyo." Still masked in the dark, the faint light showed only the top of his chest and the shadow of a trimmed goatee. With his thumb, he spun the thick gold signature ring in an unconscious, habitual manner.

"Men die senseless deaths every day," Tokyo responded, having remained silent up until then.

"That's true. And he's your problem, Furcus... always has been," UK said, addressing Ring Finger.

"If you had sent me to Tokyo back then," Ring Finger claimed, "we wouldn't be having this discussion now."

"If we had sent you to Tokyo, Furcus," Tokyo defended, "he would have sniffed you out—and me, following suit,"

"It's not him! It can't be," Asia insisted. "How many times do I have to say it? He's dead; his body burned alive. His daughter took the corpse home and buried him. His wife remarried within a year— book closed. I was on the phone when the ambassador made the call."

Europe called to order, "Alright, alright. Where is he now?" he asked the table.

"Six feet under!" Asia exclaimed.

"Enough! Where do they say he is?"

"London," came the answer.

"London?" Europe heaved a frustrated sigh, "He's in London NOW? TODAY? And staying through the weekend, no doubt?" Shaking his head, "Which of you thinks THAT is a coincidence?" he challenged.

"Coincidence or not, it's insignificant," UK interjected, shifting his eyes with a look of disinterest. Leaning back in his seat, he knuckle-rolled a gold coin, absently gazing into the dark.

Ring Finger stepped in, "Fortunately, comrades, I'm traveling to London tonight."

"What aren't you telling us, Furcus?"

"Too many cooks spoil the soup, my friends," he answered.

"All right, then," Europe resigned, "he's your problem again. Wrap it up, Furcus, we have other matters to deal with."

Heads nodded in the shadowy dark and Ring Finger once again accepted his charge.

"We've been informed the soil samples from Syria were successfully acquired," Russia spoke out, bringing the meeting into focus. "We predict they will fall in line with the thematic, multispectral satellite imagery which revealed radioactive signatures at the base of the Jabal al-Druze mountain range. The results should be conclusive following the summit."

"Then London becomes much more critical now."

"Will the summit leaders follow instructions?"

"They've had a recent change in leadership," Ring Finger flatly stated. "That should persuade full membership compliance."

The Collective looked one to another, "So, who are we thinking for London?"

"This needs to be done right; it needs to be assured," Ring Finger answered again. "We have someone in mind."

"Fine then," Europe concluded, "Nothing stands in the way of London—agreed?"

"Agreed."

*   *   *   *   *

When the meeting came to a close, figures rose from their seats in the dimness. Europe turned to Ring Finger, "Furcus, stay with me a moment."

As the others began to leave, Europe discretely addressed the large man with the gold ring, "No one questions your motives or your methods, Furcus, but you have been distracted by him in the past."

Ring Finger appeared pensive, "I disagree, old friend. Much progress has been made in my pursuit of him. In some ways, as much of an impediment as he was, he kept me focused— whereas, others at the table have become distracted; serve no real purpose, caught up in power or politics. But my devotion is unequalled."

"No question. Your focus on the grand picture has always been unwavering. Your foresight in what's required— few in the room could understand, yet alone conceive." Europe voiced with utmost respect, "Time has certainly validated your effectiveness— although your strategies are still largely questionable."

"Has the job been done?"

Europe gave a small nod.

"Then what does it matter?"

Chapter 13

IT WAS NEARLY 10:30 when Victoria awoke in her bed. She wasn't naked, but she wasn't fully dressed, either. She fluffed the pillows behind her head and rose to a seated position.

Running her tongue across her lips, she found herself wondering what her new friend might have seen the previous night considering her current state of undress. After a brief assessment, "Well, he appears to be a gentleman," she decided. "Add that to Mr. Graff's accolades, I suppose."

The door between her and Micah's rooms was partially ajar. She heard rustling and clanking coming from the adjoining room. Throwing off the covers, she searched the floor for the hotel's courtesy robe; but finding it nowhere in sight, she grabbed Micah's torn dress shirt, loosely slipped it on, and hurriedly fastened a couple mid-level buttons. Although calmly entering his room, she managed to exude the authority of an invading force.

At the kitchenette Micah sat meticulously mixing milk with his cereal before taking large bites with an oversized utility spoon. Glancing up at the menacing presence that was Victoria, he quickly looked away tending emphatically to his oatmeal raisin squares. Victoria stood firmly in the entry way, a stern look upon her face.

Darting his eyes back and forth between Victoria and the cereal bowl, Micah chewed, swallowed and finally asked, "Sleep well?" before obnoxiously filling his mouth with another extraordinary-sized bite. In the midst of his resumed crunching, his darting glance lingered a fraction of a second on Victoria; he couldn't help but notice how much better his shirt looked on her.

Slightly frustrated, Victoria was unwilling to be the first to bring up the night before. Whatever had happened in the parking lot and whatever he had done to her with the heat from his hands were definitely some things in need of explaining… but having awoken wearing nothing more than her bra and underwear was clearly another. "Hungry?" Micah asked, raising the box of oatmeal squares.

Victoria glared.

"Coffee?"

She frowned, "I am going to go shower and then we're going to have a chat. Then we are going to leave. I expect you in my room by the time I get out." With that she turned and marched to the shower.

Micah's mouth full of cereal, he mumbled loudly, "Where are we going?"

"You said you were giving me three days," she yelled back.

Micah was bewildered. "When did I say that?"

Shouting from behind the bathroom door, "We'll talk about that in the chat."

*   *   *   *   *

Victoria exited the bathroom; hair partially dried, complimentary hotel slippers, and a towel that sparsely covered her shapely body. He supposed the oversized slippers were to make up for the undersized towel. Micah fixated on Victoria's feet, refusing to raise his stare. He finally shook his head, "Those slippers don't fit."

Victoria looked down at the cushy white slippers not understanding the magnitude of his concern.

"I should call down to the front desk and request a smaller pair," he insisted.

Victoria finally understood. "Oh… you don't like my slippers?" she feigned a pout. "I can take them off if you like?" Crossing one leg behind the other, she used just her toes to step down on the backside of the slipper. Slowly sliding her foot out of the slipper, she moved her bare foot up her leg, pausing at the knee. She then slid it slowly back down along the curve of her calf to repeat the process, removing the second slipper.

Standing there barefoot, she coyly asked, "Better?"

Giving him nowhere to look, Micah's eyes hit the floor. He wasn't quite ready to confess to having a thing for ankles. He couldn't explain why, but there was something attractive about them; the shape, the contour, the softness of the skin stretched tight around them. Ankles were the base of all things forbidden. The right pair of shoes with an outfit that left a woman's ankles revealed was a surefire way to draw his attention.

Victoria, satisfied with herself for the moment, proceeded across the room and sat in a chair with her back to him. On the back of the chair, neatly folded, was the dress she had worn the night before.

Brushing her hair, she pulled the dark brown waves over her shoulder and across her chest, exposing the length of her neck. When she finished, she rested her head on her arm and ran her fingers through the back of her tresses. Her exposed neckline accented the strength of her shoulders to the sides and the softness of her hair to the back. The sensuous contour to the front led from her throat to her chest disappearing suggestively beneath the towel. *If she attempts to dress in front of me, I can't be held responsible.*

"So, are we going to talk about last night?" Victoria began.

Micah, waiting patiently, gave a start. Confused, he pointed to himself questioning, "Are you looking for me to start?"

Victoria folded her arms across her chest, "Well, I could talk about what I experienced, however I don't think you want to start this morning with an argument you don't stand a chance of winning."

"You do look extraordinarily rested."

Victoria became distracted thinking about how well she had slept. She caught herself, rapidly shaking her head, "Don't change the subject."

Micah took a deep breath and slowly exhaled through his nose, "I got a little angry," he confessed.

"THAT was anger?"

Micah struggled a bit, "Eh… mixed, I guess."

"Duly noted. So what in particular… set you off?"

"Um… again, mixed. Skepticism, mainly. But let's not go down that path." Micah got serious, "Listen, Victoria, believe it or not, I am an open book. And if you want to talk, I'll keep nothing from you." He bowed his head solemnly, "There are things I can explain and things I can't. Some things just have to be experienced."

"I'm coming to understand that. What happened in the parking lot?"

Micah was reluctant to explain. Long ago he believed the truth set people free. But sometimes ignorance was truly bliss. She had suffered for years from delusions; some manufactured by the stress of her industry, but others… he knew all too well that with Victoria, there were certainly external forces adding to the conflict. For her, knowing about them could be liberating— or could be equally paralyzing. "What do you think happened?" Micah decided.

Victoria pictured the haunting images that plagued her in the car. The sound of the wind, the predator who stalked her. They were all too similar to the images she had seen while he'd held her hands. She didn't believe it was real. She didn't believe in such things— she only lived with them.

Like the perverse bond of an abusive husband and his loving wife, she was suddenly embarrassed to say anything. This was a conversation for her psychiatrist (whom she lied to.) She became eerily insecure.

Micah stopped her, "Put it away."

"I don't want to. I know what I think, but..." she started to cry. "Do you know how scary it is to know you're crazy? To not trust yourself with your own mind... what you see? What you hear? To sit in a room full of people having to play a role, not sure how many people are real or even how many there are?"

"Put it away, Victoria, it has nothing to do with you anymore." Micah lifted his shirt. "Do you see this? Do you feel this?" Placing her hand on his wounded side, "They're gone now."

Victoria gingerly caressed the wound. "I knew it, I knew it last night..." with more surprise, "I knew it in the car— I can see them, Micah!" She abruptly pulled her hand away.

"Put it away, Victoria."

"No! Don't you see? I'm not crazy, it WAS real! When I think back... I was there, they were there, then you were there. It all makes sense. When I think back... oh, my God— they were THERE!"

"And are they here now?" Micah's voice was calm.

"No."

"That's right. Were they on the plane?"

Victoria looked down trying to remember. A look of anguish crossed her face, "They were! But then you were there— again."

"That's why I stood up. We're not so different." He raised his head, searching her eyes, "Were you able to sleep?" he questioned.

"Yes. Like a baby," she answered with sincerity.

Micah nodded with a faint smile. His expression then turned serious, "Are you threatened by me, Victoria?" he asked.

Victoria stared intently into his eyes, seeking to see into him. She glanced at the span of his hands, the breadth of his shoulders, the strength of his legs. She noted the cut of his chest and the width of his arms. He was strong, but not a large man. And she was a petite woman; no physical match for the man who stood before her.

She sat silent for a time thinking of every word they had exchanged; on the plane, in the restaurant, in the car— and now in the room. It took a few moments to even recall the seconds of anger, as brief as they were. Had he not mentioned it, she would have likely not noticed or remembered.

She recounted the events of the evening. She remembered the attack in the parking lot— it was her memory now; the fight that ensued and Micah's victory over the beasts. The glow of his hands— his core; the unbridled force— the power that followed, surging through her body and her helplessness to resist. Even the grasp of his hands; it was out of her control to stop him. *There should be fear.*

Contemplating it all, if she was to remain with this man, Victoria surmised that one day she would surely drive him to unsurmountable anger. She considered it, the whole of it. What that meant, where it came from, and where it was going. She sighed.

With confidence, she finally spoke, "You couldn't hurt me, Micah. It's not in you. You're not capable of it. You would never hurt me." Her expression was warm and sincere. She didn't understand how she knew, but she had no doubt. For reasons she couldn't explain, she trusted him— utterly and completely. "But having said that," she added, "I do truly fear for anyone who might try... to hurt me, that is."

"Me to."

"Why does it feel like that's a valid concern?"

"Another thing I can't explain."

"Okay, fine. I understand there are things we can't talk about right now, but we ARE going to circle back around to the whole electrified body... thing."

Micah shrugged his shoulders as if he knew NOT what she was talking about.

"Don't even." She blew a wisp of hair from her face, "However, on a lighter note, whatEVER are we going to do for the next three days?"

"Um... something is amiss here."

"You promised me three days."

Micah squinted searching the ceiling, "Pfft... I don't recollect anything of the sort."

"You said you forgot the code but you would give it a few days. Then you proposed we hit the tunnel, drive the Autobahn and go anywhere I wanted."

Micah winced and stammered, "Ah... what I meant... uh... well, that was a metaphor."

"About me?"

"Yes..."

"Then I don't see the problem."

Micah scoffed.

"Okay then, let me ask you this; did your CAR really not start, or did YOU just not start it?" Victoria waited.

"Um…"

"That's what I thought. Stick to the code, Micah. Three days until I feel like home. That's what you meant. If I'm wrong, just tell me."

Micah surrendered raising his hands and shaking his head feebly. She was right, that was what he'd meant.

Victoria clapped her hands together, "Good! Then, I suggest we visit the cabin."

"Cabin?"

"It's a cottage I have out in the country… in Wales."

"WALES?" Micah was now the one experiencing unescapable submission. "All right, fine, but I need to stop by the Oracle first."

"Matrix reference, I should have known. You are suddenly starting to make sense."

Micah grinned, "The Oracle Mall in Reading."

Victoria quipped sarcastically, "Shopping…? How absolutely dreadful! What IS a girl to do?" She smiled from ear to ear.

Muttering, "Why did I stand up on the plane?"

Chapter 14

THE CALMING STRETCH OF farms and fields along the M4 faded into the twilight as Micah and Victoria reached the Second Severn Crossing. The rolling green of Wales and picturesque Bristol Bay, swallowed into the encroaching night.

The uneventful drive had been a godsend; a reprieve from a long day of malls, shops, markets and cafes— and the calculated maneuvering required to traverse such places. Victoria now knew the Oracle inside and out— and Micah had a new wardrobe to testify to it.

Nearing the cabin on Swansea Bay, Victoria yawned, welcoming the normalcy of all-day-at-the-mall fatigue. "I'm actually just plain tired. It's so refreshing!"

"Glad to hear it," Micah sighed, yawning as well. It was contagious.

"I know you're tired, too. You need some sleep. And you do know I'm not expecting you to drive back tonight, right?"

"Three days. Yes, I'm aware." Micah rolled his eyes.

Victoria slapped him on the shoulder, "It's really so painful to be graced by my company?"

Micah laughed, "There's no place I'd rather be."

"That's better," she grinned, "here we are!"

The two walked the pristine stone path leading from the carport to the hand-carved double doors. The breadth of the edifice so vast, in the cloud covered moonlight Micah couldn't even make out the far end of what Victoria so casually called 'The Cabin'. Where he grew up a cabin was a drafty one or two room structure with a Ben Franklin stove and an outhouse in back. It was someplace you stayed when you went fishing or hunting; somewhere a toothbrush was optional and all you needed was a pocket knife and a sleeping bag.

After an abbreviated tour including directions to the servants' quarters, Micah sat back in the chair next to Victoria's luxurious antique bed. With comforters and more pillows than the queen-sized bed could possibly hold, it was a marvel in physics. *Beats the heck out of a sleeping bag though,* he had to admit.

Victoria emerged from the adjoining bathroom in surprisingly practical flannel pajamas; face scrubbed clean, hair loose and freshly brushed. Micah rose, ready to bid his goodnight and retire to the already prepared guest room. He really was exhausted.

Victoria spoke, "Stay with me until I fall asleep." It was neither a request nor a command.

"I can stay," he replied, knowing there was no unspoken agenda.

Falling asleep had been a challenge for Victoria for longer than she cared to remember. True, she had slept sound the night before, but in the light of day (so to speak) doubt had crept in about its apparent ease and the likeliness of doing it again.

"How do YOU sleep at night?" she asked.

"Close my eyes?" Micah smiled.

"Seriously. With all you've seen?"

"I learned to love the dark," he answered. "As a child I was afraid of the dark– what I couldn't see." He sighed. "One time, I was so afraid, I hid. I was caught, cornered in the dark, petrified. But they couldn't see me... I was looking right at them, but they couldn't see me. The more they looked, the less I feared. I guess I found my companion."

"Ewe, that sounds suspiciously evil. Isn't that the story of villains?" Victoria tried to sound ominous.

"I suppose," Micah laughed. He considered the circle. *Do I pursue justice because I've been chased by injustice, or does injustice pursue me because I try to be just? If those were the only two elements, it might be worth considering...*

He sat back down in the beautiful Victorian chair (made more for aesthetics than comfort) as Victoria readily snuggled in. The air was cool. After almost three hours in a car together with Victoria running the heater on high, Micah knew she liked to keep extremely warm. At night, however, she obviously preferred a half-dozen comforters to protect her from the chill of the night air blowing in through an intentionally opened window.

"You look uncomfortable." Victoria motioned Micah to sit on the other side of the bed. "There's plenty of room up here, I won't bite."

"No worries there. What worries me is that if I lay down, I'll be asleep in seconds."

Victoria patted the bed next to her. Micah kicked off his shoes and climbed up; she covered him with two of her three extra throw blankets.

Confident he wasn't going anywhere anytime soon, she was now ready to change the subject. "So, as I warned," Victoria started, "now that I have your undivided attention, what the heck was that all about last night?"

Micah looked at her. He simply said, "Cleansing."

"Cleansing?"

"Just knocking out the cobwebs. People too easily believe in dark things and lack faith for good. Let's just say it was a little demonstration that went a tad bit overboard."

"A tad bit overboard?"

Victoria watched him bite the inside of his lip. He shook his head as if remembering something he hadn't accounted for, "There was more to it than I expected. Something happened... there's something going on between us..." Micah stopped, regretting saying the last part aloud.

Victoria turned on her side, thinking. Noticing his discomfort, she soothed, "Thank you for being here, Micah. I think I'm okay... I mean, I KNOW I'm okay, but this is just easier. And I wanted to talk until I fell asleep."

"You're welcome." He appreciated the fact she hadn't pushed. He tried to get comfortable, shifting himself attempting to find a good reclining position.

Victoria leaned back into her mountain of gushy pillows, "Here, this helps. Lay back in your pillows."

"Really? Some of them are mine?"

Victoria gave him a dirty look, "On loan. You can have... a couple. Here." She handed him two.

"THESE are pillows? I thought these were those little cushy room deodorizers."

"Fine. Here, take this big one. Geez, it's like a slumber party with my little brother."

Pounding the pillow, "Is this feather or that stuff that feels like snot? I like feather pillows."

"Seriously? Just take your pick." Victoria leaned forward and threw an armful of pillows on him, "God, somehow I thought it would be different with..."

"With...? With what?"

She stopped and looked at Micah. Micah leaned back a bit to get a full view of her expression, "With what?" he asked again.

That is the question, isn't it? Victoria held her tongue.

Micah rolled over on his side facing her in a playful mood. He was much more comfortable lying on the bed as her obnoxious little brother.

"Take your feather pillow," Victoria instructed as if talking to a child. "There. Are you comfy now?"

Micah shrugged.

"Okay. Now, no looking at each other. Lay on your back. Just look up at the ceiling like we're camping, staring at the stars. Then you can tell me a campfire story about the beast in the parking lot, spring cleaning… oh, and the strange thing going on between you and me."

Micah rolled over on his back, stared at the ceiling, "You're right, this sorta does work. Did you do much camping growing up?" He didn't try to hide his doubt.

"Don't be so surprised, I wasn't always a…" searching for a quippy description, "…Hollywood debutant. I grew up in Washington State."

"Really?" Micah was genuinely interested. "Which part?"

"Seattle area."

"I actually lived there, about twenty years ago," he said.

"I was there twenty years ago, we could have met."

For some reason her casual comment struck Micah.

"You got quiet. Something wrong?" she asked.

"Nope." Micah relaxed, letting the thought go. "Just gazing at the stars. Listening to the crackling fire."

"I love camping."

"Me, too."

"You know, we call this the cabin."

"I do," Micah laughed, "but you do know most people would call this a castle, don't you?"

"Well, maybe a manor or a chateau," Victoria defended.

"Okay." It was strangely peaceful staring at the imaginary stars together.

"Kai," Victoria whispered, causing Micah to look in her direction, "tell me a fairytale."

Micah paused then looked away; he wasn't sure how to take that. Victoria calling him Kai took him off guard and caused him to think of his wife. No one other than his wife had ever called him that— EVER. And it was also the name of his first son; a child he had lost when the boy was only a toddler. Micah sat silent.

Victoria reached over and touched his arm, "I'm sorry." She wanted to say that she wasn't being presumptuous, but to say another word would have been. A moment of silence stood between them. Victoria's heart ached.

"It's… it's fine," Micah fidgeted. "It's fine."

She didn't blink.

He leaned toward her convincingly, "Victoria, it's fine. It's just no one has called me that or said that name in a long time. It was nice to hear... it was my first son's name as well. Just took me by surprise."

"I... um... "

"It was nice," he assured.

And it was. He really wasn't hurt by it. On the contrary, it was like hearing the voice of his wife and someone speaking fondly of his son in a single word. But she had scared him. Micah didn't believe in love; not for him anymore, not like that. And certainly not with a celebrity. She couldn't possibly understand him nor the sacrifices he had made, the life he had lived. With Micah, there was no going back and he couldn't ask her— or anyone— ever again to make the journey in the first place. There were too many unknowns; too much left to fate for those who became wrapped in his reality. It never turned out well. *We live on different planets,* he thought.

"You... I..." he struggled trying to say, *'I don't have the liberty.'* Micah sighed, "I can't ask this of you. And you really don't know what you're asking."

"What?"

"For the fairytale."

"It's just a fairytale," she said quietly.

"Right," he conceded. "Fine then, just the fairytale." Removing his emotions, he began. "So, in the fairytale, Obi-Wan Kenobi has looked for Luke his entire life."

"Ooh, this story is good!"

"Uh-huh," Micah frowned, "and Obi-Wan has been waiting so long, hiding from Darth. Problem is, he eventually realizes everyone is an Imperial stormtrooper or an Imperial loyalist. At the same time, nothing's going on and there hasn't been a rebellion for over twenty years; all the Jedi are either dead or revealed double agents... or they just flat-out hate each other— and especially me!" Micah was growing agitated.

"Okay, wait a minute, you're getting a little intense. Can you calm it down a bit?"

"You have no idea..." Micah mumbled. Realizing he was rapidly moving toward real anger, he attempted to calm down. "Breathe... breathe," he told himself.

Victoria laughed, "What does that mean?"

"My wife told me to breathe when I got angry."

"Oh? And are you all right? Do you need to take a break?" She was obviously poking fun at him.

"No, no, I'm okay. It's probably good for me to vent."

"You do realize you're venting about Luke Skywalker, don't you?"

Micah glanced at her sideways but then exhaled a deep breath, "Yes, fine, you're right."

"Better now? So, you were saying?"

Micah continued slow and solemn, "It's just that Obi-Wan is tired. He's stopped looking... doesn't know what he's looking for anymore. Smokes a carton of cigarettes a day. He still feels the Force but there's no mountain to move and no reason to walk on water. And somewhere along the way the Empire became the good guys... and the bad guys became far, far worse."

"I thought this was going to be a fun fairytale."

"So did I. But there is no rebel force."

"Well, that may be true, but what happened last night..."

"...was only the beginning. It's a preview. It's the trailer. It's a shot across the bow before the real players manifest."

Victoria held up her hand, "Excuse me? The real players? As in regular life? Like people... not shadow ghost— things?"

Micah rolled his eyes. *Curses, now ghost-things. Great.*

"Don't roll your eyes at me, I saw your side, Micah. It was real, you could have died! But you didn't. You... killed it." She then had a frightening thought, "You did kill it, didn't you?!" Her eyes got big.

"Yes, Victoria, it's 'dead'." He tried to conceal his amusement.

"Have you ever had to fight... the 'dark side of the Force' for real?"

He chuckled at her wording, "I'm sorta regretting the whole Star Wars analogy now, but do you mean in the 'real-world'?"

"Yes, that's exactly what I mean."

Micah was suddenly serious, slow to speak. A memory full of regret took hold, of his expression, "I have," he answered.

She lowered her tone to match his, "Like that?"

"Can be."

She understood his fear in the possibility. "With real people?"

"Uh-huh."

"How do you fight that?"

"You avoid it."

"And if you can't?"

"Well, usually things can be dispersed or diverted."

"And unusually?"

Micah lifted off the plush pillow to look her in the eyes. He softened his tone for seriousness, "You pray that your unavoidable actions are somehow for the greater good."

Victoria quietly questioned, "Unavoidable?"

"Believe me, you want to avoid it," Micah said seriously.

"And if it can't be helped?"

"Then it can't be helped."

Victoria nodded. She felt strangely connected, compassionate. "Micah, what did you mean by 'something's going on between us'?"

"I don't know why that came out of my mouth," he answered hastily. "Pretend I didn't say it. I've been out of the game too long, I'm reluctant to say. I doubt I'd even recognize... um… forget it. There is no rebel force."

Victoria thought about it for a moment. Then her eyes opened wide, "You think I'm Luke!"

"Pfft,' Micah scowled and looked away.

Seeing the expression on his face, "Oh, my God, you do! You think I'm Luke!"

Micah scoffed, "I've met more Anakins than Lukes. I really do regret the Star Wars thing."

Victoria rolled over towards Micah, trying to see his eyes. He turned his head to the side, darting them away from her. Micah knew if she saw his eyes, he would not be able to hide what he was not ready to believe himself.

Victoria popped up onto her knees and leaned over to see his turned face. Micah squinted, throwing his head even farther back, as far as his neck would allow, forcing her to completely bridge his body on her hands and knees. "You're getting annoying," he said.

She started to stretch further. Micah quickly flipped his head 180 degrees and buried it into the pillows like a toddler avoiding a bite of peas.

Victoria flopped back down on the bed. She laid on her side propped up on her elbow, resting her cheek in her hand. "Look at me!" she demanded playfully.

"Nuh-uh!" muffled between the two pillows on loan.

"Look at me…" She reached out to grab him.

He flipped quickly onto his back and put up his hands as if warding off a blow, "Don't. Don't touch me right now." He sounded almost serious.

"Don't touch you?" Victoria teased with a laugh. "Okay." She held her hand just millimeters from his chest, "Is this okay?"

"Huh-uh." Micah pressed his body into the bed.

"Okay…" she pulled her hand back, still less than an inch. "Is this better?"

Micah stared her down.

"Oh, come on… a little closer?" She moved her hand within a breath. Searching his face she saw earnestness in his eyes and was suddenly drawn into the passion of his fearful expression. Instantly waves of both rage and compassion overwhelmed her causing her to snatch her hand away. The heat, the energy, a barrage of emotions— all right there for her to explore. "Are you doing that?" she asked.

"No."

She held her hand close once more. It was faint, she almost couldn't see it; matter of fact she wasn't sure if she was seeing with her eyes or her desire, but there was a blue aura around him, expanding and contracting just inches off his chest and arms.

She reached out to touch it, like warming her hands on an open fire. It arched and touch her, gently shocking her, causing her to catch her breath. It was like fire without the burn. The closer her hand got, the more frequently the glow expanded.

Victoria finally raised the courage to submerge her hand into the light. In that instant, she saw flashes of him as a child with a woman who could only have been his mother, then saw the day his father walked into his bedroom to say he was leaving. As she held her hand steady she could feel Micah's frustration, elation, anger, compassion; feelings of pride for his son, love for his daughter. A collage of births and deaths. An underlying drive; a determination to be worthy of his gift— to do good— a heavy debt he yearned to repay. So hated by his enemies, a longing to be accepted, liked, and to blend in. All of his passion focused to a single point.

It didn't take an interpreter to know this was his essence, his soul. Every event in his life that caused him to stand— or to hold back. The Native Americans called it 'Achachak'; in Chinese it was 'Jingshen'; and the Hebrews had many words for soul and spirit. It was best described as 'Nashama'.

"Well if it's not you, then... how?" she whispered.

"There's something going on between us."

Looking down at him, Victoria could feel the intensity of his gaze; but this time it wasn't memories, it was directed toward her. His hands still guarding his chest, he spread his fingers open and she could feel them as if they caressed her. His gaze intensified. His body shivered. She knew he was feeling her as strongly as she could feel him— *maybe stronger,* she wondered.

Micah stared into her eyes as she felt his soul. Her expressions of surprise; her elation at his joy, her sorrow for his pain, the loneliness they shared— hers in a crowded room and his hidden all alone.

It became too much for him to remain a mere observer trapped beneath a sea of blankets and pillows. He rose slowly to a seated position, anticipating her hand would readily embrace his as he let down his guarded position. But Victoria, with a beaming smile, maintained her distance at the pre-requested gap of no less than half an inch. She somehow managed not a smidgen closer nor further away. She was now the master and Micah, the student, leading him with her maintenance of the distance.

Something about the new dynamics didn't seem fair to Micah. He joined in the game moving his hand slowly towards hers, now trying to decrease the gap.

She nodded, but with a shake of her finger whispered, "But don't touch," as she slowly scooted herself into a reclining position.

"Don't touch," he agreed, his hand moving forward.

As Micah pushed his hand closer, Victoria gradually moved hers back, retracting it deliberately up to her chest. Micah pursued, closing the distance between their palms, feeling the heightened intensity of Victoria's energy; the connection, the overwhelming sensation. At the final moment, Victoria moved her hand to allow Micah's finger tips to rest upon her heart.

Victoria caught her breath. She couldn't exhale, breathing only inward until she shook. Staring directly into her, Micah held her with his eyes.

Two, three, and then four fingers gently spread across her collarbone. Firmly laying the palm of his hand upon her chest, finally allowed her to exhale. Head slightly back, she arched her body forward accepting his touch, eyes never leaving his gaze. She was wide open; both heart and body. His touch more intimate than mere flesh.

Victoria knew this wasn't just physical. It wasn't just a game. She understood that what they shared could not be done maliciously; could not be done unintentionally. It could not be stolen nor swindled and she knew what that meant. What she must mean to him suddenly scared her. She was certain she wasn't worthy of him, not like this; he wasn't just some conquest. It was all beginning to mean too much— much more than mere sex would. She gently drew back.

Micah eased away. He feared he had gone too far, but Victoria smiled. She reached out and touched him on the face. She could feel the soft stubble of an emerging beard and passed her fingers across his lips. She started to cry.

Folding her hands together and laying back on the bed, she looked to the ceiling. Tears dried on her cheeks.

"Are you okay?" Micah asked.

"I don't know," she answered quietly. "Thank you for being here with me, Micah."

Victoria wasn't ready to define it, to even consider what they were, what they might be, what this was or was becoming. She sighed a heavy breath. *Everything is fine. Everything is good.* She was warm and safe. She was free. Her head was clear. She was tired and she could sleep.

She smiled at Micah, rolled over and spooned up against him. She took his arm and wrapped it around her.

Micah held her tight.

Chapter 15

MICAH AWOKE, STARTLED TO find himself buried in a sea of Victoria's pillows. Without thinking he sat up and began digging through them; the downy comforters, the fluffy cushions, the throw blankets. He finally stopped, eventually satisfied that Victoria was not in the bed.

It was a very large estate, she could be anywhere. He brushed his teeth and put on his shoes before venturing out on the hunt. He found her in the staff kitchen. There was no staff, but it was clearly an industrial kitchen and not the homey guest kitchen where one would expect to find a celebrity on her chef's day off.

"Breakfast is in the dayroom," Victoria sang out.

Micah was taken by her beauty. She wore a pair of sweatpants and a loose fitting t-shirt, her hair pulled up in a ponytail. There was something about the way she moved around the kitchen, it was hard to define. Youthful, came to mind.

Victoria plucked a strawberry from a bowl on the prep island and swirled it in cream. As she bit off a piece she noticed Micah hadn't moved at all since entering the room. "What? Is something wrong?" She looked at Micah as he stood there watching her.

"Nope."

"And yet you are still staring."

"Sorry. Wait, take that back. I'm really not sorry."

"Okay," she shrugged. "Do you not want breakfast?"

"Dayroom…? That way?" Micah pointed.

"Yes, it would be that way—" she answered impatiently, "toward the sun."

"Ah, the east wing," Micah added.

"Oh, come on, the house is not that big."

Micah headed out of the kitchen, Victoria following with the cream and strawberries. "Oh, by the way," she started, placing the bowls on the dayroom table, "I talked with William this morning." She casually opened the curtains of the large picture window behind him. "He's in country and will be over for lunch." She quickly turned back toward the kitchen.

"Um, oh...? William, huh? Great! What time is it now?" Micah stopped scooting his chair up to the table and fixed a strained smile on his face.

"Eight a.m." Victoria was already halfway out of the room through the swinging doors when she called over her shoulder, "I bet you feel better about last night now, don't you?" Then she was gone.

Micah's mouth dropped open. *I thought they weren't together? Divorced, split... something— but not coming over for lunch!* "Geez, I need to keep up with the tabloids better," he grumbled. Then loudly projecting so Victoria could hear him in the other room, "I'm having a tad bit of anxiety here... is this what they mean by 'morning after syndrome'? I really have no experience with it!"

She didn't respond.

Micah was dumbfounded. Meeting the husband only hours after awaking next to the wife? *Okay, not next to, but in her bed. Potato, potahto.* This had to be a universal faux pas, she couldn't be clueless to that fact. And her comment, 'feel better about last night'? Not a throw-away-over-the-shoulder comment under the circumstances. It was admittedly playful morning-after banter, but Micah had yet to hear the punch line.

"Um... Victoria? We... uh... do you have a minute?" Micah called out after her.

Victoria didn't respond.

"Hello...? We should talk about our lunch plans, don't you think?" Still nothing. Micah continued to yell into the abyss. "Okay, we both know it's totally unfounded, but I have just a few small concerns I'd like to discuss with you!" *You've got to be kidding me!* Trying not to be snide, Micah called out once more, "Hey, Vic?!"

"Yes?" Victoria's voice lilted into the dayroom from somewhere deep within the house.

"Um," clearing his throat, "do you have a minute for a quick chat?"

"Can't hear you! Go ahead and start breakfast without me, I'm busy," she called back.

Micah threw up his hands in disbelief in the SUNROOM. *It's a sunroom, not a dayroom!* With a shocked look upon his face he thought about her comment. *She could only have meant that I must feel better that I didn't sleep with her last night now that I'm meeting her husband and all.* He shook his head.

Micah got up and opened the door hoping she might hear him better. He had no idea where in the monstrous house she could have gone and knew his best bet was to stay in the sunroom and await her return. "Will you give me a couple minutes?" he shouted.

Victoria stood behind the pantry door holding it shut. Her eyes closed, breathing rapid. She listened closely at the door— car keys in hand in case she needed a quick get-a-way. She didn't know how to explain, so saying nothing and hoping he would assume she was beyond earshot seemed to be her best option. It would, however, be a challenge to maintain until lunch.

Victoria's phone rang. Answering quickly and whispering so she wouldn't be found, "Hello?"

"Hi."

"Who's this?"

"This is Micah, do you have a minute so we can talk?"

Victoria sat quiet on the phone for a moment. "I need to run to the store." *Quick thinking, Vic.*

"Happy to go with you."

Victoria sighed, "I'll be right there." She hung up the phone.

Victoria took a deep breath before re-entering the sunroom. She bounced a couple times to gain momentum and pushed through the doors, cheery, playful and oh, so innocent. "You wanted to talk?" she asked with a brilliant smile.

Micah smiled, not so brilliantly. "Have a seat."

"Okay."

"William's in country?"

Victoria stood, "I really need to go to the store…"

"Have a seat."

She sat. "It's not like it sounds," she blurted, all the cheery and innocence gone.

"Uh... you know I don't do this. I'm not the other guy."

"Micah," she paused struggling with her words, "it's so hard to say anything. If I say any one thing, it will be misconstrued. So, I need to say a bunch of things at the same time."

Micah sighed. "I understand. Listen to everything before..."

"Exactly. You and I didn't sleep together."

Micah slowly stood and said, "I think I need to leave..."

"He already knows you spent the night," Victoria said defensively.

Micah scoffed and rephrased, "Now, I know I need to leave."

"Wait, wait, wait... yes, he's my husband, but not HUSBAND like you think."

"I'm always up for learning the local vernacular. Please enlighten me."

Victoria dropped her head in her hands, "I can't believe I'm having this conversation with anyone other than my mother."

"Can I meet her instead?" Micah asked.

"You're not helping." Victoria took a deep breath, "We got married when I was young... REALLY young. And he was old. He's almost 80 now, you know. William thinks of me more like his daughter... he's been my manager and mentor forever. We misinterpreted our affection, got married, but discovered very quickly that it was the wrong kind of love. Anyway... we have our own lives. He has his own family. He's been married twice before. Hell, he's going to be a great-grandpa soon. Hollywood divorces are a scandal. And I don't even believe in love. It was just easier to stay married."

"Ugh," Micah said under his breath. He scrunched his face. "Victoria, I completely understand. You really don't have to explain to me. It's just... I don't see any reason for me to meet him. I'm not that guy. I don't have affairs. I'm not a love interest to ANYONE."

"That's exactly my point."

"Ow. Ow, ow... ugh." He rubbed his brow and shook his head, "Why do you want me to meet him?"

"Um..." Victoria blew out her cheeks and thought about it. She knew she really wanted Micah to meet William but hadn't put a finger on it. Didn't even consider it would be an issue, other than the whole guys-don't-meet-ex's thing.

But she trusted William. He loved her. He'd been her manager, her protector for so long, it wasn't even a thought.

She then realized what it was. It wasn't a profound step in her and Micah's relationship, she had no definition for that herself. She smiled and raised her eyes with a heartfelt gaze, "Because my father would have loved you."

She joyously thought of the only man she ever truly loved. "He would have loved you. He would have kept you talking all night, the two of you on the porch.

"He lost a lot of faith in people later in life… I don't know if he ever got any of it back, he died while I was on set. He got sick. He would have never told me. He was so proud of me," she paused, "but he would have LOVED you."

She put her face in her hands. "You're right," shaking her head, "you don't need to meet William if you don't want. I understand. But he does want to meet you."

Micah took a deep breath. He grunted and groaned, mumbling something about 'women' and finally conceded, "I'll come back around at 1:30 for a late lunch if you both still want me to. Is that acceptable?"

"That would be great, thank you." She didn't realize she had been holding her breath. "You will be back though, right?"

"If you call. When does he arrive?"

"Eleven-ish."

"I think it might be time to turn you over to Yoda."

"There's a Yoda?"

Chapter 16

MICAH PULLED UP TO the Cabin. Victoria met him at the door, "I seriously wasn't sure if you were going to return."

"Me neither."

"William is in the study, he's very excited to meet you." Victoria could tell Micah was still reluctant. "He's a good man, Micah, and he really does care about me. Think of him as my father… just be yourself."

"I'll be fine, Victoria, meeting people is part of the job description. It's just been a VERY long time since I've had to meet the parents; have 'the talk' with some girl's dad. I'm the dad now, I know how this goes."

As they entered the study, William rose and briskly crossed the room to shake Micah's hand. Much to Victoria's surprise, Micah, too, sprung to the event. "You're better looking than in the movies," Micah directed to William with enthusiastic sincerity.

"So I've been told," the older man answered.

Years before Victoria (or Micah for that matter) was born, William had been an up-and-comer on the big screen. However, according to the tabloids, after the scandalous divorce from his first wife, William had dropped behind the scenes in Hollywood, directing and some producing.

"Your voice is spot on, though," Micah went on, "exactly like it sounds in the theater. You could do great impressions— of you!"

"That's funny."

"Well, I've watched your movies my whole life. Seeing you in person is one thing, but when you speak… I must admit, it's a bit surreal."

"You're going to be okay, aren't you?" William lightheartedly asked.

"Oh yeah," Micah realized he may have been a bit exuberant, "I'm typically not taken by celebrities; much to say about nothing, so to speak. Uh— no offense?"

William nodded.

"But, you know, in Korea they say I look like you… although I'm sure people say that to you often."

"Hmm, it has been said," William replied politely, "but I take it as a compliment coming from you."

Victoria, puzzled by their initial exchange, decided to chime in, "Well lovers, I think I'm going to see to lunch and leave you to flirt." She headed out the door, not sure what to think of the mutual ego-stroking fest.

Micah watched her leave, "I guess I should have warned her—about being a fan, I mean… so she could have warned you… uh… should I call you 'Mr. Cleese'?"

"Please, call me William. You are much different than I pictured."

"In what way?"

"Well, you're the man who saved my wife." William was stating a fact. He truly believed it but undertones were still there; he seemed genuinely grateful yet obviously skeptical of Micah's motives.

"That's a bit of an overstatement," Micah corrected, "more like I happened to be in the right place at the right time and provided a healthier perspective."

"That, too, surprises me."

"Sorry to disappoint."

"No, I think you are being too modest. She is completely transformed. You've domesticated her. She's making lunch and that is no small thing. I honestly wouldn't have believed it if I hadn't seen it with my own eyes. I was surprised she even knew where the kitchen was."

"Not sure how I can take credit for that, William. So what kind of man did you picture? Robes? Long hair? Crystals or beads?"

"Well, yes, actually. Either that or a plaid suit," William insinuated.

"And my modesty, as you mentioned, doesn't go with either of those depictions?"

"Something like that. She says that you're the real deal."

"And what does that look like?"

"I've never met one."

Micah nodded in agreement. There was no mistaking William's misgivings about Micah. He'd all but called him a charlatan; certainly insinuated it. Micah was just waiting for the other shoe to drop with an open accusation. He knew there was nothing he could do to dissuade William's opinion, so he maintained a firm, yet cool demeanor. "I thought I met one once. Still not sure if I was wrong or not."

"How did that work out?" William asked.

"Still in the works. He doesn't like me, either."

"So you admit it, that you are a fraud?"

"I haven't claimed to be anything yet, so the jury is still out."

"Let's put that aside for a moment, shall we? Your results, Mr. Graff, are impressive."

"Micah, please."

"All right then, Micah. So what's the fee?" William bluntly asked.

"Excuse me?"

"Your fee. What do you charge for 'providing a healthier prospective'?"

Micah sighed. *This is not going to go well.* "Charge? I charge my phone," he answered wryly.

"Oh, I see." William was calm, relaxed. For him, this was just another business transaction. "When someone tells me it's free, that's when I know it's time to go to the safe deposit box." Pay the plumber, pay the psychiatrist, pay the voodoo priest.

"William, you asked me here. Is there something I can help you with?"

"I honestly don't mean to be offensive, Micah. We all need to make a living. The amount of money I've made from just a handful of films…? I have no illusions. And I inherited my real wealth. I understand much better than you think. We're the same, you and I. We're both entertainers— I just go after a larger market, make my money in volume. You target a single person, charge a higher price. In the end, I think I still come out on top."

"Maybe this is why it's harder for a rich man, William… it's not what he has to give up, it's that he's heard every con in the book."

"Clever. Almost believable. Let's cut to the chase, shall we? You've done your job well; I mean she has truly changed. There does seem to be a hint of cultic voodoo in her explanation, but you have no idea how far down she had gone. By some freakish chance your parlor tricks may have honestly saved her life— and for that I am truly grateful."

"Well, that should be good enough then."

"Yes, but you weren't the first, by any means. But I do intend for you to be the last. I don't want her to ever know you're just another phony. She's vulnerable. It would devastate her. She would spiral backwards."

"Mr. Cleese…"

"What happened to William?"

"Well, while you're open for business, I thought it would be best to stick to the appropriate formalities."

"Drop the act, Graff. What are you after? What's your biggest win? Take that, triple it."

Micah headed toward the door.

"I'd stop if I were you, son. I'm honestly being civil here." Micah kept walking. "You're not getting a dime more out of her than I'm ready to offer you right here and now. She's clinically unstable, you know. You walk out of here, I have her deemed unfit... put her back in the rehabilitation center and you'll never see her again. You won't get a dime. Or do you really think she's going to fall in love with you? Understand this— you'll never see her again."

Micah stopped with his back to the man. *Breathe... breathe...*

"That's better," William said, "are you ready to talk real now? You'll find I'm a reasonable man. I truly appreciate the change in Victoria, I know your value better than you think. Will three million dollars do?"

Micah rubbed his brow. "William," he said softly, turning to look him in the eyes, "I can see that you love her... but that is your only redeeming quality. You are more the problem than the solution here. Leave her alone, she's stronger than you think she is."

"You think you know so much?" William sat down at his desk and opened a folder. He spread more than a half-dozen pictures of men across the smooth mahogany. Micah didn't look at any of them; he kept eye contact with William.

The older man smiled. "These two are in jail; she doesn't even know. That's right, I can have you thrown in jail. The others...? beaten within an inch of their lives. And this one..." he picked up the picture of a very good looking man, "well, let's just say, this one was worse. You can't imagine what my kind of money and friends can buy."

Micah put his hands on the desk. With a grin, he leaned in towards the man, "You threatening me? Oh, William." He slowly stood back up straight. Shaking his head with condescending disapproval, "You had me with threatening Victoria... but threatening me? You've just stepped out of your depth."

William didn't know how to respond. He wasn't sure what Micah meant. How the younger man could be so confident with an absolute lack of fear, truly confused him. *What kind of man turns down millions of dollars? Cannot be bought, cannot be threatened... why? What's the angle?*

"Listen," Micah continued, "your life is over. It's only going to get worse for you. You probably have enough money to die in a warm comfortable place... good for you. But as the illusion of control you speak of starts slipping away ..." Micah shook his head, "take my advice, save yourself the pain. You don't want her around when someone has to wipe the shit from between your cheeks." Micah grimaced, "The stench... my God, the rot of man is the only assurance he can buy."

Hearing Micah's rebuke made William sick to his stomach— literally. He belched a putrid smell. Bile coated the back of his throat with an unendurable burning. Micah headed toward the door.

Finding his voice, William pleaded, "Stop!" Micah's hand was on the door knob.

The tone of William's voice changed; he suddenly sounded humble and sincere. "I had to know for sure," he started. "Micah, please, I never would have fathomed. Why would I?" The man behind the desk was now different. "You were right. We've seen every charlatan in the book, so why would YOU be for real?" His eyes were solemn. "And if you are, why would I be allowed to meet you? I've already received my reward here on Earth. Isn't more than that reserved for the meek?"

Micah turned to face William.

"You know, I've sought you— sought someone— my whole life. But I've looked in all the wrong places. I've been seeking a righteous king, so to speak..." His voice trailed off as he leaned back in his chair, resolved his fate was assured.

After a silent moment, the older man's demeanor altered; he was no longer mournful. "I've killed every phony I've found... that's got to count for something? I rid the world of them! Maybe not permanently dead, but I finished them just the same. That's got to be worth something?! And they all come to her, Mr. Graff; she's a magnet for every psychotic charlatan! They all find her, I don't know why. I was convinced for a while that she and I were a team; she was bait and I, the executioner."

Micah remained silent listening to William's confession.

"What must I do to be saved, Micah?"

"I'm not your savior, William. And from what I've seen, you're beyond redemption. You do know that, don't you?"

A cold yet honest glaze settled over William's face. He did know. "Just give me something," the man begged in spite of his resignation, "something— anything! I've been waiting my whole life!"

"I'm not who you think I am. I have noth..." Micah stopped himself. He wanted to reiterate 'nothing', but couldn't. In his mind he saw the image of a smiling boy chasing after William. He paused and said instead, "Your son."

"What of my son?" William's eyes widened.

"Your son, William. He will be the one to carry you over. He's always wanted to."

"Which one of my sons?"

"Oh, William, you disappoint me."

William looked confused for a moment but then suddenly realized what Micah had meant. "I do know." William's eyes closed. He hung his head and uttered, "Jeremy."

"Ah, there is hope for you yet."

"My son..." William's eyes welled. Jeremy was the least of his sons. For the longest time William had thought Jeremy wasn't even his; he'd been convinced his former wife had had an affair. The boy, raised in his own father's house, was a stranger, an outcast; yet as a child, Jeremy had wanted nothing more than to please the man who had rejected him. William's head fell upon his desk. He reached for Micah's hand.

"I am not your salvation, William. I'm not your prophet." *Even the misguided and corrupt seek to be led like sheep.*

Gazing upon the grief stricken man, Micah's face softened as he began to see William more clearly. Continuing compassionately, "William, your son sees because you sought; your son sought because (although you were looking) you refused to see. You, my friend, have found your righteous king in him." William hung his head, quiet tears rolling down his cheeks onto the desk's smooth surface.

"Lunch is on!" Victoria's voice chimed as she abruptly threw open the study door.

Seeing William raise a tear-stained face with Micah standing over him, Victoria stopped just inside the doorway. "Uh, I hope I'm not interrupting anything?"

The two men stared at her.

"On second thought," she decided holding up a hand, "I think I'm going to pretend I'm not seeing this." She turned back around, stepped out of the room and called over her shoulder as she pulled the study door closed once again, "We'll be eating in the dining room. I'll see you both in there." The door clicked shut.

"This probably looked worse than it was," Micah commented.

William nodded, "Yes, it wasn't good."

Chapter 17

A BLACK STRETCH LIMO DROVE slowly through the high-tech sector of Bracknell, UK. In its backseat two men sat quietly behind a tinted glass partition that separated them from the driver.

"You are toiling. Did we not remove that weakness long ago? Need we refresh your training?" A man with a gold ring asked of the second.

The second man remained silent in quiet reverence.

"You can look up, Jaharah," Ring Finger assured.

"I would never presume, my lord," maintaining a bowed head, "but have I failed you? Is this the reason for you being here?"

"Failed me?" Furcus was snide. "There lies your presumption, Jaharah; to assume I would expect anything more from a worm than to writhe upon the hook is impertinence."

When Jaharah's head sunk lower, Ring Finger smiled, satisfied with the man's submission. "I have a gift for you, Jaharah— and a task."

The abased man's eyes lit. He knew this request was most special. He often did the Collective's bidding but never with a request in person and never presented as a gift. He was well trained; void of emotion, empathy, humanity. His gift was to serve the Collective— the knowledge of their existence and the revelation of human insignificance was its own reward. He was their handyman— a tool in the shed, prepared to be discarded at their discretion. He could only presume this task would require his ultimate sacrifice.

"It is not your death I require this time... but surely that is of no concern to a warrior of God like yourself?" Ring Finger was testing him.

"I am no clergy, my lord," Jaharah meekly defended, "I leave religion to the zealots. I don't hear from God and I haven't met anyone who does. I don't need to hear from God to justify what I do to those who bring war to my people." Vengeance for a lifetime of injustice had burned away his soul— he was void. Yet the source of his callousness suddenly manifested. Teeth clenched, he remained composed in fearful respect. "If God wants to stop me," he quietly uttered, "let him send a prophet to stop me."

Furcus sneered, "Make no mistake, there will be sacrifice." His voice, cold and deadly. Jaharah quickly dropped his eyes to the floor.

Ring Finger calmed, "But that, Jaharah, is my gift to you. Out the window," he directed. The man dared to raise his head.

The limousine passed a middle-aged man walking to a car parked in a multi-tiered parking complex a few blocks down the road. Jaharah stared, "That can't be..." he questioned in disbelief, "I thought he was dead."

"No. He's quite alive," Furcus answered coolly, "and we have both his son and daughter. His son, Faakhir, has recently come of age."

Jaharah's eyes shifted upon hearing the news, a sinister grin forming at the corners of his mouth. "He has children now... how perfect." He lowered his voice; it was both solemn and hopeful, "What do you need of me... and of him?"

∗ ∗ ∗ ∗ ∗

As Raza approached his car on the bottom floor of the basement parking lot, reaching for the keys in his pocket, he noticed the figure of a man in the darkened enclave of a cement pillar a few feet away. He recognized him immediately.

Raza's face paled. He stood frozen, immobile; instantly transported to decades before— a world he had left behind over twenty years ago. The moment gave him a split second's wish that seemed to last a lifetime; a wish— an aching yearning— that he had somehow died back then no matter how brutal and regardless of how much suffering it might have required. To have died, even at the expense of all he had attained since, was truly his wish. His wife, his children, were suddenly better not born. Who could imagine the world he came from; a world where death was honored— even worshiped, rewarded and praised? His colleagues? His family?

"Hello, Raza," Jaharah greeted. "You saved me once, big brother. It's time now that I save you."

Chapter 18

BREECHING THE ENTRANCE OF Oceans Restaurant felt like stepping back in time onto the set of a 1950's movie musical. The room, fairly evenly split with free-formed seating on both sides of the main floor, gave the illusion of ballroom grandeur. In the center, a luxurious stairway led up to the balcony— a staircase one might expect Ginger Rogers and Fred Astaire to graciously traverse. The balcony hosted premium seating overlooking the entire restaurant with a 270 degree view of the city skyline; a door to outside seating remained locked until summer.

Micah instantly spotted Victoria and William already seated atop the balcony front and center. "I hope you haven't been waiting long?" he said, approaching the table.

Victoria stood and leaned across the table to give Micah a hug. "Not at all. They've only just brought the place settings."

"Micah." William stood, extending his hand.

"William. Nice to see you again."

"Likewise. Have a seat."

Micah pulled up a chair. "You look good, Victoria… energetic. You must have gotten some good sleep last night."

"Yes, I did, thank you," her smile radiant. "Isn't this place glorious?"

"That is certainly the word for it." Micah took in the view with awe.

"And the food is amazing… but the story is even better!"

Micah smiled at her enthusiasm. "Really? Do tell."

"Well, it's why the name of the restaurant is deceiving," Victoria explained. "If you hadn't noticed, although it's called Oceans, it's neither near the sea nor the genre of its cuisine." The men listened with interest. "Rumor has it that the founder who was neither poet, chef nor restaurateur, had never owned or built anything prior to this. Nothing that is, except for a broken heart over the loss of forbidden love." She sighed. "The story says he spent every cent he had to make this place in the shape of a lighthouse just so she might one day find her way home."

Micah nodded, more enamored by her ardor than the story.

"The intended title was Oceans Apart," she continued, "but at near completion he was forced to a final compromise. Because he had relentlessly insisted on the unique sign that would cut through the thickest of London fog, in the end, he could only afford six letters. So, he settled on Oceans."

"It doesn't look like a lighthouse," William dismissed, "but nice story. I think it's more marketing than truth, though. This is a newer building… what love could possibly have been forbidden in the twenty-first century?"

Briefly glancing toward Victoria, *You'd be surprised,* Micah thought. Self-conscious, he disguised an inadvertent sigh by turning his admiration to the building's architecture. "Oh, I get it," he said. "It's not really a lighthouse; the whole building is the beacon— the top of the lighthouse. The chandelier, the mirrored walls, the 270 degree view… it's the lamp of a lighthouse meant to be seen from any point in the city."

Suddenly being exposed in the center of a beacon made Micah uneasy. *What am I doing here?* He wasn't questioning the company he kept nor the luxuriousness of the environment, he had literally sat with kings in castles. This was a deeper feeling; one of being in the wrong place at the wrong time.

"I'm really looking forward to the premier tonight." Victoria's carefree voice cut into the gloom of his thoughts. "I'm so glad you decided to join us, Micah."

"Yes, we're both glad you came," William added. "The show will no doubt be excellent, the producer is a personal friend. Slightly private affair. All in all, it should be an enjoyable but quiet evening."

As William spoke, Micah's hand suddenly began to shake. He grabbed his wrist attempting to still it, looking at his palm and staring at it for longer than seemed natural.

Slowly he raised his eyes and directed his gaze down from the balcony to the seating area on the main floor. He was searching for something; not with his eyes, not with his ears; more with his breath— like tuning the pace of his breathing with the beat of his heart. Not unlike the feeling of uncontrollable panic when the body surrenders while the mind still tries to rationalize. *Something is wrong*, he thought. *Something is really wrong.*

"Micah, did we lose you?"

"You don't look good, son," William said.

"Micah?" Victoria repeated. "Micah?"

Still focused, Micah held up a finger to hush her for a moment. Her voice only added to the building tension.

A wave of nausea confirmed to Micah that whatever this was, it was more than physical. But he also feared it was more than ethereal, as well. He knew a metaphysical event could be devastating, but a physical event with this level of foreshadow undoubtedly prefaced mourning, wailing and long-term grief.

The clatter of dishes, people talking, the background music; everything silent only to him. All Micah could hear was a low, almost unnoticeable hum slowly growing louder, nearly lulling him to sleep. Even shaking off the haze he was unable to achieve a fully awake state, rather resting in a trance-like alpha.

It was something he hadn't experienced in many years; someplace between anger and peace. 'Resolve' was what he had called it. He knew resolve was the wrong word but it was the closest he could come up with. To get angry had no value, peace was reckless. So, he resolved to walk through it— whatever unavoidable circumstance was yet to come.

The uncertainty of his insight had always been something he took in faith— believed would lead to good. But the overwhelming evil crushing in on him at that moment tested that faith like it hadn't been tried for longer than his conviction allowed him to consider.

Eyes half-opened but focused; breathing calm and steady. The air, colder. Not winter, but fall— ice was yet to come. His right arm fell to his side heavy as if holding something weighty, his hand flexing. His mind was quiet, still unsure of what events would inevitably follow.

"Micah, Micah…" Victoria persisted.

With some annoyance, William looked with scrutiny at the unresponsive Micah, put-off by the strange display. "What's wrong with him?" He looked to Victoria for understanding or at least an explanation for the rudeness. She shrugged having no idea.

Micah lowered his eyes to the floor. Sound changed. Like a skipping record he heard the waiter taking an order at a table below, "Have you made your selection, sir … have you made your selection, sir?" The voices and noises surrounding Micah all began to echo, "I'll take the… I'll take the…"

A woman at the table next to them spoke to her daughter, "You're making a mess…" Micah glanced toward her quickly and watched her lips move, "You're making a mess… don't play with your food." He seemed to be hearing the words in his head before they were spoken.

Micah concentrated on the woman in an attempt to focus and shorten the gap between what was heard and what was seen. But the harder he concentrated, the greater the time-lapse became. One second became two, then three became five. He stared intently at the woman's mouth, counting the seconds between what he heard and her corresponding lip movement.

Victoria became uncomfortable with Micah's apparent fixation on the mother seated next to her. "Micah!" she nearly scolded.

Then, *"BANG!"* The sound in his head startled him out of his chair. *"BANG! BANG!"* His heart raced, his mind still counting seconds. *One, one-thousand, two, one-thousand…*

"Get under the table!" he suddenly commanded.

"You're not serious?" commented William, clearly thinking Micah was crazy.

Micah grabbed Victoria's arm and repeated forcibly, "Get under the table!"

Still not understanding but seeing the look on his face, Victoria put her head under the table. Face to face beneath the tablecloth, Micah motioned her onto the floor.

"This is absurd," William muttered as he bent over, lifting the linen to see what they were doing.

At that moment, three gunshots rang out. Screams and horrified cries followed. Terror engulfed the entire building as Micah calmly signaled Victoria to curl-up on the floor, concealed under the nearly floor-length tablecloth. Another shot and loud commanding voices thick with accent caused William to duck under the table as well.

Micah listened attentively, his eyes closed. He heard the distinct sound of a woman screaming; not in fear but waling, telling him at least one person was dead. Another voice groaning in pain was followed by the sound of scurrying that ended with gunfire. *Two dead,* Micah thought. There was at least one rifle— semi-automatic— and likely a pistol.

Three to four assailants, he calculated by the distinction of their voices, the repetition of their threats, and the overlap of their commands. *One will be ready, experienced. He will take command. Another will be quiet, speak very little; he will be angry, ruthless, and unpredictable. Another— amped on adrenaline, fear and inexperience; he will repeat everything the leader says. He's the question mark. He will either fold or make the first irreparable mistake that will put them in a no-win situation.* Micah listened for purpose in the shifting of their movements.

It can't be a robbery, there's nothing to steal, he reasoned. Still listening, he held his breath until he heard, "Allah Akbar!" He sighed loudly as his head fell in dismay.

Micah looked at Victoria; her beauty, her recognizable face. What were the odds they wouldn't notice her? *The odds are slim. And if they recognize her, they will kill her for the fame and success of their mission, the statement.* He paused. *Unless they don't? I suppose there's a chance…* but he stopped the thought, doubting too much to even think letting her go would be a possibility. *What if she was sympathetic to their cause, might they consider her a spokeswoman?* Shaking his head, *No, there are already at least two dead. The police will be cautious, hesitate; it will be too late.* He put his face in his hands attempting to push away the thoughts. He turned to Victoria, asking for the impossible, "Be unnoticeable, invisible."

The startling sound of violence reignited; running footsteps and two more shots— a fleeing patron barreled to the floor right behind their table. The little girl at the next table, screaming.

Ruffled by the sound of guns and the child's howl, Victoria could handle no more. Her desperate look of panic, the pleading in her eyes; everything she was cried out begging, 'Micah, do something! Make this go away, too!'

He saw Victoria youthful, rested, and thought of his daughter; the thought of her hiding under a table— any table, at any restaurant about anywhere in the world anymore. She was possibly sitting in a restaurant right at that moment. Lunch on Friday in New York. She was somewhere he wasn't. He couldn't get to her right now if she needed him, he couldn't be there for her— not always, not everywhere. He looked at Victoria. Her lips silently mouthed the word, 'Please.'

The mother at the next table calmly wiped tears from her crying child's eyes, softly singing in the little girl's ear. Micah listened to the mother's song, soothing like a prayer. "Take me, my God. Take me even painfully… but spare this, your child, today." It was one of the most beautiful things he had ever heard. A peace settled over him as the mother continued to sing.

Micah rose to his feet.

Quickly surveying the scene, a man appeared dead behind him. Two others— presumably hostess staff or guests waiting to be seated— down and motionless near the entrance on the lower level. He eyed a steak knife on the table. *This could play out one of a few ways with too many variables. An initial weapon? An unbalanced steak knife increases the odds of my quick execution.* He left the knife where it lay, instead unbuttoning his sleeves and pushing them up over his elbows. He exposed himself unarmed.

The broad stairway of fifteen or more steps led down to the first floor where seating was split with a section on both the right and left sides. The kitchen entrance, masked under the stairs, divided the two halves. One gunman on each side of the dining floor and commotion from the kitchen led Micah to believe a third attacker was rounding up the staff. The bottom floor was secured.

They paid little attention to the upstairs platform, most likely having staked-out the location previously. They would have known the balcony door would be locked and that there were no other exits above. Three or four attackers; Micah's initial summation seemed correct. *There will likely be an accomplice in the crowd, possibly a woman… I need to watch my back.* He proceeded down the stairway cautiously with his hands laced upon his head.

His first break— the younger, inexperienced attacker was the one closest to him. Still a question mark, young meant either hesitant or over-zealous. *I'll take my chances. Better that than the three-time murderer to the right,* he calculated.

* * * * *

Neither of the two men had seen Micah slowly descending the staircase. *Time for introductions, first impressions are everything.* The younger one was clearly British raised if not born. He carried only the slight accent of his mother tongue. Calmly, Micah spoke in Arabic, "Brother, I too, son of . . ." he intentionally trailed off, hoping the terrorist would hear enough to notice but still question what had been said.

Spinning towards Micah, the startled attacker aimed his pistol. Micah repeated, "Brother, I too… with you."

"Get on the ground!" Faakhir screamed.

Only halfway down the stairs, Micah crouched as if looking for 'ground' to lay on yet continued down the stairs to the bottom. "Brother … brother …" he repeated, bowing as he moved closer and closer to the man.

Reaching the bottom level, Micah dropped to the floor; left hand, right knee with head bowed and right hand raised in submission. His eyes clinched on target, right foot against the bottom step like a starting block; he was too small to have ever been a lineman but he'd coached enough American football to know the lower man won the position.

Micah rocked forward just enough to draw the young man's attention. Inexperienced and panicked, Faakhir rushed him drawing point blank on Micah's head.

"Allah… Allah…" Micah said, but smiled to himself. The young terrorist had made a fatal mistake. He had put a hesitant pistol within Micah's grasp.

The second attacker securing the right side of the dining area briefly turned in their direction. "Kill him!" he commanded causing the younger man to take his eyes off Micah.

As the second attacker turned back toward his charges, Micah took his opportunity. In a single motion he grabbed Faakhir's wrist and slammed the pistol away with the other. A shot exploded over Micah's shoulder as the pistol flew across the room. The scissor impact broke the terrorist's wrist and trigger finger, but Micah failed to grab the gun in the disarming move.

Continuing with the same motion, Micah's elbow jutted upward into the young man's throat, crushing his larynx and leaving him unable to call out. Micah's right knee, with the force of an NFL guard, launched into the crotch of his target. With a final downward thrust, he planted the sole of his foot into Faakhir's knee making a rag doll of the eighteen year old assailant.

Holding up the young terrorist's head to keep him from dropping to the floor, Micah used the man's falling motion to rush toward the second attacker, keeping the boy's body between him and the next assailant. *I needed that pistol!*

Everything had happened so fast the second attacker miraculously failed to notice— the pistol shot would have been expected having commanded the execution, and the sound of the following scuffle would likely have been perceived to be a dying man writhing on the floor.

Micah, now closing in being pulled by Faakhir's collapsing body, eyed the veteran assassin turning in his direction. A restaurant patron, seeing the possible thwart, stood up at his table and shouted across the room in an attempt to draw the terrorist's attention away from Micah. "Please! Please! You don't have to do this!" the man called out.

With the added seconds, Micah rushed the last few yards and shoved the young terrorist across the floor at his comrade's feet. Shocked and surprised, the veteran looked down at the younger man choking on his own blood, gaging to draw his last breaths. Faakhir's eyes rolled back in his head, his body contorted.

"What the hell...?" Jaharah exclaimed as Micah seized the advantage to step in close behind him.

*   *   *   *   *

Startled, the man swung around; his rifle flying toward Micah who, until that moment, had remained unseen. As the barrel came his direction, Micah grabbed the forearm of the weapon and forced the butt downward, lodging it full force into the attacker's genitals. Quickly using the length of the steel barrel, Micah had enough leverage to strengthen his position. He drove the man's arm backward, leaving the assailant nothing more than his over-extended shoulder to regain control of the gun.

Immobilizing Jaharah's dominant arm, the fight was all but over. All Micah needed to do now was move to the man's right, break his arm, then kick a forceful foot to the knee to put him on the ground. With the butt to the back of the head, without firing an alerting shot, Micah would be both armed and have the element of surprise for the final attacker in the kitchen. His plan was ready. "Get out of here!" Micah commanded the crowd.

But the assailant's strength was uncanny. Jaharah's right arm, stretched and twisted, was trapped by his own grip on the gun. With nothing more than an immobilized hip for balance, by sheer will alone, the assassin managed to thrust his free arm into Micah with enough force to lift Micah to his toes. Refusing to relinquish his weapon, the man violently struggled; every attempt to regain control of the rifle causing him excruciating pain.

Micah and Jaharah's faces only inches apart, Micah marveled at the man's resolve. More than competition or even the instinct for survival, the killer's determination was unprecedented. There was clearly no fear of death. On the contrary, the killer's agony and the threat of death seemed to exhilarate him. Aggravated by the struggle, the fresh jolts of searing pain from the jogging force of the rifle-butt still wedged between his legs eroticized the man; demonized, accentuated and maculated him into a frenzy. The assailant roared like an ungodly animal.

Jaharah's terrifying will was a force Micah had never experienced before— at least not in the flesh. This fight should have been over in seconds, Micah had the upper hand— but he had failed to anticipate the killer's absolute will. Evil derived its power upon fear and inciting fear which should never to be taken for granted. Even so, evil dissipated quickly when confronted by self-sacrifice or determined faith. Unfortunately, true faith was one of the rarest of characteristics while fear and doubt were readily available. In this room, the beast had his fuel.

This wasn't a façade of evil. It was unopposed, indisputable evil-incarnate with an absolute resolve for victory without the thought of defeat nor the concern or care. Humiliation was its goal and intimidation was its name. Jaharah had never been beaten— except as a child in the ritualistic fashion of an honored legacy. He was someone raised on pain as a rite of passage to manhood and greatness. He would not stop, even unconscious.

Micah suddenly remembered a video he'd once seen; a terrorist wielding an axe. Shot six times, the man in the video lay unconscious in a pool of his own blood yet his arm continued to flail. These thoughts of evil, along with Jahara's strength and sinister pain-twisted face, quickly wore Micah's faith thin. He was faced for the first time with having to kill a man.

Micah had taken life before but never as a conscious thought; rather a reflex— muscle memory during an inevitable circumstance. But this time the unavoidable truth was that he would either kill or be killed. And he could unfortunately be more persuaded toward the latter.

His faith began to falter and along with it, the tide of the struggle. He did not give up, but his tenacity weakened.

Victoria laid huddled under the table, chancing a peak now and again. Her table on the balcony was perfectly positioned over the scene, but she could not bear watching. She grimaced with every sound, every blow; every exerted breath was as if her own. She found herself cringing again and again just waiting to hear Micah call her to safety. She could believe nothing less.

All at once, a wave of black hit her. Suddenly she could feel Micah's pain— but more frightening, his despair. Everything seemed black and white, both sound and slow-motion action. She felt the assailant's blows like daggers penetrating her own flesh and soul. Desperate, she crawled out from under the table and screamed, "Kai!"

Her voice commanding, penetrating; it pierced right through Micah— a shiver surged through his body causing the beast within the assailant to roar at him, spewing. The two men pressed face to face, fighting not only with hands and feet, but even cheeks and foreheads, clashing for the dominate position.

Inches apart, the killer's breath carried the stench of hell. "Your woman calls me," the assassin taunted. "I will fill her yearning while lying on your limp corpse!"

Micah responded with venom, "I do know you, you foul creature; I banished you nights ago! You are merely an echo of the fallen. You are a zombie, a Lazarus reflex of the dead… the involuntary action of a corpse. The smell of the pit emits from your stomach! Your end— inevitable."

"If you can, I invite you… but you'll have to kill me more than once!"

"Then, so be it."

Both Micah and Jaharah eyed the knife in the military belt around the attacker's waist. With an evil sneer, the killer reached for the blade first. As he did, Micah pulled Jaharah forward by the rifle strap, simultaneously sending a knee to his abdomen and a right fist to the bridge of his nose. Micah pulled him in again and again with every frantic attempt the assailant made to reach for the blade.

Jaharah did not flinch with the blows but rather lunged into them with such force, it lifted Micah off the ground. With each punch delivered upward, Micah followed through and then back down, bringing the weight of his entire body downward with his elbow across Jaharah's face, slapping his hand away from the knife— only to cock back his elbow, ready for another round.

Round after round after round, the raging killer fought with a will of steel, thrusting forward into the full force of Micah's strikes as if attempting to break Micah's fist and elbow with the broader anvil of his face. The only care the man showed was holding the angle of his head so as not to force the splinters of his nose into his own brain.

Absolute dominance of will over matter; Jaharah believed he could not be broken nor beaten. He believed to fail would put to question the pious martyrdom of his father and grandfather's faith— dying was insignificant. He was to be seventh generation consecutive martyr of a single lineage. An honor that would put his linage at the table of Mohammad in heaven. But he was not a religious man himself and this was not the martyrdom of his fathers'— not this fight. This was no suicide bombing hoping to take as many more possible lives than one self-sacrificing loss, still he did believe in predestination. Jaharah's faith lie with the power the Collective and the knowledge their choosing.

"I will not stop!" the assassin cried out in anger as his consciousness began to fade.

"That's fine by me," Micah whispered, "but it will all be over soon. It's not your life I seek…I am the prophet you called to banish you and your brutality to the pit of hell from where you came."

With those words, the first show of fear washed over the terrorist's face.

"Ah, acceptance," Micah said. "Take it in PEACE. I assure you it's the last peace you'll ever know."

*   *   *   *   *

As Micah readied to make his final move to disarm the evil man, he heard the last sound he wanted to hear… the third assailant had rushed into the room, stopping less than twenty feet behind them.

The distinct rustle of a jacket surely indicated the raising of a weapon. No time to shift positions nor use Jaharah as a shield, Micah tightened his grip on the unconscious man and pressed up against his flak jacket. He grabbed Jaharah's belt buckle and lifted the man's pelvis up to his abdomen in hopes that merging their bodies might prevent the third attacker from firing. Briefly losing his stance with the unbalanced weight, Micah raised his foot to a chair for leverage. He heard a trigger cock and waited.

The moment slowed; seconds seemed minutes, heartbeats became hours. His plan must have worked, no gunshot rang out. But Micah was completely vulnerable and had no follow-up move.

Suddenly the man in his arms awoke. Struggling, the killer began to wriggle back and apart from him. Micah frantically buckled to bow across Jaharah's body. Then a loud CRACK and light— a trembling vibration like electricity went through Micah's body. A hollow, deafening sound echoed in his inner ear, *"Ahh… ahh… ahh…"*

"We shouldn't do that," Seth said.

"There are lots of things we do that we shouldn't," Micah responded.

"I understand, Dad, but we have to draw a line somewhere."

Micah exhaled. He rubbed his brow then rested his head in his hand. "I'm retired, son." He sighed, exhausted and tired, "I'm retired… what good ever came of it anyway?"

"You're here, Dad, and you're with me. I can carry some of the load now." Micah saw more of a man in his son than he could have ever hoped for.

"Besides," Seth continued, "you know you can retire all you want, but that'll never stop them from hunting you."

Ahh… ahh… ahh…

"What are you two doing out here?"

Micah turned, surprised to see his wife standing behind him on the veranda. "I don't know," Micah answered. He stared at the dusk sky looking for the first star. "This is my favorite color," he thought aloud. "It's not midnight... I like to look away from the sunset and its bright colors, then just watch the streaks of dark. A long day over."

"You should come in from the cold," his wife beckoned.

"It is cold." Micah looked back at her. She wasn't young anymore, but it still amazed him how he never failed to see the young woman he'd married all those years before. "Are you really here?" he whispered. She was just beyond his reach. He'd had enough visions of her to know that reaching only pushed her further beyond arm's length and caused her image to fade more quickly. Now he stood still in hopes the vision would linger.

"I'm right here. It won't be much longer."

Ahh... ahh...

Micah heard the hollow echoing. "What is that? What is that sound?" he asked Lena.

Her voice softened to a quiet whisper, "It's you, my love."

"Me?"

Ahh... ahh... ahh!

"No, Micah!" she scolded. "Not that sponge, it's halavi."

"AAHHH!" Micah woke to the sound of his own voice, howling as his knees hit the floor still holding Jaharah's body. Micah landed face on face with the man's cold lifeless corpse, staring into eyes like glazed stones. Lying upon the body, Micah remained breathlessly still.

*   *   *   *   *

The restaurant was now near empty. All the patrons from both the right and left had escaped out the main entrance clamoring over the fallen bystanders near the door. The kitchen crew flooded out next leaving only the guests in the balcony and the third attacker.

Raza moved slowly; his whole attention drawn to his fellow terrorists heaped on the floor— the body of their executioner sprawled atop of one.

Victoria and William, hunched under the table nearest the stairs, were still prisoners of the attack. To flee they would be forced to move down the center of the open banquet room, unable to avoid the terrorist. Captive in her front row seat, all Victoria could do was weep as Micah's body lie on the dead man.

Raza screamed out for his fallen men. First, to the younger, he leaned over and wept, "My son, my son... my brother! Dine in paradise, you have earned your rest!" Then moving to kick Micah's body off his second comrade, he felt his foot catch.

With a burst, Micah wrapped his arm around the leg of the third attacker and swept both legs around, knocking the man behind the knees and sending him tumbling backwards. He grabbed Raza's jacket, using the weight of the man's fall to lift himself to a kneeling position over him. Lunging his body into the attacker to increase the impact of the fall, Raza's rifle butt hit the floor, launching it upward and across the room. The older man lay flat on his back, dazed.

Micah leaned hard and tight over the terrorist, his elbow at the man's throat. Raza looked up at Micah, eyes darting to and fro. "You're not milk," Micah stated with no emotion. Blood began to seep from beneath Raza. Micah blankly watched the thick dark liquid trickle and pool. "I don't have a sponge for this, Lena," he said quietly to the air.

His attention full on the final assailant, Micah's voice was cold, bitter. "You must be thinking, 'What did I land on? What is this piercing pain?'" Taking his time, Micah slowly uttered each word, "That... is...your... lung."

There was no compassion in Micah for this man— any he may have had, died when he was forced to kill. The sympathy he showed now was sarcastic; cold, harsh. Micah mimicked and consoled, "Ooh... just breathe through it." Raza attempted to fight. Already wrapped around the man, Micah pressed himself down harder until Raza stopped.

A futile mumble, the dying man tried to speak. "No, no, shh," Micah patronized, "you won't be able to talk right now. That's okay, your statement is over."

The terrorist struggled, reaching for a rifle that wasn't there. "Huh-uh, let's just talk... my hand is starting to get cramped underneath you." Micah's hand held Jaharah's knife, plunged into Raza's back. "You're going to want to hold still," Micah whispered, "I fear even the slightest movement might hasten things for you... though I'm honestly not sure how we got wrapped into this position."

Micah continued without emotion, "I just came for dinner. Moments ago (along with the last ten minutes, I suppose) I had conceded to die. Now, here we are, you and I." Micah put his face right into the face of his now final victim. "You see, I, too, am a son of Abraham. I, too, devoted much of my life to the pursuit... oh, wait, wait, you're fading." Micah's voice held feigned disappointed. "Stay with me on this," he commanded, "if I were in your position, I would certainly want to know. Now where was I? Oh, yes, I gave a good portion of my life— with the exception of the last seven years or so." Raza's eyes met Micah's. "What happened, you wonder? Well, if you must know, I tried to run. I tried to hide." His tone began to change; annoyed now, building to anger. "I tried to mind my own business, but you wouldn't let me. You won't leave me alone!"

Micah's glare bore into the man lying under him as if all the fault were his. Raza attempted to speak, fighting the stare. "I tried to live a quiet life... no, stop, stop... don't try to talk, you're gurgling now." The terrorist's eyes were seriously fearful; not of dying but rather the rantings of the crazy man holding a blade in his back.

"You're right, you're right... I shouldn't be taking this all out on you," he confessed as Raza began to drift. "Matter of fact, was that your son? Your little brother? I heard what you said over him." Micah paused as if thinking, "I have a little brother... and he WILL go to heaven, but not for killing people."

Micah sighed. "I'll cut to the chase," beginning again, "because I want you to know that you've helped a fellow son of Abraham tonight. That's right. I can no longer run, hide, pretend to be normal. You did make a statement. It's not the one you intended, but it will motivate far more than you can imagine. You see, three armed terrorists were foiled by an unarmed, almost fifty year old man... MIRACULOUSLY. True, you managed to kill a couple of people... but far more than that my friend, you have awakened a giant."

Micah joggled the knife just a bit causing the attacker to exhale in pain, startled awake. "Oh, and one more thing." Leaning in, he whispered something in Raza's ear that caused the man to writhe. "That anger you're feeling? That's the fire of hell from where all that is unholy will dine tonight upon your burning flesh!"

And with a twist of the knife, Micah ended him.

∗　∗　∗　∗　∗

Micah knelt over Raza's body for a moment emotionless, staring without focus as it paled and became lifeless. Blood soaked his shirt and hands. He felt himself twitch and shook it off like a shiver. He opened his mouth wide, stretching his jaw from side to side to pop his ears. He tilted his head back and forth, working out a kink in his neck as if it should be accompanied by a restful morning yawn. Kneeling on the ground, he gazed toward the ceiling as if just realizing where he was. Hobbling to his feet and favoring his right leg, Micah watched the last of the upstairs patrons flee out the main entrance.

Intending to mingle out with the crowd, from behind, Micah heard the sound of Raza's semi-automatic weapon being picked up off the floor— the pullback action of the bolt chambering a bullet. *The accomplice in the crowd,* he thought to himself with dismay. Without turning around, he spoke, "You can walk away free. If Allah wanted different, would it not be?"

The sound of a higher pitched sigh hit his ears. Micah slowly turned to see a teenaged girl in a full-length, flower-print dress. Dark eyes, long hair, thin— no more than ninety pounds. "I will never be free," her voice trembled.

"There is no future in pulling that trigger. You are free NOW. You are free. Free to go home. Free to NOT go home ever again. Walk away with me," Micah said.

She hesitated. There was no malice in her eyes. Micah had seen younger girls than her surrounded by no less violence— no less dedication to death than the men that lain dead upon the floor. But she was not one of them. She was a prisoner, a victim of skewed faith that no child should know. Yet desperate people were often more dangerous than fanatical extremists. Extremists had a plan, they had a course. Although the outs were often the same, the desperate had none, saw none… and needed none to act.

"In a very few moments the option will be gone forever," Micah warned. The last people leaving the restaurant would see her with the rifle.

Micah eyed Jaharah's gun just a few inches from his feet; the strap perfectly bowed for a quick kick up into his hands. The bolt action cocked, safety off. She was shaking, hesitant; likely facing the corpses of her brother and father while staring down the man who killed them. It would be no challenge for him to end this.

Micah stilled. 'Still' was a place in the center of all things. The core. His breath, his heartbeat, sweat, tears… the wind, the rain, the tide; the earth's rotation around the sun… and God. The decision to fight or run, to live or die— it didn't matter. He could do no wrong from that 'still' place. He eyed the girl then briefly glanced to the gun at his feet. Again he beckoned, "Come with me."

She remained unmoved and Micah sighed. After a slight pause, he turned his back to the girl and calmly headed to the exit. As the door pushed open, he heard the rifle drop to the floor.

*   *   *   *   *

With one foot outside, the cool air of the upcoming evening whipped across Micah's face; the sun only now settling atop the horizon. Suddenly he sensed something he hadn't felt for a long, long while. In the relative brightness of the oncoming dusk, he could feel 'The Dark'— the same eyes in the dark he had felt many times throughout his life. Something, someone, was watching him.

The Dark stopped him dead in his tracks, immobilizing him. He could neither move nor blink. His equilibrium off balance— not a heaviness in his head but on the contrary; light and freefalling where catching his head from falling forward caused him the sensation of falling backward. Had Micah never experienced this before he would have attributed the sensation to blood loss from the gunshot wound to his backside. But he knew this feeling all too well. He suspected from where it came.

He leaned against the opened front door, now pushed open full; a remnant still scurrying from the restaurant. Unable to move his head, Micah shifted his eyes as far behind him as possible, back into the restaurant from where the feeling came.

Eyes half opened, he could barely see the darkened corner of a small supply closet near the hostess station. At that moment he knew what he suspected was true. It was not what he saw but rather what he did not. He saw a void. He saw nothing in the midst of detail— a space undefined.

Like having the wind knocked out of him, he felt loss and remorse having looked in its direction. "There lies the true enemy," he muttered to himself. "There you are in all your shining glory of NOTHING!" he yelled at The Dark.

Then whispering, "I see you," as he hung his head in quiet regret, "and now…
once again, you see me."

An obscure silhouette stepped out from the shadows. Nothing more than a
ring upon its finger captured the dim light of the entryway. Seeing the ring,
Micah scowled. But able to move now, he turned and continued into the
parking lot, disappearing into the crowd.

ACT II

WALK

Chapter 19

MICAH WALKED ACROSS THE street toward the police barricade that surrounded the restaurant. Law enforcement of all flavors prepared their incursion. He thought to stop and give his statement, but with the adrenaline rush subsiding, he was becoming lightheaded— every step shocked his senses with sharp stabs of pain. His eyes remained fixed on an ambulance a block and a half down the street.

A second layer of barriers lined with a barrage of spectators and journalists lay between Micah and the ambulance. Concerned citizens with blankets swarmed one by one to aid the fleeing patrons; reporters grabbed restaurant survivors both in front and behind him as if snatching falling money from the sky. Yet they all paid little to no attention to him. *Maybe because I didn't flee the building running like the hysterical mass?* Even the police, attempting to herd survivors for questioning, strangely were not interested in the limping man covered with blood.

Weeping and hysterical, people around him collapsed to their knees. The moment so surreal, the reality of the event was only just beginning to take hold of him. Micah stopped in the middle of the road, slowly turning 360 degrees, looking at his blood-stained hands in disbelief. He began to shake. It was impossible to reconcile the moment; the death of the victims, the life he took, the safety of Victoria and the little girl who sat behind her— his own life which he had conceded to give. And yet he walked alone, unseen, unheard. *Maybe I died. Maybe I'm still lying on the floor. Am I a ghost? A spirit without a host? What am I? Have I ever known? Why me? What have I ever done to deserve the honor, the glory, the humiliation, the loneliness... where is the peace that my insight has robbed me of? If I knelt and cried to the heavens, would they answer?*

Micah spread out his arms continuing his rotation. He looked to the dusk swallowing the cloudless evening sky and cried to the heavens; no words, no complaints, not anger nor sorrow— just a loud voice; a cheer with neither joy nor remorse, just noise. The noise of one. It was hard to describe all that was in the sound and all that was absent.

He turned back toward the restaurant with the brief thought that he might see his corpse lying on the floor. A stab of pain accompanied the turn, shooting up his back, jarring his ruminations. He decided then to continue on to the EMTs and the ambulance another half-block down the street.

"Look at that! That guy's going to lose it!" Henry Wilkens, reporter for The Register Guard News, chuckled as he watched Micah turn aimless circles until eventually heading down the street. Henry, having made his recent career on the backs of government officials' indiscretions, was unlike the wall of reporters outside of Oceans and not particularly interested in the victims unless one happened to be the lover of a married politician. But for some reason at that moment, he felt drawn to watch Micah move just beyond the wall of journalists.

Micah saw a stray police officer making his way quickly toward the inner barricade. As the man rushed past, Micah tapped him on the arm and hoarsely offered, "The place is secure, officer, the three suspects are down."

The police officer gave Micah a quick tip of his hat, scribbled down the information as if he'd just received it in a report over the radio, then barely looking up at Micah, continued on his way with resounding purpose.

Micah stared at the officer in bewilderment as the man crossed the street and relayed the statement to his commander, "The building is secure, sir, all three suspects are down."

Echoing along the patrol line Micah could hear, "Suspects are down…. suspects are down … move in! I repeat, all three suspects are down."

Being only a few yards away, Henry also overheard the exchange between Micah and the passing officer. Asking his colleague, Sara Jennings, "Did you hear that?" Henry continued to watch Micah hobble towards the EMTs.

"Hear what?" she replied.

"That guy… he just walked out of the restaurant and told a chimp the place was secure. He said three suspects were down."

"He said three suspects?" she asked with enthusiasm.

"Yes."

"Can we confirm?"

"How the hell are we going to confirm?" Henry barked. "The police haven't even gone in yet!"

Sara's eyes lit up, "Do you think we should use it anyway?"

Henry thought about it, rubbing his chin. "It's risky, but we'd have an exclusive for at least the next ten- twenty minutes… hey, Kevin!" Henry turned toward the camera man, "Did you get a shot of that guy coming out of the restaurant?"

"Which guy?"

"What do you mean, which guy? The fucking bloke with the blood all over his shirt!"

"Where?" Kevin started turning in circles.

Henry looked at him in disbelief. "God, am I the only one who sees him?" Kevin gave Henry the deer-in-the-headlights look.

"What planet am I on?" Henry ranted. "We're behind press barriers at an armed hostage situation… a guy comes out covered in blood, hobbles past you— ten fucking feet away and you're the camera man! Then you ask 'which guy?' You're in the wrong fucking profession, mate."

Henry was on a roll, "You see that ambulance?" Kevin looked the opposite direction. "Are you daft?! … THAT way!" Henry pointed toward the ambulance, shaking his head incredulously.

"Uh, yeah…?" Kevin was getting a lay of the land.

"Thirty yards in front of you, heading straight for the ambulance!"

"Oh, him? Oh, right! Uh, no. No, I didn't see him," Kevin answered.

"Well, get a bloody shot of him now walking unassisted to the ambulance," Henry commanded.

Henry was excited, "Right, right this is good … this is good." He scribbled some lines on a yellow legal pad, ripped it off and handed it to Sara. "Run with this. Send it now then stay here. See if you can get an early update from the police." With a second thought he added, "Better yet… get a shot of the bobbies saying the WRONG thing." Henry smiled smugly hoping this would confirm that the Guard knew the crime details before the authorities did.

Sara stared at the note, "Really? You haven't got anything close to this, Henry."

"Just do it. I've got a feeling on this one."

"Henry, this is not journalism."

"Hey, I'm sticking my neck out. Aren't you always telling me I play it too safe?" He gathered his bag and headed toward the ambulance.

"YOU'RE sticking your neck out?" Sara called out after him, "Is that why you're having ME on camera?"

"You're prettier than I am. You'll be great."

"Henry, I'm the producer, YOU are the reporter."

"Well, now you're the correspondent-reporting-producer."

"Where are you going?"

"I'm going after the only guy who's talking. If I don't catch him here, I'll catch him at the hospital."

With an exasperated sigh Sara conceded. "All right then, Kevin… lead in with a shot of the gent in the blood-stained shirt, then scan over to me in five, four, three…"

*   *   *   *   *

Heading toward the ambulance, the EMTs saw Micah coming and rushed to his aid. As the medics fawned over him assisting him to the vehicle, Micah glanced over the crowd scanning for Victoria or William. After only a moment he stopped, realizing it might not be wise for them to be seen with him.

Strangely, the EMTs weren't interested in asking Micah any questions, either. Quickly stripping his blood-soaked shirt and seeing the bullet wound exit in his abdomen, their attentiveness grew serious. "How were you able to walk the block and a half, sir?" Micah just shrugged. He did look worse for the wear but was certainly conscious and coherent.

Just then, Henry Wilkens peeked into the ambulance doorway. The reporter challenged Micah with a stare. "Did you say there were THREE suspects and all three were down?" Seeing the press badge dangling around Henry's neck, Micah turned toward the EMT as if not hearing the question.

Henry persisted, "Were there ONLY three suspects? How were they subdued? Are they dead? What's your name? How were you shot?"

In an act to avoid the reporter, Micah quickly thought to buckle over in pain, "Ahh... ahh!" then flopped himself back onto the gurney and began to hyperventilate.

Henry stepped back—barely. "Is he going to be okay?" he asked the EMT closest to him.

She threw up her hands, "Get out of here, this man has been shot!"

"Where are you taking him?"

"Get the hell out!" she yelled again.

Another set of ambulances arrived on the scene. The EMT grabbed the radio transmitter attached to the shoulder of her jacket, "GSW victim with substantial blood loss. In route to Mercy General... this is turning critical."

Henry was a veteran reporter. He'd spent the greater portion of his early career covering 10 Downing Street until he pissed-off the wrong people one too many times. At the end, Henry reported a military raid that never took place— a report he swore was confirmed at the highest level only as part of an elaborate conspiracy to personally ruin his career (although he could never prove it.) As a result, Henry wound up making his living chasing police cars and ambulances— with the occasional dirty politician thrown in for fun. Now he refused to take chances with a story. He knew that just one more blatantly inaccurate report and he'd be flipping burgers.

One thing Downing Street had taught him however, was he did know a brushoff when he got one. Bullet in the belly or not, Henry wasn't convinced; there was something off about this guy. "Why would a wounded victim not want to tell his story?" He continued to mull as he headed back to his crew, trying to make sense of the contradiction. By the time he reached his colleagues, Henry had derived the only conclusion— *He's NOT a victim!*

For a brief moment he felt a fleeting sense of civic duty— he should probably report the man's suspicious behavior to the authorities. But Henry quickly dismissed the notion— an absurd, unprecedented encounter with moral conscience was something Henry Wilkens could never be accused of having. He chuckled aloud, "What was I thinking? This is a bloody exclusive!"

*   *   *   *   *

A younger EMT jumped from the back of the van to close the outer cabinets. He then circled around front to signal the driver off a cigarette break while the female EMT (who had runoff Henry) was still busy giving a pass-down to the newly arrived ambulance teams. Alone for a moment, nowhere near as critical as he portrayed, Micah pulled his passports and credit cards from his back pocket, loosened his boot, and put them under the inner sole of his shoe.

Micah was slipping his shoe back on when the young man re-entered the van and readied to shut the main door. To disguise any possibly suspicious action, Micah rushed to make a feeble attempt to exit the ambulance. "I forgot my coat, my phone… I didn't pay for dinner," he said before falling back onto the gurney, moaning.

"Stay calm, stay down. We'll get your coat," the young man said.

Hopping into the back and slamming the doors, the senior EMT gave the signal and the ambulance took off. Micah had both EMTs' full attention once more as the younger one leaned over him. "Approximately forty year-old GSW victim, blood pressure 98 over 60; heart rate in the low 60s and dropping…" The man checked his watch, "55 now," he told his boss.

"Kick it into high gear!" she commanded over the airwave.

Micah had been a runner and an athlete his entire life. And although in his upper forties, his heart rate was still exceptionally low. Plus, he had always been able to control his pulse to some extent— his resting rate, in the mid-forties. He also hadn't bothered to mention that much of the blood on his shirt was not his own. But considering the circumstances, toying with a young EMT in an attempt to get away from the scene and avoid any questions, seemed like a good idea.

Chapter 20

HENRY TUCKED HIS PRESS badge in his shirt as he made his way through the crowd up to the emergency room reception counter at Mercy General. "Gunshot wound patient was just brought in from the hostage crisis, yeah?"

"Yes. Who are you?" the nurse at reception asked.

"I'm a friend of the family. I was with him at the restaurant. How's he doing?"

"He's in surgery."

"Is he going to make it?" Henry drummed his fingers on the counter as if he had somewhere better to be.

The receptionist glared, sarcasm in her voice, "You look all broken up about it."

"Yeah, yeah, it's a tragedy. Hard to contain myself here."

"I see that."

"Right, right. One minute you're carving a piece of fillet minion, next minute they're carving a bullet out of your ass. So, will he be out of surgery soon?"

"There's really no telling. You can wait over there, I'll let you know."

Henry frowned and looked up at the TV in the emergency room waiting area.

"This is a Register Guard Exclusive Report. We are now switching live to Sara Jennings reporting from Oceans Restaurant in Kensington. Hello Sara, what can you tell us?"

"Well, Frank, we've been told that three suspects were subdued and neutralized prior to police incursion. We have yet to receive confirmation, but initial reports suggest there were three armed suspects, all apparently killed. Early reports indicate victim fatalities as well, but those, too, are still too early to confirm. We do know, however, that at least one man sustained a gunshot wound as seen here in our initial footage. This man walked out unassisted to an ambulance stationed a block and a half down the road.

"Currently, it does appear that all other hostages— both patrons and the Oceans' staff— are safely out of the building. As you can see, Frank, the police are only now moving in to secure the area."

"Thank you, Sara, we can see that. Please keep us posted."

"I will, Frank. And again, sources from inside the restaurant have indicated that all three suspects have been neutralized, which leaves us only one primary question... WHO subdued the assailants?"

"Yes, quite! Very good question, Sara," Frank agreed, turning full-front to the camera. "Again, that was Sara Jennings reporting with a Register Guard Exclusive. The hostage nightmare is finally over."

Henry glanced back to the nurse. "You see that coverage from the Guard?" With a grin and a wink, "They got the exclusive on this one."

Grimacing at the creepy man, the receptionist raised her brows and clenched her teeth hoping it might pass for a smile.

Before Henry walked away, he turned back and leaned into the woman, "Did he happen to say anything?"

"Did who saying anything?" she answered.

"You know... my friend."

"Like what?"

Henry glanced from side to side, securing the area of eavesdroppers. He moved closer and brought his voice to almost a whisper, "I don't know... maybe like how many victims there were? How many suspects? Who took out the suspects?"

The woman narrowed her eyes, "I thought you said you were with him?"

Backpedaling, "Right, right I was," standing up straight and trying to sound casual, "but I was hiding in the loo." Henry leaned in again, "So he didn't say bugger all, eh?"

The nurse was clearly annoyed. "The gentleman was quite out of it when he came in. They rushed him straightaway to surgery."

"Any other family or friends come for him?"

"No, you're the first."

"So what's his name?" Henry asked.

"Who's name?"

"The guy… the guy in surgery?"

The nurse pulled back in her seat, "You're asking me the name of your friend-of-the-family whom you had dinner with?"

"Yeah, yeah… never mind. Let me know if he makes it."

The woman shook her head, speechless.

Chapter 21

"IT IS HIM," RING Finger announced with a mix of satisfaction and concern in his voice.

"Did he see you?" The question seemed imperative.

Ring Finger took a long drag from the cigarette he held cupped in his large hand. He slowly exhaled as he watched the dim glow of the cherry all but extinguished in the clasp of his palm. After a moment, he finally responded, "No."

"Are you sure?"

"Yes," he answered annoyed.

UK slapped his hands down on to the table, "What caused this little man to crawl out from under the rock where he was hiding? And why now?"

"Is he going to be a problem?" Europe chimed in.

"Hard to say," Ring Finger explained, "there's a bit of a media crisis here in London now."

"What kind of crisis?"

"We initiated a cell in an attempt to alleviate the problem, but he's in better form than I expected. Matter of fact, age hasn't slowed him down a bit." He took another drag from his cigarette, "The good news, however, is that he still avoids the press. And that's the last thing we need… but there will still likely be a manhunt."

"Can we use that?"

"Possibly," Ring Finger continued, "but he got out of Tokyo. If a white man can stage his own death and get out of Tokyo unnoticed dead or alive, I don't see how London is going to hold him."

"Let him leave," Europe conceded. "But he cannot be allowed to get in the way of the ecological summit or our plans. You need to use whatever force necessary."

"We've just tried that."

"Maybe best thing for us to do is to force him back under the fucking rock!" UK seemed less than happy about the situation.

"Why now? Why did he show up now?" Europe asked.

"We must be close."

"He's nothing… he's nothing more than an annoyance," the Brit argued. "He has no idea. It is foolish to talk about him like one man is an omnipotent force against us! He's an anomaly at best; he's dust in the cog of the machine. You are too close to him, Furcus. Honestly, what has he done? Nothing!"

Furcus spun the big gold ring round his right middle finger with apparent disregard for UK's opinion. Equal voice in the Collective was one thing, but he alone had seen them through the process since the beginning and deserved more than a little respect— and UK gave none. "You should stick to things you know like your lust for degeneracy," Ring Finger rebuked, "we don't need to hear the opinion of a whore mongering sodomite like yourself."

"You know better than that, Furcus, his opinion is just as valid," Europe corrected.

"Well, then let him deal with the man," Ring Finger challenged.

"I have other responsibilities," protested UK.

"I think you both have valid positions. But you have gotten too close, my friend," Europe told Ring Finger. "You think too much of this man, Furcus. We need a new perspective."

"Then we are in agreement?" Furcus offered.

"I'm not," UK injected.

"Your opinion is valid, but the council decision stands."

"Fine," UK conceded. "But if I'm to deal with him," he proclaimed as he nonchalantly displayed a solid gold coin, rubbing it gently in the palm of his right hand, "I want no complaints about my methods." He revealed the coin gone from his right hand, instantly manifested in his left. Then right to left, left to right knuckle roll, and the coin once again disappeared.

Furcus abhorred UK's arrogance but also recognized its value. *Perhaps he's right, maybe I have been duped.* It was not in Ring Finger's nature to consider— much less care about— an insignificant pawn. *Still, there is something familiar with this one man.* Like being unable to remember or feeling a haunting itch, Furcus pondered. *Why does this man gnaw at my conscience?*

"A conscience is a dangerous thing," UK remarked, having intruded into Ring Finger's thoughts. "Who would ever have thought you even had one," he mocked.

Furcus was infuriated. His eyes turned a blackened hollow; how dare UK touch his mind without invitation? "You of all the members should not play mind tricks," Ring Finger spat at the man seated across from him. "Shall I open YOUR thoughts? Tell you what you REALLY think?"

Furcus rose to his feet. He placed two fingers against his temple and leaned across the table, drumming his fingers against his own hardened skull in a hypnotic motion. When he stopped, he slowly turned his fingers toward UK and held them suspended above the table before returning once again to a casual upright stance. "Better yet, comrade, I shall SHOW you."

The intensity of Ring Finger's stare burned into the depths of UK's mind. "You want to read my mind?" Furcus continued, countering, "Very well. Then see you as I see you!"

Upon Ring Finger's command, images of cannibalistic orgies flooded UK's mind. Furcus narrated in a sinister tone, "Don't confuse your delicacies with empathy—" while scenes played one after another of violated and shamed youths weeping at UK's feet, "don't confuse your LUST with compassion," he scorned.

Then Ring Finger's voice calmed slightly, "What pleasure does that bide the soulless? Can you even feel their body's pain twitch, wrapped around your member, comrade?"

UK did not appreciate Furcus' illustration. But having opened the window first, there was nothing he could do to prevent the intrusion into his mind. Though it was not the images that bothered him— they were true; his comrade's interpretation of the events was where the disparity between the two lay. Morals were neither's strong suit. Definition of motive was the difference.

UK shrugged off the reproach and scoffed, "You are demented, Furcus. My research is critical. If we're to remain anonymous, we need an arsenal. You only kill them, I elevate man to his potential. Besides, you utilize my weaponry—Jaharah graduated top in his class from my 'academy', just as his father and grandfather before him."

Ring Finger laughed, shaking his head, "Haven't you heard? My boy killed your armed Magna Cum Laude legacy with his bare hands."

"With his bare hands?" UK puzzled. *How is that possible?* He was instantly intrigued. Pain was an aphrodisiac to Jaharah; all of his so-called students fed upon lashes.

Sarcastically Furcus added, "It will be good for you to come to know my boy, comrade, then you will see the depth of your emptiness. You will yearn for more than flesh and find no capacity within yourself to satisfy it."

"You speak foolishness."

"Oh, I forgot myself. You can't even understand the words I speak. Don't take it too hard." Ring Finger almost sounded remorseful, "Neither can I."

Europe cleared his throat, "Settle this between yourselves. Enough has been said. Adjourned."

As the members of the Collective took their leave, Furcus lit a fresh cigarette and rolled the hot ember of the cherry against the inside of his broad, gold ring. Europe joined him, taking his time relishing the taste of his nearly extinguished Havana.

"Look, old friend," Europe began, "I truly don't understand. We all want off this rock, we agree. You execute the plan, see it through. We have our part, but what is it about this MAN that so distracts you?"

"Nothing," Ring Finger immediately answered. Then putting the cigarette to his lips, "Nothing," he repeated thoughtfully. "It's merely a sense… a wariness. I don't have the word."

It was always as if a word were on the tip of his tongue; this was nowhere near the first time he had tried to reach for it. He had searched his mind many times but the thought had always alluded him, constantly toying at the edge of his consciousness. "What do you remember?" he posed to his old friend.

"Before?" Europe considered. "Only images— power and light, mostly. Over time I've added my assumptions. But he will know."

"He will know," Furcus agreed.

Europe nodded solemnly.

Taking another drag from his cigarette, "As you recall, I was awakened before you," Furcus mused. "Those of us who did, wandered at first. Ruled… were called monsters." Visions of burning villages and terrified townspeople's screams echoed in his head. He paused, letting the vision subside. It was always that way. Though the Collective's origins alluded them, since their awakening, with every thought or recalled memory, the past played fresh upon their minds like a haunting three dimensional, high definition, surround-sound nightmare.

"But it was easy for us to be forgotten," Ring Finger continued with contemplation. "Man's history becomes wives-tales— myths and legends within a few short generations. So, we scattered, each to his own region. But the others had no vision, no direction. And that was not enough for me. So, I searched for him."

"We all remember him. He will bring order." Both men lowered their heads in agreement.

Furcus then raised his eyes. Hesitant to speak, he rotated his ring. "I remember another, as well," he confessed.

Europe looked up astounded. He searched his memory in curiosity but came up with nothing, "Let me see!" he demanded, wanting a view into Ring Finger's mind. "Who?!"

"In time my friend, when things are clearer."

"Are you telling me you think this MAN…?"

"I think nothing!" Furcus rebuked. "I think nothing but the Collective!" To be accused of thinking anything of a man infuriated him. "Let the sodomite kill him."

Europe smiled wryly, "I hear skepticism in your voice, Furcus."

Ring Finger crushed out his cigarette, "Very well, you are correct. Shall I say… let him try."

Chapter 22

"THIS WILL BE THE end of us," the Mayor said, rubbing his temples, "the end of us all. How many terrorist attacks does that make this year?"

"Six in the Kingdom, the fourth in London."

"And this is only April, the media will have a field day." The mayor shook his head. "You know how this is going to go, Philips— keep it contained…" the chauffer pulled over a block from Oceans Restaurant, "…and keep me appraised."

Chief Superintendent Philips nodded curtly and exited the limousine. Scowling at the barrage of reporters lining the police barricade outside of London's most recent terrorist attack, the chief attempted to avoid exposing his clear disregard for the media.

"Chief! Chief Superintendent Philips! Is this officially the fourth terrorist attack in London this year? Were all the terrorists apprehended? How many fatalities? Why didn't Scotland Yard know about this?" Cries from a wall of reporters flooded the street.

With a halfhearted wince posing as a smile, Philips held up his hands, "Representatives of the press… please grant me a chance for a first-hand assessment. As you've come to expect, I will be glad to share what I know as soon as I know it."

Crouching under the crime scene tape barring the entrance of the elegant yet aging Oceans Restaurant, Philips solemnly surveyed the scene. Blood splattered the wall at coat check; two bodies lay face down near the hostess station. A yellow plastic foldout sign read, 'Caution – Slippery When Wet'.

Seeing Sergeant Tilman, Philips approached. "Tilman, what do we have?"

"So far five dead, two injured, Chief."

"Jesus."

"Two over there— one's a hostess and the other is apparently a patron; I'm guessing by the attire. We haven't got names on the vics yet, but there's another possible patron still on the balcony above, as well." Tilman walked the Chief Superintendent further into the restaurant, "And over there, two apparent perpetrators— both dead."

"Why haven't you got any names on the victims? They must be carrying ID."

"We were told not to touch anything, Chief. We've only just secured the scene."

Philips shook his head, "How did we miss this one, Sergeant?"

"Not positive, sir," Tilman answered, "but if it is as it appears, the perpetrators are locals, sir." Tilman was a stickler for 'innocent until proven guilty'.

"What do you mean, 'as it appears'?"

"I just mean that if the three men with the ammo were the terrorists... well, um... then yeah, we've discovered that they're locals, sir."

"I don't think that's too much of a leap, Sergeant, they're wearing flak jackets and masks." Chief Philips was annoyed. "So, for this conversation only, let's move forward on that assumption, shall we? You know— cautiously."

"Right," Tilman conceded. "The, um... suspects..."

"Yes," Philips prompted with sarcastic encouragement, "that's the word you're looking for. Innocent until proven guilty, but suspects just the same, yeah?"

"I get you, Chief. Anyway, the suspects are locals. Well, not natives, but this one here..." Tilman pointed at the older of the two suspects, "is Raza Mohammed Ahluwalia; early forties. He works in high-tech in Bracknell; makes a good living, father of six children. His eldest child— Faakhir Ahluwalia, eighteen years old, was among the suspects, as well. He was rushed to Mercy General."

"He's alive?"

"Yes. His throat was crushed, he nearly chocked to death on his own blood. He had a faint heartbeat, though, and with a tracheotomy, they got him breathing on his own. Not sure how long he wasn't breathing— may not come out of it. The EMTs mentioned the possibility of brain damage."

"You let me know as soon as you know anything on the boy. He's secure, right?"

"Yes, there's a policeman with him now."

"Let's double-down on that. If this gets out to the media… we don't want a riot at the hospital."

"Consider it done, sir." Before turning to go the sergeant added, "One more thing, Chief… the boy may have been born abroad, but he was definitely raised here."

"Bloody hell, this is turning into ugly." Philips rubbed his hand down his face. "So, Tilman, without searching their clothing, how'd you get this information so fast?"

"Raza's eldest daughter was at the restaurant, too… one of the last people to come out. She was obviously distraught, but it all came out when we initially questioned her. She's clammed up since then, though. Not sure of her involvement, if any, yet.

"The media didn't catch any of this, did they?"

"The girl didn't talk to the media. We moved her quite quickly."

"Right. Was she a participant?" the chief asked.

"That's hard to say. She obviously wasn't at the restaurant by accident. It'll come out in the investigation fairly fast. She's a scared kid; I can't imagine she stormed the building, but I'll let you know what we find out."

Chief Philips nodded as a tall, well-dressed young man walked into the restaurant foyer asking questions of the Metro officer guarding the front entrance. Whatever the questions were, the officer pointed the man toward the chief. "Here we go," Philips said, "looks to be a political officer of some sort. Let's avoid him as long as possible. Continue, Tilman."

"I assume you're talking about the suit heading this way, sir?"

"Yes. Just continue."

Tilman stepped closer and knelt down next to the second terrorist suspect's body; this one in his mid-thirties. "He's the wild card, sir. He's the only possibly remote radical element. We're not certain who he is and the daughter didn't say. But when witnesses were questioned, descriptions of the primary shooter indicate it was likely him. Again, we haven't moved anything, but if eyewitness accounts are accurate— and there is a common thread building— this man did all the shooting… or at least shot the two victims in the front and the man on the balcony."

"See?" Philips said, patting Tilman on the back, "Now THAT'S how I want you to report an initial investigation! First, you called him a suspect— quite honorable. And now you've gone on to accuse him of three murders based on the accounts of idiots on an assembly line."

"I'm sorry, Chief."

"No, no... no, no, I was just ribbing you. You were brilliant."

Approaching the chief and Sergeant Tilman, the handsome young suit attempted to join in the conversation, "What do we know so far, gentlemen?"

Chief Philips ignored the man, speaking only to Tilman, "So, where are the bullet wounds on the these two in the flak jackets?" Chief Philips waved his hand over the dead terrorists.

"Well, sir, we were told not to touch or move the bodies. SIS is already here."

"SIS?" the chief asked surprised.

"That's the badge he showed. Told us not to touch anything." The sergeant pointed to another suit up on the balcony.

"Really... SIS? Does he have a name?"

"Um, it's an older name... Rothery, I believe, sir."

"What's his first name?"

"Rothery is his first name. Last name is, um... Taylor, yeah. Last name's Taylor. Rothery Taylor. Do you want me to call him down?"

"Nah, he looks busy. So, how did we take these two out?"

"We didn't, sir."

"What do you mean, we didn't? Who did? They kill themselves?"

"No, Chief, that's why SIS wouldn't let us touch the bodies. According to eyewitnesses, it was actually a patron who took them out... sir."

"Right, then. So, where is he— the patron? Why aren't we talking to him? Why isn't HE talking to him?" the chief motioned to the SIS agent.

"We don't know where he is, Chief. He walked out of here. No one noticed."

"Off-duty policeman? Detective or something?"

"I don't think so. They wouldn't have left the scene."

The chief frowned.

The good-looking young man, still patiently standing with the officers, found his chance to interject. "Excuse me, Chief?"

"I'll be with you in a minute, lad," Philips said holding up his hand. "Tilman, humor me here… I see there are two automatic weapons and a pistol— the kid likely holding the pistol. And this man here— clearly a deranged murderer. The boy's body was right there, with all three in one pile, correct? They wouldn't have all congregated, would they? They would have spread out, secured the building.

"So, let's just say, it was an off duty policeman, an incredible marksman— hell, maybe an MI6 agent which would explain why SIS is here so quickly— but it doesn't look like whoever it was dragged the bodies. How did he get them all together?"

Tilman laughed nervously, "The man didn't shoot them, sir. As far as we know, he didn't have a gun."

"What? One bloke took out three armed men without a gun and then 'poof', disappeared?" Philips pondered. "I think we need to talk to Mr. Rothery Taylor."

"Right," Tilman agreed. "Oh, and we also were told that the Prime Minister's Office had members of their Terrorist Taskforce in route."

"Member," the youthful suit said, slightly raising his hand.

"Excuse me?" Tilman asked.

"Member, as in singular. That's me. I'm with the PM's taskforce."

Chief Philips acknowledged the young man with mock delight, "So, you're with the PM's taskforce?"

"That's right. My name's Dylan Vasko— Dylan is fine. I was sent immediately upon hearing of the incident."

"Huh." Chief Philips motioned Dylan to follow him toward the balcony stairway. "Well, I worked extensively with the taskforce of the former Prime Minister… can't say I've felt the same level of cooperation from YOUR boss's administration."

"I assure you, Chief, we at the Prime Minister's Office are as eager to work with Scotland Yard as any previous administration."

"Right. Well, when your boss decides it's prudent to make the customary curtsies to Scotland Yard— including looking at the piles of inquiries made regarding his recent budget reductions, I will be more than eager to cooperate." The chief's tone was less than accommodating. "Also, please tell his majesty that a terrorist attack that leaves five people dead most definitely requires a PM representative who has at least a secondary school diploma. This is no place for a class project, lad."

"I turn twenty-six in July," Dylan informed the chief.

Philips stopped. He stared blankly at the young man, blinking his eyes in disbelief. "Eh... Dylan Crisco, is it?"

"Vasko."

"Right. Well, here in Great Britain, Mr. Dylan Vasko, we stop including the month of our birth to validate our credentials somewhere around primary school. For example, I don't say that I am fifty-six AND A HALF years old... generally." Laughing, Philips walked away.

"I understand your reservations, sir," Dylan followed close behind, "but I assure you, the PM has the utmost faith in my abilities."

"Laddy," continuing to laugh out loud, "that only makes one question the PM's credentials."

"Uh, I understand, sir. Eh, um... this is not my first... I mean, I've done this before. I mean..." Dylan seemed eager to build a level of rapport with the chief, but faltering only diminished his credibility further.

Chief Philips stood at the bottom of the stairway leading up to the balcony, "Mr. Taylor?" he called up.

Rothery Taylor stood on the top step looking at dabs of blood splattered on the first few stairs. He looked back down toward the suspects bodies on the left side of the main banquet hall.

"Mr. Taylor?" the chief repeated.

Rothery glanced toward the wall behind him. He then took three steps down, viewing a second set of blood splatters on the wall to his right. He crouched, squinted, then turned back; his hand to his chin, face scrunched in thought. He sighed.

Chief Philips and Dylan made their way to the top of the stairs; the chief a bit worse for the wear having concluded that traversing the stairway was his only option if he didn't want to continue being ignored. Careful to not disturb the crime scene— though the blood on the stairs had already been trampled through presumably by fleeing guests— "Mr. Taylor," the chief addressed again, this time touching the man on the shoulder.

"Yes, Chief?" Taylor responded, briefly looking up before continuing his investigation of the floor.

"Do you mind if I see your identification?"

Rothery Taylor now appeared particularly interested in the design of the wall paper. "You were saying, Chief?"

"Your identification, please."

"Oh. Certainly." Rothery reached in his jacket's left inner pocket. He handed the chief his wallet while remaining fixed on the wallpaper.

"Rothery. That's a bit of an unusual name for a man your age."

"Third generation."

"What does that mean?"

Running his hand across an unstained portion of the carpet, Rothery pointed to himself in rhythm, "Rothery... Wyndham... Taylor..." then looking to the ceiling, "the third."

"I see. Will there be a fourth?"

"A fourth what?"

"Rothery?"

For some reason, the question was the first that seemed to interest the agent. Although the man's concentration was not easily penetrated, the look on his face progressively changed. At first distracted, the question finally pulled his mind from his investigating. "Why do you ask?"

"Curiosity mainly," the chief replied. "I've heard of a number of thirds in my time, but don't know if I've ever met a fourth."

"Really?" Rothery stopped to ponder. His entire countenance began to reflect intense calculation; his eyes rapidly shifted as if searching the room for an answer, his fingers drummed his chin and lips. After nearly a minute, breaking the silence, "I think you are correct, sir, I've never met a fourth, either." He appeared clearly disappointed. "Damn all, Chief," he declared, glancing briefly back at the scene, "this entire evening has been an enigma beyond proportions, and that just took the cake."

The chief scoffed out loud. He looked around the room, puzzled, "You must enlighten me, agent. I have many unanswered questions about this night, but unless I have mysteriously entered into one of Sir Conan Doyle's chronicles, for the life of me, I cannot see how the future name of your child is the top conundrum of the evening."

"There are those days, Chief, when you think, 'I shouldn't have gotten out of bed'…" he paused, "but this is not one."

Philips, still puzzled, "Okay, I think I'm with you so far…"

"Then there are those days when everything seems to rotate in the same direction as if playing out on a stage. Do you know what I'm talking about?"

"Not really."

"Have you ever had one of those mornings where you've known you're going to remember that day for the rest of your life?"

"Yes, but I'm always wrong. I still don't see the correlation with the name of your future son."

"My wife went into labor this very evening, Chief, with our first child— a boy. I swore my whole life that I would not curse my son with the name Rothery Wyndham. However, had there not been a terrorist attack on this side of town under unexplainable circumstances, I would not be here… you would not have asked me about my name, and my son would be called Liam Taylor. Isn't that a lovely name— Liam Taylor? But in my entire thirty-one years, no one has ever mentioned the extinction of fourths, and you said it tonight of all nights. Tomorrow wouldn't have mattered. Doesn't that reek of pre-designed coincidence? His great-granddad will be ecstatic."

"Well, congratulations to your grandfather and my sincerest condolences to the boy," Philips sarcastically replied. "Now moving on… out of curiosity, what does the feel of the carpet or design of the wallpaper have to do with the crime?"

Rothery's eyes shifted; his eyebrows lifted with a slight look of insecurity, "Excuse me, Chief, I'll be with you in one moment."

Rothery had an obsession with textiles; in particular, the feel of textures. His processing method included walking away from the scene and doing something unrelated, mindless, to generate spontaneous thought. It was not a method for detective work, although he was certain that one day a case would hinge on the distinct texture of something— the design of the wallpaper was going to be the ultimate tell. But the fact was, he just liked the way things felt.

"Do you want me to call you Rothery or Taylor?" Philips interrupted.

"Suppose you can call me anything you want, that's what most people do."

"Right," the chief answered, "Rothery it is." It clearly didn't matter to the agent. "I know you boys have national security concerns, but I need to know which jar we can dip our hands into," Philips continued.

"Sorry, Chief, once again you have me at a disadvantage. I am unaware of any jars pertaining to this case." Rothery thumbed through a small notepad he kept in his breast pocket.

"I'm just a little surprised that SIS is on the scene so rapidly." The chief was cautious, "Why is SIS here, Mr. Taylor? Our initial assessment has the suspects as local British citizens." Philips was now more than suspicious.

"Terrorism is a global issue, Chief Superintendent Philips. Besides, the Prime Minister needs an extremely rapid response."

"That explains the PM Taskforce's presence, not yours."

"That's me! Dylan Vasko with the Prime Minster's Taskforce." He held out his hand to Rothery.

Rothery shook hands with Dylan, "No offense to the taskforce."

"None taken," Dylan said, finding it to be the first civil response to his presence at the crime scene.

"We at SIS are better prepared to deal with any potential international collaboration," Rothery told Philips.

"And you in particular? On the night of your child's birth?" the chief interrogated.

"I have… a perceived skillset in matters such as this; unique," Rothery responded. "What's with the inquiry, Chief? Hasn't your department complained about a lack of cooperation between divisions? Especially in dealing with terrorism? We thought you might be grateful."

"So, we're collaborating?"

"That would certainly be helpful."

"Right then. How can we help?" the chief asked.

"Please don't let me get in your way. I'm here for an initial investigative assessment only. I would, however, be grateful to have access to Scotland Yard's forensic data."

"Then we're free to take lead on the investigation?" Philips assumed.

"Certainly. We're primarily concerned with gathering information that might help us prevent further incidences. And, of course, bring to justice any potential participants that either move or currently reside beyond the borders of Her Majesty's Kingdom."

"I didn't pick you for a Royalist."

"I'm not, just a romantic."

"A romantic…" the chief laughed, "a pocket-protector, carpet-sniffing romantic. This is my first-time meeting one of them."

Rothery might have been insulted, but as respectfully as the chief had initiated his engagement, Rothery attributed the comment to either the chief's lack of social graces or a flawed attempt at playful male banter. Either way, he didn't have a suitable response, so instead pealed the left side of his suit jacket open and pulled a set of tweezers from the hidden pocket-protector in his dress shirt pocket. The chief nodded. He was not surprised that Rothery actually wore a pocket-protector but rather that he revealed it so blatantly.

While briefly distracted from the actual investigation, in an effort for efficiency and to prevent further interruptions, Rothery turned to the PM's taskforce representative to get the formal introductions out of the way. "And your involvement, slash, expertise, Mr. Vasko?"

"Please, call me Dylan. My responsibilities include but are not limited to, the assessment of terrorist activity within the greater United Kingdom."

"So, are you authorized to make arrests or execute the right of search and seizure and the likes?" Chief Philips inquired.

"I work primarily as a liaison between Scotland Yard and other national investigative bodies such as SIS and the Prime Minister's Office. My responsibilities stop at the investigative, slash, advisory role. I am not personally authorized to make arrests or use deadly force, if that is what you are asking… but there are members of my organization who are licensed to do so. I'm here to help work in collaboration with Scotland Yard— and now apparently MI6. Though it is still unclear to me their involvement considering the preliminary identification of the suspects constitutes a domestic threat and not an international one."

"Okay, you done?" the chief asked. Dylan certainly did not catch that Rothery's intent was to merely satisfy the customary divisional roll call. Dylan's shoulders sunk; he blew his GQ bangs out of his eyes, pursed his lips and returned to being the silent observer.

Chief Philips shook his head returning to ignoring Dylan. "So, if you don't mind, Agent Taylor, take me through this."

"Yes, all right then," Rothery nodded. "However, before we begin, what shall we call our mystery individual— the foiler?"

"Vigilante," the chief responded decisively.

Rothery raised a brow, "That's a bit harsh, wouldn't you agree? I was actually thinking something more along the lines of 'Samaritan'."

"Samaritan?" Philips almost scoffed. "Do you MI6 agents think everyone is an asset?"

Rothery surprisingly pondered the idea, "Possibly, Chief," he replied after a brief pause, "I've never considered it."

Before Philips could comment, the SIS agent began, "Now, gentlemen, this is a bit early… but lined with some preliminary assumptions and presuming that the three subdued men were the only perpetrators actively involved, the larger man of the deceased suspects is our shooter." Rothery motioned to one of the bodies wearing a flak jacket, lying on the lower floor of the restaurant. "He was second in the door. He came in shooting with the intent to kill immediately thereby squelching any and all thoughts of bravery."

"How do you know he was second in the door?" The chief sounded skeptical.

"The door opens to the right."

Chief Philips and Dylan exchanged a confused look, waiting for the agent to expound.

"If he was first in the door," Taylor went on to explain, "he would've had to have held the door with his right hand, correct? Or, had he opened it with his left hand, the barrel of his gun would have rested on or across his left arm resulting in misses— or more shots fired." Rothery looked down from the balcony toward the front entryway. "And, had the attacker opened the door with his gun, people in the center or right of the room would have been his easiest targets… where, as we can see, the first casualties were clearly to the left of the entrance."

Rothery pointed over the rail to the slightly smaller corpse of an older man in his forties, also wearing a flak jacket and lying motionless in a drying pool of blood. "This concludes that the older man was the first to enter; he opened the door then moved to the right giving the shooter an open shot to the left upon entry; the first two restaurant victims killed with what appeared to have been no more than four bullets— three, of which remain in their bodies. The shooter then naturally proceeded immediately to his left leaving us only the teenager. The youth would not have entered the building first— the shooter wouldn't have had him in his way, so he had to have entered last."

Making one more visual appraisal of the scene, the MI6 agent concluded his summation. "This was planned, gentlemen. Likely we'll find a restaurant layout at their home or lair. The shooter was military trained; the older man was the shepherd."

"Shepherd? You mean, the leader of the flock?" Dylan asked.

"No, English Shepherd, like the dog. His job was to corral the sheep; random killings only, until the execution phase. The youth was the doorman; prevents anyone from attempting to enter or exit." Rothery considered, "He's the weak spot, the anomaly. In a building like this with two of the three being seemingly well-trained men, the doorman should have been number two." Taylor shook his head, "The whole thing doesn't make sense."

Glancing at the unrecognizable body of a well-dressed man lying near his feet, Rothery looked to the elegant stairway leading down from the balcony. "The shooter then fired two rounds at this patron fleeing up to the balcony…" pointing to the left side of the lower floor, "from there. Two shots— both kill shots— on a running target in the midst of the corral stage from lower ground and around a corner. I'd say from the angle, the shooter had about a 3-inch window to even make the first shot." He confidently turned to the chief, "Therefore, we can call him the assassin."

Philips spied the angle, the wall; the blood streak leading to the bullet lodged in it. "That's some impressive shooting."

"You think that's tough," Rothery walked Philips three steps back, "look at the angle of the head shot. Second shot fired— two to three seconds after the first. Had to miss, right? But he threaded the bar."

"What do you mean?"

The balcony wall was made of 3-foot by 8-foot glass sections with a classic, brass rail above and below. Multiple 3-inch brass mounts divided the suspended walls. "He didn't hit the glass," Rothery explained. "He shot between the panels using this brass mount as his sight," indicating a slightly singed mount with his extended pocket pointer. "He hit not only a moving target, but a randomly falling target— right below the cheekbone in a profile shot, crushing his brain instantly. A target, he must have known from the first shot, was already inevitably dead."

"So, what are you saying?"

Rothery held his chin in thought and drummed a finger against his cheek. When he stopped, he spoke with authority. "He did it for fun, Chief. He was showing off. An assassin of that caliber wouldn't have walked in here... not like this. Not with a teenager watching his back."

"Bloody hell!" Philips exclaimed. "He's not a zealot, he's paid for hire!"

"Exactly," Rothery nodded. "This was no terrorist attack."

Wide-eyed, Philips gave the MI6 agent his undivided attention, "What else?"

"No answers, only questions. The restaurant is all wrong. It's too easy; three rooms plus a balcony. The crowd is too diverse; four stars, not five. No political affiliation, owners not Jewish— clam chowder on Friday. It's too random," Rothery postulated.

"Do they really serve clam chowder?" Dylan asked.

"I don't know," Rothery answered, "I didn't read the menu."

With a slight scowl to the young man, the chief moved on, "So, our vigilante... off-duty policeman?"

"No, the 'Samarian' didn't have a gun," Rothery replied.

"SIS?"

Agent Taylor raised a brow and eyed the chief, assessing the blatant inference. "Even an MI6 agent wouldn't have taken the risk unarmed. If he was SIS, Chief, he may have disappeared into the crowd but I would have known about it by now. And he would have been carrying."

"I notice that you're not carrying a gun, agent" the chief quipped.

"It's in the glovebox of my car."

"Uh-huh. And how long has your car been in the parking lot?"

Rothery didn't bother to entertain the insinuation.

Deferring his suspicion, "Do you think the Samaritan was an accomplice?" Chief Philips questioned.

Rothery sighed, thought about it, and scanned the room. "Why?"

Philips explained, "Bear with me, Taylor… the buyer wants a front row seat to the execution; he leaves no strings attached, no witnesses."

"Interesting, but without a weapon?"

"Hmm," the chief thought, "so, who does that leave us then?"

"The target," Rothery asserted.

Chief Superintendent Philip's eyes widened, "An unarmed target of an assassination attempt takes out three men— one of whom is a trained assassin? Who the hell is this guy?!" he demanded.

"That, Chief, I don't know…" Rothery answered, "…not yet."

Chapter 23

SEEING MICAH COME TO, the attending nurse stepped up to the side of his bed, "There you are!" she smiled. "Can you hear me?" she asked. "Sir, can you hear me?"

Micah blinked his eyes hard. More than his hearing was a bit blurry. "Do you know where you are?" she probed.

Micah scanned the room. He nodded 'yes' while yawning to pop his ears. "How am I?"

"Well, I'm Nurse Joan and you'll be just fine. Do you know what happened to you?"

"Uh, horrible taste in my mouth…"

"Yes, that's possible, probably from the anesthesia." Nurse Joan spoke as if to a child, "But you were SHOT, as well. Not just the anesthesia shot either— which was actually more likely gas or could have been put in your IV…" she tapped her nails on the IV tube above his head, "I mean you were shot by a GUN."

"Uh-huh… this is a hospital, right? A medical hospital? You're a nurse, right?"

"Yes, yes, yes." She pointed to her name tag with a bubbly bobble of her head.

If Micah didn't have doubts before, he did then. "Okay, how long have I been out? Can I speak with the doctor?" Just as Micah knew he needed to leave the restaurant scene before he could be questioned concerning the terrorists, he likewise knew he needed to get out of the hospital as soon as possible. And, as he had already come to find out, the fact that he was likely the only surviving gunshot victim made him a story of interest to the media, as well. Something else he needed to avoid with Ring Finger now in the picture.

"The doctor will check on you in a bit," Nurse Joan informed, "but I need to get some information from you first. You didn't have any identification when you were brought into the hospital."

"Yes, my coat and phone were left at the restaurant. I tried to have the ambulance go back to retrieve them."

"That's all right, you can get them later. It sounds like you're American, eh?"

"Yes, that's right," Micah answered.

"And what's your name?"

"Allen Steinbeck. I'm from New York."

Joan wrote the details on her clipboard. "Do you have any allergies or are you taking any medication, Mr. Steinbeck?"

"No and no. I'm pretty healthy… fairly active, you know. Sports, etcetera."

"Yes, quite. I can see that." She lifted the blankets to view the bandage on his lower abdomen. "Age? How old are you?"

"Thirty-six."

"You look young for your age."

"Thank you, so I've been told. Feel much older today, though."

"That's the medication talking," Joan comforted. "A thirty-six year old athlete… well, that actually explains a lot, Mr. Steinbeck. The EMT said you were in your forties and she couldn't understand how your heart rate and blood pressure could be so low." She made a note. "All right. Next… do you remember how you were shot?"

"Yes, in the commotion at the beginning… by the door. I pretended to be dead."

"Were you with anyone? Anyone who may have suffered an injury as well?" Nurse Joan kept a watchful eye on Micah as she asked the question knowing that often during a tragic event where actual fatalities occurred, the nursing staff could be called to assist in finding separated victims. In the worst of cases, Joan might need to be the bearer of bad news— the part of her job she liked least. Due to the risk of shock or the possible need for counseling, the question had to be on her list.

Micah understood the intent behind the line of questioning; the last thing he needed was prolonged counseling. He gave himself a moment for the pretense of sincerity before responding, "Actually no," he answered. "I was supposed to meet someone but they called and cancelled. I was retrieving my coat from coat-check when men with guns entered the building. I didn't know anyone else in the restaurant, thank God."

Hearing his own words, Micah stopped himself. Rebuking his callousness, "I'm really sorry… I don't mean to be inconsiderate of the victims." The thought of loss brought heaviness to his heart. Micah had enough real emotion to make his eyes misty, but leaving the hospital still remained his main goal. "I just want to go home to my family," he said. "I need to be with people who know me, you know?" He choked back any real tears, "You know… to be with people I can feel like myself with?"

Nurse Joan patted Micah on the shoulder, "I understand, sir, it's all right. It's good to cry. You've been through quite a lot."

"Yes, but I guess I actually should be thankful, shouldn't I? There are people that have no one to go home to tonight because they were at that restaurant."

Before remorse could overwhelmed him, the doctor entered the room cutting off his thoughts. "You're awake. How do you feel?" The nurse handed him Micah's chart.

"Sore."

"Mr. Stein… Steinbeck. Do you know where you are and why you are here?"

"Yes sir, I don't think I'll ever forget it."

"I suspect not," the doctor agreed. He turned to Joan, "Joan, can you prep Mrs. Beckham for her examination?"

"Right away, doctor," she bobbed, quickly exiting the room.

"Mr. Steinbeck, my name is Dr. Wilson. I'm the attending physician who gave you this scar." He peeled back the bandage on Micah's stomach to check on the exit wound. "How do you feel— other than sore?" he asked.

"I feel okay. I didn't get the worst of it. I wasn't even positive that I'd really been shot until I was walking out the door."

"Well, I have to tell you that you are an extraordinarily lucky man."

"Somehow I don't feel lucky today, sir."

"Well, you should. Maybe not today, but you should. There was no bullet in your body, Mr. Steinbeck. It passed right through you. Matter of fact, we don't exactly understand how that was possible."

"How's that? Don't bullets fly straight?"

"Well, for the most part... apart from a ricochet off a hard object or a drop over a long distance. There are also bullets designed to burrow and others designed to explode upon impact— none of which applies in your case." Dr. Wilson examined Micah's expression. "You're shockingly coherent for a gunshot victim, Mr. Steinbeck."

"I don't feel very coherent. Like I said, I didn't even know I'd been shot."

"That's not all that unusual. In hindsight, do you remember the moment? What position you were in? Were you standing, sitting, kneeling, lying on the floor?"

"Yes, I do. If you don't mind, why are you asking?"

A frantic knock on the hospital room's door sounded as it flew open. Victoria and William entered.

Seeing the couple, Micah gave a subtle shake of his head. William, catching the hint, nodded, "We'll be right outside," he said turning.

"Oh, no we won't!" Victoria announced, pulling her arm free of William's guiding grasp. "We've been waiting here for HOURS! We checked every hospital in London tonight and couldn't find you anywhere! We only came back here in the hopes that this might be you... believe it or not, you're the SECOND unidentified person we've waited to see tonight! And they wouldn't even let us check right away if you were you no matter how much money William offered them." The trauma of the day flowed out of her mouth, filling the sterile air. She was obviously more relieved now than upset.

"The nurse at the emergency room reception station must really be having a bad night," Victoria continued. "After she wouldn't take our money, she told me (and I quote) 'I'm sorry Ms. Adams, but even YOU are going to have to wait until the patient is awake and suitable for visitors. Let him rest, Lord knows the poor bloke most certainly won't have any peace once he leaves here.' End quote. Not sure what she meant by that, but I really didn't like her tone."

Victoria rushed to Micah's side and took his hand.

"Now I'm certain that I will wait outside." William gave Micah a helpless shrug and moved into the waiting area.

"Victoria, dear, the doctor was speaking." Micah held her hand but eyed the doctor.

"Oh, sorry, don't mind me. Please continue, doctor," she apologized cordially.

Dr. Wilson struggled to conceal his surprised that it was THE Victoria Adams now holding his patient's hand. He gave her a second look before clearing his throat, "As I was saying," he began again, "we're having difficulty calculating the route. The bullet went in low at an upward angle; through your buttocks and missing the pelvic bone, then on a path through the small intestine— which is still completely intact."

"I was standing with my back to the shooter, if that helps?"

"All right then, we should be able to draw the line; meaning it should have hit your bladder or your prostrate... your rectum, your reproductive organs, spinal cord— something. Mind you, even the needle-threading of the bullet past your pelvic bone was by design. Had it hit your pelvis, you wouldn't have been able to walk to assistance. But then, what's more the wonder, is that the exit wound itself split the right and left rectus abdominis, failing to even tear the rectus sheath."

"Okay, I'm not completely sure what all that means."

"Your right and left abdomen muscles— the proverbial six-pack— were split, so there was no muscle damage, either." The doctor's brow furrowed, "Mr. Steinbeck, we spent close to an hour looking for something to repair. I'd say we almost did more damage looking than the bullet that traveled through your body."

Victoria frowned confused, "Steinbeck?"

Micah quickly squeezed her hand, "Well, that's good news, right, doctor? So, what's with the questions?"

"Curiosity more than anything, I suppose."

"At least it explains how I walked out the door without knowing I'd been shot, right?"

"Actually, it's not surprising you were able to walk away. There are numerous cases evident to that, especially in the military. But those are usually flesh wounds, shoulder wounds, profile buttocks wounds; your case is strange because the bullet traveled through a concentration of vital organs yet left you unscathed."

"So, doc, can I leave?"

"Hold on there… I'd like to keep you at least a couple of days for observation."

"Dr. Wilson, my hotel is close by, I need to get to a phone. I need to call my family. Can we do this on an outpatient basis? Honestly, after today, I'm much more stressed about being in a crowded, open environment like this hospital than about any other aspect of my health. I want to be locked behind doors that are locked behind doors, if you know what I mean. And no offense to my bunkmate over there, but I don't think I could sleep here. Not tonight."

"Well…" Dr. Wilson paused thinking; he had more problem with a patient requesting to leave than with actually letting him go. "Being that you are not a citizen, we also need to sum up the bill. From what I understand, we didn't have any information for you upon your arrival."

"I'm most certain the restaurant insurance will cover that, but if not…"

Victoria chimed in, "I'll cover any expenses."

The doctor had purposely tried to ignore the fact that he was in the room with a celebrity. Now she was speaking to him. "Ah, well… billing is not really my department, Ms. Adams."

Victoria smiled sweetly, "Of course it isn't. So, about leaving… you were saying, doctor?"

Intentionally avoiding Victoria and addressing only Micah, "You, uh… won't be alone tonight, correct?" he asked.

"Oh, no," Victoria obnoxiously replied instead, "I can assure you he will be well tended to."

Dr. Wilson blushed. "This goes beyond my better judgment, Mr. Steinbeck, but I suppose it is possible if you are close by and being cared for." He didn't dare look towards Victoria. "But don't do anything that may re-open your stitches."

Micah shook his head emphatically, assuring him there were no worries in that department.

"And you will be back in the morning, won't you?" Dr. Wilson's request was more accurately a stern demand. "My office is just across the parking lot. I want to check your stats as an exit examination before we consider how soon you're on a plane for home."

"That's great, doc!" Micah resounded.

"I'll send Nurse Joan back in to help you gather your belongings and settle the expenses. Please feel free to take your time. I'll see you tomorrow." The doctor exited with an awkward nod to Ms. Adams.

Chapter 24

WHAT ARE YOU LOOKING for now?" Dylan asked. After following the MI6 agent through the restaurant for hours, he found it hard to image there might possibly be something the man had missed.

Rothery, consumed in the moment, was uninterruptable.

"Agent Taylor? Is there something specific you're looking for?" Dylan tried again.

Ignoring the young investigator, Rothery looked to the ceiling. Suddenly he called over the balcony rail, "Chief Philips!"

"What do you got?" Philips responded from the main floor.

"We may have caught a break, Chief."

The chief motioned to Sergeant Tilman, "We'll be right up."

As the two men from Scotland Yard reached the top of the stairs, Rothery continued to stand at the first table on the balcony, scanning for surveillance cameras.

"I'm waiting," Philips announced, his patience exhausted.

Taking another moment to calculate, "Well, Chief," the agent finally explained, "this place may not have any known political affiliations, but its cameras are D-Link DCS series with HD color. The restaurant's three cameras should have caught the entire establishment. And they're networked."

"That's not unusual, everyone's a geek now. We've already got our men working on it. Why? You think HD quality to film their customers' indiscretions? A side source of income?" Philips suggested.

"Restaurants don't stay in business blackmailing their patrons, Chief, but you're right; my brother-in-law has as good, if not better, surveillance system protecting the riding lawnmower in his storage shed."

"Has anyone seen the film?" Dylan asked.

"Server's intact but it's encrypted," Tilman answered. "We're waiting."

Rothery sat down at the table. "He sat here."

"Who?" the chief asked.

"The Samaritan."

"Are you certain? What makes you say that?" Dylan asked.

"Well, again, all this is preliminary speculation, but I knew fairly early on that he came down from the balcony to engage the terrorists." Rothery got up and walked four steps down the stairs. There was a half-moon, un-smudged blood print on the edge of the top step. "This is our man," Rothery said, motioning to the blood stain.

"There are footprints all over," Tilman pointed out. "The customers from the top of the balcony ran through the blood while fleeing the restaurant."

"Yes, but this print is darker, thicker— not a trampled stain. It was dried before the customers made their escape from the building." Rothery crouched on the step. "And it's just the instep of a right foot. I propose the Samaritan was up there under the first table when victim number three was shot and fell to the ground near the table next to his." The agent stood. "See how he avoided walking through the blood splatters on the stair?" He pointed, "First there, missing a step for his left foot then stepping over here. It's on the right and then on the left side. He didn't walk a straight path down the stairs. He must have wiped off his shoes on the carpet before heading down to the floor."

"Where did he wipe off his feet?" Phillips asked. "You'd definitely see smudge marks."

"Right, you would think. Unless he wiped them off where the victim's blood was about to stream. In that case, the fresh seeping blood covered his footprints before our investigation."

"Hmm," Philips considered doubtfully.

"These crescent moon-shaped blood stains are made from high on the instep of the shoe. Shuffling his feet upon the carpet failed to clean the blood in the shoe's crevice. He caught the edge of the step with his instep because he tipped-toed down the stairs. See how it's thin? The customers ran flat footed down the center of the steps." Rothery moved back toward the first table, "So, for a person to get fresh blood on his shoe, he must have been seated here."

"Seriously Wyndham, now you're just getting cocky," Philips challenged. "I admit you have impressed me so far, but I'm no novice sleuth slayer, myself. And that's a huge leap— a ridiculously huge leap, don't you think?"

"I thought so, too…" Rothery sat back down in the chair, "until I noticed that this seat is the only seat in the house that does not give a frontal view of its occupant to the cameras."

Shocked, the chief looked at all three cameras' angles. "Bloody hell, you're right! And that makes the…" pausing for effect, "VIGILANTE a bad guy, doesn't it? Good Samaritans don't worry about things like that."

Rothery, also assessing the camera angles, spoke quietly, "Either that, or he's extraordinarily lucky."

"Lucky? Another coincidence? Like your son now being named Rothery Wyndham?" Philips waited for the agent's response. Rothery seemed engrossed in thought. "What are you thinking, Taylor?"

"Hmm? Nothing. We'll get a portrait of the fight when we have the video."

"Right. Keep me informed if you have any further details." Chief Philips and Tilman headed back down the stairs.

"Mr. Taylor," Dylan said, "impressive demonstration."

"It's just a preliminary."

"Well, brilliant; outstanding theory."

"I'd rather, hypothesis."

"Would you consider, sir— taking into account Chief Philips' blatant conflict with the PM's office— that we pull our resources on this one? I can provide some political insight and possibly alleviate any unanticipated roadblocks?"

Rothery was used to working alone but less by desire than due to his unique skillset in the department. Plus, the techies were envious and the field agents felt threatened. Apart from his superiors, Rothery had more enemies than allies within the firm. A partner had only slowed him down in the past... but possibly one from outside his department might be different?

He had made no judgment of Dylan; the young man's enthusiasm a bit over the top but admirable. *What's the worst that could happen?* he thought.

"You've made quite the impression on me, Agent Taylor, I feel there is so much I can learn from you," the young man flattered.

Rothery answered as if not having heard the compliment, "Listen, I'm quite cautious when filing reports. You mustn't speak of our unconfirmed theories."

"Discretion ... absolutely! So, that's a 'yes', yeah?"

Rothery nodded.

Chapter 25

IN THE BACK PARKING lot of Mercy General Hospital, Henry and Kevin sat in the front seat of Henry's late-model Peugeot. An assortment of paper cups, candy wrappers and fast food containers littered the floorboards.

"What are we still waiting for?" Kevin whined. "We got a name almost an hour ago. We know he's being released, let's just go up and interview him." Pedestrian traffic in the well-lit area was gradually slowing as the hours ticked further into the night.

Henry frowned, "I'm telling you, this Allen Steinbeck guy is dirty. He knows something he's not saying."

"A man's shot by terrorists, but because he doesn't want to talk to a reporter with his trousers down and a bullet in his ass, he's a bad guy?"

"It's not that he didn't want to talk to me, it's HOW he didn't want to talk. There's a reason why I'm the famous investigative reporter and you're just the cameraman."

"What? You say famous?"

"Before your time, lad."

"And how'd that work out for you?" Kevin smirked. "Let's just go up. It's creepy sitting out here with you. And I'm not the only one who thinks so. So does the girl who just walked by our car."

"I didn't see any girl."

"No, I know you didn't. You were leaning across the seat grabbing your sandwich out of the glovebox." Kevin sat back, crossing his arms, "I waved at her, she looked at me and smiled. Lovely, right? Well, as it figures, I had this stupid 'pretty-girl-just-looked-at-me' grin on my face just about the time you raised your head up from the glovebox— which from her angle, was right out of my lap. If that wasn't bad enough, you took the first bite of your sandwich straightaway, so you're wiping off your mouth as she walks by. So, there I am, smiling and waving like a fucking adolescent in the parking lot of a school prom. No surprise she ran the rest of the way to her car."

"It's a good sandwich!" Laughing, Henry took another big bite and continued with his mouth full, "Gave me a laugh, gave her a thrill... and you always look like a fucking adolescent. Good story, good stakeout." Henry swallowed. "What did you think? She was going to join you in the backseat of my car for the other half of the sandwich?"

"Do you know how creepy you sound? Let's just go in."

"Listen, if we go in, we may or may not get our interview. But if he comes out the back door of the hospital..." Henry shook his sandwich like a teacher emphasizing with a ruler, "then I'll know my suspicions are correct."

"Some people park in the back, Henry. Means nothing."

"He came in an ambulance, he'll leave in a cab. And that..." Henry hesitated, "comes to the front door." He frowned.

"Right, and you're sitting in the back. So, what if he's already left, eh? But you hadn't noticed because you were hanging out in the back?"

Henry stopped, shifting his eyes to and fro. He hadn't thought of that. Decidedly, he shook the doubt aside, "No, no, no, I'm right on this one."

Kevin let out an exasperated sigh, "Let me go in, I'll wait in the lobby— just in case he leaves out the front. I'll SMS you; you can circle round and get your interview while he's waiting for a cab, yeah?"

"Hmm. That'll work, I suppose." It did make a measure of sense.

As Kevin readied to open the door, Henry reached his arm across the passenger seat to stop him, "Well, well, Kevin, look at that! That's our boy… coming out the BACK."

"Hey, who's the girl with him? She's hot from fifty yards!"

"Shut up!" Henry jumped out of the car. "If I signal, you get some pictures, right? If I call you over, video and don't stop filming for nothing, got it?"

"Right, what's the signal?"

"I'll raise my hand, just watch."

An attendant was pushing Micah in a wheelchair down the backdoor ramp, Victoria close to Micah's side. Henry hollered across the parking lot, "Mr. Steinbeck! Mr. Steinbeck!"

Micah failed to respond.

Crossing the lot at a half jaunt wheezing, "Mr. Steinbeck…!" the reporter finally reached the trio at the base of the switchback ramp.

Hands on his knees catching his breath, "Mr. Steinbeck," Henry gasped. Victoria squeezed Micah's hand with a nod in his direction.

"Oh, I'm sorry," Micah acknowledged, subtly directing Victoria to move behind the attendant, "how may I help you?"

Henry, in a bent-over recuperating position, looked eye-level at Micah sitting in the wheelchair. "Do you remember me, Mr. Steinbeck?"

Micah did recognize him but nodded no. He purposefully kept eye-contact with Henry in hopes the man wouldn't look up and recognize Victoria.

"You know, I've never seen anyone take so long to recognize their own name," Henry insinuated, carefully watching for a reaction. "I suppose you've had quite a long day, sir."

Micah maintained a cool demeanor. He sensed that what had previously been a reluctance to talk to the press had now become much more. Henry's insinuation that he might actually know Micah's real name (or at least have a suspicion that he had lied to the hospital) was not something to be taken lightly.

Micah seriously sized-up Henry. At first glance he didn't appear to be one of those Micah had spent years avoiding; but they were known to change their appearance. He couldn't be too careful. Out of habit, Micah scanned the parking lot for accomplices then toward the alley for a possible quick escape. In his assessment, he noticed the cameraman fifty yards back, clearly watching their interaction.

Still wary, Micah inconspicuously adjusted his wheelchair further away from Victoria. He kept up the façade, "And yours?"

"My what?" Henry stuttered as he finally stood upright. "Name? You want my name?"

"Well, suddenly we seem to be at that point in our relationship, don't you agree?" Though the words exchanged between the men were superficial niceties, there was still something about their conversation resonating beyond the surface keeping Micah on guard.

Henry considered a nom d' plum but instead answered, "Wilkens... Henry Wilkens. Ring a bell?"

"Should it?" Micah asked casually.

Henry thought about it. "Nah."

"Is there something I can help you with, Mr. Wilkens?"

"I was at Oceans as you exited," he stated.

"Ah, yes, you were asking questions at the ambulance."

"That's right." Henry attempted to turn on what little charm he had, "Are you going to be alright? Took a shot in the backside, yeah?"

"Yes, went right through me. Barely noticed." Micah smiled pleasantly.

"I suppose that explains how you walked out on your own. Awful lot of blood, though."

"Really? I hadn't noticed. Busy with having been shot, and all."

"Yeah, really. I served in the Gulf... was an embedded reporter in every skirmish. I've seen my share of bullet wounds."

"I haven't."

"You were covered in it, mate. I mean, front and back, trousers, shoes. Man loses that much blood he goes home in a body bag, if you know what I mean. How do you explain that?"

Micah was slightly shocked by the reporter's intuitiveness; shocked but relieved the man was nothing more than a suspicious reporter and not his worst case scenario. He could tell Henry was suspicious, possibly suspecting he was an escaping terrorist. Not great, but also not his primary concern— Micah had bigger things to worry about. Eventually this reporter would get his story. Micah just hoped it would be long after he was gone.

"Do you know what you are looking for, Mr. Wilkens? Can I help you find it?" Micah needed to bring this meeting to an end as quickly as possible.

"Are you avoiding the question? And it's Henry."

"I know you think I am. So, what do you want to hear? I'll give you a story, Henry." *If you think I'm going to lie and you know I can lie, why bother asking the question?*

Henry smiled, "Let me guess… you pretended to be dead lying next to the other victims, who in turn, bled out on your clothes."

Micah smiled. "That works for me," chuckling, "though I might not have come up with it as quickly as you did."

Henry paused. *Did he just confess?* The reporter frowned, "You do realize I can print what you just said, don't you?"

Micah winked with a grin, "Anything else, Mr. Wilkens?" Micah motioned the orderly into the parking lot towards the Avis rental car.

"Damn it all," Henry grumbled. He turned and stomped back across the parking lot.

*   *   *   *   *

As the attendant made his way back through the hospital doors with wheelchair in tow, Micah and Victoria settled into the car. "Who's Allen Steinbeck?" Victoria asked.

Micah laughed, "He's a friend of mine; always wanted to be a superhero."

"Well, you just made him one."

"Yeah, I suppose." His smile began to fade. "I'm afraid he'll likely be less appreciative than he might have thought, though. But on the other hand," he added, "if this goes south, he'll know I'm in trouble."

Chapter 26

MICAH OPENED THE HOTEL room door, walked straight to the television, and turned it on.

Victoria followed close behind, sensing his anxiety. "I don't understand. You're a hero. You saved seventy-five people or better."

"Trust me, I can't afford this kind of attention. There were cameras throughout the restaurant, it's only a matter of time. The police will want to question me. And someone is sure to have recognized you. I need to get out of town."

"This may sound strange coming from me, but I think you're being paranoid."

Micah sat silent, hesitant to speak. To say anything further only endangered her.

As if on cue, the television news coverage showed the Guard video gone viral, all channels broadcasting a crafty display of police-blues encircling the restaurant, body bags on gurneys, and Micah covered in blood. The commentator's final statement, "The question still remains— who subdued the terrorists? Back to you, Frank."

"Great." Micah put his head in his hands. He was exhausted, sore, and too tired to consider any more that night.

Victoria took a seat across from him. She considered everything she knew, yet a thousand questions ran through her mind. Unfortunately, tonight was probably not the best time to pry. "I've seen you chase away shadows in the night," she began tentatively. "I saw you take down terrorists. You walked away from the hospital when you clearly needed to stay. Why, Micah," she questioned, "what are you afraid of?"

Micah remained silent although she could tell he wanted to speak. She knew the look on his face far too well; the look of wanting to share with someone but knowing they'd think you were crazy. Suddenly it hit her, "It's me isn't it? You're concerned for me?"

Micah tried to look at her, but in his exhaustion his eyes could not conceal his emotion. He shifted them to the floor.

Part of living as a target— combating that which came against him— was a resignation; a surrender of his life and his own safety to whatever fate might send his way. For the most part, good won out over evil; but there were no guarantees and the odds were too great to expect the risk from another. There had been those who'd chosen to delve into his strange reality with him, but reviews were mixed on how that had worked out for them.

The two sat silent for a time. Victoria's mind reeled, searching for the source of his concern. "You once mentioned the real players…"

Micah took a slow drink of water maintaining his solemn disposition. "I need sleep."

"Are you okay?"

"I can't think about this tonight, let's talk in the morning."

"Okay. Can I take your extra key?" She carefully watched for a response. "In case I feel the need to check on you during the night?"

"No. Stay with me," Micah said, surprising her.

Victoria glanced at the undersized double bed in the simple, single room and replied, "Okay."

Chapter 27

ARRIVING AT THE BULL pen of the Guard, Henry turned on the British Journalism Award statue lamp on his desk. One of the most prestigious awards for journalism given in the UK and Henry owned two. The one for foreign affairs was considered by his colleagues to be the more impressive, but his baby was the one for investigative journalism from fifteen years back. Though no one understood why he took his prized possession and converted it into the base of a gaudy lamp, Henry knew far too well that today's late-breaking news lined the birdcages of tomorrow.

Few positions were less forgiving than that of a journalist. Reporters were praised for unadulterated, even brazen reporting… until the target of their report was nominated to an exalted position with just enough power and intelligence to exact revenge. Due to a single bit of shoddy reporting (or more accurately, an unintended 'political collision') Henry now had a stream of investigative competitors waiting in the wings to take his place. But this reminder of his achievement was now too gaudy to steal and the perfect excuse to never take off his desk.

Henry powered up his laptop as he eyed the windowed offices above, following the row all the way to the corner office with the wall-to-ceiling view of the city— the office he had once-upon-a-time inhabited. The upper hallway was now dark; at two in the morning, the entire building was all but empty with only a few members of the foreign affairs' night shift mulling about their sparsely lit, mid-sized bullpen of average-looking, open cubicles.

Seeing the desk light flip-on, Henry's boss dropped by. "Brilliant job on the terrorist piece, Henry," Pete said, taking a sip of his lukewarm coffee. "How'd you pull that off?"

"Right place at the right time, I suppose." Henry could have done without seeing Pete that evening.

"Yeah? I'd long given up on you ever being at the right place at the right time again."

Henry started to frown but refrained; he didn't want Pete to think he'd gotten to him.

"What I can't understand, Henry, is why you allowed Sara to enter the entire nation's living rooms to tell the tale when it was your scoop? You saw she got a corner seat upfront at the desk with Frank on the 10 PM broadcast, didn't you?"

"She anchored with Frank at 10?" Henry mourned.

"Of course she did. She was the only person in the world— other than you, of course— to know the story. Hell, Scotland Yard and the PM's Office had agents here to interview her by 11. The only reason anyone even knows it was your story is that when the MI6 agent threatened her, she gave you up."

"MI6 agent?" Henry openly began to cry. "Why the hell is SIS involved?"

"It's terrorism, Henry. Besides, no worries, I'm certain they'll want to talk to you by morning. I'm a bit surprised they haven't found you yet."

"I suppose. Is that why you're working late, Pete?"

"No, it's my week to put the dailies on the trucks."

"Dailies, huh? Do people still read paper anymore?"

"Nope. It lines the..." both men in unison, "...waste can."

"Still the cheapest paper-towel-multi-purpose-gift-wrap in town," Pete finished.

Henry sighed, "It won't be for much longer. With Reuters online, they won't need us anymore."

"Yeah, no one cares about anything anymore. PM shags a whore and it's all fodder unless you have ink..." again, both men finished together, "...and it'd better be pink!" Pete laughed.

Henry mustered a chuckle though it was painful to do so. Many of the common phrases that still circulated the newsroom were invented while Henry sat at the table if not literally created by him over a beer at the Pressroom Pub— the place reporters gathered every night to wind down and banter over their war stories. Ten to fifteen years ago, Henry held the crowd there with actual war stories and tales from 10 Downing Street.

He forced a smile as a reminder of what was— that, and to keep on Pete's good side. It was still up to Pete to publish his daily drag, but enduring the boss' slaughter of his old quotes was more than Henry could tolerate that night. "Well, goodnight, Pete," he said abruptly, directly ending their conversation.

"All right Henry, I'll let you get back to it." Pete's unsuccessful attempt at authority as he sheepishly backed away from Henry's desk was nothing new. He knew not to interrupt Henry (or any of the reporters, for that matter) in the midst of a story. Pete might have been the editor and chief, but as even he himself would admit, his shoes and mouth were bigger than his bite.

Even so, no one bothered to correct Pete's brutal butchering of idioms and metaphors, either. On the contrary, it was more fun to get the boss to coin a new phrase. The reporters often asked him for a line or title for the paper; the life goal of the team to finally get one of Pete's quotes past the executive staff and published as a front page headline.

Pete had never been a reporter; he was never invited to the pub. But he was legacy—fourth generation. Legend had it that Pete's great-grandfather had been the reporter who wrote the front page Daily Mail headline of September 3rd, 1939— the headline that consisted of one word: WAR.

'Great Britain and France are at war with Germany. We now fight against the blackest tyranny that ever held men in bondage. We fight to defend, and to restore, freedom and justice on earth.'

Henry never liked the use of commas in subtitles and he would have capitalized Earth. But it wasn't grammar that lit his desk at night; it was his nose for the story and the guts to see it through— something he hadn't paid much attention to for the better part of a decade.

Sitting at his desk, the familiar dim light of his ridiculous award-lamp comforting him, the barely recognizable smell of a good story began to haunt him. He couldn't put his finger on why this particular story interested him. Now that the Guard had won credit for the exclusive and humiliated the police in the process, (a police force that had harassed Henry for many years) what more did he want? He could not for the life of him determine why this one guy shot in the rear gnawed at him so much. *It's over,* he thought. *There's no story in it.*

He shrugged, "Who cares, right? An American survivor, so what? There's plenty of Yanks trolling about the isle…" He sat up straight in his chair, "An AMERICAN survivor!"

Henry began to muse out loud, "Wait a minute, wait a minute… wait a bloody minute! The police have got to be looking for him— and who knows he's an American?" He began to laugh, "The nurse is a divvy, the doc is embarrassed… they're no good to anyone. But I've talked to Mr. I-Don't-Think-Your-Name-Is-Steinbeck— TWICE." Henry's laugh became almost sinister.

He hunkered down and started typing.

Chapter 28

ROTHERY ENTERED THE MEDICAL examiner's morgue at Scotland Yard followed by Chief Philips. "Helen?" Philips called out.

As the men came through the examining room doors, a slight woman— silver-haired, bun loose yet neatly at the nape of her neck; eyeglasses (sporting a delicate gold chain) perched on the end of her nose— held up her hand without looking up from the body of a man in his mid-thirties. Her petite gloved fingers motioned a countdown. Goggles strapped behind her ears and mounted on her forehead, with something similar to a multifunction otoscope, she peered into the ear of the corpse. She unclipped a sharp set of micro tweezers from the lapel of her lab jacket, inserted them into the ear, and pulled out a tiny fragment.

Though Helen had only motioned a count of three, Rothery noted that precisely ten seconds had passed before the chief began to speak again, "Helen?" Rothery also noticed it was the exact amount of time required to remove whatever it was she had found in the dead man's ear.

"Lawrence," Helen responded curtly.

Philips cleared his throat, "Mrs. Goff," he corrected, "this is Rothery Taylor, special agent for SIS."

"Lawrence, I'm in the middle of a forensic investigation. Do I bother you during the mayor's gala or whatever such things they have you do around here now?"

Philips took a deep breath and sighed. Attempting to redeem the illusion of his authority, he officially inquired, "Are these the suspects from the Oceans Restaurant terrorist attack?"

"This is not Israel, Lawrence," Mrs. Goff lectured, facing him off, "was there more than one terrorist attack in London last night?"

Now clearly annoyed, Philips refused to answer.

"Lawrence? A bi-directional flow of communication is required for all of us to do our jobs efficiently."

Clearing his throat, "No, ma'am, there was only one."

"One what, Lawrence? Clear communication requires concise, accurate and fully descriptive sentences, don't you agree? I would have thought they'd have taught you that in your special inspector's course."

Clearing his throat for the third time since entering the room, "There was only one terrorist attack in London last night, ma'am. And I'm the Chief Superintendent now."

"Do you have a cold, Lawrence? Do you need a lozenge?"

"No, ma'am, I don't."

"Hmm. All right then." Helen returned her attention to the body on the table.

"So these are the suspects?" Philips ventured again.

Helen stopped, removed the glasses from her nose and allowed them to fall to her chest, suspended by the chain around her neck. "And if these were the victims of the shooting, would they be in my laboratory, Lawrence?"

Philips drew a clenched fist to his mouth now hesitant to answer incorrectly, "No."

"Hmph… that's not entirely accurate." Helen shook her head, disappointed.

The small woman exhaled an exhausted breath, took off her rubber gloves; and though still bothered by the interruption, with an opportunity to educate, she felt obliged to continue. "There are many gunshot victims brought to my laboratory. However, considering the weapons were found at the scene, there was no reason as of yet to order the victims' bodies from this particular incident to my crime lab. Does the city coroner suspect the victims have died from something other than bullet wounds?"

"No, ma'am," Philips answered. Rothery joined Chief Philips in a bewildered stare at the small, intimidating woman.

Helen rolled her eyes and attempted to summarize, "If there was only one terrorist attack in London, gentlemen, and there was no reason to bring the victims' bodies to the crime lab, then these are most definitely the suspects of last night's shooting."

"Thank you, Mrs. Goff," they replied in unison.

"I don't know what... without me... when I'm gone... God help London," Helen mumbled.

"Rothery," the chief said calmly, "I will leave you in the capable hands of our most senior officer and forensic specialist." Philips then hurriedly left through the swinging double doors.

"I haven't yet received the ballistics report on the victim, Lawrence!" she called out after him.

"Mrs. Goff, ma'am?"

"Yes, Rothery?" Helen answered in a tone he had not heard since the third grade.

"What can you tell me about the suspects?"

"Well, Rothery, what do you know about forensic medicine?"

Rothery had actually started his studies in medicine at Cambridge. He then received an MSc in criminology and criminal justice at Oxford with a PhD in mathematics at the same. All of which told him to answer as thus, "I'm just an agent, ma'am."

"All right, then." Helen perched her glasses back upon her nose, reading from the clipboard, "Raza Mohammed Ahluwalia— the older gentlemen— died from a puncture wound starting from behind and under the ribcage, upward to the heart. His killer was either quite skilled or extremely lucky."

"Why do you say that?"

"He nearly bled out to the point of death just prior to the fatal puncture to his heart."

"So, he would have bled to death without the second wound?"

"There was only one incision, he was only stabbed once. The same initial stab was slightly retracted then pushed and twisted, puncturing the heart and killing him instantly."

"Could he have been stabbed and then fallen on the knife causing the deeper wound?"

"I considered that, but the thickness of the cartilage the blade had to have penetrated, plus the amount of force needed to do so; the knife at that angle and the precision... it required a strong amount of force. Falling hard against a solid object could have caused enough force, however, with the amount of prior blood loss, he wouldn't have been conscious enough to have remained standing to then fall on his own. He most definitely was stabbed and held in that position for an extended period of time. Then in a forceful, precise blow and twist, killed instantly.

"The killer tortured him."

"Hmm, there would have been pain… however, a benefit of the final stage of blood loss is the masking of pain, leading to a lack of consciousness. In my experience, a sure sign of a tortured victim is the grinding of teeth and self-inflicted abrasions in the mouth. Mr. Ahluwalia had none. Therefore, I wouldn't say tortured… but the man would have definitely been cold, which to me, is torture."

"How long to bleed out— or nearly bleed out, from that incision?"

"I'd have to say approximately five to seven minutes."

"So, why would the killer stick around for five to seven minutes before finishing the job? Do you have a hypothesis?"

Helen thought for a moment, "To guess, I would say the killer was talking to him. What else would you do?"

"Could he have known him?"

"Rothery, I'm a doctor not a social worker."

"I apologize, Mrs. Goff. I was thinking out loud."

"My husband used to think out loud… caused us all sorts of trouble in the early years of our marriage. Later, however, it became somewhat of an aphrodisiac."

"Mrs. Goff!" laughed Rothery.

"Oh, pish-posh, young man, don't give me that look! In all my years I've never been one minute inappropriate— and especially not in the work place. However, my James passed 13 years ago, and you don't work for the Yard."

Rothery grinned, "Then you are quite free to elaborate."

The coroner smiled playfully, "Why is it you men think a woman who mentions a moment of promiscuity spends a lifelong journey traversing the streets of infidelity?"

"I'm not certain how to take that, Mrs. Goff."

"Well, in a phrase, my young SIS agent… you can call me Helen."

"The pleasure is certainly mine." Rothery smiled from ear to ear, completely infatuated with the other side of Scotland Yard's prim and proper school mum.

He comfortably continued, "So, he was talking to him; either getting information or giving information to him. What does a tech-worker from Bracknell know?"

"Possibly where Malcolm X came from," Helen surmised.

"Malcolm?"

"We don't have a name on Mr. X, so Mr. X likely being a Muslim, became Malcolm X."

"That could be offensive."

"It could be offensive for you to say, Mr. Taylor. I've only six months to go before retirement; how do you think I get away with calling the chief Lawrence?" Helen winked.

"Does anyone else know how duplicitous you are?"

The woman smiled deviously, "As I said, Mr. Taylor, you don't work here. You go right ahead— go along and tell them I'm actually a sweet, lovely lady. Which of us will they think is crazy, eh?" She lowered her voice to a whisper, "I've been acting this way for 46 years… insanely maniacal!"

Rothery warded off a chuckle.

"Forty years ago, no one would have worried about what we called a brutal, ruthless killer." Helen shook her head in disapproval, "Besides, they only let me talk to dead bodies anymore. None of these men are going to snitch on me."

"You, Mrs. Goff…"

"Helen," she corrected.

"You may be my favorite character of all time, Helen."

"Why, thank you, agent. Though you say 'character' like you're writing a book."

"I always am."

"Then write me well," she grinned.

Rothery gave a respectful nod. "So, what can you tell me about Malcolm, Helen?"

"Here lies the mystery." She was suddenly all business. "I can't determine a single cause of death other than the *single* bullet that traveled his entire body." She uncovered Malcolm, opened from chin to testicles.

"I don't understand," the agent questioned, "the bullet must have either hit a vital organ or the man bled out externally or internally, correct?"

"Yes."

"Am I missing something, then?"

"All right, I'll start from the beginning." Helen flipped through the pages on her clipboard. "Single gunshot wound— took me awhile to find it. Unlike Mr. Ahluwalia who was delivered with little blood left in him, Malcolm lost almost no blood apart from a nose bleed from the severe shattering of his left and right nasal bones and both the frontal process of the maxilla with its anterior nasal spines. His septal, lesser alar, lateral crus and medial crus cartilage were hanging from his face completely detached, held on by skin alone. These bones were not merely fractured or even broken, they were nearly pulverized."

"What could cause that?"

"Nothing in that banquet room. A serious car accident, perhaps; although I've seen bodies thrown face-first out a windshield with far less focused facial damage. Upon discovery, I wanted to label cause of death as head trauma. The nasal bone is a dangerous weapon when shoved upward into the brain, but on this subject, it never penetrated the brain cavity."

"So, apart from in the room, what could cause the likes of that?"

"Jackhammer. Wrecking ball. Even a cricket bat would break only one side or the other; the cartilage, broken bone and blood would absorb a second blow leaving at least pieces of something. The real conundrum is that this damage would require the victim to stand there long enough to see it done. Theoretically, the first blow would knock him down or cause him to shift. And if he were lying on his back, there would be evidence of impact— flattening of the skull or even fracturing the back of the head."

"So, he was standing," Rothery agreed with a frown.

"In one spot quite firmly— and unmovable, somehow."

Rothery moved closer to the corpse, inspecting the facial mutilation. "What's this... the glaze over his eyes, the distorted conjunctiva?"

"Yes," Helen answered, refusing to look. "If I didn't know better, I would say he was blind."

It surprised Rothery that she wouldn't look at the subject's eyes. It was as if she were afraid. She was the coroner; she had cut this man from chin to nuts. His brain (or what was left of it) was in a jar. She had obviously already examined the man's eyes, but now she was afraid to look at them. This seemed to Rothery to be more bizarre than anything else that had been discussed in the lab. "Could the nose injury possibly have caused this?" he asked.

"Blindness? Yes, but those are scales." Helen pulled the sheet up over the corpse covering his face. "I don't have a guess, and truthfully I don't want to. I have seen this before, Mr. Taylor, but not in my lab."

"Where?" The agent was more than a little curious.

"You'd have to ask my priest."

"I don't understand."

Helen turned and faced Rothery, "Well, if you must know, when I was a small child, my mother died." She defiantly crossed her arms across her chest. "My father sent me away to a nunnery— boarding school for girls back then. I was just a little girl…" Helen stopped. "Mr. Taylor, that's all I'm going to say. But if you are still curious, you'll have to find a priest."

Unsure of what more to say, Rothery returned his attention to the unidentified terrorist now draped with a clean white sheet.

Helen pulled the sheet up again; this time starting from the feet to mid-thigh. "There were no other bludgeon injuries other than this bruise on his right knee. But if it is a mystery you seek, Mr. Taylor, cause of death is the big one."

"The facial wounds didn't kill him?"

"No, no. It was definitely a bullet. There was a single bullet wound, no exit. Actually took me a while to discover it due to the severity of the facial mutilation and the lack of blood loss. Frankly, I wasn't even looking."

With a remote control Helen turned on a touchscreen monitor above the autopsy table. She expertly flowed through a series of pre-autopsy pictures of the corpse. "The bullet entered underneath his scrotum and ran straight through his body upward all the way through to his brain, ultimately lodging in the roof of his cranium skull."

Puzzled, Rothery questioned, "How do you shoot a person from rectum to brain? Do you think Malcom straddled our shooter who then shot him straight upward from the floor?"

"That was my first thought exactly… until I removed the bullet and found the caliber matched the RIFLE from the scene of the crime."

"There really is nothing easy about this case, is there?" Rothery pulled out his notepad.

Sergeant Tilman cautiously entered the room. He knew better than to interrupt Helen while she was doing anything— or nothing— ever.

Both Rothery and Helen stared at the waiting officer until the silence made him begin to squirm. "Well?" Mrs. Goff finally said, indirectly granting Tilman permission to speak.

"Rothery. Ma'am," Tilman started, nodding respectfully to the coroner.

"Do you have something for us or not, Nathaniel? Speak up, I'm not a mind-reader." The tone of Helen's voice caused the hair to stand up on the back of Tilman's neck. Rothery was amused.

Tilman cleared his throat (something that happened often in the Scotland Yard coroner's office), "I've sent the bullet out for ballistics, ma'am. However, considering the caliber of weapons found, unless someone carried another weapon out of the crime scene... this man—Malcolm, ma'am— was shot with the weapon believed to be carried by Raza." He pointed to the older terrorist lying on the adjacent table.

"We know the Kalashnikov was Raza's gun," Tilman clarified. "Malcolm's rifle was still strapped across his shoulder when we examined the bodies at the scene. Besides, we believe this Malcom was too good of a marksman to be using a Kalashnikov, being that he was carrying an L96— a precise weapon. It was a strange choice for an indoor, close range attack, however. The whole thing had the feeling of being a bit staged."

Rothery pondered. "Intriguing. Now, this is where it becomes quite confusing. We are fairly certain that the suspects were killed where they lay, correct? There was no evidence that the bodies were moved postmortem. So, the question remains, how do you shoot someone with a rifle from scrotum to brain?"

"They're lying on the floor; the rifle's on the floor, you pull the trigger," Helen surmised.

Rothery started to laugh, "Quite! You first beat his nose with a jack hammer while he's standing up, then once he's on the floor, you shoot him in the bollocks!"

Even Helen couldn't help but laugh and added, "But there's another thing to consider here, agent."

"You're quite right, Helen," Rothery resounded.

"Really? You know?" She sounded suspicious. "I was saving the whammy for you, but instead, I think I'll let you impress me with your brilliant deductive skills."

Rothery paused, looking from one corpse to the next, then finally stated the question, "How could our Samaritan possibly have killed Malcolm with Raza's gun?"

Helen was pleased. "You're spot on, Mr. Taylor. That IS the question."

"Our discussion," Rothery suggested, "presumes that Raza (Mr. Ahluwalia) died last, according to the length of time the Samaritan took to finish him; more than five minutes kneeling over him holding the knife in his back while most likely talking to him. If that holds true and Raza did die last, how was it that our Samaritan was able to acquire Raza's gun BEFOREHAND to shoot Malcolm? AND if the Samaritan had Raza's gun, why would he stab the man with a knife?"

Rothery's eyes widened with his own question, a lightbulb going off in his head. "Sergeant Tilman, there was another gunshot victim… a man wounded, not dead."

"Five dead, two wounded from the hospital's initial report."

Snapping his fingers repetitively at the sergeant, "The guy, the guy… the bloke from the telly…"

"Yeah, right, the man who walked out on his own. Yes, our hospital report indicates he was the only surviving gunshot victim."

"Yes, yes. Where is he? Who is he?"

"I know I have his name on my desk…" Scratching his head, Tilman pulled out his extensive notepad.

Rothery pressed, "Has anyone talked to him?"

"Everyone in the restaurant was interviewed, I'd have to go over the files."

"I don't understand, he shouldn't be too hard to find, he's one of two surviving wounded and the other is a suspected terrorist."

Tilman thumbed through his notepad, "Oh… um… uh… no. No one has talked to him, agent. He was one of the first taken to the hospital but was then released last night."

"Gunshot victim was released from the hospital the same night?" Rothery questioned.

"Actually, doctor's report said that the bullet…"

"…went right through him," Rothery finished with an exasperated sigh.

"Yeah, that's right," Tilman confirmed, a bit puzzled. "The doctor's report specified that the bullet went through him clean… he didn't incur any damage."

"No damage?" Helen asked. "What do you mean by no damage?"

"The report said the bullet passed through his body." Tilman skimmed down his notes, "Passed through him on an upward angle from his buttocks and out the stomach without hitting any vitals or ripping the stomach muscles. They released him only a couple hours after surgery."

Helen appeared stunned, "What's the name of the doctor?" she asked solemnly. "I want to see that report along with any images."

"Why? What are you thinking, Helen?" Rothery asked.

Tilman read, "Doctor Trey Wilson, attending physician… um, Steinbeck… Allen Steinbeck, name of the victim."

Deep in thought, Helen walked over and uncovered Malcolm's corpse. She motioned the men to join her as she carefully took a thin stainless steel probe to the completely opened body. She carefully wove it from Malcolm's exposed lower stomach inward, toward his back and downward. "The viscera of this lower abdomen are loose now because he's been split open. Our organs are obviously much tighter, held closer together. Either way, as you can see here, how does a bullet travel through the lower abdomen without causing any damage? The small intestines alone could not have been missed." She paused to ponder, "And I thought I had a whammy."

Tilman, still confused, turned to Rothery, "How did you know the bullet passed right through the man?"

"Because," Rothery offered, "once you eliminate the impossible, whatever remains, no matter how improbable, must be the truth."

"Great quote," Tilman commented.

"And quite relevant to our situation," Rothery stated. "If Raza died second, then Malcolm could not have been shot by the Samaritan with Raza's gun before he'd had a chance to retrieve it. If the Samaritan had shot Malcolm with Raza's gun first, then the Samaritan wouldn't have needed to stab Raza, he would have shot him. Then you add the question, how do you shoot a man in the scrotum with a rifle?"

Helen crossed her arms and tapped a finger to her cheek, "So you're suggesting, agent, that Raza shot the Samaritan and that the same bullet traveled through the Samaritan's body and into Malcolm, making it the only bullet fired?"

"That's my thought. They were wrestling when Raza shot the Samaritan killing Malcolm." Rothery turned to Tilman, "How many bullets were missing from Raza's clip?"

Tilman looked through his notepad, "One. That's one hell of a bullet."

"I'd say you have your poles reversed, Nathaniel," Helen corrected Tilman.

"Not following you, ma'am."

"It's what I've been trying to tell you. If this bullet completely passed through the 'Good Samaritan' without harming him, yet killed the 'bad guy' seven ways to Sunday… gentlemen, I can't single out a specific cause of death for Malcom because that one bullet killed this subject seven times over. It sliced through his femoral artery– death was inevitable. It gashed his kidney, it split his heart. It punctured his lung, tore through his esophagus, then mutilated his brain."

"That's only six," Rothery commented.

"The bullet castrated him, gentlemen."

"Blotted out his lineage, as if he never were," Rothery rephrased. "That's especially damaging to a possible Muslim."

"That's bloody creepy! So, which religion believes in seven levels of hell? Because this guy may be at the bottom of it." Tilman shivered at the thought.

"That's out of our jurisdiction, Sergeant Tilman. Let's just stick to the hell we live in, shall we?" Rothery turned to Helen and smiled, "Helen… uh, I mean, Mrs. Goff? Thank you. You are a peach."

"Thank you, agent."

"If you discover anything further, you'll contact me, won't you?"

Helen briefly shifted her eyes in Tilman's direction. "That, Mr. Rothery Taylor, would not be the proper channel. I don't know how you conduct business in your spy organization, but we are professional here at Scotland Yard. We have proper protocols to abide. They've been developed and refined over the past 400 years for good reason."

"Yes, Mrs. Goff," Rothery replied.

Helen winked with a smile and the agent could not have been more relieved.

"Ma'am," Tilman nodded as he and Rothery made their way through the swinging doors.

Outside the office Tilman checked over his shoulder then leaned into Rothery almost whispering, "Really, mate? Mrs. Goff, a peach?"

Rothery just shrugged.

Chapter 29

"I DON'T LIKE THE DIRECTION this is heading," Dr. Arrhenius objected. "How is it that an ecological consortium is turning into a pro-nuclear proliferation summit?"

"I do understand your reservations, doctor. You share the same sentiments as our late chairman, Dr. Phelps." Dark undertones colored the man's words. "Tragic, really. Rest his soul."

"That almost sounds like a threat, sir."

Expressionless, the man cocked his head, "Your insinuation is abhorrent, doctor; we are people of science, not terrorists. I realize, however, that you as a confined lab researcher, may not be well suited for multicultural diplomacy. Still, I encourage you and each member to put aside differences so that we might utilize this opportunity and our expertise for the betterment of mankind. If my demeanor fails to exhibit an acceptable measure of grief, I assure you, I suffered the most at the untimely demise of our colleague." The man cracked a kink from his neck, stroking his goatee.

"And your credentials, sir?" Arrhenius called into question, "I don't recall seeing you during the consortium."

"My credentials, you'll soon find, are most useful… but first thing this morning, I suggest we nominate a new chair in the absence of the late Dr. Phelps."

"I suspect your name is in the hat?"

"Why, thank you, I appreciate your vote of confidence." The man lit a cigarette. "However, my current responsibilities preclude such time-extensive involvement; although I do intend to maintain a strong level of oversight— even in my absence, I assure you." Tapping the butt against his gold ring, the man flicked an ash on the table. "Actually, my vote for chair resides with Dr. Merlo Charles," he stated. Reclining confidently in his seat, "And with that, doctors, I yield back my time— to 'the chair'," motioning to his nominee. In as much, the arrogant man had relinquished his right for the seat while implying that his was the only vote that mattered.

With a look of warning from the smoking man, Dr. Charles knew he'd better corral his new flock. He shifted uncomfortably in his seat. Nervously clearing his throat, "Thank you, esteemed colleagues, I look forward to the lively debate. In the meantime— perhaps prior to the vote... some clarification is in order?" Turning to Dr. Arrhenius, "I, too, share your concerns, doctor," he began, "however, 97% of world scientists agree the planet is warming." The doctor paused, addressing all the members, "Are there any among us who disagree?"

The group remained silent.

"Members, I suggest we seize this opportunity to make a lasting impact on the preservation of our planet— no longer abide the academic advisory role permitted by the UN and its syndicate of industrial super powers."

"I don't dispute global warming, Dr. Charles, but nuclear? What of potential disasters? Chernobyl in the Ukraine; Japan with Fukushima— hell, Three Mile Island?"

"No question that our research be predicated with the utmost caution. On the other hand," he stated firmly, "we can no longer afford political stifling. The 1988 Intergovernmental Panel Report outlined worse case scenarios for 2050 and we have already surpassed their estimates. Keep in mind, this report also failed to account for escalated domino effect.

"We need to consider all possibilities, ladies and gentlemen. To be clear, we will never influence the vast worldwide industrial complex of global powers on theory alone. China, Russia, South East Asia— or even the United States, will not be swayed unless we provide a viable solution. And whether the long-term solution is cold fusion or not, we also can't be so naïve or dissuaded to rule out nuclear fission as a potential temporary alternative to the destructiveness of existing fossil fuels— of carbon energy and its emissions."

"You'll find no objections here, Dr. Charles. But right wing delegates refuse to recognize the existence of global warming while the left hold anti-nuclear rallies. We'll be labeled crazy conspiracy-theorists and lose our funding."

"Funding will no longer be a problem," Ring Finger interjected. "Even as we speak, a non-profit organization is making a sizable donation to appropriate research."

The US representative laughed, "Privately funded alternative-fuel research that includes nuclear fusion? What private organization could afford that? Not to mention afford going to war against the oil and gas lobbyists that line the pockets of the House of Representatives' Energy and Commerce Committee?"

Furcus smiled, "How very astute of you. A bit defeatist, but a very fine point. If I may alleviate your concerns, you have all been chosen for that very reason. This venture cannot be a single-state pursuit. Keeping in mind that all previous attempts at collaboration have failed drastically, this time we intend to avoid the restrictions of regulatory bodies. I won't bore you with the meaningless details, but suffice to say, mechanisms have been put in place to assure compliance. Anonymity and secrecy will be critical."

"Secrecy?" The Japanese member laughed. "Where would one hide a nuclear test facility out of the global community's sight?"

"As I've said, details are forthcoming. However, we are aware of locations outside the interests of most government entities."

"This is all very exciting— even seductive," the delegate from Australia spoke up, "a scientist dreams of endless private funding without the restrictive logistics of governmental oversight." Careful not to offend the dark investor, "Don't misinterpret my colleagues' concerns, sir. Even their objective mannerism is why they are leaders in their fields."

The confident man nodded, taking another drag of his cigarette as the Australian environmentalist continued. "However," the representative stated, "this consortium is being hosted by the UK due to support received from the House of Commons Energy and Climate Change Committee. As you know, their oversight ensures us credibility.

"Unfortunately, as it were, Eleanor Aldous, the MP leading the campaign, will not likely be our best advocate. She has long been a promoter of arms reduction— specifically nuclear development. She participated in START III (the Strategic Arms Reduction Treaty) and Putin/Bush's SORT. I believe she was even a keynote speaker at the Seoul Environmental Impact Assessment of 2012."

"Then we'll merely need to have parallel agendas and documented results. I don't believe that's beyond the capabilities of anyone in this room now, is it?" Furcus passed a challenging appraisal over the congregated scientists. Satisfied, he summarized, "Keep in mind we're not seeking approbation for our efforts, doctors, but rather having them stay out of our way." He rose to his feet, "I will leave you now to vote."

Heading for the door, the man with the gold ring dropped his cigarette in Dr. Arrhenius' coffee mug and marked him the only member excluded from his endorsement for chairman.

Chapter 30

ROTHERY, TILMAN AND DYLAN, waiting in a Mercy General meeting room, rose to their feet as Dr. Wilson entered. "Dr. Wilson, thank you for taking time out of your day to meet with us," Rothery greeted, extending his hand.

"Anything to help. I've already told the other policeman everything I know."

"Which other policeman?" Rothery asked.

"The policeman that asked all the questions about Mr. Steinbeck earlier this morning."

"Right. Yes, of course." Rothery pulled out his phone and typed a message while he continued. "I apologize for having to repeat the process, Dr. Wilson. As you can imagine, with an international terrorist attack, we're dotting our 'i's and crossing our 't's."

Tilman received a text message from Rothery:

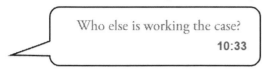

Who else is working the case?
10:33

"I understand, agent. It's not a problem. Joan Perperdex was the attending nurse, she may be able to answer some of your questions, as well."

"That would be lovely," Rothery replied.

Rothery's response from Tilman read:

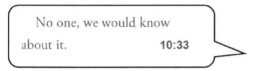

No one, we would know
about it.   **10:33**

Tilman received a second text:

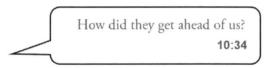

How did they get ahead of us?
10:34

Rothery smiled pleasantly and continued, "So, you discharged Mr. Steinbeck only a few hours after surgery?"

"You must understand, agent," the doctor began, "I didn't want to, but it was a remarkable situation. The patient sustained no injury from the bullet; I've never seen anything like it. And the poor man was quite shaken by the incident and didn't want to stay. A crowded, open environment and all, was making him understandably nervous. As you might well suspect, emotional and mental factors must always be taken into consideration when evaluating the effectiveness of the recovery and healing process."

Dr. Wilson was feeling a bit defensive. Problem was, he honestly WASN'T sure why he had let the patient leave. "He's staying at a nearby hotel. If there were any complications, he could have been here quickly." Finishing his statement confidently, the doctor added, "We treated it as we would an out-patient procedure. I really had no room to object to the patient's wishes."

"He's staying in a hotel?" Dylan asked. "He doesn't live in London?"

"No, he's an American. How do you not know that?" Dr. Wilson was puzzled. "The other policeman carried a profile on Mr. Steinbeck along with Mr. Steinbeck's police statement… said he was here to have him sign it."

180

The three men looked at each other causing the doctor to suddenly suspect their credentials. "May I see your identification, gentlemen?" Wilson requested.

Quickly flipping his badge, Rothery continued the inquiry, "Tell me doctor, how is it that a surgical patient was released before the 72-hour mandatory observation period? Septic doesn't even manifest prior to twelve hours post-surgery… the possibility of internal bleeding? Should I also mention a GSW victim in an ongoing criminal investigation was under your care?" Rothery rapidly rattled off protocols while continuing to text on his phone. He sent to Tilman:

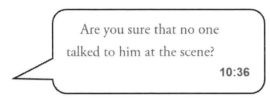

Are you sure that no one talked to him at the scene?
10:36

Dr. Wilson appeared at a loss and called in Nurse Joan to confirm. "I can tell you, officers, there has been no intentional neglect, if that's what you are suggesting."

"I believe you doctor," Rothery assured.

Tilman's text response:

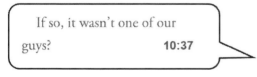

If so, it wasn't one of our guys?
10:37

And Tilman again:

And there is no one else other than SIS and Dylan.
10:37

Dylan had become skeptical of the doctor, finding his actions not only suspicious, but potentially illegal. "Doctor, I understand how busy it can become at a hospital— especially on the night of a terrorist attack. But this man was the only surviving gunshot victim of the incident, correct?"

"Yes, but actually the young man with the crushed thorax was much more critical. Though alive, there are still concerns of possible brain damage from lack of oxygen. He wasn't shot, but all and all, he was much more severely injured."

"How is he doing now?" Dylan questioned.

"He was conscious briefly but seemed to be suffering from delusions."

"Did he say anything?" Rothery probed.

"Yes, but mostly incoherent ramblings."

"Anything intelligible?" the agent pushed.

"Not especially. He seemed to be experiencing delusions of men in the room; creatures climbing the walls. We had to chemically induce a comatose state."

A young nurse entered the room. "Doctor, you sent for me?"

"Yes, thank you. Come in. Gentlemen, this is Nurse Joan Perpedex, the nurse on duty during the incident. Joan, this is SIS Agent Taylor and Sergeant Tilman with Metro."

"And I'm Dylan Vasko with the Prime Minister's Office." Dylan shook Joan's hand.

"These men are asking questions concerning Mr. Steinbeck, the GSW victim from the terrorist attack," Dr. Wilson told her.

"Nurse Joan," Rothery began, "you attended to Mr. Steinbeck post-surgery, is that correct?"

"Yes, I was present when he awoke."

"Did he say anything to you?" Tilman asked.

"He was quite coherent coming out of anesthesia. He knew where he was, what had happened to him. He didn't say anything unusual."

"You take pictures of all your patients, don't you?" Dylan inquired.

"Yes, we do; upon admittance."

"We'll need a copy."

"I can get you a copy," Dr. Wilson offered.

Rothery politely declined. "We're in a bit of a time crunch, doctor," he began, "and we understand that you are a busy man. We would hate for you to get called away while you were out on our little errand." Dr. Wilson's posture became ridged. "So if you don't mind, would you perhaps have someone else retrieve the picture? We'd like to finish our questions while we have your undivided attention."

Wilson was instantly concerned. The agent's refusal to let him leave surely insinuated guilt of sorts.

"I can get it for you, doctor," Joan suggested.

"That's alright," Rothery replied instead, "I'm certain there is a hospital volunteer available."

Wilson frowned, "Are we under suspicion, agent?"

"No, no, I assure you. We just want to be as little of a burden to you as possible." The MI6 agent's authority was suddenly intimidating. "Let's all get comfortable and get through this quickly, shall we?"

Reaching for his phone, Wilson addressed Rothery, "If you don't mind, Agent Taylor, I'd like to call in the hospital administrator— in full cooperation with Metro and the likes… to expedite your requests."

Rothery nodded, "Very well. Have a seat, doctor. So you were saying, Nurse Joan, he didn't say anything unusual?"

The young woman was now nervous. She looked to the doctor, then to the officers and back. "Doctor Wilson signed the patient's release while I was out of the room, sirs."

Rothery smiled, "That is interesting. However, we didn't ask about his release. Why? Was there something unusual about the doctor releasing a GSW patient that had just undergone abdomen surgery three hours prior?"

"Listen, agent," Dr. Wilson interrupted, "there was some confusion. Although, for the life of me, I still don't understand. I honestly don't know why I released him. I'm not a new attending, I'm the head of general surgery. I know hospital policy, I know the legalities and I know the dangers. I've seen the consequences. I play it over and over in my head and I can't make sense of it… I wasn't even taken by her. She's beautiful and all— and I've seen her movies… but I was not star-struck."

"Taken by whom?" Rothery asked.

"Victoria Adams."

Rothery looked puzzled. Tilman jumped in, "The actress?"

"Yes, the actress." Dr. Wilson was bewildered, "I don't mean any disrespect, but you blokes really don't know anything, do you?"

"How could we possibly?" Dylan raised his voice, "While we were body-bagging bad guys, the hospital was releasing our only detainable witness… AND apparently gave the whereabouts and information to a fifth suspect."

Rothery raised his hands to stifle the growing tension, "This is needlessly getting out of control. Shall we settle down and start from the beginning? Please stop me if I miss anything."

Rothery took out his notepad and began. "He's an American. He was with the film star, Victoria Adams. You released him— for reasons beyond your own reasoning. He is staying at a hotel nearby. A policeman showed up first thing this morning with a full dossier on Mr. Steinbeck and an unsigned witness statement suggesting Steinbeck had been previously interviewed. How am I doing so far?"

"That's right," Wilson agreed.

"Did he say which hotel?" There was a pause. "Either of you feel free to answer," Rothery prompted.

"He didn't say," Joan replied.

"So, he left with Miss Adams?"

Dr. Wilson and Nurse Joan both nodded.

Joan meekly raised her hand, "Actually, it's Mrs. not Miss… though I only saw her briefly here at the hospital because Teresa had me fetch the paper work." Although the young woman seemed disappointed about that part of her story, with growing exuberance, she continued telling it just the same. "I have seen her before, though. Once in Piccadilly Square… I was less than twenty feet from her! She looked right in my direction, but I was in the middle of a crowd so I can't say for certain that she saw me personally— though I always believed. And I did have the sense that she recognized me last night, but she obviously couldn't place me under the stressful circumstances and all."

"Joan…"

"Sorry, sir. Anyways, she's married to William Cleese." She paused and looked at the men. "I mean, if she didn't take his last name, is she still called Mrs.?" The nurse was met with blank stares.

Joan felt need to expound. "So, would you say Mrs. Adams if that's not his name? Or do you think her name is actually Mrs. Cleese on their marriage certificate? I suppose it doesn't really matter. After all, their marriage has been on the rocks for many years— she's been seen in questionable situations with quite a few other male celebrities, if you know what I mean. I understand that in her early relationship with Mr. Cleese, he took her from small time to the show… you know he's more than thirty years older than she is!

"I've never understood their relationship, though… whereas, on the other hand, Mr. Steinbeck was quite nice— and charming! I can see the attraction. And he was so down to earth… hmm… do you think he's in an upcoming film with her?" The possibility spurred the woman on.

"Do you think they are here shooting on location?!" Joan's excitement increased, "I mean, I haven't heard anything on the circuit— and I usually know since I was an actress in secondary school— but do you think? I don't want to toot my own horn, but I could have made a brilliant character actress… not big name, but maybe on Dr. Who or the likes. The girls on Doctor Who are much too common for the role, don't you agree? Though, now that I think about it, I guess that's quite what they're going for, isn't it?"

"Joan, please… for the love of God, STOP!" Dr. Wilson interrupted.

"Actually Joan, you seem to be a wealth of knowledge on Ms. Adams. Does Ms. Adams have a home in London?" Rothery inquired.

"It's not believed that she owns anything in London; she usually stays at one of the studio flats when she's on location."

"Where might that be?"

"Well, Kensington, for one. I can get you the exact address, but…"

"Oceans restaurant is in Kensington," Tilman interjected.

Joan lowered her voice to a whisper, "Well, I've got one better for you. What is not known— and I mean by ANYONE… and it can't leave this room…"

The four men glanced around the meeting room to insure they were alone and leaned in closer. "Yes?" they said in unison.

"My sister, Penelope, has a flat-mate…"

"Right…"

"…whose mum is a housekeeper in Swansea, Wales…"

"Yes…?"

"Okay, you REALLY have to promise me you won't tell anyone. If this gets out…"

"JOAN!" Wilson yelled.

"Right, right. But you need to know this has taken years of research to confirm." Joan shifted her eyes from one man to the next, demanding their undivided attention. She took in a deep breath and finally announced, "William bought Victoria the Victorian!" Joan nodded, drawing the connection between Victoria and Victorian. "A royal hunting lodge— but more like a castle, I'd say. And they call it, 'The Cabin'."

"The Cabin."

"Right. They stay there when they're in Britain. They bought it through their publicist so it's not in their name— for anonymity reasons and all, I suppose. But I did the research and it was purchased the year they were married. A wedding gift, I'll bet. Hmm… I wonder if she'll keep it after the divorce."

"How much of this…" Rothery paused looking for the correct word, "BRILLIANT investigative information was given to the other policeman this morning?"

"None of it, sir! No one outside of this room— except my sister, Penelope; Silvia, her flat-mate; and of course, Phyllis know anything about it!"

"Who's Phyllis?" Dylan asked.

Rothery shook his head matching Joan's tone, inflection, intensity and gender, "Her sister's flat-mate's MUM, obviously."

Dylan nodded, stepping back from Rothery.

Rothery addressed Dr. Wilson, "Doctor, if you can pull a surveillance photo of the Metro policeman, we'll need a shot of him as well."

"Why, was he not a cop?" Dr. Wilson was suddenly alarmed. "What the hell are we into? Are we in danger?"

"I don't believe so, but I recommend all discussion of Mr. Steinbeck be filed with the same level of caution and security as the residence of Ms. Adams," Rothery recommended.

Nurse Joan nodded in agreement, "They're connected."

Dr. Wilson looked at Rothery and Joan nodding in unison. Raising a confused eyebrow, he reluctantly agreed.

A knock came from the hallway as the meeting room door slowly opened. A tall, well-dressed woman entered the room, "Good afternoon gentlemen, I hope I'm not interrupting?" There was a look of concern on the woman's face.

Doctor Wilson stood, "Agent, this is our hospital administrator, Evelyn Beltane."

"Yes, I've had the pleasure. Mrs. Beltane."

"Agent Taylor, the pictures are missing." Evelyn went straight to the point.

"Mr. Steinbeck's picture? How about his file? Medical records? Address?"

Evelyn rubbed her forehead, shaking her head. "I know how this looks."

"CIA?" Tilman questioned.

"That's utterly ridicu..." Rothery was prepared to rebuff the sergeant, but seeing the hushed attention of everyone in the room, he conceded with a slight scoff, "Highly unlikely, Tilman. If he were CIA, he would be working with British Intelligence, wouldn't you agree?"

"Then who?"

"Tilman, this is not the time..." Rothery motioned him to drop the subject, but the anticipation of everyone else (especially Nurse Joan's wide-eyed look of excitement) prompted Rothery to instead clear his throat. He threw up his hands, "Well, we know he's not Chinese." He could almost hear the proverbial 'ooh' echo in everyone's mind as they looked to each other with raised eyebrows— now all part of a small, elite group in the international-espionage-know.

With a gesture, the agent washed his hands of the moment and continued, "We're going to need your cooperation, Ms. Beltane," Rothery continued, "this investigation has taken some unforeseen turns. You will be contacted by an agent— name's Stover. Please don't talk to anyone other than Agent Stover unless you hear from me first. Agreed?"

"All right, then."

"Very well."

Rothery and Dylan headed for the door— Tilman still chatting with the young nurse. "Tilman? You coming?"

"Yes, sir," clearing his throat, "right away, agent." The sergeant turned back to Joan with a last nod, "I've got to go, but maybe we can get together later... discuss the case? Your connections were really quite helpful..."

"Tilman!"

Joan nodded with enthusiasm.

Chapter 31

IT WAS AFTER NOON and Micah hadn't yet begun to stir. Victoria had made as much of the morning as possible leaving him for less than thirty minutes per interval, not wanting to be away in case he woke. From what she could tell his vitals were good; he had slept hard with an occasional stir, though it appeared he'd had disturbing dreams throughout the night.

She liked caring for someone; tending instead of always being attended to. It was new to her— made her ponder whether she had been selfish much of her life. *You have to care for someone to enjoy tending to them. And they have to need you.* William got sick often later in life but had a host of servants and professionals surrounding him. Her father, on the other hand, never told her he was sick— even at the end, which robbed her of the privilege. Suddenly, she was finding it missing in her life; the gratifying value of giving and being needed.

Victoria was gone when Micah awoke at nearly 1:00 PM but she'd returned before he surfaced from the shower. "How did you sleep? How do you feel? Should we go back to the hospital?" Her face showed concern.

"I'm okay. I shouldn't have slept so long."

"You needed it, you were shot, remember?"

"I can't afford it." His voice was stern, almost accusing.

Victoria's eyes narrowed. She sat back in the chair and crossed her arms, unsure where this emerging hostility was coming from.

"Go back to the States, Victoria. Be with your family."

Her jaw dropped. She parted her lips as if to speak but didn't know what to say. There had been no conversation; no discussion the night before or in the car ride from the hospital to prepare her for the severity of what Micah felt nor the implications of what he had said.

Micah, unemotional, seriously instructed, "If you are questioned by anyone— and I mean ANYONE, you tell them I was a guy you met at the airport. You just took me out for dinner as a gesture of appreciation; tell them I told you my name was Allen. It will take a while before they suspect you're lying, but by then they'll have forgotten what you said."

The finality of their relationship hit Victoria all at once. His candid, matter-of-fact attitude multiplied her emotion.

"So that's it?" She looked at him in disbelief, "Can you really do that?"

Micah didn't answer.

"You can walk away?" Hurt and unable to let it go, "Is this a weekly thing for you?" she accused. "Save a damsel in distress then dump her off at a hotel?"

The air got thin. Micah stood silent. She waited for his behavior to turn but he didn't move.

After an agonizing moment, her face dropped in despair, a tear flowing down her cheek. His silence was devastating. Take away all the cameras and all her shallow friends… the realization that she had never truly felt so much for anyone suddenly impacted her.

Victoria stood motionless in complete disbelief. Her paranoia gone and the coldness she had nurtured over the years broken left her absolutely vulnerable. Someone could reach in and crush her— take her heart from her. But although it was painful, with a stiff inhale through her nose, she realized she had no regrets. She could feel again.

Her tears weren't for Micah. She did fear the loss of him, a man she barely knew; but only because he was the instrument of her deliverance. She could see now that he was not her strength, not her savior. She did love him (if she had ever loved anyone) but the tears were for herself— for the person whom she was coming to know, coming to love. And that made her cry.

Micah mocked himself in his silence. No words came out of his mouth, nothing consoling. Only silence. He found it hard to breathe. But he knew he could say nothing. *How can I take the only life she knows? She has everything. A Hollywood movie star…? She can still return to fame and adulation.* He barely understood himself the sacrifice he was making right then and there… how could he ask the same of her? *A hero to remain a hero must forfeit the prize.* And for Micah, that meant being alone. Every chance he'd ever had at the least amount of happiness had always turned just as quickly.

He looked at Victoria. He had been moved, connected, touched by this woman; something that was far from common for him. *Am I being selfish even considering asking her to go with me? I can't! The risk, too high; the guarantee, nil.*

Still, he could say nothing though he ached to reach for her hand; to touch her, to hug her, to hold her; to bump playfully into her. She had no idea how lonely his life was. She had no idea how few understood him; how few would ever come as close as she had in only a few short days. To find one— to find her; she had no idea she was his one-in-a-million.

Micah attempted to appear stone cold, though nothing could have been further from the truth. As a matter of fact, the inevitability of their fate insisted he distance himself, protect them from his own dismay. If he gave it one second, one moment, one ounce of the most remote thought to what could be between them, she would find him heaped upon the floor inconsolable. And that would likely get them both killed.

The silence overtook him— too much for any man to take. When he finally spoke, it was slowly; catering his words trying to hold back the flood, "This is not a movie, Victoria. This is not a set. These are not actors. Last night I killed a man, maybe two. Do you understand that? There's no coming back for those men... barely men. I saw a look in that man's eyes as they rolled back in his head... so cold, it made a demon pleasant to gaze upon."

Micah lowered his head, "And the boy...? Have you spent any time around the dead? It's hard to imagine a body once danced, once sang, once laughed..." he began to tremble.

"They weren't men, they were monsters!" Victoria reproached. "They were no different than the beasts that attacked us in the parking lot! Micah!"

Micah remained motionless.

Softening her voice, Victoria repeated, "Micah?" Bringing her back into focus, Micah met her eyes. "Who are you really?" she asked.

It was not the question Victoria intended, it was simply the closest one she could muster. Her heart continued to rise to her throat until the true question finally manifested, "Are you a man, Micah?"

Micah's eyes fell to the floor. "A man... human?" he mumbled mutely.

The air was still and so was Victoria. It was as if she had discovered something; as if she had asked the right question. Though she heard him speak nothing, his eyes spoke volumes.

In all honesty, she couldn't fathom the answer— and that realization startled her. The silence between them hung thick in the room. She watched as Micah raised the courage to speak, "Victoria... I..." Her eyes widened, paused in anticipation.

Then the reality of what his next utterance might be (or not be) frightened her. She quickly put her hand over his mouth not wanting to know what he might say. "I'm not ready, I'm not ready," she whispered.

Micah abruptly stopped. A cold shudder ran through his body. His shoulders dropped, his mouth closed— and with it, his heart. He gingerly removed Victoria's hand from his lips, his demeanor rigid and focused. His bag was packed in seconds.

Victoria hadn't quite expected such a cold response. "Do you ever do anything lighthearted?" she quizzed sarcastically.

Micah was less than amused. He gave her a half-hearted sneer.

Victoria instantly grinned. She LIKED IT! His sneer— it was nasty, it was mean. It was an unadulterated expression of pure anger, annoyance, and blatant disappointment. It was HUMAN. It warmed her heart like nothing else could.

"Ugh. What are you smiling about now?" Micah grumbled, "I didn't think I could feel worse."

Victoria was strangely relieved. The emotional overload had fled the room. For some reason she was content now just to watch him toil. "Watching you pack, is all. Where are you going?"

"Not sure yet, but there's a man we need to see."

Chapter 32

"HENRY WILKENS?"

"Yes, sir." Henry barely glanced up from his typing.

Rothery pulled up a chair from the neighboring desk, spun it around and sat down next to Henry. Three separate coffee cups littered the desktop; one purchased from a café outside of town, two from the same 24-hour coffee shop across the street. A plastic container with remnants of steak-fat and a few pathetic fries swimming in mayonnaise sat next to a half-eaten McDonald's breakfast burrito. In spite of the desk's disheveled state, the waste can with a fresh liner indicated the graveyard janitorial staff had done their job.

A suitcoat matching the trousers Henry wore lay balled-up on the floor. "Pulled an all-nighter, eh?"

Henry stopped typing and glared. "May I help you, officer?"

"What makes you think I'm police?"

"All dressed up, suit and tie. 100 quid shoes, 50 pound wedding band." Rothery smiled.

"Don't get me wrong," Henry continued, "I agree with you. Other than the tassels, your shoes are worth twice as much as your marriage, I'm certain."

Rothery chuckled, "You're in the wrong line of work, Mr. Wilkens."

"Why do you say that?"

"You should be a detective."

Henry flinched, offended, "I AM an investigator, thank you very much. An INVESTIGATIVE reporter. Difference is, people don't HAVE TO talk to me. I can't take them downtown. I can't hold them for 36 hours; subpoena, sequester, hold them in contempt or ask them questions at gun point. Still, my work is published every day. How about yours?"

"Very well, is that how you knew there were three terrorists— all subdued before the police entered the building?"

Henry sized the man up, "Well you're not with Metro; you're underdressed for the PM's Office. So, you must be the SIS agent."

"Why couldn't I be from Metro?"

"You would have threatened me by now."

"Well, if you must know, I'm underdressed because it's a Saturday."

"Seriously? You wear that tie on your day off on purpose? And I don't know where they even sell tassel shoes anymore."

Rothery looked down at his clothing. He was a bit self-conscious, though Henry's attire was far worse. *I like the tassels on my shoes. My grandfather had a pair just like these.* He began to retort but refrained; fashion sense was not his strong suit— even against Henry. He blew it off as he straighten his 10 pound tie. "I can see Metro's reason for hostility. What are you working on there?"

"Nothing. Finishing up a piece for the column."

"Hmm, I didn't know you had a column, Mr. Wilkens. Under a pseudonym?" Rothery chanced a look over Henry's shoulder.

Henry slammed closed his laptop, "It's more of a feature."

"Something to do with the terrorist attack in Kensington? Surely you're not impeding a criminal investigation?"

"Ah, there it is. The threat. I expected more from MI6," Henry scorned, shaking his head.

"With the time you've spent abroad, Mr. Wilkens, I would think you'd know MI6 doesn't threaten to have you arrested. Our methods are a bit more *direct*."

Henry laughed, "Listen, Bond… for starters, you don't pull it off. You look more like a squeamish version of 'Q'." Henry chuckled, too pleased with his use of 007 idioms. "I admit I'm not real technical, but I suspect your watch is not the exploding type. Those are historically Omegas. If your Casio detonated, it would rain plastic bits all over us!"

Laughing hysterically, Henry abruptly turned completely serious. He leaned across the desk, moved in close to Rothery's face and lowered his voice, "What are you really, Mr. Taylor?" He glanced over his shoulder, assuring their privacy, "Come on, you can tell me— off the record. You're the guy that picks up the laundry, aren't you?" Henry laughed mercilessly.

Rothery was not amused but had to admit he was slightly impressed the reporter had known his name.

"Oh come now, don't be offended, I was just fooling. Honestly, I met a few of your colleagues 20 years ago in the Middle East; former SAS muscle-heads. Hey, if you're the future, the Kingdom stands a chance."

"Five people are dead, Mr. Wilkens."

"Believe me, I know. Not that I need to tell you, but my column... okay, my article, is based on the PM and Parliament's failure to appropriately fight the war on terrorism... their refusal to recognize the growing attack on British identity and freedom of speech and the press by succumbing to the PC rhetoric of the left wing liberal Nazis. Every time ISIS, Al Qaeda, or the likes attack, they displace the threat by 5000 miles at the pleasure of the current administration."

"I read through your last ten years of articles, Mr. Wilkens. I don't recall any mention of the failure of pluralism or of immigration policies; nor any objections to the wars in Iraq, Afghanistan, or the pull out of troops. Matter of fact, you made a career off both Gulf Wars, didn't you? And even then, your political stance was admirably neutral. Any particular reason for the change in politics now?"

It had been so long since anyone had taken an interest in his work, it was hard for Henry to resist the temptation to say something really subversive and drive more suspicion and intrigue his direction. An SIS investigation would do wonders for his career. But Henry refrained. "Well, I don't completely agree with your assessment of my life's work... I wouldn't say *change*, but last night's tragic event..." Henry bowed his head in a pathetic attempt to portray sympathy, "has really impacted— or rather, amplified my perspective."

"Yes, I can see that. You seem to be a real sensitive guy."

"You know, others have said the same of me this very week. Wait a minute... you read all my articles because I knew the terrorists had been apprehended? Huh." Henry thought about what that could imply. Putting one finger to his forehead, "That's great intel, Agent Taylor."

"What do you mean?"

"Well, I said they were apprehended, I didn't say how or when. Stands to reason that if an MI6 agent stayed up all night reading my articles, it means you think I know the 'who'. I took the only picture of the survivor... which means YOU think the survivor was the one who subdued the bad guys."

"I didn't say that."

"Uh, yes you did."

Rothery sized up the unshaved, unkempt man sitting in his fast-food refuse. "Are you certain you are just a reporter?"

"Agent, you've put me in such a good mood, I'm going to pretend you didn't say that." Henry crossed his arms and leaned back in his chair, nodding his head thoughtfully. Smiling he said, "You want to guess what my second article today will be about?"

Rothery sighed, "You are an interesting man, sir; initially suspicious, but clearly a man of singular motive."

"Thank you."

"That wasn't intended to be a compliment. But you are no traitor, Mr. Wilkens."

"Traitor? I'll have you know I served in Her Majesty's Army. I'm a bloody war hero!"

"You were a chef."

"You're bloody hell right! That's what Alec Baldwin said on the 'Hunt for Red October' and look how that turned out. Have you ever seen 'The Siege'? Scoff all you want, but you feed 250 troops in the desert where the only women they see are eyelids behind burkas… I deserved a bloody medal!"

Rothery broke into laughter. Shaking his head, he casually rose from his chair. He turned around, laughing all the way out of the bull pen, leaving Henry to his story. Rothery didn't even bother to say goodbye.

Henry didn't mind. He grabbed his wadded jacket off the floor, on a mission. "Ooh, Mr. Steinbeck, the police are looking for you... and I'm going to make you a fucking hero!" He grinned at the irony of the scheme, "'The Hero of Kensington.' Brilliant! I'm going to make the bloody PM have to crucify you on public television. No offense, Allen Steinbeck, but you're MY martyr now. When I'm done, women will weep for you— and I'll update my lamp!"

Chapter 33

AS MICAH AND VICTORIA approached the storefront of a mid-sized appliance shop, Victoria pointed out televisions in the display window playing the BBC news channel coverage of the Oceans Restaurant terrorist attack. A tickertape at the bottom read, "Police are looking for a person of interest possibly involved in the restaurant shooting…" Micah's head dropped to his chest.

"It doesn't mean they're looking for you," Victoria tried to console, "surely they're looking for accomplices who may have helped plan the attack?"

Micah knew better but mustered a shrug anyway, more convinced than ever that Victoria needed to distance herself from him… and that he needed to leave the UK as soon as possible.

An old-fashioned bell over the entryway began to clatter as Micah opened the front door. Quickly stepping through, he raised his hand and silenced the bell, keeping it from finishing its chime. The sound stopped mid-clamor so suddenly that even having seen it, Victoria still questioned if the bell had rung at all. Micah raised a finger to his mouth to silence her as well.

Victoria caught his intention, but easily seeing the girl working behind the counter, she was bewildered at how long this apparent sneak approach would last. It seemed childish but she played along.

From that point Micah proceeded into the store casually, which also caught Victoria's attention. If he intended a surprise, shouldn't he have tiptoed across the old wooden floor that was bound to creak?

The girl cooking the inventory books at the counter happened to glance up just as they reached the desk. Her eyes opened wide. She turned pale, a horrified look on her face.

Micah held a finger to his lips to shush her but realized instantly it was pointless. He rushed quickly to the other side of the desk and subdued the young woman from behind, wrapping her up in his arms and pulling her away from the desk to give her no time to trigger an alarm. He then shot a quick glance to the patrons in the refrigerator section, relieved they appeared not to have noticed.

Mouth covered, tears flowing, the woman's eyes shifted back and forth in panic, straining to see Micah over her shoulder as he continued to shush her to no avail. The girl's stifled screams forced Micah to tighten his grip over her mouth, her eyes fluttering as she became light-headed. Then, even loosening his hold against his better judgment, she still fainted into his arms.

Micah rolled his eyes. "Great."

Setting the girl back down in her chair, he kicked the recline lever to a comfortable seated position. Assured she wouldn't fall out, he put the ledger in her lap and left her tucked safely away behind the front counter as if deeply engrossed in the store's bookkeeping. Grabbing Victoria's hand, they proceeded to the swinging double doors leading to the back room. Victoria, not at all sure what they were doing, was certain it was beyond trespassing.

All the way in the back at the far side of the building, they entered the manager's office of Kipley's Appliances. A tall man sat at a large weathered desk with his back to the door. Hearing their entrance, he looked slightly up toward the multiple surveillance monitors mounted on the wall in front of him. He hadn't been particularly keeping a keen eye on them that afternoon, but he could see Kasandria sitting undisturbed at the front desk and the couple who had now moved on from refrigerators to washer and dryer sets. Another patron was just entering the shop.

Without turning around, the man behind the desk aggressively began rubbing his circle beard. Micah didn't move; Victoria followed suit. For minutes even, Micah stood firm, a serious look developing upon his face. Victoria could not tell if he was expressing anger, sorrow, or preparing for an offensive attack.

Victoria presumed the man was Kipley based on the size of the store and the lone employee watching the front. It was clearly not a thriving enterprise that would require a residing manager (at least not from what she had seen so far), but more likely suggested an owner/operator establishment. There was no mirror in front of the man so he couldn't possibly have seen them enter. Still, he seemed strangely determined not to turn around; his beard stroking having become progressively more aggressive.

Suddenly the man stopped. He dropped his shoulders and unemotionally said, "I thought you were dead."

Micah remained silent.

"I saw the footage back then... still play it every once in a while."

Micah maintained a pensive scowl, his face stern. Victoria remained still but considered whereto she might flee if the situation became a physical confrontation.

"Seven years and still I knew you would walk back into this room one day; your unpaid debt."

Victoria sensed a flavor of remorse in Micah's evolving expression; his eyes shifted to the floor in his continued silence. A television mounted in the corner of the good-sized office quietly played the terrorist attack newsreel.

Refusing to turn around, Kipley announced as if reprimanding, "You know, I had offers to sell this place. Did you know that? I turned down an offer to retire while I was still young." He paused to reflect, "I'd seen your grave. I visited. I saw your grave and still I didn't sell because I KNEW one day you'd walk back through this door." The silence between the men was deafening. "Are you going to say something or just let me keep rambling, questioning whether or not I'm sitting alone talking to myself like a crazy man?"

Micah inhaled a deep breath. Kipley echoed the sound, knowing now for sure he was not alone in the room. He tilted his face toward the ceiling, both ears attuned to whatever the next utterance would be. "How's this going to go down?"

Micah's voice finally broke its silence, "It would be just as easy for you to turn around, old friend."

Kipley exhaled, choking on emotion. He sucked it up putting a hand over his eyes, clearing his throat and swiping a stray tear. He spun his chair around to finally face Micah.

"Damn all, I'm not crazy after all!" Kip blustered into cheer, jumping out of his chair. He crossed the room and hugged Micah into his 6'4" frame, lifting him off the floor.

"Easy," Micah flinched.

"You're friends?" Victoria asked. "Then what did you do to that poor girl in the front room?"

"What did you do to Kassandria?" Kip questioned.

Micah threw up his hands, "I didn't do anything! You know how she is, Kip... she gets very emotional. She had no idea I was... uh... 'in town'. She would have screamed and fainted whether I grabbed her or not."

"What?!" Kip looked again at his monitors. Out of habit, he grabbed the remote to silence the TV. Glancing at the coverage, he hesitated.

The store owner looked back at Micah, this time a frown forming upon his face. Using the remote in his hand to increase the volume now, he shifted his attention to the television, listening to the news anchor announce, "Police are looking for a man of possible interest from yesterday's terrorist attack at Oceans Restaurant."

Kipley pushed mute and stared at Micah. He began gesturing with his eyes up to the TV and then back to Micah, careful not to mention in front of Victoria what he was suddenly and understandably thinking. He had no idea whose side she resided on.

"Yes," Micah said, motioning to the news coverage, "and she was there."

Kip aggressively sat back down in his chair and rebuked Micah. "You son of a bitch. You son of a bitch! Seven years?" Kip waved his hands in the air, "You don't walk in here until you need me?"

"I haven't walked into anywhere for seven years, Kip."

"What does that even mean, David? What? Are you Elijah?"

Victoria's curiosity was instantly aroused, "Yeah, David, what does that mean?"

Micah put a hand up toward each of them. Shaking one at Victoria suggesting he'd explain in a minute; the other toward Kip trying to keep him from loosely spewing anything else from his mouth. Micah paused to consider how to best respond given the circumstances.

Victoria and Kip began to speak at the same time. Holding both hands higher Micah yelled, "Give me a second!" Pointing first to Victoria, he spoke firmly, "I'll get to you in a minute," then back to Kip— he chewed on his lip.

"I don't need you to make up a story," Kipley retorted.

Micah looked the tall man in the eye, "No, Kip, I'm not Elijah."

"Who's Elijah?" Victoria asked. Both men ignored her.

"I had to fall off the grid. I mean *completely* off."

"Who's grid?" Kip questioned without a pause.

Micah just stared at Kip initiating a strange, speechless communication between them made up of bizarre, progressive gestures and facial expressions.

Kip thought of a grid and looked at Micah. Micah stared him in the eyes then shook his head no, raising his eyebrows to indicate higher. Kip thought again, this time adding a hand gesture and a slight head-tilt conveying a higher, mid-range but obviously significant grid. Micah again signaled "no" and used his hand to gesture "higher". Kip scowled in disbelief and gestured obnoxiously to the highest grid. Still, Micah indicated, "higher."

Bewildered, Kip dropped his hands and just spoke, "Higher?"

Micah's head nodded slowly as if counting the seconds it would take for Kip to guess. Then Kip's eyes suddenly opened wide in disbelief. Micah nodded, "Yes," with raised eyebrows.

"THE grid?" Kip answered.

"Well, they don't really call it a grid," Micah corrected.

Victoria had waited long enough, "Okay, how is it that I have no idea what you're NOT talking about and yet I do?"

"You do. Well, wait... actually, no you don't." Then Micah thought about it, "Okay, you might." He paused again, finally shaking his head, "No, no you don't. You might think you do, but you really don't," he decided.

Kip finished for Micah, "You really don't want to."

Victoria nodded. *I can't believe I almost caught that. I'm getting pretty good at this.* Victoria laughed to herself, *This is going to make a great movie! Who will I get to play Micah?*

Suddenly Micah was hit in the back by Kip's heavy office door. Before he could turn around, he was nearly tackled by Kassandria, the store clerk.

"Ow, ow, ow..." Micah complained, covering his head with his hands, "did you know you're stronger than Kip is?"

"Yes, I DID know that!" Kassandria wrapped her arms around Micah, emotions overwhelming her, "And I KNEW you were alive! I KNEW IT!"

"Hello, sweetheart." Micah grabbed her into his arms for a proper hug and held her. "I wanted to tell you... you know I would have if I could..."

"I know, I know... I'm just so glad you're ALIVE!" she hugged him even tighter. "It's okay, I know you would have told me. I know the kids would have told me, too, if they could have. I message with Rachel, with Seth… they've never said anything but I still knew." Drying her eyes on his shoulder, "I get it. If anyone understands, it has to be us, right Kip?" Kassandria and Kipley exchanged a shared look of relief.

Micah gently moved the young woman off him, "Is he treating you okay, Kassy?"

She gave Kip a playful scowl, "Well, besides beggar wages, he's nice enough."

Micah smiled, "The other reason you refused to sell, huh, Kip?"

Kipley shrugged, "What can I say? I collect strays."

"Hey!" Kassandria punched Kip in the arm.

"Ow… you're right, she IS stronger than I am." Kip rubbed his arm.

"But are you okay now?" Kassandria looked at Micah with concern.

"Same ol' same ol', but I'll be alright."

"Am I going to get to see you more before you leave?" Kassandria had spent many of her teenage years in Micah's house and knew this seemingly simple assumption wasn't necessarily a given.

"I don't know, sweetheart… maybe it's time you came home for a little while."

Kassandria obnoxiously glared at Kip, "I'd love to, but not sure if he'll take the chains off."

"Just drug him while he sleeps," Micah teased.

"Sounds like a plan." Kassy winked at Kip then kissed Micah on the cheek. She gave him another hug as if it might be her last, then reluctantly went back to watch the front.

"How's she doing?" Micah asked Kip.

"She keeps me honest."

Micah nodded like a proud father, "She's good that way."

"So DAVID," Victoria interrupted, "about time for introductions, don't you think?"

Grimacing, Micah obliged. "Victoria Adams, meet Kipley Holland."

"Victoria Adams," Kip commended, "David, dang!" Turning back to Victoria, "I thought you were just a remarkable lookalike."

"Kip, David Finch died in Japan seven years ago, remember? I'm Micah Graff."

Kip held out his hand, "Well, then it's damn good to meet you, Micah."

Micah shook hands with a half-hearted smile, "I guess we'll see how 'good' it really is soon enough, won't we?"

Chapter 34

PETER WIGHTMAN, SCOTLAND YARD'S IT specialist, entered the investigation room. "All right, Chief, we've finally decrypted the Oceans' video footage. We're running through it now, it's going to take some time."

"Why's that?"

"First off, Ocean's on-site IT guy was on vacation. We had to hunt him down. Didn't get him here until this morning."

"You mean the heavyset guy who bought up all the Ho-Hos from our vending machines?"

"That's the one. He eats those non-stop, doesn't he? Pops them in his mouth like Jelly Babies. Anyway... second thing, the main onsite server at the restaurant was corrupt. We had to pull the files from their on-premise storage and decrypt each file individually. Even with the encryption key it took hours. Now we're running the video on a third-party player; meaning there's no time-sync anymore. We've isolated the day but we have hours of footage to run through."

"Can't you just go to the end and back up an hour or so?"

"That would be nice, but no one shut off the cameras, they're still running. And the backup application de-duplicates all the files down to block level with a random name generator for security purposes. We've tried to just restore the files from their backup application to another server, but that had been mysteriously corrupted as well."

"What does that mean?"

"Needle in a field of haystacks. But the good news, Chief, is that we're in the final stretch."

"All right, that's good to hear. Could the corruption have been… deliberate?" Chief Philips hesitated to suggest.

"Well, I've already pulled their hard drives— there were no viruses or worms on their server; the operating system and other applications seemed to be intact. It's not completely improbable that two specific applications were corrupted unintentionally, however, the restaurant uses FIPs 140-2 encryption which is the same as we use for government level security— which makes the circumstances that much more unlikely."

"Government level security, eh? What then? An inside job?"

"That's the question, sir. And the follow up question is, if it wasn't an inside job and someone hacked the place, then it had to have been government level espionage hacking." Wightman paused at the thought, "It would take some added resources but I think I could possibly determine that."

Philips waved it off, "Not now, Wightman… but you're saying our files could be out there?"

Wightman laughed, "Not likely, sir. And even if they were, we have their onsite IT guy; we have the encryption key. It would take years for anyone to decrypt those files— arrange them in order to view or make any sense of them…"

"The whole bloody thing is on YouTube!" Tilman rushed into the room, winded.

Philips refused to even look at Tilman. He raised his hand to stop the sergeant from saying another word, slowly shifting a glare to his IT technician. "Wightman? Tilman can't possibly be talking about YOUR video files, can he? You've just assured me in enough techno-babble to give Bill Fucking Gates a headache that it would be impossible."

"Actually, sir, had you said Steve Wozniak…"

Chief Philips moved his raised hand, now stopping Wightman mid-sentence. He directed his words to the sergeant while keeping a paralyzing stare on Scotland Yard's IT specialist, "You were saying, Tilman?" He wanted to relish the career-limiting expression upon Wightman's face.

Tilman, wide-eyed and enthusiastic, expounded, "The Oceans terrorist attack is on YouTube! It's got our lad in color. Whoever edited it did a splendid job, too. It's an entire music video with slow motion effects and bullet-path animation."

Wightman's face paled. The chief just continued to nod, refusing to relent his stare, shifting it from Wightman's eyes to the man's Scotland Yard employee badge.

"He's added the 'pows' and 'bangs', as well, Chief," Tilman added, pantomiming a fistfight with his hands, "you know, like from the old Batman TV series of the 70s? It's quite wicked!"

With that the chief raised his hand again, this time stopping Tilman. "Sergeant, get that fat fuck back in here immediately… send three squad cars, lights blaring. Wightman, I'd like you to check every floor of this building— the entire campus for that matter— for Ho-Hos. Don't come back short of a dozen!"

∗　∗　∗　∗　∗

Sergeant Tilman brought in Stuart Buckley, IT consultant for Oceans Restaurant. They entered the Scotland Yard conference room to find Rothery and Dylan already seated, both men fixated on a laptop on the table.

Dylan looked up, "Have a seat, Mr. Buckley. Would you like some coffee? a pastry?"

"No, I'm fine," the large man stated. "Where's Wightman? Shouldn't we be in the server room?"

"Chief Philips has him doing errands and he's still running through the video files," Tilman answered.

"Ha," Buckley laughed, "that's going to take him a while." He shifted uncomfortably in the chair. "Listen, I'm all about civic duty and the likes, but I have an hourly rate for consultation."

"Yes, of course. May I call you Stuart?" Dylan asked.

"Certainly."

"So, Stuart, are you incorporated? You have a tax number for billing purposes, I assume? We may have you here for quite some time."

Stuart's eyes widened with enthusiasm, "Righto! Business cards and everything."

Rothery sat quietly watching the laptop screen. Less than entertained with the direction Dylan's conversation was taking, he shifted his attention and cleared his throat. "So, Stuart," he began, "how do you explain this?" Rothery rotated the laptop and displayed the YouTube music video of the terrorist attack for Mr. Buckley.

Stuart's expression immediately changed from jovial enthusiasm to suspicious nervousness. "Uh, that is hard to explain," stammering, "but you should know, those files are backed up offsite, too— in case of fire or the likes; so, our cloud storage provider gets copies, as well."

"Then we'll need their name, as well. Where are they located?" Rothery's question was bland.

"Down near the East India Docks. But I'm sure they have additional backups with a big service provider like Amazon, MS Azure, or HP Helion, too."

"Those files were encrypted, were they not?" The SIS agent's patience was thin.

"Yes, the entire hard drive was encrypted."

"That's 256 bit encryption?"

"Yes, that's right."

"Who could decrypt 256 bit encryption, Mr. Buckley?"

"No one— not that fast, at least. I mean, I suppose it's not impossible, but it's highly improbable."

Rothery laughed, "You do realize those slim odds of improbability are the same odds you'll have of being acquitted of an international indictment for obstructing justice?"

"Whoa , whoa, whoa… I'm just an IT guy! You need to be far more sophisticated than I am to do that."

"Like who? Could a hacker do it?"

"I don't know."

"Well, if a hacker couldn't do it, that means it was an inside job, doesn't it? And that has us looking right back at you, Mr. Buckley. Are you certain you don't fancy a pastry?"

Stuart frowned, ignoring Rothery's offer. "Yeah, yeah, if anybody could do it, it would be a hacker, right? There are all sorts of guys out there… in fact, China broke into some government databases quite recently, you know."

"That's quite a defense, Mr. Buckley— 'China did it'. You sticking with that, eh?"

"There ARE hackers out there who could do it!" Buckley insisted.

"Hmm, possibly someone like MorbiX?" Rothery pulled a folder from his attaché case. He laid it open on the table displaying an array of pictures and documents. Stuart sat back in his chair, the color draining from his rosy cheeks. Strewn in front of him was an entire dossier on his extracurricular activities.

"Listen," Rothery leaned in, "we know you didn't do this alone. Just the time it required suggests an accomplice— it's actually a well-made video. However, given the fact you were on vacation, I suppose you did have plenty of time. So, as I see it, Mr. Buckley, the real issue is you impeding our investigation. I suggest you first tell us who all was involved then give us the complete video file. Not the edited joker version; the unedited footage. Then we will certainly show at least a bit of leniency."

A man like Stuart Buckley waits a lifetime for an opportunity like this one. "Yeah?" he began smugly. "Well, that sounds like a pretty good deal. But I think I may have a better one. How about I give you the finger..." he flipped off the agent, "and you give me my phone call." His Keanu Reeves' Neo impersonation was actually fairly good.

"So, that's the way you want to play it? I'm disappointed, Mr. Anderson."

"Listen 5-0, I know my rights. I want a solicitor and I want one now. This conversation is over."

"Oh, I understand now, you think I'm a cop? Didn't I introduce myself?" Rothery pulled out his ID and slapped it on the table. Rothery Taylor – SIS Special Agent. "There is not going to be any trial, Mr. Buckley. This was an international terrorist attack. There will be a tribunal years from now after all the potential associates of the Syrian-based, Islamic extremists group are brought into custody. And only then will we determine the nature of your involvement. Until that day (however many years into the future it might be), we will release some of the detainees we feel may lead us to higher ranking members in the echelons of ISIS or the likes. But unfortunately for you, sir, I don't see you being able to lead us to the Caliphate."

Buckley suddenly broke, now in a cooperative panic, "All right, all right, let's get real here! First of all, MorbiX is made up. I'm no hacker! That personal profile is a gimmick… gets me in the door for small-time IT jobs. I'm honestly not your guy, gents. Personally, I get squeamish just looking at a command line… I have to take an online course every time Windows releases a bloody new OS update. I can barely find my way around the Yahoo email interface… you've got to believe me!"

Rothery leaned forward, tightened his lips and narrowed his eyes in disgust, "Actually, I do. Wannabe-bloody-hackers… I would have hated you in college except I'm certain you weren't there. While I was writing my thesis on counter cyber-terrorism at Cambridge, you were likely taking an Excel course at the local technical institute." Rothery pushed a pen and tablet in front of Buckley. "Start writing. Every name, every number. Anyone you've even mentioned Oceans to."

Shaking his head, Rothery got up to leave the room, Dylan following close behind. Sergeant Tilman stepped up to the table and took Rothery's now empty seat. "You heard the man, Buckley… write!"

Once out of the room and heading down the hallway, Dylan slugged Rothery in the shoulder, "Brilliant, Agent Smith! That was so wicked… how fast you broke Fat Neo in there? 'I give you the finger…' and Agent Taylor waterboards his ass in Guantanamo!" Dylan couldn't help laughing.

Rothery gave a boyish grin and chuckle, appreciative of Dylan's youthful admiration. It was something he was not accustom to.

Chapter 35

"TURN IT UP," MICAH said pointing to the TV in Kip's office, now displaying a full color, HD quality still of Micah in the middle of his battle with the terrorists.

"We now have late-breaking video footage from the Oceans Restaurant surveillance feed. Police are looking for any information regarding the whereabouts of this man in link to the Oceans terrorist attack. Anyone with information is requested to contact Metro Police authority immediately. Do not attempt to approach him, he may be armed and dangerous. Again, police are looking for..."

Kip muted the television. "What did you do?"

"He saved me and everyone else in that building!" Victoria defended. "How did you know they would turn this on you, Micah? I really thought you were just being paranoid after everything that happened yesterday."

Micah remained silent.

"What aren't you telling me?" she pushed.

"I told you this morning that it's important you distance yourself from me— for your own sake."

"Oh, so that whole cold, morning-after thing today was for my sake?"

"Morning after, huh?" Kip nodded, giving Micah a thumbs-up.

"Really?!" Micah snapped at Kip.

Victoria pleaded, "Just turn yourself in, Micah! There were enough witnesses— they have a video. They have to know you're a hero."

Kip looked at Micah and shook his head adamantly, "Ooh, you know that's not a good idea," then sorrowfully, "but it's still good to have you back, old friend."

The TV screen now maintained the full-sized photo of Micah. "Can you get me off the island, Kip?"

"Not for a couple days," he replied. "Maybe Tuesday. What is it, Saturday? Too risky now," pointing to the television.

"Couple days is a long time, they will have closed down the airports by now. Train stops outside of Canterbury before the tunnel. I'm sure they're checking every car," Micah conjectured.

"Just turn yourself in," Victoria insisted. "I have connections. We can get you a lawyer..."

Kip interrupted, "It will never go to trial. How did you get out of Japan, Micah?"

"I died. Didn't you see the footage?"

"Do they know you're here?"

"Japan?"

"No, THEY?"

Micah sighed, "Yeah, he was at the restaurant."

"He was at the restaurant? Shit!" Kip paused to consider all that implied. "Damn it to hell! You know what that means? You know what this means, don't you?!"

"What does what mean?" Victoria was almost afraid to ask.

"That means, my dear love, that this was no terrorist attack," Kip explained.

Kip's words drained the color from Micah's face. "You're jumping, Kip," Micah disputed, shaking his head at the thought. "You're jumping."

"I know why you want to believe it's a leap, but…" Kip started.

"Why?" asked Victoria.

"Shut up, Kip!" Micah scowled. His hands shook, his finger pointed at the tall man, "Just give me this for a moment, will you?"

Kip silenced.

Seeing how much Micah was disturbed, Victoria knew that whatever it was, it was something deeply rooted. *Why was he hidden all these years? What happened in Japan? Was it something like this?* She had to wonder.

Victoria thought about what Kip had said, *'This was no terrorist attack.'* And suddenly she knew. If it wasn't a terrorist attack— if it was about Micah instead— then all the people who had died in that restaurant… their lives were over because of him. Their families would never be the same again because he got on a plane.

Victoria saw Micah— all of him. She could see through him like he saw through her. It suddenly seemed too easy, too obvious; like putting on a pair of glasses to adjust her sight, her perspective. The strangest thing was that it felt like she had always known this conviction about him— his concern, his compassion for life, his deep sense of responsibility; and even more, it was as if she had always known *him*. Her imaginary, childhood playmate suddenly was always Micah.

The three sat quiet for a while until Micah spoke. Sounding less emotional, "It's interesting that both incidences happened on self-contained islands," he said.

"You're right, that's actually quite a coincidence," Kip agreed.

Micah raised a brow, "I thought you didn't believe in coincidence."

"I don't," Kip frowned. "Nah, I guess it's not that big of a coincidence."

"Started making exceptions?" Micah poked.

"I don't know how you can joke around at a time like this," Kip scoffed, "I never got that about you."

"The three of us sitting in the back of an appliance store while they're closing down the airports…? I don't see myself going anywhere anytime soon. If I can't joke now, when can I— in prison?"

"You know THEY will never let you get to prison," Kip warned.

"Who's THEY?" Victoria demanded.

Micah and Kipley looked at each other; Kip watching to see how far Micah wanted to go with it. Micah rubbed his head, "I suspect we'll get to that eventually."

"You know," Kip interjected, "this really is a red-letter day. I should call Felix."

"Ugh," Micah groaned.

"What? You know what this will do for him."

Victoria chimed in, "Who's Felix?"

"Zealot. Religious zealot," Micah answered.

"And you should talk?" Kip retorted.

"I… I can talk. EVERYTHING is religion to Felix. Food is religion to Felix."

"Food IS religion to Felix," Kip agreed with a chuckle.

"You'll understand when you meet him, Victoria… IF you meet him."

Victoria put her hand dramatically upon Micah's shoulder then spoke specifically to Kip, "As you can see (and I'm sure you already know), Micah can be a bit remiss in his explanations. So, I'd like to ask you…"

"Anything, sweetheart," Kip obliged.

"…what are we talking about here? WHO are we talking about? I've seen more in the last three days than in a lifetime… and I'm older than I look," she added with a wink.

Straightforward, Kip declared, "The battle between good and evil!"

"Oh brother," Micah scoffed. "PLEASE don't get him started."

"You shush, DAVID," Victoria teased. "So, we're talking religion?"

"Oh, no, no, no… never say that word in front of him," Kip sarcastically warned, "he's AFRAID to talk about religion."

"Now he's attempting to goad me into an argument." Micah shook his head and balked, "Fine, go ahead, hear it from him. Then I'll just seem more reasonable."

Kip laughed, "Oh, yeah, your theories are textbook."

"Mine aren't theories, Kip. Can't we save this conversation for another time— like over a beer in Munich or something?"

"The lady asked ME a question, Micah. And as you know, I have a well-defined theory."

Micah rolled his eyes shaking his head, "Has it changed over the past seven years?"

"I'd like to think so." Kip thought about it for a moment then decided, "No, not really. Matter of fact, your presence here today confirms it all quite nicely." Kip smiled, pleased with himself.

"Is there nothing I can do to stop the two of you?"

"Nope," from Victoria.

"Then I'm going to just sit down over there." Micah planted himself on the tan leather couch, his hands behind his head.

Kip walked Victoria to his desk, "You see these magnets?"

"You still have the magnets?!" Micah mocked.

"I thought you were going to shut up?"

"Yeah!" Victoria agreed.

Kip had an arrangement of magnets on his desk, constantly moving in well-balanced placement. "In these magnets, the north and south polarities retract from each other while at the same time pulling toward their compatibles causing movement."

"Interesting. So, how long have they been spinning?" Victoria questioned.

"At least twelve years," Micah interjected.

"He can answer for himself, thank you," Victoria retorted.

"Yeah. Um, yeah… about twelve years," Kip said.

"Yes!" Micah raised his hands in victory.

"ANYWAY," Kip continued, "if I change the polarity of the southern half and offset the stage weighting more heavily toward one polarity than the other; it doesn't restrict the minority but increases its speed."

"Hmm, that's rather cool. So, what are you saying?"

"Well, whether you believe in creative design or nature; at least on this planet, there is a fundamental foundation to science that balance is inevitably maintained. Storms, for example, are a reaction to equalize Earth's temperatures like an automatic air conditioner or a fire sprinkler system."

"Or a fever in our bodies to fight off the flu?" Victoria suggested.

"Exactly!" Kip was becoming excited.

"You're only encouraging him," Micah grumbled. "Three years from now he'll retell this story back to you using your 'body fever' example."

"Take a nap," Victoria frowned.

"Yes, like the body," Kip explained. "Or chemistry, for instance. There are a perfect number of electrons required for the combining of elements. Whether it's two, ten, eighteen. . . there is no exception."

"Oh, my gosh! You HAVE expanded your theory!" Micah threw back his head.

"MEANING. . ." Kip gave Micah a dirty look, "a disregard for BALANCE (by definition) creates radioactivity. An imbalance causes decay of the nucleus because the nucleus experiences intense conflict between two of the strongest forces in nature. If the nucleus decays it emits alpha or beta particles and becomes a new element."

"I warned you," Micah told Victoria, "but that's actually a pretty good addition, Kip."

Kip nodded. "Thank you."

"Do you know where he's going with all this?" Victoria asked.

"Unfortunately, yes," Micah responded. He turned to Kip, "You're only confusing her, you know. Hell, I've heard this before and you're confusing me."

"Where are you going with all this?" she asked.

Kip shook his head, "Okay, okay. Let's look at another angle in my theory. Did you ever watch Michael Jordan play basketball?"

"Sure."

"There were plenty of men taller and great players who were shorter, but Michael Jordan's body was perfectly designed for the game of basketball. He was only 6'6", but the span of his hand in comparison to the ball was incredible. Michael had an 11.5-inch spread, thumb to pinky. He had the second largest hands of all time in the NBA, second only to Wilt Chamberlin. There were (and are) players almost a foot taller than Jordan with smaller hands, but his ball control, grip, precision as he shot— amazing! Also, with his leg to body ratio…"

"Are you coming to a point?" Micah butted in.

"I haven't seen the guy in seven years and he's already impatient," Kip gibed. "Anyway, Jordan's lateral leap and hang time… it looked like he could fly. The physics of his hang time, the sheer velocity and acceleration; he remained in the air nearly twice as long as average players. He could hang, switch hands, wait for a taller player to descend and then take an unchecked shot for the basket. It looked like he actually gained altitude after his initial burst."

"I have another explanation for that," Micah mumbled.

"I know you do. You want to tell her your version or mine? Which is she more likely to believe?"

Micah laid back on the couch, picked up a magazine and put it over his head as if to sleep.

"As I was SAYING… besides Jordan, look at Srinivasa Ramanujan. At the end of the nineteenth century, an Indian boy with no formal mathematical training baffled all of Europe with mathematical theories which could not be proven until the use of computers. His natural brain was DESIGNED to calculate numbers.

"Suffice to say, now, in the twenty-first century when we can map synapses and follow the stimulated brainwave patterns across the cortex, this can be proven. We can determine which minds are geared to spawn abstract, calculative or creative thought. Mozart or Einstein would be other good examples."

"I get it. Men extraordinaire," Victoria said. "Go ahead and say what you mean."

"These men were physically designed for specific thought processes like Michael Jordan was designed to play the game of basketball…"

"O-kaay…"

"… and natural design is not limited to sports or mathematics. I'm suggesting (with evidence) that as the world polarizes overly toward the negative, the universe will balance (like the magnets) and undoubtedly birth a Moses."

"Or a Neo," Micah added sarcastically.

Kip shot him a quick frown. "Imagine, Victoria, if someone was distinctly tuned to spiritual polarities? Evil would find him, be drawn to him, stack up against him. But it would lose. What I'm suggesting is if you put someone like that in a room with three evil guys, he'll be three times as strong, three times as fast. He'll see what they're doing before they do it." Kip lightened his tone, "Of course, in your average environment I could still beat him at arm wrestling."

Micah smirked, "I was drunk and you cheated. Don't ever play cards with him either."

The levity faded and the men briefly exchanged a somber look. "Micah won't die in a room of ten evil people, Victoria... he'll die in a room with ten good ones."

"Because he wouldn't be needed then. The balance would be going the other way," she said quietly.

"Oh, now THAT'S science," Micah loudly scoffed, interrupting the solemn moment.

"Okay, smart guy, then you tell her the truth," Kip challenged.

"It's not my department," Micah responded, aloof.

"It used to be," Kip said cautiously.

"Yeah, and you saw how well that turned out, didn't you?"

"I've seen you cause a priest to confess, my friend."

Victoria ventured into the brotherly bickering. "Okay then, Micah... other than being snarky, you've been pretty quiet through all this. What's your theory?"

Micah gave a reluctant sigh, "People believe what they want to believe, Victoria. And good for them. You can't teach anyone anything."

"You've taught me."

"No, Victoria. No, I did not. You EXPERIENCED something. Nothing— everything. I can't even presume that what you see as blue is not red to me."

"Micah, that's really harsh," she said with true remorse.

He lowered his eyes knowing he had become cynical over the years. He looked back at her apologetically, "I'm learning."

She smiled faintly, "Oh, that's not fair. You're saying that you're learning from me but I can't say the same."

"You're a better teacher than me."

She narrowed her eyes at his comment, "Yeah, I'll bet. So, you have nothing to say to any of this?"

"Nope."

She frowned.

Folding his arms across his chest, Micah sighed reluctantly, "Well, first of all, Kip's battle-between-good-verses-evil... that's a slippery slope. Once your goal is to exterminate evil, no matter how good your intentions, you will likely find yourself fighting against God himself."

"So are we supposed to let Evil rule in fear of misguided good intentions?" Kip argued.

"No, I didn't say that. I just caution you. Your harmony is a balance. Evil is not unlike life itself— it just is. You can't eliminate it. Where there is man, there is evil. Evil is man's shadow as he basks in the light. It's a gage of our distance from the sun. True faith trusts good to win out over evil. It doesn't fear nor is it bent on evil's extermination... it's faith." Micah shifted in his seat, "Can we talk politics instead?"

Kip raised a knowing brow, "I don't know, can we?"

"NO!"

Micah looked away, gazing absently at the muted television. The new video footage of his fight rolled across the screen. "Hey, if they've already gone over the entire tape, by now they have to know I was with you, Victoria," he realized. "They're bound to try to reach you. You still have your phone on you, don't you?"

"Oh, for the love of god, give me your phone!" Kip demanded.

"Hey, I might need that!" Victoria protested.

Kip snatched the phone out of her hands and immediately snapped the screen in half, throwing it in a very large fish tank that sat against the wall opposite the TV. "I'll give you a Samsung from up front."

Victoria pouted. "So, where's YOUR phone, Micah?" She didn't even try to hide the snotty undertone.

Micah smiled smugly. "They don't know who I am," he retorted.

"What?!" Kip gasped.

"Hey, I'm not a famous actor or anything..."

"Oh... my... god!" Kip blurted, exasperated. "Morons! I'm with morons. Give me your fucking phone, Micah."

"They don't know who I am, I've got at least a day. I just bought it!"

"What, are you stupid?"

"I haven't uploaded my pictures. It's a new iPhone."

"If it's a new phone, what pictures could you possibly have on it?"

Micah signaled Kip with a few stealthy head jerks towards Victoria.

"What?" Kip asked.

Micah rolled his eyes and shifted them in Victoria's direction.

"I'm right here, Micah, I can see you," she said. "You've got pictures of me on your phone?"

"Appropriate ones," he defended. "I took a selfie while you were sleeping. You know, in case anything happened, no one would believe me…" Micah almost started to blush.

Victoria smiled, "That's so sweet."

"Give me your damn phone." Kip grabbed the new iPhone, cracked the screen and threw it into the tank with Victoria's.

"I didn't really take a selfie with you," Micah said, leaning into Victoria, "I was just messing with Kip."

Victoria gave a knowing grin, "Sure, you were."

"Listen," Kip spoke up, "I can ship you out maybe Monday— more likely Tuesday. I was going to suggest you use the room, but if they've got her location and know she's here… that would lead to the room AND everywhere I go. Sorry my friend, you have to go. You've got to go now— and you're on your own for the meantime. Let me get you a couple of untraceable phones from the front. Leave me your passport and when I have safe passage prepared, I'll call. Don't call me. You be safe."

"Well," Micah resigned, "I guess we've seen worse."

Chapter 36

LEAVING THE BACK OF Kipley's Appliances, "Taking in the sites?" a voice quipped out of nowhere.

Micah stopped dead in his tracks. Without turning he knew it was Henry. "You know you're in the wrong line of business, Mr. Wilkens."

"That's the second time I've heard that today. And it's Henry. Didn't anyone see 'All the President's Men'? Police don't get their man, investigative reporters do." Henry pushed up his sleeve and glanced at an imaginary watch. "From reports on my police scanner, I'd say you have less than three minutes now."

Micah shot Kip a quick look. Kip nodded.

With a satisfied smirk, Henry went on, "Unfortunately for you, mate, I've already copied down the license plate of your Avis rental— unless, of course, you want to leave another body behind?" Henry placed his hands inviting to his own chest. "Though I doubt your car was rented to Victoria Adams or Allen Steinbeck, you still won't be getting far today. So, what are you going to do, Mr. Steinbeck?" He paused, waiting for Micah's response.

"I'm thinking about it," Micah grumbled, more annoyed than anything else. He wasn't worried about the license plate considering the decommissioned Avis car hadn't actually been rented to anyone, but the reporter could be a problem.

"Oh, come now! YouTube has provided a stimulating documentary of your physical abilities, sir, but we both know you're not capable of cold blood."

Micah moved quickly toward Henry invading his personal space. Six inches from his face and backing him against a car, "Are you certain, Mr. Wilkens?"

Henry grinned, pleased with himself. "I am now."

"Enlighten me."

"Well, most obviously– I would already be dead."

"And less obviously?"

"You're sad."

Micah pulled back and turned away, "I'd love to chat about my emotions, Henry, but I really need to go."

"Mind if I come along?" the reporter asked flippantly.

Micah paused to actually think about it. "I'll tell you what," Henry proposed, "I'll leave my phone behind with the big guy. I won't be able to call anyone and no one can trace me. Sound fair?"

Micah's eyes shifted, considering the alternatives. He finally shook his head in annoyance, "Whatever." Henry threw his phone to Kip and prepared to jump into the backseat of their car.

"Hold on," Kip told Henry, fiddling with the phone.

"Don't bother, mate, its password protected." Henry was smug until Kip began thumbing through his contacts seconds later. "Hey! How'd you do that?"

"Trade secret."

A mobile phone ring came from inside Henry's jacket. Kip spun the reporter around, grabbed his lapel, and pulled a second phone from the man's inner pocket. "Forgot that was there," Henry tried to play off.

"Sure, you did," Kip responded.

Henry defiantly eyed the tall man, "I'm going to need those back, you know."

"No problem. I'll keep them with Victoria's phone in the back office."

Henry raised his eyebrows expectantly then leaned in and whispered, "How much for *her* phone?"

"Maybe we can work something out. Stop by the store," replied Kip with a wink.

Henry smiled, jumping into the backseat. Micah and Victoria tried to hide their laughter as they both climbed into the front.

*　*　*　*　*

The dark blue Avis car pulled out of the back parking lot unseen as the police turned the corner into the front. Henry leaned up against the front seats, "Don't you want to know how I found you?"

"Not really. Will you put your seatbelt on?" Micah didn't care whether Henry put his seatbelt on or not, but he did prefer to have him out of his face.

"Mine really is a thankless job," Henry complained as he sat back. "Not unlike yours, I'm certain... being a hero, and all."

"I am a bit interested how you found us," Victoria said.

"Please don't encourage him," Micah pleaded.

Victoria mused, "I suppose this does feel a bit like Lethal Weapon, doesn't it?"

"One or two?" asked Henry.

"Three."

Henry frowned. "Are you suggesting I'm Joe Pesci riding in the backseat?"

Victoria turned and smiled.

Henry sneered, "So, what do I call you, Mr...?"

"I don't remember asking you to call me at all," Micah said curtly.

"Ah, I'll know soon enough. But I refuse to call you Steinbeck."

"No questions, please."

"That's fine. Though in the process of due diligence, I thought to give you an opportunity to comment before the release of the evening news."

Micah didn't respond.

"The headline WAS going to read, *'Hero or Terrorist?'*, but after the unfortunate release of that YouTube video it will need to be changed. None the less, the content remains. I'll paraphrase... *'Scotland Yard, the Prime Minister and Her Majesty's SS blunder protocol number one— contain the scene of the crime...'* might suggest to at least consider interviewing the victims? *'How secure are our borders when an American— lone survivor— can walk past thirty of London's finest covered in blood, unaided, unimpeded and unquestioned?'* *'Never fear, the hunt is on; although the gunshot-wounded man continues to elude Britain's finest...'* Then of course, *'This is just another fine example of Downing Street's PC objectives; three Muslim terrorists kill three people— extremists wave ISIS flags in victory in the boroughs of Newham and Tower Hamlets while the Prime Minister's Office has three divisions of British national security exhausting efforts to unsuccessfully subdue the white, Anglo Saxon American for questioning.'* And my favorite... *'The question remains, what does he know that they don't?'* Or should I say, what doesn't he? End article."

Henry waited for Micah's response, "Comments?"

"I think it's nice," Victoria answered.

"Oh, lovely. That'll change their intentions," Micah griped.

"Could you repeat that with a tad less sarcasm?" Henry chided.

"If I did, it would give you a clear and concise quote. Forgive me if I'm less than eager. Besides, you appear to be the true vigilante here."

"Just informing the public, sir."

"Oh, you're quite the conscientious civic servant, I can tell, Mr. Wilkens. I'm sure this ride will also make the morning news."

"On the contrary, your capture is the last thing I want. I have an exclusive and I intend to protect it."

"I see that. Anywhere in particular I can drop you?"

"Actually, my calendar is wide open." Henry leaned back getting comfortable.

"If you're traveling around with us, who is going to publish your article?" Victoria asked.

"I sent that before getting into the car."

"Then you don't need a quote from me," Micah said.

"Hmm… can I borrow one of your phones?"

"NO!" Victoria and Micah responded in unison. Micah pulled over, "I believe this is your spot."

Henry looked up to see the back entrance of the Pressroom Pub. "As good as any," he smiled.

Exiting the car, Henry leaned his head back in before shutting the door. "It's truly been my pleasure. I'll keep Ms. Adams out of the story as long as I can— or until they catch you. Try not to take it personally, mate, after all, I am rooting for you. If you need anything… a place to stay…?" looking at Victoria and winking, "…maybe a ménage à trois?"

"We'll let you know," Victory finished. And with that, Micah drove away.

* * * * *

"You do need to distance yourself from me, Victoria— for now."

"What will you do?"

"I have to disappear for a few days."

"Where will you go?"

"I need to pay a visit to an old acquaintance. He knows I'm in town and he'll be looking for me. It's best if I find him first."

Victoria sighed, "I don't like the sound of that."

"Can you get the car back to Kip's?"

She nodded.

"He'll know what to do. If for any reason you need to get ahold of me, call Kip." Micah got out of the car.

"Micah?"

He turned back. A moment of silence was broken by her smile. Micah nodded, warmly returning her look, "I'll see you." He quickly disappeared down an alley in the city.

Chapter 37

"MAY I HELP YOU, officers?" Kip asked in a thick Scottish accent as he entered from the back room to the showroom floor.

"We're not policemen. I'm Dylan Vasko with the PM's Terrorist Task Force and this is Rothery Taylor, Special Agent with MI6."

"MI6? Sure you are. I'm a Kingsman, myself. This store is just a front. We have an underground tunnel directly to Buckingham, so you laddies have come to the right place!" Kip's pronunciation of 'laddies' was suspiciously close to 'ladies'.

"Can I interest you gents in upgrading your surveillance equipment?" Kip continued. "Make you a good deal— you boys being on the job, and all."

"Surveillance equipment?"

"I have a penlight camera here... popular with the boys like yourself. Fits in tight places." Kip gave them a wink, "I don't ask, don't want to know, I just sell the instruments. But the real specialty equipment is in the back room." He turned to head toward the double doors.

"That's alright, maybe another time," Dylan replied with a smirk.

"Suit yourself." Kip sat down at the front desk.

Rothery grabbed a business card off the counter and read it out loud, "Kipley Holland, proprietor."

"Aye, that be me. Is there something particular I can interest ya in, gentlemen?"

"We hope so. We're investigating the recent terrorist attack at Ocean's restaurant."

"Really? I thought they caught da terrorists. What might this have to do with my store?"

"Was Victoria Adams in your establishment this afternoon?"

"Victoria Adams?"

"The film star."

Kip openly laughed, "Victoria Adams, the film star?" But seeing the serious looks upon their faces, he adjusted to disbelief. "You're not serious? Victoria Adams here in Soho?" He laughed again, "You ARE serious." Kip tossed the stack of papers he held upon the counter. "Well, I'm here every day, and I've never seen the likes of her. Wish I had!"

Rothery, pointing to the in-store surveillance cameras, "Do those work?"

"Of course they work," Kip answered, a bit offended.

"Do you mind if we view the tapes?"

"Tapes? They stream direct to disk. I can download all three angles to a thumb drive, if you'd like. I suggest the 64GB Sandisk. It's USB3 and looks as slick as your boyfriend's suit."

Rothery pulled a USB drive from his jacket pocket. "I have my own."

Kip shrugged, "No offense laddy, but I don't allow anyone to plug their media into my domain, if you know what I mean. Viruses and all. That's like asking a man to drink from another man's beer... a feller gets AIDS that way." Kip overtly assessed the male couple in front of him.

"Oh, we're not... I mean... we're just colleagues," Rothery stammered.

Kip threw up his hands, "Don't ask, don't want to know."

Entertained, Dylan delicately brushed a piece of lint from Rothery's shoulder. Rothery scowled as he pulled out his wallet to pay for the pen-drive.

"How far back do you want me to go?" Kip asked concerning the video download. "I can give you the whole week, but you'd need a terabyte drive for that. The Western Digital is on sale?" he pitched.

"No, just the last couple hours will be fine."

"Splendid. That'd be 74 quid."

"74 pounds for a 64GB thumb drive? Thought you were giving us a deal?"

"Time spent, gents. Can't help me other customers while downloading the video." Dylan looked around the completely empty store.

Rothery joined Kip behind the counter. The files were in directories dated and time-stamped in ten-minute increments. Rothery also noticed the next directory already auto-generating as Kip began downloading the first file with the current date and time displayed. "Why don't you give us the last three hours," Rothery requested, "up until the moment we walked into the store."

Kip looked at his watch then moused-over the last three hours' worth of directories, highlighting them. Pressing Ctrl-C to copy and Ctrl-N to open a new Explorer window, he then scrolled to the USB drive and opened it. With Ctrl-V, he copied the video directories over to the pen-drive.

"Can you play the last ten minutes while it copies?"

"Of course I can," Kip replied. He opened the last directory and played the video. "Would you like me to fast forward to when you entered the store?"

Rothery nodded.

The video played through as expected with a three-way split screen of all three angles of the store. "Now, can you go back to about an hour ago?" Rothery requested.

"We'll have to watch in 10-minute increments," Kip explained.

"Yes, that's fine."

Kip opened the 17:30 folder and began to play the video at 4-times speed. On the video display, a couple had just entered the store. Kassandria came out from behind the counter to greet them. Then a young man entered. Kip was shown making his way from the back room to assist. The 10-minute footage was entirely uneventful.

"Do you mind if we look around the place?" Dylan asked.

"I don't mind, but while my assistant is out, might we all stay together? No offense, I trust you lads... this might not look like much, but it's all I've got."

Kip led them to the back room and gave them the nickel tour. "Nice fish tank," Rothery commented. "Where are the fish?"

"Kept getting trapped under falling phones. That was a display for the waterproof Samsung. Ya interested?"

Rothery took a closer look at the phones at the bottom, "Not a big fan of Apple?"

"Aye, they're nice and all, but no margins for the working man. They tie their phones to the large carriers."

"Where does this door lead?" Dylan asked.

"Back parking lot."

"Do you use it much?"

"Every day. My Volvo's parked just beyond."

"Interesting book collection, Mr. Holland," Rothery remarked, glancing at the books above a bench in the small workshop attached to the larger office. "Thank you again for your time."

"Don't mention it, gents. Always willing to help out our men in… well, I guess you don't really wear the bobby-blue."

* * * * *

Leaving the store, the men got into their car. "You cut that short," Dylan observed, "why? What do you think?"

"It's exactly what he said it is," Rothery stated, flatly.

"What's that?"

"It's a front."

"A front? Seriously, like secret service? That guy? How do you know?"

"Well, to begin with, in the video he's wearing the same store jacket but his shoes were different from the ones in the first and second video. He was wearing brown shoes in the video, black shoes today."

"Weren't there brown shoes by the back door?"

"Yes, but no water marks. It's raining today. Those shoes have been drying by the door at least a day. Also, there were four new phones disposed of in the fish tank with remnant air bubbles still lodged in the cracks of recent breaks; couldn't have happened more than an hour ago. I don't know how he pulled off the rapid video switch, I was watching closely. Possibly has dual servers with a script running in the background… he did hesitate before opening the second video. Either way, it's too sophisticated for the Scottish dolt he was playing. And thirdly, his book library would put John Le Carre's guide to underworld espionage to shame."

"Well, that's quite obvious though, don't you think? Would a real spy have that sort of material on display?"

"That's actually my point. I didn't say Ian Fleming's guide; he didn't have the imaginative works of 'James Bond for Dummies'. He had an impressive, everything-you-would-need-to-know-without-anyone-knowing-you're-looking collection. I have that same collection at home."

"Well, buggers! Let's go back in and bust him."

"Can't do it. This is no small-time pawn shop; he probably DOES have a tunnel under the building. We'd need to check back channels before breeching his cover. None the less, it's no coincidence that Ms. Adam's phone was here."

"So, that suggests that our Samaritan is connected— government and all?"

"Question is, why hasn't anyone claimed him?" Rothery muttered to himself, "It doesn't make any sense."

"There have been recent speculations of even the US infiltrating its ally governments like the UK," Dylan postulated.

"Yes, but if he were spying on the UK, why would he risk being exposed over a restaurant? I just don't know," he toiled. "I've known men deep undercover; everything they risk is FOR their cover, not against it."

Chapter 38

TWO SAT IN THE furthest dark corner at an undisturbed table. The Rumpus Room at the Mondrian luxury hotel was near empty, its evening's patrons still strolling the adjacent Thames or fighting London traffic on their way home from a Sunday's outing.

Spinning a gold signet ring, a large, well-dressed man sat at a dimly-lit table with his back to the bar. At ease with the chic décor and the panoramic river view, he appeared to be enjoying his environment like a mafia boss in his own establishment. The other, cloaked and well hidden, purposely leaned back into the decorative curtains to disguise his appearance.

"I don't like meeting out in the open like this," the cloaked man declared.

"You worry too much. Besides, we're not in the open. Believe me, this is far more private than you can imagine."

"Is this a corporate asset?" UK asked.

"Let's just say it's a subsidiary under the umbrella of influence."

"That explains the Twisted Circus on Halloween."

Ring Finger shook his head with disapproval, "I really don't understand with all you have at your disposal why a circus entertains you; nor do I understand your appetite for impregnating Cirque du Soleil starlets. Tell me, do you perform the act yourself or do you hire a stand-in? I'm certainly aware they don't meet your usual criteria— too old and too buxom."

"It's but a mere aphrodisiac for a night's festivities! I didn't know you took such interest in my hobbies, Furcus. After sharing your perspective on the subject the last time we met, I'd have thought you would pay less attention, not more. But my extracurricular activities aside, I seriously don't like being kept in the dark. You're in my territory, now."

"Have I been amiss?"

"You initiated an unapproved operation in London. Why wasn't I informed?"

"You were in Moldova, you were at our last meeting— surely you were aware. Besides, I've always carried cart blanch approval to execute operations at my discretion, regardless of territory."

"Well, your recent event was not on the agenda. And it did nothing for Syria."

"Though I could enlighten your apparent misguidance, rather I'm obliged to remind you that there is a hierarchy to order, each with their role. You chose your assignment. You prefer the limelight. Real power must remain hidden in the wings, and to that, you're not particularly suited."

"Fine, but I don't like taking orders from you. I'm never certain if it's the will of the Collective."

"Well, let me clear it up for you," Ring Finger's eyes turned fierce as fire, "I AM the Collective, and the Collective is me. By my hand and through my direction we aspire. There was no Collective before me. In this, there is no question. I don't speak for myself, neither do I have illusions of grandeur. I don't seek human adulation; I made my sacrifice long ago."

The cloaked man smirked, "What, are you a priest? Why do you deny yourself mortal pleasure? Why make such a sacrifice? To what god do you serve? We are the gods of this planet."

"Gods? God's? God?" Furcus scorned. "I believed as you once, centuries ago. Actually, no I didn't. That is a feeble explanation. We do not supersede the nature of this planet, we defy it."

"Therefore making us gods in position to rule," UK declared.

"You are not unique in your thinking," Ring Finger chuckled. "There were those who thought their awaking was like a birth to evolve to greatness, but our amnesia is evidence to the contrary. We were banished and forgotten here long ago. If we were the gods of this planet, we would not defy it; we would be the inherent principium. But I cannot make the rain fall nor the wind cease. We don't belong here and will find no answers until we leave."

"Well, the one thing we all hold in common... soon HE will bring order to the Collective— or more likely disband it all together."

Ring Finger's eyes hollowed black, "I did not call you here to speak philosophy. With Jaharah out of the picture, we'll need another to execute the plan."

"I assumed."

Ring Finger remained quiet with a suggestive glance at his comrade, waiting.

UK startled, "Me? No. We can't afford to expose my position. Besides, I'm a bit busy with YOUR boy."

"Your position is irrelevant. It is temporal, at best. Hell, Great Britain is becoming less and less significant."

"I don't like this, Furcus. There must be someone else. We have always used disposables for projects such as these."

"That is true."

"I am not disposable!"

Ring Finger leaned over the table, "As far as we know, perhaps. But your position is. In the event of an error, you can start over elsewhere."

The cloaked man shook his head in contempt, "I've worked hard... I'm perfectly positioned! Is'polnu'vanje."

"Call a meeting if you like, you'll see that I speak for the Collective."

UK frowned, then noticed someone new walking into the Rumpus Room. Becoming apprehensive, he rose to his feet looking back at Ring Finger with reluctant submission. "Fine," he relented, "we all know there is no one better to handle the situation than I— as regrettable as that is. You do know, however, that it was your collective fuck-up that put us here in the first place… and I WILL get confirmation, just the same."

"You don't trust me?" Furcus smiled. "You need to learn to trust your friends." Adding what he only sensed, "You've been out too long, comrade. You're assimilated."

With an indignant glare, the cloaked man exited through the decorative curtain behind the corner table where a hidden door resided.

*　*　*　*　*

The man who entered the bar removed a dusty old coat and hat, draping them over a chair. Peeling off a synthetic beard and latex nose revealed Micah Graff. He walked up and took a seat at the table behind Furcus.

Ring Finger lowered his head with a humorous sigh, "You're a hard man to find."

"How did you know it was me?"

"No one else could get pass the doorman."

"Really? I didn't notice."

"Apparently, neither did he."

Micah rose and moved to the seat across from Ring Finger. The man took a sip of his drink but couldn't avoid the feel of Micah's glare. This was a first for Furcus; no one had ever walked up on him before. No one would want to nor dare.

The hunter was out of his element but remained cool, confident. He was in unchartered waters; something he should have grown accustomed to with Micah. "You found me. Should I thank you for saving me the trouble?"

"Why Furcus, you haven't changed. Actually haven't aged a day, either," Micah said.

"Thank you for noticing. I dressed for the occasion. I knew I was going to be meeting someone *special*." Ring Finger's voice held a menacing tone.

"I hope I didn't chase off your friend."

A half-smile slowly evolved into a grimace, "Actually, he's more a friend of yours."

"I should have taken a closer look then."

"Now, that wouldn't have been very good for you."

The two men sat silently for a time with an occasional glance in the other's direction. Micah was content to wait him out.

"Comforting isn't it?" Ring Finger posed in the silence.

"It's not bad." Micah knew the man was suggesting that sitting in the company of one's enemy left no room for unwarranted fear.

"I might just doze off," Furcus said casually.

"Haven't been sleeping lately?"

He haphazardly shrugged, "I wonder if you could say the same."

Micah echoed the man's same lack of concern; tilted himself back in his chair, hands clasped behind his head.

"You know, I've seen you on television lately, they're causing quite a fuss. You need a room somewhere to relax?" Furcus offered.

Micah pondered the thought, almost questioning whether he could trust him or if Ring Finger would try to kill him in his bed as he slept.

Furcus answered Micah's thoughts, "That would be unsporting, don't you agree?"

"I appreciate your ethics. Still, Oceans? I really hope you didn't go to all that trouble on my account," Micah quipped.

"No, no… it was a multifaceted necessity." Watching the look on Micah's face, Furcus continued, "I see that relieves you."

"I appreciate your concern, however, if you hadn't noticed, I was GONE. Out of your way. RETIRED. Wasn't that enough for you?"

"Rising from the dead spawns a whole new category of concern."

"So, where do we go from here?" Micah asked.

"You are no longer my responsibility."

Micah sighed, "Someone less accommodating, I suppose."

Ring Finger shrugged.

"Your kind— you don't belong here."

"We are very aware of that."

"That's good to hear, how can I help?"

"Stay out of the way this time," Furcus said firmly, methodically twisting the gold ring round and round.

Micah frowned, "Nice ring." He rose and walked out with his back to Ring Finger, leaving the disguise on the table.

"He's done hiding," Furcus said unemotionally.

"It won't matter," came a voice from behind the curtain.

Chapter 39

ROTHERY AND DYLAN ARRIVED early afternoon through the gates of the Victorian hunting lodge— more fondly known as 'The Cabin'. Rothery stopped short, "Do we just proceed up the driveway?"

"Why not?" Dylan asked.

"I don't know, do you think they have guards? Dogs?"

"Who do you work for?" the younger man mocked sarcastically. "What, are you star-struck? They are witnesses to a crime. Just drive, I'll knock on the door."

"Front door?"

"Just follow me."

The front of the house seemed vacant. Dylan knocked on the beautifully crafted door. An older gentleman eventually answered. "May I help you?"

"Hello, sir, I'm with the PM's Office; my partner is an investigator. Is Victoria Adams and/or William Cleese present?"

"May I see some identification?"

"Right." The two men showed their ID.

"This must be concerning the incident at the restaurant?"

"Yes, sir. They were witnesses and we're doing some follow-on investigating. The Prime Minister also wants to assure that Ms. Adams— and Mr. Cleese, for that matter— are doing well."

"They are doing as well as can be expected, although Ms. Adams has just laid down for a nap."

"Well, if Mr. Cleese is available? We drove out from London, sir."

"Please follow me, I'll see if he is available." The gentleman led them into a simply furnished lounge. "Please make yourselves comfortable. May I offer you some refreshments; a snack? something to nibble?"

"Water would be lovely, thank you."

"Of course. Please feel free to help yourself to the bar." The man motioned to a generously stocked wet bar on the other side of the room.

Dylan nodded, "Thank you, that is most gracious."

"By all means. Ms. Adams would have it no other way."

"And your name, sir?" Rothery asked.

"Nigel, sir." Nigel nodded and exited the lounge.

"Nigel. Quite nice." Rothery seemed a bit taken.

"He's a butler or grounds keeper or maintenance man," Dylan scoffed, "what's wrong with you?"

"I don't know. However, I do believe I understand Doctor Wilson's momentary lapse of judgement; the idea of meeting a celebrity is quite overwhelming."

The two were seated comfortably in leather recliners when the lounge door opened. It was Nigel. "Gentlemen, Mr. Cleese."

The men stood. "And that's not intimidating?" Rothery whispered to Dylan.

William entered the room, "That will be all, Nigel."

Nigel nodded, "Very good, sir." He gracefully pivoted and promptly left the lounge. Rothery raised his eyebrows looking to Dylan. Dylan ignored him.

Stepping up to William and offering a hand, "Mr. Cleese, thank you for your time. My name is Dylan Vasko with the PM's Office, and this is my colleague, Agent Rothery Taylor with SIS. We understand that you have gone through a horrible ordeal and we're sorry to have to bother you."

"Please, no bother at all. How can I help?"

After also shaking William's hand, Rothery returned to his seat. Recomposed, he began, "Your statement to the police, sir, failed to mention that the man who subdued the terrorists was part of your dinner party. Matter of fact, it didn't mention the apprehension of the terrorists at all. Doesn't that seem odd to you?"

"Well, that's right to the point now, isn't it?" William replied. The agent was obviously no longer star-struck.

"Pardon my colleague," Dylan apologized, "his expertise in these matters lies more behind the scenes. His bedside manner has a tad to be desired."

"Mr. Taylor," William began, "the gunshots started almost immediately as we sat down. I had barely met the man before the three of us were under the table. Honestly, I didn't see any of the exchange. Victoria has declared him a hero, but when the police asked me what I heard and saw, I told them just that. I heard gunshots fired and sometime later Victoria grabbed me by the hand and we ran out of the restaurant. The only thing I remember is the blood on my shoes from the man who died behind us." William frowned, "I heard a man die, agent— his last breath, choking on blood. I honestly don't want to consider it much more than that."

"What can you tell us about Mr. Steinbeck?" Dylan asked.

William paused, "What do you mean?"

Unexpectedly, Victoria entered the room with an assortment of snacks. Her hair in a ponytail, she wore tight jeans and an equally tight sweatshirt with no bra. "William, have you offered them something to drink?"

"Nigel told them to make themselves at home and offered the bar."

"Not everyone is as presumptuous as you are, dear. You would have poured yourself a drink regardless of an invitation. Clearly both of these men have better manners." She smiled charmingly and set down the food. "You must be parched from the trip in from London. What can I get you to drink, gentlemen?"

The men's eyes were set on Victoria. "Water would be fine," Rothery managed. Dylan nodded in agreement.

"Really? Hmm… I've been in the room less than thirty seconds and I'm certain I saw both of you eye my husband's crystal decanter?" She moved toward the bar. It was an overt suggestion.

The men nodded no— unconvincingly. Victoria smiled and winked, turning over three glasses and pouring a healthy portion from the decanter into each. Her ponytail bouncing playfully, she returned from the bar carrying two glasses in one hand and one in the other. She delivered the drinks to her guests while William held out his hand for the third. She gave her husband a saucy look and shrugged. She then sat down across from the two detectives. Crossing her legs and holding onto the third glass, "So, where were we?" she asked sweetly, taking a sip of William's best scotch herself.

Captivated, both men failed to respond.

Looking back and forth between the two men, "I believe you asked William about Allen?" she said, breaking the silence.

"Excuse me?"

"Mr. Steinbeck?"

"Oh, yes, yes. That is correct, Ms. Adams," Dylan recomposed.

"I'm sorry to say, neither of us know much," Victoria began, "I met him less than a week ago. As is customary, I invited him to dinner. William and I like to repay courtesy with dinner at a nice restaurant, you see. Obviously, we aren't comfortable having complete strangers to our home— we only invite family or friends here… our home is personal to us and it can be awkward. Neutral ground is much more fitting, don't you agree? Besides, when you invite someone to your home, the night's end is too often at their discretion not yours, whereas you can leave a restaurant anytime you'd like."

"Ms. Adams, you seem to be doing remarkably well under the circumstances," Rothery commented.

"I am a professional actress," she defended, "it's actually been a horrible ordeal." Her eyes immediately hollowed, "To be frank, I'm actually having to play a role." She stammered a moment, "So, what is your interest in Mr. Steinbeck?"

"Tying up loose ends, Ms. Adams," Dylan answered. "The incident was quite remarkable. If I hadn't seen the surveillance footage, I'd never have believed it myself."

"Did you watch Mr. Steinbeck apprehended the terrorists?" Rothery questioned Victoria.

"I saw bits and pieces. For the most part I was hiding with William."

"Do you know where Mr. Steinbeck is now?" he asked.

"No."

"Do you know how to get ahold of him? Do you have a phone number for him?"

"I do. Oh, wait a minute, I don't. I lost my phone. His number was in my phone."

Rothery chuckled, "Sleeping with the fishes."

"Oh?" William cut in eagerly, "Are you a Godfather fan?"

"Oh, god, William!" Victoria exclaimed. She turned to her guests, "He is now going to tell you how he turned down the role of Sonny in the Godfather because he felt he'd have been better cast as Michael Corleone. If you let him, he'll tell you how he re-wrote the dinner scene before they gave the part to James Caan!"

"You make a mockery of that, but you weren't even born, darling," William boasted.

"Please forgive my husband. He's not as bright as he appears in the movies. If he realized what it said of him to admit that his wife wasn't born when he was PASSED UP for the role of an almost 30-year-old Michael Corleone back then, he'd be beside himself."

"Darling, I will never be ashamed of winning you at whatever age," William flattered.

"Winning?" Victoria teased, "These men are law officers, dear... the term is ROBBING— as in 'the cradle'. It's a much better fit."

"Your wit, Ms. Adams, is entertaining," Rothery complimented with a smile.

"Do you regret giving up the part?" Dylan asked William.

"It hasn't hurt me," he replied. Adding graciously, "And I will confess, Pacino was a much better Michael than I would have been."

"Ms. Adams?" Rothery addressed.

"Please, call me Victoria."

"How did you meet Mr. Steinbeck, Victoria?"

"I met him in London on Tuesday."

"Where in London?"

"At..." she paused, "the airport." With the answer, she was suddenly trapped. She grieved she hadn't considered the simplest question. That bit of information alone would likely lead to them identifying Micah.

"You flew in on Tuesday?"

"That's right."

"Did you meet him at baggage claim, immigration, on the plane?"

"I was waiting for the car," she answered without missing a beat. "We use a service if no one knows we're coming to town."

"So, it was after baggage, beyond immigration?"

"Yes. But my typical driver wasn't there. I wanted to just take a cab— but I hate to admit, I don't usually carry all my luggage myself, it's also picked up by a service. So, I couldn't very well leave the airport until that was taken care of, could I? Anyway, my phone was dead from the long flight and Allen was there at baggage service near the Terminal 5 exit."

"You have such trouble with your phone, madam. So, had he just arrived?"

"Hmm... I don't think so. I believe he was dropping someone off or picking someone up. I didn't even think to ask. I really don't deal with such complications very well. I was a bit... frustrated."

"You have no idea," William mumbled.

Victoria gave William a dirty look but found inspiration for her role. "As I was saying, Allen happened to be there. He... how should I say... helped me convince the baggage attendant of the seriousness of my situation."

William chuckled, "You mean, he calmed you down and prevented you from pulverizing the poor employee behind the counter?"

Victoria frowned harder at William, "Let's just say, I was unable to optimally express myself at the time, so Allen mediated the inconvenience on my behalf. And then he let me borrow his phone to call a car."

"Picture Tasmanian-Devil-meets-Tweety-Bird," William explained.

"Awe... you think I'm Tweety Bird? How sweet!"

William, nodded in bewilderment, "Yes, of course... Tweety." The men snickered.

"So, you invited Mr. Steinbeck to dinner to repay the courtesy?" Rothery surmised.

"Yes."

"And you haven't seen him since the restaurant?"

"No... I mean, yes. He was shot, so we went to the hospital to make sure he was alright. He was understandably distraught and I offered to pay for his bill. There wasn't much more to it than that. They released him and he went to his hotel, I suspect. He mentioned wanting to go home. He's probably stateside by now."

"You know you can replace your SIM and contact your service provider to get your service up and running immediately," Rothery mentioned.

Shaking her head, "I'm sorry, I didn't understand a word you just said there."

"He's talking about getting your phone working again, Victoria," William explained.

"If you do, and Mr. Steinbeck should ring, you'll give us a call, won't you?"

"Absolutely."

"I still don't understand why you are looking for him," William said. "What has he done?"

The two men thought to answer. Dylan explained, "What he did was clearly heroic. But the fact that he has disappeared is curious, don't you agree? And I'm certain you understand that a man with such abilities, in any case, is a potential risk, as well."

"He's a good man," Victoria defended.

"What caused him to engage the criminals?" Rothery questioned. "Do you remember? You were under the table with him... what caused him to get up?"

Victoria thought a moment. "I asked him to."

Rothery stopped. "You asked him to," he repeated thoughtfully. "Hmm, you're a beautiful woman... but you asked a complete stranger, not your husband, to face down three armed men— killers? What are you not telling us?"

"If you met him..." Victoria's voice trailed off. She knew her ruse was faltering.

"Oh, I intend to," Dylan said with uncharacteristic venom.

Victoria glared at Dylan, turning back to Rothery, "If you met him for even a moment, you would have asked him, too. And he would have."

"Ms. Adams, that's sounds like an extraordinary man. Help me understand. Had you seen him kill before?"

"That's quite a question," she retorted.

William hadn't considered that possibility. True, Victoria was changed, but the restaurant video was hard to ignore. Maybe he had been duped? "Victoria has gone through an extraordinary event— we both have. I'm not sure that any of us who were at the restaurant know exactly what happened or what was said. To be quite honest, I keep expecting to wake up and find this whole incident was a dream." He cleared his throat, glancing hesitantly at Victoria, "But then again, if I were to be entirely forthcoming..."

"Don't you dare, William," Victoria warned.

William paused but continued, "Victoria has been under a lot of stress lately, gentlemen."

"William!"

"She is under physician care and medication. She has been..."

"Screw you, William!" Victoria got up, threw her scotch glass, and stormed out of the room. Multiple doors slamming trailed her exit.

Her husband shook his head. "She's not been herself. Matter of fact, she has gone off her meds. This trip was an unscheduled vacation for her. I didn't even know where she was until she called after meeting Mi..."

"Mr. Steinbeck?"

"Yes. It's not completely uncommon for her to find a hero of sorts. It's a by-product of the industry we work in; always looking for the knight in shining armor. As you can imagine, it makes her easily persuadable and often entangles her with the wrong sorts."

"I understand. And I'm here to tell you, Mr. Cleese, that Mr. Steinbeck is NOT the right sorts," Dylan warned vehemently.

Rothery covered his mouth in thought. He rose and paced the room.

"As I said, Victoria's vulnerable. I made an urgent trip to London because of her detailed description of him."

"And what were your initial thoughts on Steinbeck?" Dylan probed.

William earnestly considered. "Well, prior to the incident, he would have been a typical find for her. Still, I have to admit, there was something different about him."

"Different how?"

"He was not as cocky as the usual charlatans, he had a humble demeanor. Of course I do realize that could be part of the ruse, but it seemed extremely genuine. Why? What do you know about him? I would greatly appreciate any information you can give me. Our marriage is not traditional, but I am still Victoria's benefactor."

"Steinbeck is definitely powerful. But he's secretive which also makes him dangerous. Brilliant sociopaths have motives, Mr. Cleese." Dylan's answer caused Rothery to frown.

"You think he's a sociopath?" William's face showed concern.

"Or a psychopath. How else might you explain a man casually facing down three armed terrorists without conscience of harm?"

"Oh, my god." William covered his head, closing his eyes to consider what Dylan was suggesting. He was tempted to tell the police everything. He rose and walked about the room, toiling with the realization of what kind of danger Victoria could have been in. William poured himself a double from the crystal decanter. Remembering the YouTube video, he pictured the force of Micah's hand around the neck of the young terrorist; the rage it must have taken. He thought of how that could have easily been Victoria. He looked toward the men, their anticipation blatant. He felt like an injured gazelle.

Victoria listened outside the door, "Please, William... please don't," she begged under her breath.

William sat back down in his chair, staring into his drink. He slowly rose his head to speak.

For some reason he couldn't. William couldn't get passed what Micah had said about his son— his moment with him in the study. But at the same time he also remembered Micah's words declaring there was no hope for him. And he would never forgive himself if he allowed Victoria to fall into danger.

"Mr. Cleese? Mr. Cleese? Is there something you want to tell us?" Dylan pushed.

"Yes."

Victoria held her breath outside the door, touching the knob. Rothery heard the creek and saw the shadow of her feet under the door.

William was slow to speak, definitely something heavy upon his tongue, "You're wrong about Mi... my wife's friend. You're wrong. I don't remember much from the restaurant, but there was a little girl crying at the table next to ours—and Victoria's plea. I saw his face... the look on his face."

Tears hid behind the curtain of William's eyelids as he pictured his son who had taken so much abuse from him yet still wanted nothing more than to please him. William let the first tear flow then proudly wiped it away. "I saw a man ready to die, gentlemen— had conceded to die to save a child. The little girl next to us, a girl he didn't know. Her mother's prayers, not for herself but for her daughter, still echo in my head. And I saw a man willing to rise to his feet. And I hate that I didn't." William could barely speak. "He conceded to die. That's what I saw."

Victoria whimpered in relief, embracing the door. Rothery, standing on the other side, heard her gesture and subtly reached his hand out as if to touch the knob. Deciding against it, he turned back toward William.

"That's a sweet story." Dylan was unconvincing in his attempt to sympathize. "Quite touching. I'm certain the tragic events have affected all those involved in different ways. It's impossible to know what REALLY happened. As I'm sure you know, eyewitnesses are most unreliable under duress, but it is a nice story. Stories like that are why sociopaths run loose in our streets victimizing people like your wife. But as you said, she's easily tempted."

"Dylan," Rothery warned.

William stared at Dylan, his face void of emotion.

"I feel sorry for you, William. What she must put you through. You... and your son."

Rothery interrupted, "Dylan, I think we have bothered these fine people long enough. We won't keep you any longer, Mr. Cleese." He rose to his feet, "If you hear from Mr. Steinbeck, please contact us. If he's the hero you say he is, then he should be celebrated."

William remained curt, "We certainly will. Thank you for your trouble. Please tell the PM we appreciate his sympathies."

Dylan took in a deep breath returning to his usual pleasant demeanor, "I will."

"Thank you again for your time, Mr. Cleese," Rothery concluded, "and tell Ms. Adams we didn't mean to upset her."

Victoria slipped away from the door to remain unseen as William showed the men to the front of the manor.

As they walked to the car Dylan looked to Rothery, "Thoughts?"

"I'm hungry," he responded blandly.

"I'll buy. Italian?"

"Fine."

"Italian's splendid for pork," Dylan grunted. "God, some people are just nuts, yeah?"

"Hmm."

"That's it? Have you nothing to say?"

"Processing."

"I thought your specialty was processing quickly?"

Rothery looked thoughtfully at Dylan. He sighed, "Well, she loves him."

"Cleese?"

"Perhaps. But certainly our avenger. I suppose it's to be expected; him having saved her life. His name is not Allen Steinbeck, by the way."

"Why do you say that?"

"Never did Mr. Cleese say either name, Allen or Steinbeck— almost uncomfortably. Though he almost gave it up at one point. My guess is that his name starts with an M, or at least the name he gave does... possibly Michael."

"Michael, huh?" Dylan considered. "I think William is in love with him too," he added sarcastically. "Do you think they had a little ménage à trois?"

Rothery remained serious, biting his lip, "No, I don't think so. Their affection is genuine. It seems like a strange form of reverse Erotomania."

"Euro what?"

"Erotomania is a syndrome where a person believes a celebrity loves them and is sending telepathic messages through images in the media. I suspect Victoria Adams has her share of eroto-admirers. I would also guess the reverse affect is possibly equally common; celebrities seeking some reality in their fantastic lifestyle." It sounded plausible. *Still, Mr. Cleese's toil did indicate such sincerity.*

Rothery wished he had gotten more. "What was your rant at the end, Dylan? He wanted to give us more information. All of a sudden you became insulting."

"I don't know, I got carried away. I'm new to this— thought, good cop/bad cop? But honestly, Rothery, he needed to see the seriousness of his situation. Could you imagine if this thrill-seeking, self-appointed vigilante wanted eternal fame? He could certainly attain that by killing them both in their own house— and they would let him in the front door!"

"Well, Cleese was believable enough. You do remember, though, that Mr. Steinbeck has yet to do anything besides defend himself and the people he was with, don't you?" the agent reminded.

"Yes, yes, of course," Dylan replied flippantly. "But these sorts are dangerous. Take my advice, mate... when we find him, if he flinches, don't hesitate. I know I won't."

Chapter 40

"VIC!" WILLIAM CALLED.

Victoria walked sullenly into the study.

"I didn't mean to..." William started.

"I know," she responded, "I know, I was trapped. Once he asked where I met Micah, I knew I'd lost my footing. But you jumped in at the right moment... the bit about my delusions was actually perfect. I heard the whole conversation, I was listening behind the door."

"I really don't understand their obsession with hunting him down. Shouldn't they be honoring his heroics?"

"You'd think."

"God, that Dylan guy? He's bent."

"You saw that too?" Victoria frowned.

"Oh, and he got worse after you left. He seemed to be fishing."

"What was the name of the other guy?"

"Rothery Taylor," he answered.

"That guy is scary."

"Why?"

"He's smart. He was reading right through me."

"Something's bothering you about it," William observed.

"It's nothing. I don't care about those guys, I don't care what they think."

"I didn't think so, but you're somewhere else."

"It's hard to come up with what is real, William. I don't know how to move on from here." She shook her head. "I can't make sense of everything... it's like my whole world has been turned upside down. I'm not sure how to apply..." she stopped to think.

"Apply what?"

Shaking her head, "...anything. Everything."

"You've been through a traumatic experience, dear, it will take time. You'll be different— you ARE different, but you'll be the same, too. That's not to say that it may not be difficult for a while to distinguish between the two."

"He has something though— Micah, I mean. Doesn't he?"

"It's hard to say but he got to me, too," William laughed.

"That's saying a lot. You're a sorry son of a bitch."

"Thanks for noticing."

Introspectively, William put his head in his hands considering his entire life. "We traverse this mess called life leaving wreckage in our wake," he began. He thought about everything they'd been through in recent days, "We've done alright. We've done alright, but I can't contemplate it... my own reconciliation is impossible." With a sorrowful frown he sat speechless for a moment, occasionally closing his eyes and shaking his head with obvious, hard-to-dismiss regret.

Victoria sat silently, stunned by the words coming from her husband's mouth.

"I think the best we can do is repair what's laying before us, pray for what lies beyond, and try to do better," he finally summarized.

"Who the hell are you?" The stoic, tower of a man Victoria had known her whole life was now remorseful, regretful, grateful— changed.

"I can't fix anything, Victoria. I'm too old. No one would believe me anyway. My life has been a con."

Victoria hadn't considered the impact the terrorist attack may have had on William. He had been a driving force in her life; an unwavering SOB but consistent, reliable— and for the most part in her defense.

"You know, your magic man said something to me," he said quietly.

"What was that?" she asked.

"He said that I was beyond..."

"What?"

William paused, deciding on second thought to refrain from disparaging Micah. "He said that Jeremy was special. That Jeremy was my pursuit's reward."

"How did that come up?"

"I made him angry. It was strange; he thought to curse me and instead said Jeremy was the king I sought."

"Hmm. I told you."

"Honestly, when Dylan pressed," he continued, "it wasn't that I didn't want to sellout Micah. I was tempted to rid us of this. It was just I couldn't sell out my son... give up the hope I have for him now— for the both of us." He straightened his shoulders, "But that still doesn't change my daily life, Victoria, and it shouldn't change yours. Be happy, dear, and enjoy your newfound freedom. I can see you're thinking about throwing it away. Honestly, what can Micah offer? A life on the run?"

"It's more fundamental than that, William."

"It's an adventure, sure. But the cost? You've had plenty of adventures. And believe me, between you and him, there are far more people who would rather be you."

The words hit Victoria wrong— or just right. They summed up her entire life. She had everything; money, fame, freedom to go and do whatever, wherever she wanted. William was right. No sane person wouldn't want the life she had lived. *I have everything to lose... the rest of my life slowly depreciating into nothing. And for the rest of my life I would have just kept looking back at what I was had I not met this man.*

Then it dawned on her. "Had I met anyone else, William... do you realize that anyone else would have wanted MY life? Anyone else would have wanted one tenth of what I have— it's the American Dream. I AM the American Dream." She thought about it some more, "Anyone, but him."

"Then by definition, he is crazy," William replied.

"No, it's just something about him that very few can understand. That's why... what if..."

William looked at her.

"I was in Seattle," Victoria continued, surprise in her voice.

"Yes, so? What the hell does that mean?"

"I was in Seattle," she explained, "not long after high school, remember? That's where I met Kramer."

"I hated that guy. What he did to you..."

"He was..." she stammered to speak, "he was the devil. But..." she stopped mid-stream, "Oh, my god!"

"What?"

She had an epiphany, "He WAS the devil! He's why I left Seattle, why I flew to New York!"

"I'm not following you."

"Micah lived in Seattle."

"Honey, you're starting to sound like him now."

Her eyes opened wide, "I am!" Victoria's head began to nod, she was excited. "Do you think he knows?"

"Do I think who knows?"

"Micah."

"Knows what?"

"I've got to go." She turned to head towards the door.

"Where are you going? Does Micah know what?"

"That he is the life I was supposed to live," she declared, running out of the room and calling over her shoulder, "or better yet... that I am the life HE was supposed to live!"

"Can he act?" William called back.

Victoria's laughter floated down the hallway.

Chapter 41

SITTING ON A BENCH in Chinatown near Piccadilly Square as evening settled in, Micah wore a long, black wool coat with a matching fedora brimmed low to cover his appearance from passersby. He was waiting for Victoria.

She was fifteen minutes late. He hadn't known her long enough to know whether she was typically prompt or late, but he knew, given their circumstances, she would not have left him waiting. Not today.

A couple passed by. He glanced up to see them smiling and cheerful as were most in Piccadilly Square any day of the year. But as they gazed in his direction it appeared their faces distorted; stretched with elongated snouts and fangs. Then the howl of a caged cat lost in the background noise of the usual hustle and bustle of the square, suddenly crept to the surface and roared just beneath a conscious plane causing Micah's fingernails to grow sensitive.

He closed his eyes. These things were not a threat. They were mere receptacles of his presence. Not of Micah's, but of the hunter's— the one Ring Finger had spoken of.

Micah knew he was close by. He sat still, eyes remaining closed until a sharp pain like a migraine struck him like an icepick above his right brow. The pain showed him where the hunter stood. Opening his eyes, Micah quickly turned his head, looking across the street and down a darkened alley. He didn't need to see the hunter with his physical eyes, he knew he was there.

"What are you waiting for?" Micah whispered to the air. "I know you can hear me. Did you also know I can feel you?" Disgust in his voice, "You're not moving? Why? Run away or come for me!" he commanded. Still, there was no movement from the dark thoroughfare.

It was in the absence of action that Micah suddenly understood. *You're just a decoy.* Raising his gaze to the left, he saw two men a half-block down the road. They were dressed as tourists but unmistakably agents. *SIS or less,* Micah thought. "They can't be with you... or are they?" The possibility was puzzling. *Since when have you played with the authorities... you command SIS now? Interesting.* "What are you doing in London?"

With that question, the presence was gone. It was like waking from a dream. The hunter's presence when felt was all encompassing— only a fine line lay between being drawn in and controlled by it, and Micah's ability to see beyond the natural. It was dangerous to engage with such energy, even for him. Like pitching a tent toward Sodom, he could find himself living in the middle of it.

"What scared you?" Micah hollered toward the alley, "What chased you away?" He lowered his voice and spoke quietly as he pondered. "Your purpose in London is more than me," he accused the air. Though knowing the presence was gone, Micah still believed his words were not spoken in vain. "You've dedicated much time in pursuit of me, but I'm not the only reason you're here. Or am I? What is it you fear? I must be close once again."

The two agents moved slowly, waiting for backup. Micah, sure they had identified him, knew his leash was short. He wouldn't get away naturally. As he considered the unlikeliness of escape, he noticed an Asian restaurant across the street that seemed familiar like déjà vu, just beyond his recollection. Having learned to trust that feeling over the years, he stood up quickly and headed in the restaurant's direction. All the lights, glass and brass of Chinatown made for nice reflections to watch for people coming up from behind.

Upon entering the establishment, Micah was certain the building had an upstairs. *Why am I looking for stairs?* he scoffed at himself. *The second biggest get-away blunder— never, EVER run upstairs when being chased by bad guys.* The authorities might not have been terrible, but THEY thought HE was, which made them equally dangerous. The last thing Micah wanted to do was to hurt someone who was less than a bad guy. He had seen enough bloodshed to last a life-time— even two.

He found the staircase at the front of the restaurant. Against his better judgment, Micah alighted the steps swiftly, ignoring his natural hesitation. Down the hall, *One, two, three… the third door on the right,* he thought as if he had been there before. He could hear the men coming up the stairs after him as he shut himself in the third room. *This is crazy! Certainly I've trapped myself.*

Looking around the room Micah was startled— there were chains fastened to the floor. "What the…?" But then he remembered the dream he'd had almost a week before. *A Chinese restaurant, chained to the floor.* "It was here."

In the dream there had been a spiral staircase, but in reality there wasn't one to be seen. *There's got to be one somewhere…* Desperately searching with his gut as much as his eyes, he rolled back a worn ornamental rug, hoping his memory hadn't elaborated on the vision. There, under the carpet, a trapdoor concealed a thin spiral staircase.

Shutting the trapdoor behind to give himself a few extra seconds' distance between himself and his pursuers, Micah rushed down the stairs into the back of a kitchen supply closet. At the bottom he spotted the back door leading into a blocked alley behind the run-down establishment. He quickly pushed through it.

The dimness of the alley revealed no alcoves or doorways for refuge; it was a 100-yard dash down the passage and back to the lit street. *I'll never make it unseen, backup has got to be closing down the neighborhood.* Micah had been a runner his entire life and could still make the distance, but the dash? It was doubtful.

Footsteps closed in clattering down the flight of stairs. Assuming that the front was already covered meant his pursuers would be heading for the back either through or around the building. He saw no hope of doing anything but running smack into the authorities. *What's with this restaurant and the chains on the floor? Why a vision that most assuredly leads to my demise?* Detrimental foretelling was not what he'd come to expect over the years.

With no options, Micah took off running, his toes digging into the ground like the track star of his youth. He ran with surprising ease giving him a strange sense of confidence that didn't falter, even as the young agents hit the backdoor hard and continued their pursuit. The sound of their feet on the worn alley pavement growing louder, he was less than thirty yards from capture.

As Micah approached the street he knew agents were likely on the other side in both directions. They would undoubtable see him whichever direction he chose. Twenty yards or less from the main thoroughfare and the awaiting agents; his attempt at escape seemed futile until suddenly a cab pulled up and stopped directly in front of him. The door opened and a couple hurriedly exited the cab in perfect timing. Not losing a moment's momentum, Micah leaped into the hackney, "Drive!" he ordered, trying to catch his breath.

Without hesitation the driver pulled away, "Where to, governor?"

"Saint Paul's Cathedral."

"Might I suggest Hyde Park at this time of night?'

"That's all the way on the other side of town and in the opposite direction."

"I know a short cut," the cabby offered.

Micah smiled wryly, "That's still in the opposite direction."

The driver turned right when Micah knew he needed to go left, then turned swiftly into an alley veering into an underground parking garage. The cab drove three levels down and four levels back up until the hackney emerged from the other side of the building. They took a sharp right and maneuvered a few lane changes until the vehicle miraculously disappeared, leisurely heading west toward Hyde Park in a stream of identical hackney taxicabs.

Micah was speechless. A year of planning could not have timed such an assured getaway. Only blocks from an army of SIS agents and he was unquestionably gone. Still, Micah wasn't ready to heave a sigh of relief as an even more important question hit his mind… was this driver friend or foe? "Do you know something I don't?" Micah asked the cabby when they stopped at a light.

The driver turned around. He removed a hat and glasses, pealed-off a ginger beard and plastic nose. The familiar voice of Kip answered, "I know a number of things you don't."

"What the hell?!" Micah was utterly stunned.

"I set up the meeting, remember? I've been watching you for over half an hour."

"Really? Then wouldn't it have been easier to have just pulled up and picked me up at the bench?!"

"Sure— if those goons hadn't been following you."

"Oh, you saw them, too, huh?"

"Yeah, looks like they followed Victoria. Clever girl by the way, she texted me when she suspected as much. Wasn't sure if this was it for you, actually… but quite honestly, I was more interested to know if this was it for ME."

"Thanks, I appreciate your concern," Micah, said half sarcastically. "But how did you know I would be coming out the back alley?"

"If you came out the front door, you would have been in hand-cuffs and you wouldn't have needed a cab."

Micah thought about it for a second but couldn't argue the insensitive logic. "Then how'd you time it so perfect— opening the door just in time for me to jump in at full sprint?"

"I thought I was a bit late," Kip confessed.

"Hold on… who were the people in the car?"

"Oh, that was my son and his fiancé. I offered to buy them dinner if they'd sit in the car with me until you were ready to take their place. By the way, that

Chinese restaurant you ran through...? Excellent moo goo gai pan! We were trying to read their menu-board from the cab."

"Huh," Micah resigned, rather impressed.

"So?" Kip inquired, "Where to, governor?"

"I don't know."

"Things are way too hot to get you out now."

"Yeah, it may be a foregone conclusion. It's only a matter of time. It's time to call Dale."

"Ow. Don't call him."

"What's wrong with Dale?"

"He hates me."

"No, he doesn't," Micah argued.

"He always gives me shit."

"That's just how he is."

"To everyone?"

"Yeah."

"What do you see in that guy?" Kip shook his head.

"He's funny, he makes me laugh."

"He's not funny. You do know he doesn't joke, don't you? He isn't sarcastic, he's really like that. He's an ass."

"Yeah, that's funny."

"Sometimes you amaze me, my friend." Kip rolled his eyes, "You're like Shakespeare enjoying a Jim Carey movie. Seriously, what do you of all people see in that guy?"

"He's my left arm."

"You can say that again, he throws like a damn girl."

"Well, he's my right brain, then. If he was a girl, I would have married him long ago."

"The things you say," Kip shook his head in disbelief.

"You can't assume to know someone's thoughts or prayers. I'd take ten Dales any day. You do know why he acts like that, don't you?"

"Not a clue."

"Because he believes in people far more than you or I do. His behavior, his demeanor? That's his façade of humility. He acts that way so people of less-conviction feel more comfortable around the likes of you and me." Micah spoke with sincere respect. "In the end, we may find Dale obtains sainthood long before either of us. He would die for me without a thought or hesitation... Dale would have picked me up on the bench."

"Hey, careful. I would have picked you up on the bench, I just had my kids in the car."

Micah nodded, "I know you would of." Then he grinned, "Dale would have picked YOU up on the bench."

"Really?" Kip was clearly surprised, even a bit touched. "Me?"

"Hell, no," Micah chuckled, "he hates you." Micah burst into laughter.

Kip grumbled under his breath, "Knew it."

Chapter 42

"THIS IS CAROL CUMMINGS with Sky News Morning Edition. We're here talking with Henry Wilkens, investigative reporter for the Register Guard; two-time winner of the prestigious British Journalism award and author of Brutal Blinds, an insider's look at political decision-making in Parliament. Mr. Wilkens, good to have you back."

"Thank you, it's a pleasure to be here."

"We haven't heard from you for some time, Henry, and now it appears you are topping the charts— or at least in the political circles of London." Carol's voice resonated with captivating intrigue.

"Well, that was certainly not my intention."

"Still, these charges leveled against you on grandstanding regarding the recent terrorist attack must be taking a toll?"

"It's to be expected, Carol. It seems to be plan of record— or should I say, the strategy of the occupants of Downing Street to bash the messenger."

"And you're not immune to such accusations, are you, Henry? I hate to admit I am old enough to remember that bit you bumbled during the Cameron administration."

"Did I?" Henry laughed, although he was surprised to hear a reference to the decade-old issue that ruined his career. He was under the impression he had been invited onto the show to discuss his recent work uncovering the details of the terrorist attack— his exposing the inadequacies of Scotland Yard and the PM's Office, along with their pursuit of a hero rather than dealing with another Islamic extremist terrorist attack— not to discuss his claim to shame.

"Something you'd like to add?"

Henry smiled, "No. Public opinion was biased in favor of Washington and the PM's war at the time… but clearly now, mistakes have been brought to light. There is no value in vendetta, Carol, the issues of today are quite sufficient for the day."

"How do you respond to the accusation leveled by the BBC concerning you politicizing a terrorist attack?"

"I think the British people are tired of the same old montage of character assassinations brought on by the media and its supporters. We used to speak of the media as supporters of political policies. Now I think the reverse is true; politicians seem to be puppets of the media's agenda. We certainly saw that true in the American elections of 2016. But neither side truly represents the will of the people, and inevitably in time, that will be changed by due process prodded by an open market. That is why I appreciate the a-political liberty I am given at the Guard… and of course here, at Sky News."

"It's great you've mentioned the Register Guard; have you seen the latest video they've got on their site? It's gone viral."

"How recent?" Henry asked with concern.

"Only moments before you came on," Carol smiled. "Let's watch now."

The video opened with a scene Henry knew all too well; outside his ex-wife's place of employment, the 'Booty Nail Manicure and Wax Shop' near Liverpool station.

Henry's cheekbones strained from his attempt to maintain a smile— the studio cameraman mere inches from a side-profile of his face. His eyes rapidly blinking, holding back a grimacing squint; he pursed his lips together in anticipation of the inevitable pain soon to befall him.

Time dragged before none other than his second ex-wife was center stage.

Henry realized by this point he was sporting a wide-eyed, sphincter face with an uncontrollable protruding tongue. His head was shaking a twitch not uncommon to the average drug addict or mental patient. He quickly covered his mouth with his hand, trying to maintain control of his bobbing head.

Carol smiled with eager anticipation.

The video started with Sara Jennings announcing, "We're here today with Mrs. Henry Wilkens."

"Former Mrs. Wilkens, thank you," Beatrice corrected.

"The former Mrs. Wilkens, wife of Henry Wilkens, reporter and self-appointed political critic. Mrs. Wilkens, what do you think of the recent allegations leveled against your husband?"

"Former."

"Former husband, concerning his aggrandizing on the backs of victims?"

Beatrice pulled up her spandex tights, adjusted a minor wardrobe creep both in the front and backside, spit her gum into her hand and responded in a thick Cockney accent, "That's Henry, it is. He'll do anything for a story. Loves the limelight, he does. But it always comes back 'round to bite him on the arse. Can I say 'arse' on the telly?"

By the time the camera pulled back around to Henry, he sat composed with a thought provoking ponder and a saddened disposition. Carol Cummings, still smiling, "Henry? Comments?"

"Well, Carol, it's tragic to say the least. Just seeing her there..." Henry bowed his head in a sorrowful display.

"Tragic?"

Henry nodded, pausing momentarily. He started to speak but then looked up toward the ceiling searching for the right sympathetic words. "It's clear... that rehab... has been less than successful for the former Mrs. Wilkens," too choked-up to continue.

"Take your time, Henry."

"In some strange and bizarre way— despite all I tried to do— I blame myself for her condition."

With an attempt to appear sincere, Carol slowly nodded, "Oh, that's quite awful, isn't it? So, it was the drink that ruined your marriage?"

Henry just bowed his head, nodding in agreement. "The drink and…" with a poetic pause emphasizing his regretful expression, "…and worse."

"Oohh," the studio audience expressed with sympathy. Henry hid his pleasure.

Carol at first appeared sympathetic but quickly changed, "That's interesting Henry, because she tells a different story. Let's continue, shall we?"

Henry's eyes got big.

"Please, go on Beatrice."

"Righto. So, one time my folks had gone on holiday…"

Henry's mouth dropped, "Oh, God!" he choked.

"I went over to water the plants and I found Henry bumping uglies with the press secretary of the local MK… in my parent's bed, I did! And when I say uglies, I don't know how the two of them fit comfortably on my mother's queen, if you know what I mean."

"I think we do," Sara commented.

"When I confronted him, he told me it was all part of an investigative reporter's job to get the dirt on crooked politicians and all."

The camera spun back to Henry to find his hand over his mouth, eyebrows furrowed; eyes wide in a look of panic. He quickly adjusted back to his sorrowful expression of concern.

Carol asked with too much unconcealed pleasure, "Henry, any comments?"

When Henry held up a hand to speak, Carol gave him a look of disgust and held up her own hand, stopping him from any further self-mutilation. "Don't bother, Henry," she said as she turned back to the monitor where the video continued.

Beatrice was speaking, "It was right hideous, it was… I couldn't help but film it all." Beatrice held up her phone.

Carol, squinting at the video feed, "That's the new Samsung 7-inch display. Lovely."

Sara Jennings asked the cameraman, "Zoom in, yeah?"

Henry heard Kevin's voice, "Righto," as the video zoomed into Beatrice's display flaunting the consistent motion of Henry's unmistakable ass in midair, barely covering most of the big woman's private parts.

"You can't show that on the air!" Henry immediately objected.

"Oh, no?" Carol taunted. "No, Henry, we won't show the phone video. When we do air, we will just cut to the YouTube version in full HD. Our video technician is working now to blur out the unmentionables for appropriate television discretion. This is a family show."

Camera one back on Henry. Carol asked, "Working hard there for the story, Henry?"

Henry paused, head bowed. Finally he raised it with a nod. "As reporters—journalists, Carol…" with a sniff and a tear, "we try hard to separate our personal lives, our opinions. We don't have the luxury to taint the issues with our preferences, our politics; only reporting the facts. It's for the people to decide."

Carol, becoming irritated, wondered where he was going.

"But every once in a while our lives, our opinions, our challenges do matter. Maybe our lives can make a difference. You see…" dramatic pause, "…the real reason for the dissolution of my marriage… the real reason for my poor, unfortunate wife's ongoing DRUG ADDICTIONS and BI-POLAR MENTAL tendencies…"

Carol, now completely annoyed, "Stay on point, Henry."

"…was that I was not true to her." The audience gasped in unison.

"Not in the way that you think, mind you," Henry continued, mustering tears now, "*true*, in the fact that I wasn't being *true* to MYSELF.

"You see, my father was a war hero; raised in a house of discipline and with certain expectations. I've spent a lifetime trying to honor him (God rest his soul!) But now that he has since passed, I suppose it is finally time that I tell him—tell you, tell the world… and, blimey, tell myself…

"My dear friends, my sexual improprieties were not cheating on my lovely wife; I was cheating on ME, trying to live up to my father. You see, I've been a liar. Not in the column (that is my sacred oath!) and not on camera… but my whole life has been a lie because I've been trying to be the man my father was.

"But I think today, with your help, Carol, and with the help of the lovely audience here and at home, I can truly be TRUE; by finally admitting to the world… to you, to my former wives and to myself…" (dramatic pause) "…that I am a homosexual."

"Awwe," the audience sighed. The producer and other staff members cheered and clapped in unison. The cameraman gave Henry a thoughtful nod and thumbs up. Henry just nodded and smiled, wiping tears from the corners of his eyes.

The camera view returned to Carol. Her face hurt from the strain of maintaining a smile. Her eyes now rapidly blinking, holding back a grimace; her lips, pressed tightly together. Attempting composure, she smoothed her lipstick with her tongue as if to remove a bad taste from her mouth as she quickly and uncomfortably pulled herself together.

Her head bobbing with so many things she desired to say as she gazed over the applauding live audience; the cameramen focusing, the blinking red light— she emulated a heartfelt gasp and turned to the camera for a close-up, "Well, you heard it here; the touching, heartfelt story of a man… being true… to himself… on national television, no less."

"And we're off!" the producer called. "Quite touching, Henry."

"Way to go, mate!" the cameraman cheered. The audience continued to clap as Henry rose from his seat, graciously nodding and making his way backstage.

"What a total load of shit!" Carol accused, pulling her earpiece out of her ear. "You were trying to look up my skirt the entire interview!"

"So? Take the Jaws of Life to separate those knees," Henry retorted. "What are you hiding up there? It can't be all that."

"You're a piece of work, Henry."

"What are you complaining about? I'm sure I just boosted your ratings. You and this corporate whorehouse you call a news room… by next week they will have redone the entire studio in rainbows and changed the name of the show to 'Coming Out with Carol'. Byline will read, 'See who Carol finds in her closet this week!' "

"Hey, that isn't bad," the producer responded thoughtfully, "did you hear that audience?"

"Ah, fuck all!" spouted Carol.

"No seriously…" the producer chased after Carol, "I bet we could get married politicians on the show if their constituent demographics matched. What do you think?"

Henry wiped his face with a stage rag and headed toward the door.

Chapter 43

"WELL, THIS IS A LITTLE sooner than expected," Micah said with playful sarcasm suggesting that three days apart was not nearly long enough.

"Oh, really? Your mouth says one thing but your eyes say another, Micah Graff."

"Hmm, that obvious, huh? They give me away?"

Victoria tilted her head with a slight smile and shrug.

Micah, taken by the coy response, raised a surprised brow. "There is something different about you, Victoria Adams. This is not the same woman I met on the plane a week ago."

"Do tell."

"I could say your eyes betray you, as well. They're a deeper shade of blue."

"What might that mean? And I expect to be dazzled by your perceptiveness and wit."

"Ugh, the pressure," Micah smiled. "Then pray, allow me a second moment's gaze."

"So be it, good sir."

Victoria, a tad taken by the poetic weave of his request, dawned a flirtatious countenance, closed her eyes for dramatic effect, removed the sunglasses from her brow. She brushed back her flowing chestnut hair, fastened it into a bun atop her head, and moved in close until he could feel her breath upon his chest. With a slow, sensual gesture she opened her eyes. To her delight, his expression was speechless— though his mouth did not refrain from clamor:

"Hope has never been more
satisfied… thirst never been so
quenched than to gaze upon the
piercing blade atop cupid's
arrowhead.
Am I the first to see the sky above,
am I first to ocean's depth… does
my heart fail me now— leave me
here to dream; if so, I pray never
awake, for waking eyes have
never seen."

"Keep going," she cooed.

"I can until my eyes pluck out and
ears fail to hear; and even so, I
sense and know whether you be
near.
I suspect that when my heart
gives out and I lay beneath the
Earth; your presence today I take
with me since long before my
birth.
If He be true who placed the stars
and counts them in the sky; He
gave to me one simple thing, and I
see it now… in your eyes.

"Stop," she whispered. Victoria smiled from ear to ear, closed her eyes and leaned upon his chest. "God help me."

They stood silent for some time until Victoria finally spoke, "How do you do that?"

"I hope you are speaking of more than my rhyme."

"I think you know I am."

"I do."

"A girl waits a lifetime to hear those words."

Micah laughed.

* * * * *

Victoria and Micah strolled the Tower Castle waiting for their rooms to be prepared. Having missed their rendezvous the day before, Victoria had used the extra time to covertly arrange their meeting. More people and not less seemed to be an acceptable strategy.

"Have you taken the tour?" she asked.

"Maybe, I can't remember. I've been to Windsor, though."

"Windsor is nice," Victoria said, "but the Tower is a real, in-the-heart-of-the-city fortress; ancient. Not a vacation spot for royalty."

As they entered the Jewel House vault, Micah wasn't sure why, but a sense of mourning suddenly fell upon him. At first he questioned whether it was because they were out in the open. *Am I endangering Victoria?* A rebuke echoed in Micah's head, *You're going to get her killed!* "This is not a game. It is NOT a game," he spoke just under his breath.

"Are you alright?" Victoria looked over at him with concern.

"I don't know." Micah glanced suspiciously around the main exhibit hall. A sword, mounted among the crown jewels, caught his attention. There was no fear, but for some reason he was unable to look directly upon the relic while at the same time, he was unable to turn his head away, either. It was as though the sword, too, was covered in guilt. Curious, Micah stopped straining to see it. He relaxed and closed his eyes.

Instantly, he was able to see the sword clearly in his mind. He saw the height, the breadth of it; the hilt, the pommel and the inscription surrounding the stone. It was familiar to him. In his mind he could turn the sword and see it from different angles, but more so, he could feel the weight of it as if it were in his hand— as if he had held it many times before. It was almost like remembering a dream; or more like waking from a dream to remember reality. But there was no reality for him and this sword— although it did remind him of a gift he had been given many years before. His eyes thoroughly closed, he read the inscription encompassing the pommel, *"Shame be to him who thinks evil of this."*

Micah opened his eyes and found he was now able to move his head. He turned to examine the sword in the display. But the inscription he could see with his eyes was written in French and too worn to read. Stepping up to the redcoat exhibit attendant he asked, "Excuse me, sir, what is written on the sword?"

The old man quickly responded with British pride, "'Honi soit qui mal y pense', which is French for 'Shame be to him…' "

"'…who thinks evil of this'," Micah finished.

"Aye. You know French?" asked the attendant.

"Apparently."

"Brilliant, sir!" The man smiled, nodded, and went off about his duties.

"Are you okay?" Victoria asked again.

"Getting better." But Micah still felt quiet, solemn. "Can you hold these for me?" He slipped off his shoes and socks.

* * * * *

Barefoot, Micah slowly walked the stone floor around the sword; a floor that dated back to the foundation of the castle or to at least one of the earliest renovations. His eyes, staring toward the floor, occasionally rose to the ceiling or walls. He was clearly looking past the tourists as if he were the only person in the room. His expression was fluid, changing— at first sad, then staring as if entertained watching an event play out. Other moments, he lowered his eyes refusing to look; like a child afraid of their parent's scorn, or as if witnessing something so horrific he couldn't bear to watch.

At one point Micah turned away from Victoria's direction, fearful. His expression so convincing, Victoria was afraid. She nearly screamed out, forcing to keep herself from rushing toward him. Although she refrained, the idea of even standing in the proximity of something that emotionally disturbed him so frightened her.

Then, after a few moments more (and more than a few gawking stares) Micah stopped wandering as he appeared to have found what he was looking for. An expression of accomplishment grew upon his face, his eyes shifting back and forth absorbing a great deal all at once.

His left foot already planted upon the floor, his right slid slowly over the stone looking for its place. First the balls of his toes; then once they, too, were planted, his heal fell into place like a baseball pitcher at the mound. Now standing firmly upon the ancient floor, Micah's stance suggested he was no longer an observer but a participant in the room's history— in the imagery he was seeing and now experiencing. Watching his eyes rapidly dart back and forth as if speedreading his surroundings, Victoria could only imagine he was traveling the room through time.

Finally his gaze slowed. Micah's hand began to rise from his side, preparing to gently touch something Victoria couldn't see. One of the guards, noticing this particular action as more peculiar than any of his previous ones (either that, or it was the straw that broke the proverbial camel's back), took a step towards them. Spying the guard, Victoria quickly moved into the man's line of sight, reaching her hand toward Micah as if preparing to join him in an embrace. In an attempt to conceal the odd gesture and lead the attendant and spectators to believe he was interacting with her rather than mindlessly meandering barefoot in a public place, Victoria complemented Micah's motions like a dance.

As she glanced over her shoulder to assure her act was convincing, Micah leaned forward and touched her. Startled, she quickly regained her composure, cautiously focusing on their dance, careful to not further alarm the guard nor disturb Micah from what she assumed must have been a vision of some kind.

Micah's eyes slowly rose up toward Victoria. *What is he seeing?* she wondered in awe. His expression was so full, so intense. *Is it his child? His deceased wife?*

Micah's eyes followed his hand, both slowly raising them in a motion destined to meet Victoria's cheek. *How can one man feel so much? It's emotionally exhausting just to watch.* "He will surely be the end of me," she sighed. Compassion, love, sadness, joy; even gratefulness in the face of loss— all written upon his beautiful face.

She found herself once again playing a role, a stand in. But not on a stage nor in front of a camera; this time at a historical monument surrounded by tourists and guards… with a man who was either gifted and brilliant, or absolutely insane. Victoria took in a resigned breath. Either way, she needed to keep him safe. This man was being sought by every authority in the country, as well as god-knows-who-else. *Kip's southern polarized magnets,* Victoria thought, lacking a better description of the bad guys. This spectacle of barefoot dancing (with a celebrity, no less) at a premium tourist location amidst the crown jewels and a host of guards, was probably the least prudent thing Micah could do given his situation. Still, she not only couldn't help feeling it was necessary, but after seeing the emotion in his eyes, she also couldn't help wanting to be the object of such intense passion.

"What if he looks right through me? Could I bear it?" Victoria wasn't even aware she had whispered aloud.

At that moment, Micah's rising hand intersected with her cheek. His look was elation, his touch a gentle brush. The tandem movement of his eyes and hand ending, left his fingertips resting upon her face. His eyes then shifted to her lips. His look of hunger— thirst— caused her desire. His gaze rose to meet hers. He now looked at her, not through her— passion and love near to tears. Though receptive, Victoria was unsure; still fearful she might merely be a stand-in for some unseen affection in Micah's vision.

Almost laughing, Micah smiled at her look of insecurity. He touched his other hand softly to her face.

Heart pounding, Victoria laid her palms upon his chest, gently pushing back enough to see all of him and more than just the emotion in his eyes. Staring earnestly, she needed to know if he was there with her or still in the vision miles (or centuries) away. Without thinking she whispered, "Am I the vision?"

Micah slowly ran his hands down Victoria's arms and laced his fingers with hers, "You certainly are. Let's go."

"Yes," was all she could manage. A hotel room seemed like a very good idea.

* * * * *

As they entered the Innermost Ward courtyard, Victoria noticed a man watching Micah. "Micah, there's a man at two o'clock looking at you."

Micah looked behind him. Victoria, correcting, "No, honey, our two o'clock... over there, to the right."

Looking to the right then back to Victoria, Micah appeared surprised. "Which man?"

"The tall man just standing there staring right at us." Victoria could not believe he'd asked.

Micah, still gawking, caused Victoria to sigh, "The only one not moving...? wearing black?"

"Stay here for a minute, okay? I'll call you over if..." Micah shrugged, "whatever."

"Okay. Fine, I guess." *Hmm...* Victoria mused, *I'm really getting into this whole cloak and dagger thing.* She proudly summarized to herself, *'Honey, he's at two o'clock'.* She smiled, *I noticed the man first!*

Micah walked directly to the tall stranger. There was no hesitation nor caution in his step, though when he stopped, Victoria thought it odd that Micah left just a bit more space between himself and the man than what seemed natural.

In what appeared to be squinting to an outside observer, Victoria watched the men's exchange from about fifty yards across the expansive courtyard. *What does the extra distance mean?* she wondered, proceeding to deduce. *If the man was a serious threat, Micah would have stayed back even further to better allow for reaction time. If it did move to violence, he would then likely close the gap. That doesn't seem to be the case here. Hmm. If it was a friend like Kip, on the other hand, Micah would have gone up a bit closer... and Kip would have broken all the rules of personal space and got up in his grill with a hug.* Victoria was stumped. *So, what does that distance mean?*

She folded her arms across her chest. *And look at how they're both standing; Micah's feet are close together while the other man's feet are spread a bit broader than shoulder-width. That's new, that's different.*

Victoria was now completely concentrated on the exchange. "He's reaching for you..." she commentated aloud. "Why aren't you reacting? Wait, is he handing you something? No, what are you holding? Why are you just standing there? Okay, that was sorta strange."

Victoria's thoughts were cut short when someone noticed her talking to herself, "Pardon me, but aren't you Victoria Adams?"

Always the master of improv, Victoria barely looked up. Answering in a heavy British accent, "Lookalike, mate... rehearsing for an advert."

With a could-have-fooled-me look, the man shrugged and backed away into the crowd leaving Victoria to return to her observations.

She slowly began walking toward Micah and the stranger in black. *I'll just act like I ran into them. Oh, wait, that won't work, he was watching us first.* Her steps hesitated. *Oh, screw it, I'm prom queen today.* And Victoria picked up the pace.

The courtyard suddenly became busy and more crowded. People began to bump into her, holding her up in what appeared to be almost intentional actions. "Turn around, it's none of your business," a stern voice came from behind her.

"Excuse me?" But when Victoria looked over her shoulder, it was a woman speaking to her daughter.

Victoria stepped aside trying to continue through the crowd. "Don't get any closer, stay back!" a man yelled in her face, glaring right at her and causing her to recoil. But that man, too, briskly passed by unnoticing, purposefully heading to stop another child from reaching an open display.

Trying to recommence her mission as the wave of people recessed, an even smaller boy playing in the courtyard ran just ahead of her with outstretched arms like an airplane, weaving back and forth.

Victoria veered right and the boy inadvertently changed directions. She then veered left. And although the child's back was turned, he followed suit over and over again in an awkward dance until she had no choice but to stop dead in her tracks. He seemed to be on an unavoidable collision course with her; each time she thought to step forward, the 'flying boy' soared past.

Just before running smack into her, the small child stopped abruptly. He spun and met Victoria's eyes, "What are you doing?!" he yelled sternly.

Victoria blinked, "What did you say?"

"I said, I'm flying an airplane... what are you doing?" The child looked long and hard at Victoria with innocent eyes, apparently waiting for an answer.

Victoria couldn't find the words. She just stood there staring. *What AM I doing? I guess I was supposed to wait, wasn't I?* An overwhelming feeling of apprehension held her for minutes.

The boy finally relinquished his stare, smiled and ran off giggling into a new tide of people.

No longer able to see Micah through the reemerged crowd, Victoria lowered her head continuing slowly. By the time she reached him, he was looking for her. The tall man in black was gone.

Victoria glanced around briefly, hoping to see where he had gone, "Who was that? Friend of yours and Kip's? Was that Felix or Dale?"

"No."

"Did he give you something?" she asked somberly.

"Advice."

"What was it?"

"The advice?"

"No, Micah, what was in your hand?"

"I don't what you are talking about."

"What do you mean...?" she questioned, bewildered. "The thing the tall man and you were holding."

"Maybe it looked like it from over here, but I don't have anything..." Micah stopped his sentence short.

Victoria watched the color leave Micah's cheeks, "Maybe you should go lay down, you look pale."

Micah was suddenly panicked. "Wait... he held it? He didn't take it, did he?"

"You're asking me? I was over here." Victoria was now becoming worried, "You really should sit down."

"What did it look like?" Micah was seriously concerned.

"Are you joking?"

"No, Victoria," he said sternly.

"I don't know, it was long and thin... two, maybe three feet long."

Micah gave an emotional sigh, "Did he take it from me?" his voice cracked.

"No, you were holding it, he just touched it or something. How do you not know what you had in your hand?"

Micah became queasy, his eyes rolling back into his head as he began to collapse into Victoria. "Whoa, whoa... I've got you," she assured.

"I do have to sit down," Micah mumbled as they sank to a squat in the center of the courtyard.

"Sit. Drink some water." Victoria pulled a bottle out of his knapsack.

"I need some food."

"Then we'll get you some food."

Chapter 44

"AGENT TAYLOR, DYLAN VASKO… this is Sergeant Calvin Poe, the head of our strike force. He's the best we've got and these are his men. His team has been together for years. They eat, drink and sleep this stuff."

"Splendid to meet you, Sergeant," Rothery said as they shook hands.

"Likewise."

"You do understand the situation?" Dylan asked.

"We've studied the footage," Poe stated with authority. "The target is likely trained in some form of Krav Maga or possibly Brazilian grappling, although his technique was quite rudimentary. My guess is he's forgotten much of what he's learned— there was a sense of panic in his movements. Matter of fact, he basically got lucky. His second victim…"

"Victim?" Rothery questioned, taking a bite of his breakfast croissant.

"The second victim," Poe continued to explain, "would have likely taken him down had it not been for the bullet he took from friendly fire."

Rothery nearly choked on his pastry, "Friendly fire? You mean when the third terrorist shot the second terrorist?"

Dylan, intent on Sergeant Poe, nodded in agreement waving Rothery off, "Go on, Sergeant."

Poe nodded. He went on efficiently, "Gentlemen, this is Charles Norton, second in command of our strike force. He's Scotland Yard's expert in incursion, hand to hand combat, and military-grade weaponry."

"Perfect!" Dylan all but cheered, bobbing his head as if watching blows at a boxing match. The youthful PM representative seemed swept away by the obviously high levels of testosterone in the air. Rothery's eyebrows furrowed.

Sergeant Norton spoke, "We've examined the target's every move in prep; simulated multiple counter strikes. He will not get the upper hand, sirs. Our riffles are equipped with smartgun technology. Even if he disarms one of our men, he will not be able to use the gun against us or any innocent civilians. Each gun has a triple locking mechanism including an RFID proximity chip with fingerprint recognition— he can't fire our weapons. Nothing is coming back on us. NOTHING. In fact, you gentlemen should leave your guns behind; there's no need and they're not safe."

"You needn't worry, Sergeant," Rothery commented, "neither of us make a habit of going armed."

"Although we should still err on the side of caution on this, shouldn't we, Sergeants? After all, he could have his own weapon," Dylan warned.

"Quite right," both Poe and Norton agreed.

"Listen up!" Chief Philips addressed the assembly of men. "This is Agent Taylor with SIS and Dylan Vasko with the PM's Terrorist Task Force. I want to be quite clear here; we're taking lead on this incursion, but these agents are in control of the suspect once he's in custody. Do not deviate from plan."

Motioning to blueprints of the Tower Hotel, Philips continued, "The target's potential exits are here, here and here. Those will be barricaded by the Yard— he's not getting out of the building, gents. There are two staircases, one on both the east and west sides of the building. There is a service lift in the center of the building near the housekeeping supply closets…" he pointed, "…here."

The men examined the blueprints as the chief concluded, "Also, be aware that civilians may be in the building and fall into harm's way. We cannot evacuate and risk alerting the suspect, so let's not have any casualties, shall we? Agents? Would you like to address the men?"

"Thank you, Chief," Dylan answered, standing. "The target is a white male in his mid-forties. You've all seen the video. He is highly trained, likely military special ops. He's extraordinarily skillful in manipulation, as well. He is a delusional psychopath who faced off three armed men with low to no fear for himself. He likely thinks himself immortal or immune to harm, or possibly on a mission of great importance— which makes him see authority as a potential threat. This also makes him extremely dangerous. Do not engage him alone… he may appear compliant but then turn quite rapidly."

Rothery was taken aback by Dylan's description. He cleared his throat. "Everything Mr. Vasko has said is likely true," he started, "however, let's remember the man has not committed a crime and has only acted in self-defense.

A good portion of the public still believes he is a hero, so we'd like to avoid an incident, if at all possible. Therefore, remain diligent until he is subdued, but do not provoke him."

"Though the target may not have committed any crimes we are aware of," Dylan quickly reiterated, "he has most certainly killed three men without hesitation. That is not by accident and does not come without experience. These were not likely his first kills, gentlemen, but let's make them his last! If he engages you, don't take any chances— put him down. Remember, he killed the third man at the restaurant after being shot, and he did it by luring his victim in close."

"Right!" Chief Philips announced. "Let's roll! Be safe and make quick work of it."

Chapter 45

MID-MORNING, VICTORIA SAT upon the balcony outside her suite at the Tower Castle Hotel. Enjoying the fresh air, she heard sounds coming from Micah's adjoining room— the sound of talking. She hadn't wakened him considering the prior day's events on top of everything else he'd been through, but now that she knew he was up, she went back inside and knocked on his door.

There was no answer. She listened again, sure he had been speaking to someone. She knocked once more.

When Micah finally answered, he was wearing plain white silk pajamas (a Japanese gee of sorts) and unwrapping a leather strap from his wrist. "Who were you talking to? Did you sleep okay? Are you feeling better?" she asked in rapid-fire succession.

"Not much… and I'm fine. Though I'm not quite sure how I feel, yet."

"Well, you look much better. You had me worried yesterday." Victoria watched as he turned to finish packing up his suitcase. She could tell something was different about him and that he didn't want to talk about his morning conversation, but she was waiting for the right moment— her questions were far from over.

After dressing in the bathroom, Micah eventually took a seat; legs parted, rubbing his hands on his knees and thighs. "So, Micah…" she began casually, trying to be playful, "now that I have committed to the chaos I have to ask."

Micah groaned. "Uh-huh?"

"Where does your power come from?"

That was blunt. "What power?"

Victoria's rolled her eyes. Micah scoffed. Annoyed, she demanded, "Then how do you explain it, huh? What you did in the restaurant was impossible— and I know it wasn't your first fight, either. Your dance in the castle…?" her eyes widened, "…our 'aura sex'? Everything!"

"Oh, dear, God. You do know that your descriptions are really not making this any easier." Scratching the back of his head with a wince, "It's not that I'm keeping things from you, Victoria. It's just that it's not believable— I don't even believe it myself most of the time. I can't give time to think about it. If I did, I'd doubt it all even more. All I can commit to is that in the moment, I find I have no choice."

"You really need to work on your salesmanship. I've seen the evidence that it DOES exist, so now convince me."

"Alright, fine," then trying to be less serious, "however, I do believe a bargain is in order."

"Okay, I'm listening."

"Whether I manage to convince you or not… number one, we don't bring this up again.

Victoria squinted disappointed.

"Two; see addendum one. And three… most importantly, you must promise to never tell Kip."

Victoria scrunched her face and blew out her cheeks, dramatically thinking about it. "Um, tough bargain."

"Take it or leave it."

"Together Kip and I could wreak havoc on you, you know."

"Hence the agreement."

Grinning, Victoria agreed.

"Okay, first, it's no one thing. It's hard to explain. There's no formula. There's no wand... however," he grimaced, "there may be kryptonite."

"Now, THIS sounds more fun than the fairytale!"

"For you, maybe." Micah searched the ceiling for a starting place. Shaking his head, "There's just far more that surrounds us that we DON'T understand than that we do."

Victoria nodded, "I'm following you," she encouraged, "keep going."

"Again, it's no one thing." He drew in a deep breath, "For now and for simplicity sake— and to assure no misinterpretation nor corruption— let's call it inertia. An object at rest stays at rest and an object in motion stays in motion unless acted upon by an unbalanced force, and the acceleration of the resting object depends upon the force acting upon it. So, for every action, there is an equal and opposite reaction."

"So, you're the Force," she poked.

"Ugh. We're never going to get over the Star Wars analogy, are we?"

"It's simpler. Say you're the Force and everyone understands."

"I wish it was that simple, but actually, we're the object, not the force. The object is at rest until the force acts upon it. Then the speed of the object depends upon the action of the force. If receptive... well, that's probably not the right word... but we are the opposite, equal reaction to the imbalance."

"WE, huh?" Victoria raised an eyebrow, "So, you're saying Kip was right?"

Micah scoffed, "I don't know. It really doesn't matter because you can't talk to anyone about it anyway— even if you wanted to. They won't believe you."

She smiled, "I see why you get so annoyed by skepticism."

"Skepticism doesn't bother me, it's one-sidedness." Then shaking his head, "Wait, I take that back. Skepticism is like ignorant racism— it's just blind, taught ignorance which IS annoying.

"For example, people arrogantly state there is nothing beyond known physics while at the same time accepting whatever they're fed. Like the fact that the tiniest of particles— so small they're invisible to the human eye, so prevalent that they're literally in the air we breathe and the water we drink— if split, can destroy an entire city. No problem, people swallow that with no questions asked. It boggles the mind.

"Imagine…" Micah held his fingers a millimeter apart, squinting to see the tiny gap, "how is it physically possible that between my fingers resides the power to bring fire down from heaven?"

"An atomic blast?"

Micah shrugged, "Okay."

"I've never really thought about it."

"Most don't. That's what I'm saying. They just accept that while putting tangible restrictions on everything else."

Victoria considered, "Something smaller than the eye can see, all around us, can destroy a whole city. God, that is frightening."

"The point being is," Micah continued, "there's more that we don't know than we do, and the least of all things is power. A nuclear blast is beyond physics; a near weightless object that devours incomprehensible mass as if the source of the universe resides in its most fundamental element— an element with an electron of one."

"So, big, bad-ass things come in very small packages and defy logic."

"The biggest of the baddest-ass of all things come in the smallest of logic defying packages. Wait until you meet my mother."

He blew out his breath, resigned to get it over with. "If I was to contribute it to a single thing, it would not be insight or knowledge of the unknown but rather acceptance of what's beyond comprehension. That's what puts you in harmony with all things at that moment." He bowed his head, "That… and being willing to suffer the consequences."

"My, God," Victoria expressed.

"And that's a good place to start when considering a nuclear blast."

"No…" she continued, speaking slowly as if to herself, seeing for the first time. "If the power of the universe resides in its smallest element while at the same time all life depends upon that same element…" quieting, considering, "the air, the water, the tide crashing; the moon, the Earth, the sun— all rotating around the universe for the single purpose of maintaining balance." She paused solemnly with a sense of awe.

Just then the clouds in the morning sky shifted causing sunlight to pour in through the open curtains and cast rays upon a crystal lamp sitting on the desk. Rainbow-colored lights moved along the wall through the prism momentarily blinding Victoria. As she held her hand to her forehead to block the light, she watched the colors dance over her fingertips. "To maintain that balance..." she whispered, "a universal correction... a universal gravitational pull... oh, God, how much is truly beyond our grasp?"

Micah's eyes widened, amazed, "Did you just cause the light to move across your hand?"

Victoria looked up. "That's silly."

"Is it?" Micah smiled.

"Isn't it?" gazing at the dancing light, the warmth of the sun.

"I'm not sure," Micah jested. "I've never considered the gravitational pull of the universe as an available source of power... you just did."

Beyond the outward levity, Micah could see Victoria was not the same person he had met days ago. As crazy as it sounded, it was clear that the change was more than his imagination; more than cultic acceptance. Her new found revelation would cause even Kip to cringe— to conceive of such a thing; consider yet alone believe it. Maybe Micah's intuition about her on the plane was right... the reluctant, retired hero had seen something in this woman he couldn't deny.

Victoria remained thoughtful for a moment, then a serious intensity clouded her expression. She looked away before asking her next question. Partly for fear of the answer, but mostly lest her question make Micah uncomfortable.

Seeing she was afraid to speak, he softly coaxed, "Go ahead, Victoria."

"Micah..." she paused, "...are you immortal?"

Micah turned somber, taking his time to answer. "My hair is turning gray," he answered with a smile.

She smiled back, "But you look so young."

"Are we done for now?"

"I think that will hold me." Victoria laughed, "Now I see why I can't tell Kip."

"Speaking of Kip... we should go see him today."

"Why, what's wrong?"

Micah got up, stared out the balcony window, "I don't know. Something has changed."

Victoria teased, "You would be certain of it if you hadn't pretty much passed out on me last night."

"Ah," Micah smiled, his eyes sparkling. He bit the corner of his lip, "You are beyond my wildest imagination, Victoria."

"Well, if you keep falling asleep on me, that might be all it ever is."

"So," Micah flirted, "on that subject… how are you with mornings?"

Victoria grinned, "Oh, I have a strict rule. Double digits."

"What in the world does that mean?"

"10, 11, 12… up to 24-zero-zero, military time. Occasionally I bend for 1 or 2 AM, but mornings are for coffee."

"Ah, yes…" Micah considered, looking at his watch, "10 AM, huh?"

Victoria smirked, "Hmm, not quite optimal for a couple's first I don't think."

Micah squinted one eye closed, the other looking upward for an answer. He sighed, "I suppose not."

Looking a bit nervous, "I do have something to tell you though, Micah." It was one thing to flirt but entirely another for Victoria to take the next step in a relationship. It was only fair to let him know how much it would mean— and how long it had really been since she'd even considered it.

"What?"

Before she was able to say another word she received a text message. "They've just arrived at the building!" she blurted, obviously startled.

"Who?"

"The police!"

"How do you know?'

"Okay… I guess I have two things I need to tell you."

"Start with the police-thing," Micah frowned.

"I have people watching the hotel."

"What?"

"The agents that visited the cabin… they wanted to catch you, they wanted to kill you. Our reporter friend has made fools of all of them, so now they're calling you armed and dangerous; a delusional psycho– a threat! They're going to shoot first, Micah. So, I had my publicist hire a few private investigators to inform us if the police showed up."

"Really. Might they inform the police, too?"

"I already thought of that," Victoria continued without hesitation, proud of her strategy, "that's why I had my publicist hire them. They don't know who they're working for or who they're protecting. They don't even know there are five others watching the same building. Isn't that awesome?"

Micah chuckled, "You hired six detectives. That's…"

"Awesome, isn't it? And there's more!"

"Please, do tell."

"My publicist also hired a couple of actors to stay at this hotel playing like mafia kingpins. They suspiciously enter and exit the building when we do… they even get into hired limousines— the whole thing. So, the private investigators think they are protecting mob bosses," Victoria finished.

Micah nodded, bewildered, "And you chose now, when the police are entering the building, to tell me this?"

"Can we discuss this later, Micah? We do need to move. Time to pull another rabbit out of your hat."

Quiet and serious, the lightheartedness abruptly left the room. Micah sighed, *This is not going to end well. We're on the top floor, the lifts and stairs are certainly blocked.* Having escaped twice before, he knew his options were bleak. *They'll be ready this time.*

But turning toward Victoria, he had to smile. Seeing her faith for an eventful escape confirmed how different she really was and made him consider the difference he had felt that morning. Suddenly understanding, he grinned and continued packing his suitcase; Victoria had asked him how he felt earlier and now he knew.

Victoria looked at her phone, "They're moving to our floor… I can get us a lawyer?" Now she was panicked.

"You won't need one."

"Micah!" she implored.

"It's okay." As those few short words left his mouth, Micah was certain of their truth. "This is all part of the plan, Victoria," he said confidently, "besides, I want to meet my formidable adversary." Micah managed a smile, shaking his head, "How many millions of people in this town? How many tourists? I could have and should have been out long ago." He contemplated. "No, we'll stick to the original story. You were never an accomplice. If need be, tell them I lured you here and held you captive."

"Why? I'm not afraid for me."

"I know. Surprisingly, neither am I. But if they want to charge me with kidnaping or holding a hostage, it's only an insignificant add-on… however, aiding and abetting is a serious charge for you. Just stick to the plan. Say nothing. As far as they can prove, I'm stalking you and you didn't even know I was in the room next door."

"What about what Kip said…? that they'd never let it go to trial?"

Micah smiled, eyes gleaming at her awareness, "It's possible I may only be the distraction." Pensively considering the possibility, he playfully touched her on the nose.

"If you're the distraction…" shaking her head.

"…then they'll never see YOU coming."

"What?" Victoria didn't understand. "Micah…"

The couple heard a parade of footsteps coming down the hall. "They're coming, Micah…"

"Go to your room, Victoria. Just stay seated no matter what happens. It will all be fine," he assured.

For some reason beyond logic, she knew he believed that.

Chapter 46

MICAH POSITIONED HIMSELF IN the middle of his room facing the door. Pulling an armchair from the dining table he sat backwards— legs through the armrests and hands through the holes in the backrest to pose no threat to the invading force. He left the hotel door ajar, blocked from shutting by the lock-bar. He wrapped his feet around the chair legs.

The stormtroopers broke first into Victoria's room; at least four of them in military fashion. Following Micah's orders, she remained seated on the couch as they quietly and efficiently secured her four-room suite.

"He's not here," one of the men said over the radio attached to his shoulder. He waved silently, prompting two of the officers to breakoff and join three others in the hallway, already prepared to enter the suite next door.

As the incursion team took Micah's room, Rothery and Dylan entered Victoria's salon.

"Good day, Ms. Adams."

"Agents."

"Where is he, Ms. Adams?"

Victoria smiled knowing that in seconds they would finally have their man. However, Rothery had just given her the perfect opportunity to rob them of their victory. "Today, Mr. Taylor, he decided he had put you through enough."

"What does that mean?" he asked.

She held up a finger suggesting to 'wait for it', then tilted her head to listen. As if on cue, an abrupt sound came from the suite next door. Seconds later over the radio, *"Target is secure. I repeat, the target is secure."*

"Ms. Adams, why don't you just stay here," Rothery said with a frown, "I will be with you shortly." He pointed at the two remaining men signaling them to keep Victoria there, neither officer looking disappointed in having to wait with the attractive actress.

When Rothery entered the adjoining room, Micah laid flat on his back still wrapped around the now broken chair, Norton's boot in the middle of his chest. Micah was blinking heavily from a compression hit to the back of his head brought about by the violent slam to the floor; his lip split open from what could only have been a rifle butt to the mouth.

Surprised to see the target's condition, Rothery's initial assumption was that the team had wrapped him around the chair. But after a brief assessment it wasn't difficult for the agent to deduce that Micah must have positioned himself that way for surrender on purpose.

"Pick him up," Rothery commanded. Two large soldiers immediately lifted Micah chair and all, then slammed him down to the floor in a seated position. "Get him out of that bloody chair!" he added.

Sucking blood from his lip, "If you don't mind?" Micah quietly gestured he could manage himself, giving the agent a stern look of disapproval.

With a small, embarrassed nod from Rothery, Micah slipped his arms and legs from the broken chair back, adjusting himself to an uncomfortable sitting position. "You'll have to forgive the..." Rothery didn't even know how to begin apologizing. "They're trained for a different type of assailant," he decided, trying to play apathetic.

Micah winced in pain, "Well, it's slightly encouraging that you possibly see the shades of gray."

Rothery pulled up a chair, spun it around backwards straddling it, and sat across from Micah. Dylan took a seat on the lounge at Micah's back. "You're a hard man to find," Rothery began.

Still dabbing his mouth and rubbing the back of his head, "You'll have to pardon me, agent, I'm only catching about every third word." Micah held his head with a squint, his sight slightly blurred.

Rothery nodded, "Give him that bottle of water."

"Thank you." Micah took a large swallow. "Now, where were we? Oh, yes... it's been so long since anyone has been this eager to see me, you really can't blame me for playing a little hard to get."

"I see now we've made much to do about nothing," Dylan remarked with condescension.

"Well, personally, I would rather you hadn't." Micah glanced over his shoulder in time to catch a glimpse of Dylan's contemptible glare— a sharp streak of pain and a popping jaw accompanying the turn of his neck. Too nauseated to engage in a staring contest with the man behind him, Micah returned his attention to Rothery. "Never the less, agent, my congratulations. You clearly are very intuitive."

"I'm not certain of your sincerity, but thank you just the same. It was fun," Rothery admitted, "a bit of my best work."

"Truly, my sincerest admiration," Micah reiterated. "It was as if you were being assisted all along the way. And you got your man."

"Did I? You most certainly don't look the part."

"How's that?" Micah evaluated the man.

"CIA hasn't claimed you. You don't sound Russian or look Chinese."

"Is that what you think?"

"I had hoped so, for your sake. If not, you are just a fugitive."

"Fugitive from what?" Micah snapped. "Is it my responsibility to know that you're looking for me? I don't remember receiving a subpoena."

"Come now, with all the television coverage?" Rothery accused.

"I spent the week with Victoria Adams... surely you don't think I was watching re-runs of 'Highway to Heaven'?"

Rothery smiled, "I suppose not. Hmm, 'Highway to Heaven'... wasn't that the Michael Landon serial from the 80's?"

"Would you rather I'd said 'Family Ties'?" Micah shook his head. "You're a bit of a surprise to me as well, agent. Double-aught involvement? Wasn't a bucket list item for me, but I suppose I'm Sir Hugo Drax, aren't I?"

"Who?" Dylan asked.

Rothery answered, "James Bond reference." Then addressing Micah, "Actually, Vladimir Scorpius is more fitting."

"Really? That's disappointing."

"You do know we're not the only ones looking for you," Rothery commented.

Micah sighed, "You caught that, huh?"

"Yes, fairly early on. Old friends of yours?"

"Very old."

Rothery nodded and filed the information away for processing. "The boy is awake, by the way," he added.

Micah had to think about it for a moment before he realized Rothery was speaking of the young terrorist. A look of relief swept across Micah's face. He exhaled deeply, nodding repeatedly.

The reaction surprised Rothery, "What? You didn't want to kill him?"

Micah said nothing.

Rothery bit his lip and sat up straight, "Nothing about this case makes sense—you, least of all."

Micah looked him in the eye; Rothery stared back in turn. "Who are you, Mr. Steinbeck? There are three Allen Steinbecks in the UK, all accounted for. You are none of them. Then I was shocked to find out how many Allen Steinbecks reside in the state of New York alone. And you don't appear to be any one of them either."

Micah nodded in agreement. "So, who are you?" Rothery questioned again.

"No one of significance, I assure you."

The agent sighed feeling more and more as if he were with the right man in the wrong situation. Micah let his gaze wander while Rothery stewed.

Watching the patrolling police officers, Micah noticed the strange stride of one of the men. He avoided catching eyes with the officer only observing him move. It was the manner of the man's pace that caught Micah's attention; the stride of his step seemed uncharacteristic of a soldier or police officer.

Micah continued to watch nonchalantly looking to see if any of the other men appeared to notice, too, wondering if they were aware of the officer who walked with the strange gait— or if they actually even knew him. Any team has an unmistakably developed comradery which can be observed in how they position themselves in a room; how they watch each other's back— an eye gesture or nod. It's something apparent in their proximity to one another— the closeness or spread of their position; their movement and countermovement like the rotation of a basketball team on a court. When trained in the field (having dug one another's latrines), the natural gap between men is distinctive.

But this was more than that; this member appeared out of place. His pace and distance were wrong. There was something in his step. The others didn't appear to notice him or at least didn't flow in conjunction with him.

"All right," Rothery said, interrupting his thoughts, "maybe the more interesting topic might be who's chasing you, yeah? So... who IS chasing you, Mr. Steinbeck?"

With Rothery's question, the odd officer immediately tightened the grip on his rifle. It was a subtle gesture but enough for Micah to catch. The man wasn't looking at Micah, though... his focus was on the back of Rothery's head. Micah's brows raised slightly. *So, you've found me, too?* Concerned, he chanced another look towards Dylan, but the younger agent had already risen and was quickly walking out of the living room.

Micah straightened purposefully and looked directly at Rothery, "But I like you, Mr. Taylor." Micah knew far too well that mere knowledge of THEIR existence would make the agent a target. He briefly darted his eyes toward the circling police.

The glance prompted Rothery to note how strangely attentive the surrounding officers were. The apparent lack of privacy made him recant his question. "All right then, Mr. Steinbeck, tell me this… Ms. Adams said you allowed me to catch you. I'm not at all certain she wasn't correct. Why now?"

Micah chuckled, "Who's hiding?"

Agent Taylor shook his head back and forth, then stood and walked around the suite. He took a pen from his lapel and used it to look through Micah's suitcase. "Splendid clothing. What's in the sample jelly container?"

"That? Coconut oil. Airplanes dry out my skin. Coat your face with that stuff before a long flight, arrive baby soft. You'll still feel like shit, but no one will notice."

"Good tip."

"You'll find I'm a wealth of information if you ask me about something I know."

"I'll keep that in mind. And is this your hand purse?" Rothery picked up Victoria's handbag left accidently in his room.

"Sure, it matches my luggage," Micah quipped.

"As well as your eyes," Rothery added sarcastically. "What kind of leather is this? It's particularly soft; feels thin, water resistant yet strong. And the color…"

"Well, if you like it that much… oh, wait a minute," shaking his head, "I would say you can keep it, but…"

"You'd have to ask Ms. Adams?"

"I was going say… but it goes with my suitcase."

Rothery smirked, holding up the beautiful, deep navy designer purse over Micah's rugged, black carry-on.

Just then the odd officer exited the room heading into Victoria's suite through the adjoining door. Moments later a second officer passed by the open hallway door, and a third entered Micah's suite from Victoria's. From Micah's count he had already calculated seven officers plus the two agents, so when the final officer entered the gathering in Micah's salon, he knew Victoria had been left alone with the strange cop.

"You've suddenly gotten fidgety, Mr. Steinbeck," Rothery observed. "I would normally assume the reality of your situation was sinking in, but you've never given any sign of concern in that regard."

* * * * *

Victoria had remained seated on the sofa. She'd barely noticed the comings and goings of the men in uniform, their exchange constant in synchronized rotation... with the exception, that is, of an occasional star struck glance, a less than subtle masculine flex of muscle; an officer's lean against the kitchenette counter a bit too contrived to be natural.

A twenty-year celebrity (even under house arrest) no longer noticed such behavior and wasn't interested in making any new fans or friends under the circumstances. But when the out of place officer entered, the atmosphere instantly changed. It wasn't colder as often suggested, it was denser. Thick like humid— a smell like sweat but clean... too clean, like the pretense of clean.

There was a taste in the air. Not like dust, but irritation. Her throat closed, her breath shallowed. Her lips almost pursed, subconsciously cautious of intake. Like breathing through your mouth to avoid a bad smell simply from reflex, it was without reason— the body's defense of something the mind had yet to acknowledge.

Her gaze moved slowly to the officer who had just entered the room. There was something off about him she couldn't put a finger on; something different. It was nothing her eyes saw but her senses were alert. She subtly held out her hand— not toward him but elevated above her lap, feeling the thickness in the air.

A vibrant energy just beyond tangible flowed through the room like static electricity; pulling, combining, forming what seemed like a microcosm just prior to lightening's strike. Most amazing, though, was her realization that this was not natural (nor possibly even real) and was instead her soul's instinctual response to this 'person'... but without the panic and fear she had learned to embrace for so many years.

Victoria turned to the man. His pretense too nonchalant. She knew. "You're not like the others," she boldly accused.

The officer stopped, stone still.

A mounting consolidation of focused energy seemed within her grasp. Victoria blinked slowly absorbing the sensation, looking down to see if the carpet was standing on end. But when she raised her eyes, she found him gone.

* * * * *

Rothery looked back toward the door that joined Micah's and Victoria's rooms. "Ms. Adams?" Rothery pried.

Though Micah's surveillance of the policemen had been very subtle and his actual attention to Victoria's room even less, there was a difference in his behavior when Rothery mentioned her. "Is it Ms. Adams?" the agent repeated. Micah turned a harsh glare. "Aiding and abetting, perhaps?" Rothery tested.

The accusation was utterly ridiculous and Micah's expression indicated as much. They both knew that would never stick. Besides, a celebrity scandal was the last thing anyone would want at trial.

"No," Rothery surmised. Still, something about Victoria Adams threw off the man in front of him. *The officers,* Rothery thought. *The imposter; the counterfeit policeman at the hospital...* "Who is with Ms. Adams now?" he inquired of Sergeant Poe standing by the doorway.

"Uh..." Poe stuttered.

Rothery instantly became distressed. This team he was sure, always knew who controlled each room. They'd never leave a room unattended. They'd never not know who had their back. No one moved without a call— 'alpha on the stairs', 'delta secured the kitchen'— they never didn't know. That's how people got dead. "Secure Ms. Adams," Rothery immediately commanded.

Poe went to open the adjoining door, "It's locked." Grabbing his transceiver handset, "Who's with Adams?"

There was no response. "Secure Adams!"

"The room door is locked, sir."

"Break it down!"

Micah immediately rose to his feet. Rothery sternly pointed at him, "Sit down!" but Micah refused, taking a step toward the adjoining door. Noting the concern on his face, with a calmer hand, "We've got this," Rothery tried to console.

Dylan rushed into the room to see Micah on his feet refusing an order from Rothery. Hearing the sound of agents breaking down Victoria's door in the hallway, Dylan pulled out his 45 with such speed it caught Micah's attention. Micah instantly threw his hands behind his head.

"He's moving!" Dylan yelled.

Two of the soldiers rapidly turned their weapons on Micah. Rothery, witnessing the escalated situation, stepped between the officers and Micah, holding out his hands. "This is not happening! Hold your weapons!" he called out. With as much authority as he could muster, he yelled, "Sergeant!"

"Stand down!" Poe ordered.

The soldiers immediately lowered their weapons, but Dylan remained poised; gun cocked, finger pulling on the trigger. Micah's eyes focused on the young man.

"Dylan," Rothery calmly spoke, "there is no justification. This is beyond reason."

Without blinking or moving his eyes away from the gun, Micah slowly seated himself back onto the chair. Dylan, taking a deep breath, still refused to lower his weapon.

Rothery stepped up to his partner, cautiously placing his hand on the gun. He pushed it down to the man's side. After a moment, Dylan exhaled through his nose and relaxed. He resumed a demeanor as if nothing had happened. "Thought you were going to leave your gun behind," Rothery whispered.

"I'm not getting caught with my trousers down," Dylan replied. "You're going to get us killed, Taylor."

Sergeant Norton unlocked the adjoining room door and entered Micah's suite from the other side. "The room is secure, sir. Ms. Adams remains on the couch where we left her. The room is empty. She was alone."

"She was alone?" Poe questioned.

Rothery moved to the connecting door, saw Victoria sitting on the couch. "Did you lock the doors?" he asked her.

"You told me not to move."

"Where's the officer that was with you?"

"I don't know, I wasn't paying attention."

"You didn't move?"

"No, I didn't move. Those assholes would have shot me."

"Poe, take a head count," Rothery requested.

Poe grabbed the handset on his shoulder, "Count it off!"

"Alpha, Beta, Gamma, Delta..."

Poe looked at Norton, "All account for, sir."

"There was a seventh. Where is the other man?" Rothery inquired.

"Not one of ours."

Agent Taylor addressed Poe, "Is there any reason to keep your men dispersed?"

"Yes sir, to secure the scene."

"This isn't the Prime Minister, Sergeant, no one is coming for Mr. Steinbeck. Can we all gather for a moment?"

Reluctantly, Poe commanded, "Fall in!"

"Ms. Adams, will you please join us?" Rothery invited.

Victoria entered the room, saw the gash on Micah's lip. "What the hell?! He was just sitting in a chair surrendering!" Quickly moving toward Micah, Dylan reached to grab her. She rushed forward slapping his hand away and easily avoided his attempt to stop her.

As she briskly darted past the surprised young agent, Micah held up his hand, "I'm alright," he said.

Victoria hesitated, glaring at Dylan, but she obediently took a seat upon the couch. Dylan, on the other hand, with a slightly bewildered look, stepped back out of Micah's sight and returned to the lounge situated on the far wall.

The strike team efficiently congregated in the suite's large, luxurious living room. "Is this all of them?" Rothery asked.

"Plus Chuck and myself," Poe confirmed, pointing at Norton.

"There was a seventh man, Sergeant." Rothery sounded adamant.

The team looked one to another, one soldier finally responding, "The Italian looking guy, sir? We thought he was with you."

"He was dressed identical to your men and carrying one of YOUR weapons!" Rothery bellowed.

Poe radioed down, "Chief, has anyone come down from the twelfth floor?"

"No, no one, Poe."

"All exits secured?"

"Yes, before you went up. The lift hasn't moved. No one in the stairwells."

"Hand me that," Rothery said, grabbing for Poe's radio. "Chief, this is Rothery. No one has come down?"

"All stairwells and lifts are secure. No one could have gotten even to the eleventh floor unless they went through a window."

"Might someone have gone up? Lift shaft?" Rothery deduced.

There was a pause over the radio.

Rothery shook his head painfully, then calmly addressed the sergeant in charge, "Poe, would you mind having your men secure this floor— every room."

"You heard him, men!"

"Best of the best," Rothery muttered under his breath, rubbing his forehead and the bridge of his nose, "most definitely not our finest moment."

Agent Taylor paced the room, sizing-up Victoria and Micah as the team raced to the door. "Let's get the two of them out of here, first," he ordered shaking his head. A hopeless look crossed his face.

ACT III

RUN

Chapter 47

"IF THESE STONE WALLS could talk. What is it about the air down here? The taste, the stench? What does it tell us?" Ring Finger ran his hand slowly across the slate wall.

"Moist. Damp." Europe gazed around the uniquely shaped chamber with disinterest.

"It's invigorating. It's pure, untapped energy."

"All I smell is mold. Old, trapped."

Ring Finger dismissed his friend's lack of perceptiveness. He approached from another angle, "An octagon, 12-foot high... is it a mere coincidence or by natural selection that we find ourselves at a table of eight? Why not twelve? Why not seven? Why not one?"

"Have you forgotten the ninth seat or do you wish to contend for the chair, Furcus?"

Ring Finger glared at the ridiculous insinuation and continued, "The ancients built this. Why? Is it a reminder or clue to our past? A temple or prison? Can't you feel that?" He stretched out his hands as if feeling bursts of electricity emanating from the blank space of the room.

Europe's eyes narrowed, "You're changing my friend."

"How am I changing?"

"For more than a century we've gathered in this room and never once have you mentioned such a thing."

"I'm certain I have. I remember you stood there," Furcus pointed to one of the eight identical corners.

Europe laughed, "Are you sure it wasn't over there?" waving flippantly to the other side of the room. "This room is made of unblemished single slate. How on earth could you be certain I wasn't standing in any one of the other seven corners?"

Furcus smiled darkly, "How on Earth, indeed?"

"Perhaps this is a sign," Europe posed as five more entered the large chamber, "maybe your memory returns. Maybe HE comes sooner than we'd hoped." He shifted his eyes toward the congregating members, "Shall we present your new perspective to the Collective?"

Considering only briefly, Furcus dismissed with a shrug, "It's insignificant."

"Is it?" Europe eyed his friend suspiciously.

Arriving after the five, the young Brit entered the chamber. As he joined the others, Ring Finger looked him over with scrutiny, shaking his head. He turned to Europe in reply, "They wouldn't know what to do with it, friend."

Furcus and Europe parted, the eight now each taking a place against separate walls facing each other. Other than its occupants, the room was empty but for a single, exalted stone stool in the center— no back nor armrests on the ornament precluded any member a backside view if one were to sit upon the seat. Standing along the walls in equal position, the stool was for HIM alone to sit upon— to address or dismiss the Collective by simply facing or turning his back to any member in the round.

Maybe HE will have eight eyes. Or perhaps he will have none with only omnipotence to guide him. Ring Finger's thoughts swirled amidst his own unique memories. But even as he considered, the room spoke too little to spawn what had long been forgotten yet gave just enough symbolism to demand adherence, servitude, and absolute surrender.

The eight stood in dark silence, eyes lowered; the acoustics of the room perfect. A whisper could be equally heard by the member furthest away; the exception— the speaker— whose own voice seemed to dissipate from his mouth leaving only the echo for his own ears. Had an outsider witnessed the display, he'd be certain it was by design— a council chamber for telepathic demigods.

"The nation states will not interfere."

"And the ecological science consortium?"

"They've been made to believe in their privileged participation, though they are less significant than they think. Now isolated in their designated location, we have means to assure their complete compliance."

"What if they talk?"

"Communication is restricted. And if they cease to be useful… there are other options."

"Fine. Anything further?"

"We will require one more persuasive demonstration to incentivize the West's enthusiasm."

"Another terrorist attack? Are we not unopposed?" the Brit injected. "Are there any among the nations who wield power comparable to our own? What is the purpose of this facade? Why not be exposed and rule as we once did?"

"Have we forgotten how that turned out?"

"Por qué compañeros? We continue to go around and around with this," his rolling 'r's accentuated. "What we have accomplished could not have been done any other way; to take man from horse and cart to space exploration— we must remain behind the scenes."

"I agree. What we have accomplished had to be done with anonymity," Asia resonated. "No one nation could bear the cost to put a man on the moon yet alone reach the stars. It required a stock market, globalization, global economy— a unified world power. We agreed that only democracy creates a strong enough illusion. Enslaving nations would never have been enough, nor is any army today able to maintain the vast number of slave nations required to achieve it."

"Yes, but that spawned two world wars and a dozen other skirmishes."

"War is useful. Balance of power keeps a competitive atmosphere and provides an enemy to encourage progress. The global power struggle aggressively keeps funding flowing and allows our induction of technological advancements acceptance without question."

"Yes, but in the Middle East? These are unpredictable religious zealots."

"Religion? There is no difference between the religious and political zealots— both have martyrs and terrorists; they can be easily controlled through propaganda. Matter of fact, controlled religion is equally useful; blindly unites the people, justifies the means. Islam is merely the new communism— with equal power of persuasion on both sides of the border."

"That worked for a time, but now with the growth of atheists…"

"Nothing has changed. Darwinists are no different. They have their priest and patriarchs and are more dogmatic and vocal than Islamic extremists. Besides, their numbers are exaggerated."

"Fine, but Syria? What would be gained?"

Eyeing the chair Ring Finger commented contemplatively, "Sometimes it's not about gain but rather what we refuse to lose."

"All right, then. What of the impediment?"

"He's no more than a distraction— a remotely intriguing anomaly," the Brit stated. "We have him in custody now. He's made far too many mistakes." He rolled a gold coin between his fingers adding, "He should be studied for academic purposes."

Ring Finger turned in the direction of UK knowing his comrade's methods of 'academia'. He shrugged it off just the same and nodded, "Yes. It would be... good... to get a better understanding of such an anomaly in the unlikely event that we meet another." There was something smug in his agreement.

Two things puzzled UK; first, Furcus' use of the word 'good' which seldom (if ever) accompanied the man with the gold ring's assessment of anything UK had ever suggested; and secondly, to receive consent so quickly surprised him.

"Fine," Europe conceded. "Then we all agree."

The assembly eyed the empty chair and nodded.

Chapter 48

"WHAT IS HE DOING?" Rothery asked.

"He hasn't done anything, sir. He just lays there, back to the door. When we enter, he doesn't even turn to look at us."

"Keep a vigil on him."

"Why? He's not going anywhere."

"I want to know if there is any difference in his behavior."

"What are you looking for?"

"I'm not certain, but you'll know it when you see it." Rothery turned to leave, "Wait until 19:00, then take him to the interrogation room."

∗   ∗   ∗   ∗   ∗

Scotland Yard interrogation room number three was fifteen by ten feet with a three-way mirror spanning its width starting mid-way up the wall; a surveillance camera mounted in the corner.

Entering with a manila folder, Rothery placed it on the table. "How's your lip?"

"Sore, thanks for asking." Micah sat still; elbows on the table, hands covering his eyes.

"Do you need something for your head?" Rothery offered.

"I'll be fine. It's the lighting."

"So, if I put a bright light in your eyes, you would talk to me, eh?"

"I can't tell you what I don't know," Micah said mournfully.

"Can I call you Michael?" Rothery asked.

"I like the name. It's not my name, but I wouldn't mind."

"It's a better fit than Allen."

"I'd like to think so," Micah agreed.

"All right then, Michael."

Referring to the seventh imposter policeman at the raid, Rothery began, "I saw firsthand why you may have been reluctant to stick around the crime scene, let alone respond to the media's inquiry of you."

Micah chewed on the inside of his cheek, subtly nodding in agreement.

Pointing at the camera mounted on the interrogation room wall, "It's off, Michael. We can talk. You're safe now."

Micah chuckled.

The agent paused, processing the reaction. "I'm saying this to alleviate any apprehension you may have... although I don't receive the impression you are concerned. How is that?"

Micah glanced at the walls and securely locked door. He nodded once, suggesting he agreed the room was a fortress.

Rothery then laughed, suddenly realizing the irony. "Now you're making me laugh. Come now, a man infiltrated a top strike force team led by the head of

Scotland Yard, the Secret Service AND the PM's Terrorist Task Force. He then disappeared without a trace from a controlled, secured building— with an automatic weapon, no less. Now you look at these walls as if they keep you safe?"

"No, sir, I don't. You do."

"So, are you suggesting we're in danger? Who was he, Michael?"

"I'd never seen him before."

"Really? Once he moved into Ms. Adam's room, you were unmistakably agitated. If you had never seen him before, how did you know he wasn't with us?"

"Cadence, demeanor, the grip on his gun."

"Impressive. Was he there to kill you?" Rothery thought about it and answered his own question, "No, I suppose not. If he wanted to kill you, you would have been dead upon the team's entry, no questions asked. With Sergeant Poe's men, they would have given the bloke a medal before they realized he wasn't even a cop."

Micah cracked a smile.

Rothery calculated, "So, why did he lock the door? Why didn't he injure Ms. Adams?" He sat with a blank stare upon his face gazing at the floor and ceiling, mouth opened wide. His tongue began to move slowly about the inside of his mouth as if he would find the answer lodged somewhere between his teeth. With a contemplative mumble he asked again, "Why would that man lock her door from the inside and then disappear, exposing himself? The typical thug or covert-operator would not have given up his position so easily.

"Hmm…" he pondered. "The man was delivering a message— an important message; a onetime, career-limiting message he would never be able to deliver again."

Micah gave a remiss shrug.

"The message was to you, Mr. Steinbeck, wasn't it? That they can be anywhere, anyplace they want to be. And they are able to reach anyone… even in the middle of a Scotland Yard investigation! Even with the best of the best…"

Quietly interrupting, "You think too much of them, agent. Or should I say, they think very little of you. They don't even consider us."

Rothery stared at his captive with a furrowed brow.

Micah half-smiled, "But it is fun to watch you think, Mr. Taylor. I mean, you don't smoke a pipe or play the violin, but the way your tongue follows your thoughts, it's like watching Michael Jordan in his prime."

Rothery quickly closed his mouth. "They? So you DO know more than you are saying." He stood and began to pace. "You are almost believable— unbelievably, Michael." Considering, "My partner warned me not to get caught up in your delusions, but…" he shook his head, "'they'? Really?"

The agent took on a sarcastic tone, "Are they the infamous 'they'? THEY don't fear Scotland Yard, MI6… THEY don't even consider us? My, oh, my!" Rothery scoffed.

In a drastic change of disposition, Micah sat back in his chair aggressively throwing up a hand. "It's your story, man, I'm just a guy!" Micah's expression hard, his voice raised in harsh rebuke, "Who saved seventy-five people from three fucking terrorists, Taylor? And here **I** sit in a detention cell beaten and bloody… all orchestrated by the all-powerful PM, Scotland Yard, AND MI6's special agent extraordinaire! You believe whatever the fuck you want to believe. Five people are dead and the 'THEY' have YOU hunting ME!"

Rothery was taken aback by the complete shift in Micah's behavior. The man had been extremely cordial— polite even. With every word Micah spoke, Rothery became mournfully convicted that his hunt was potentially misguided.

His prisoner leaned forward. In a near whisper with equally commanding caution, "He wasn't there to kill *me*."

"Who, then?" Rothery asked sincerely.

"Next question, please." Micah sat back.

Rothery pondered the statement. *They weren't there to kill you or Victoria… the message was delivered to you. I see why Dylan warned me, it's easy to get distracted. Hmm.* "Who's Raza Mohammed Ahluwalia?

"I have no idea."

"Who was the assassin?"

"Excuse me?"

"The man you pulverized with your fist and elbow."

Micah closed his eyes with a regretful sigh, "Oh. I don't know his name… but I can't get his face out of my head."

"Why did he want to kill you?"

"Thought he wanted to kill everyone in the room."

"No, Michael, that was no terrorist attack. Took us a while, but that man was a grade-A assassin with a portfolio of suspicion a mile long. He's known as 'The Ghost'. We assume the other two men succumbed to bribery or religious zealousness, but that man was a gun for hire. So, tell me, Michael, who was he there to kill? Or is it Allen? We've run a check on all restaurant patrons from that night and the only possible motive lies with our man with no name."

Micah gave no indication of concern nor acknowledgement.

Rothery opened a folder, "We've run your fingerprints, DNA— no hits so far. Haven't found your passport. We've checked immigration entry photos dating back over a month. The whole country has seen your face yet no one has claimed you— the CIA are now assisting us. You are not leaving here without a story." Rothery leaned in, "Who wants you dead, Michael... badly?"

"Who doesn't?"

"You're not giving me much to work with here." Rothery stood, walked over to the side table, picked up a pitcher and offered, "More water?"

Micah nodded.

He filled the glass. Casually, "So, what brings you to London, Michael?"

"Wanted to see that play, 'Wicked'. I'm not a Wizard of Oz fan but it sounded interesting. You know, 'things are never as they seem'? The whole world is on a witch-hunt while the witch is actually the good guy. And in the end she saves the day, rides off into the sunset with prince charming... none are the wiser. It's a real tear-jerker."

Rothery chuckled, "Should have seen that coming. Is that how this is going to end?"

Micah just looked at him.

Dylan entered the room and took a seat at the table across from Micah. Rothery stepped back, giving him the floor. "Hello, Mr. Steinbeck. I don't think we have been properly introduced. My name is Dylan Vasko, I work for the PM's Office as an advisor on the Terrorist Task Force. We're working in conjunction with Scotland Yard and Secret Service investigating the recent terrorist attack that you seem to be right in the middle of. If you don't mind, I have a few questions for you."

"All right."

Looking down at his clipboard but clearly not reading it, Dylan proceeded, "For the record, what is your full name?"

"Nemo Tenetur se ipsum Accusare," Micah stated.

"How do you spell that… is it Italian?" Dylan asked.

"No, it's Latin," Rothery answered. "It means 'no man is bound to accuse himself'. Or in other words, he has the right to remain silent."

"Right," Dylan scoffed. "Your Miranda Rights will not serve you here. And if there were to be a trial, this is an international terrorist attack, so it most definitely would be executed more aptly like a military tribunal. Same rules don't apply, Mr. Steinbeck."

"That's surprising, considering the phrase was first cited in this country during the sixteenth century Star Chamber Tribunals. As I'm sure you know, it wasn't until afterwards that much of the rest of the world followed your lead by initiating their own versions of the 'right to remain silent'. For that matter, 'due process' was also mentioned here first in a statute by Edward III in the thirteenth century giving right to council. Of course, none of that really matters, now does it, considering I've not been read any rights (whatever they may be) nor been made aware of any charge."

"You're an educated man," Dylan commented.

"Google, mostly."

"You looked up UK Miranda Rights before coming to Britain?" he accused.

"I believe it's called 'Police Warning' here."

"That lends to consciousness of forethought or the premeditated act of a crime, Mr. Steinbeck."

"Well, I certainly wouldn't be the first person convicted of a crime in London for having had knowledge of the law, would I?"

"Why so inhospitable, Mr. Steinbeck? Why so secretive? Who are you protecting?"

"Agent Vasko, I'm not sure what you want from me. Ask me a question I can answer. Ask me something pertinent to my detention and I'll be happy to comply."

"You knew the victims of your rage, didn't you? And I suspect there are other bodies you don't want us to find, as well. You were a cohort, Mr. Steinbeck…

for all I know, the mastermind. Likely, this was a brilliant setup to aggrandize you as a savior."

"If that was the case, agent, why wouldn't I have stuck around for the media finale and a hero's welcome?"

Dylan ignored him, "Least case scenario, you are a vigilante who took the law into his own hands and people died. Be aware that your attempt at anonymity only exacerbates your situation. The only reason for you to remain silent is guilt."

"Wow. There is a long list of falsely accused defendants who have heard that same spiel." Micah folded his arms, "I'm still waiting for a reasonable accusation to respond to, agent, though I suppose I could respond to your last one."

Micah changed his tone, speaking slowly as if to consider the scenario, "So, you're proposing that I knew the terrorists, masterminded the situation, then invited Victoria Adams for a front row seat. Interesting, I'll give you that. Why would someone do that? Hmm… maximize media exposure, I suppose. Okay, but how do you get a celebrity to invite you to dinner? Two celebrities, no less. And then why leave the scene?"

Micah held up a finger getting into the role-play, "Wait, wait, wait, I've got it… avoiding capture from the authorities? Whoa! That would definitely push it to the next level, wouldn't it? Then to be arrested…? Now we're talking Mandela status! What do you think? I'll be crown prince by morning."

"Do you think this is a joke? You think it wise to mock the authorities?" As Dylan spoke, Micah stared him in the eyes. There was something about the man's speech. Not quite a lisp or physical impediment but more a conscious or subconscious idiosyncrasy as if Dylan either didn't believe the words he was saying, or was saying them with such conviction it caused him a tick of sorts— the way someone's eyes shifted when they lie.

Though Micah knew the myth about lying was not always true. A statement someone believed whole heartedly but feared they lacked substantial evidence of, could cause the same reaction. They might increase the speed of their speech only pausing at points where evidence or argument could be viably authenticated. They might clutter uncertainties around undeniable truths, trying to convince themselves (more than anyone else) that nine indisputable true statements substantiated the tenth. Very few things were more annoying to Micah than that. Blatant lies were humorous in comparison.

On the other hand, maybe Dylan was just young— maybe this was his first media op. Maybe he wanted to impress the Prime Minister. At any rate, Micah had seen this subtle form of eccentricity before but couldn't place it. "You work for a politician," Micah observed, "what I'm hearing from you surprises me. The wind changes fairly rapidly, agent, and tomorrow I may be heralded a hero. Your alliances will then flee you like... well, like a flea from a bathed dog."

"This is ridiculous!" Dylan abruptly stood. "Rothery, we don't have to let him go. He's a foreigner under suspicion of coercion in terrorist activity. Hold him in contempt until we find out who the hell he is, then we'll charge him with whatever crimes I'm certain he has committed!" He pushed away from the table and left the room.

"Where is he going?" Micah asked Rothery.

"I don't know."

"Sort of left right in the middle of things, don't you think? I was just getting warmed up."

Rothery was noncommittal.

"That boy could win a staring contest," Micah remarked offhand.

The agent looked at him with curiosity. "Why do you say that?"

Ignoring the question, Micah had another thought, "How long was he in here?"

"A couple of minutes."

"Less than three?" Micah questioned suspiciously.

"I believe so."

"Hmm."

Rothery's turn to change the subject. "You know, you have a rather slow heartbeat, Michael. Are you an athlete?"

Micah eyed the agent. "I used to be a runner... or I should have been. Why?"

"That makes sense."

"Not following you."

"In the hotel your heart rate was erratic. I assumed it was due to the incursion— the ensuing jeopardy of Ms. Adams. But now I see you could possibly challenge a standard polygraph. That could play well for you."

"I don't see how. If you don't know whether I'm telling the truth, I remain guilty until proven innocent, it appears."

"Well, if it's any consolation," Rothery said, "I believe you. Or at least, I believe YOU believe you. Your pupil dilation has remained consistent even though your heart rate has been a bit harder to determine."

Rothery had been judging whether or not Micah had been telling the truth by the consistency of his story, the strong pulse at the base of his neck, and the dilation of his pupils. He knew none were 100% accurate, but whether subconscious or deliberate, he believed his own mind would catch any subtle change and consider it as a contributing factor in his calculations. "I appreciated your conversation— even with Mr. Vasko. Quite enlightening."

Micah looked at Rothery, questioning.

The agent moved in close to Micah, confident in his assessment. "So, Michael... WHO are you protecting?"

Exasperated, Micah sighed, running his hands down his face. He paused then shook his head. "You wouldn't believe me, Mr. Taylor. Even if I told you." The agent was asking for a target on his back.

Chapter 49

ROTHERY ENTERED THE OFFICE of the Chief Crown Prosecutor to find it empty. Checking the calendar on his phone, he was certain their meeting was then.

Hearing the door, the prosecutor's assistant, Steven Marsh, peeked his head in from the hallway, "May I help you?"

"I have a meeting with Prosecutor Evans."

"Yes, Mr. Taylor, they are in the main conference room."

"They?"

"Follow me." Mr. Marsh led the way. "It's the door at the end of the hall."

"Aren't you coming?"

Marsh laughed, "Special invitation only, sir."

"I thought this was a one-on-one?"

The assistant smiled coaxing the clearly nervous agent down the hallway. "You'll be fine."

Rothery was the last to enter the room finding only a single seat unoccupied. He was astounded to see a gathering of dignitaries that included the Chief Crown Prosecutor, the Deputy Commissioner (head of Scotland Yard), the Mayor of London, and the Home Secretary. A couple of right-wing members of the House of Commons were there, as well. All had joined Rothery's meeting under the pretense of just 'being in the neighborhood'. Having no real stake-hold in the matter, there was still definite interest in the investigation's outcome; political hacks looking for a bit of up-to-date insight— or if all went well, a by-line in the capture of a controversial fugitive with whom they had publicly refused to take a side. At any rate, when conversation in the room began, there was no reservation in the opinions expressed by those present.

Rothery took the last open chair at the table of eight, surprised to find Dylan (the youngest member of the chamber) seated at the head. "I think we need to be cautious, the public thinks him a hero," the mayor was stating.

"The public is fickle," interjected the Home Secretary. "We could announce it was a CIA plot to drive down the pound and tomorrow they'd hang him on Tower Hill."

"Possibly. But as we're all quite aware, that journalist from the Register Guard is attempting to wreak havoc on Downing Street."

"Maybe rightfully so," a right wing MK asserted. "Hasn't our beloved PM ignored the growing immigration problem for far too long?"

"I just want to know who the bloody hell this guy is," the Deputy Commissioner piped in. "Why won't he give us his name?"

Rubbing his forehead Rothery thought to answer. He considered offering Micah's statement including mention of the imposter policeman who had infiltrated the Tower raid. It was certainly valid if not pertinent to the conversation, but he was struggling with how to introduce the information. He knew that relaying some elaborate conspiracy theory about an all-powerful entity bent on killing the State's captive would definitely sound crazy; in fact, just thinking those words caused him to doubt the insinuated lunacy himself.

"Well, Mr. Taylor, you ran lead on the investigation. Brilliant work, by the way, I couldn't have found my wife out shopping! How you found him amazes me," complimented the Chief Crown Prosecutor. "So, who is he?"

Still debating with himself, Rothery hesitated with a stammer. Dylan seized the opportunity, "He's a psychopath, sir," the younger agent quickly answered. "He thinks he's on a secret mission. The man's not evil but he is extremely dangerous. He's a vigilante who was in the right place at the right time and somehow came out on top. Now I fear that having been so successful, his delusions will only multiply."

Dylan stood continuing to address the small assembly. "We can't have him on the streets, ladies and gentlemen. This bloke could start a revolution. Imagine if the wrong sort— say the English Defense League— got a hold of him and made him their poster-child, we'd have violence in the street! The police and magistrates would be made to side with the Islamic victims and all would escalate out of control." He carefully eyed his intrigued audience. "Once we find out who this man is, I recommend we deport him. That is of course, assuming we don't find skeletons in his closet. In which case, we would have the pleasure of extraditing him." An accelerated clamor spread across the room following the summation.

Elaborating in agreement, member after member began to accuse Micah of various terrorist affiliations as if substantiated facts. Rothery, stunned at the unbridled allegations coming from senior influential dignitaries from every department of State, could not help but feel obliged to chime in. "I beg your pardon to play devil's advocate here…" *even that phrase sounds suspiciously inappropriate,* "but need I mention that this man acted in self-defense?"

The agent's comment appeared to fall to the floor unheard. Frustrated, Rothery pulled out his phone and laid it in his lap as the mock trial escalated.

"What's the timing?" the mayor questioned. "We have three days before a charge, haven't we?"

"No, sir. Actually according to the Terrorist Act of 2005, a person can be held until proven otherwise," Dylan informed. "So, until he begins talking, he looks like Al-Qaida to me."

"Don't say things like that out loud," MP Eleanor Aldous retorted, "you represent the Prime Minister's Office."

"Listen, I'm just trying to prevent an all-out street war," Dylan defended.

"Slow down, lad, we have all the tanks," the second MP said, "revolution can be a healthy thing every once in a while."

While Dylan frowned, the debate continued.

"What about the celebrity? Could she cause a media scandal?"

"Her movies have fallen off."

"True. Though while the public loved her when she was young, we all know they still hate when Hollywood pretends to know something about politics."

"Quite right! The poor white-boy facade will serve our vigilante much better than being aligned with a movie star."

"And, if we apply a bit of pressure," the Chief Crown Prosecutor injected, "her agent will certainly whisk her out of here and back to California." A unanimous consensus formulated in the room.

Although the conversation seemed calm and articulate as each member spouted justifiable legal precedence, to Rothery, watching a room full of Britain's top legal minds delegating sentence was more disheartening to his sense of national pride than the football hooligans at a Manchester United match. "Shouldn't at least one of you use the phrase, 'It's for the greater good,' if we are going to go down this path?" he commented.

"We're only talking about detaining one foreign national until he talks and then deporting him. You're MI6, agent," the Deputy Commissioner challenged, "shall we discuss the collateral damage your department has caused worldwide this year alone?"

Ignoring the Deputy Commissioner and disgusted with the direction of the ongoing conversation, Rothery picked up his phone pretending to peruse his email, inconspicuously scanning the room.

Following a few unsavory remarks regarding the roles and responsibilities of the secret service, the Chief Crown Prosecutor diplomatically backpedaled and approached the seemingly disheartened agent. "Listen, Taylor. You and Dylan here have done a splendid job. You caught him, yeah?" Rothery didn't respond. "I'll take your partner's recommendation and concede that he's not linked to a terrorist organization but could still be a danger under the circumstances. So, unless you have something to add, I suggest you go home— see to your wife and that new baby of yours. Just move on."

"You're absolutely right, sir," Dylan agreed.

"Right, then." The Chief Crown Prosecutor looked toward the Deputy Commissioner, "Let's get the man to talk, shall we? How difficult can that be if he hasn't done anything wrong? Or …" shaking his head, "on second thought, I don't even care. Let's just get him on a plane!"

*　*　*　*　*

"As I said, much to do about nothing," Dylan whispered as he and Rothery left the chamber, his voice laced with cocky undertones.

Rothery eyed his partner. "Are you threatened by the Samaritan, Dylan?"

The good-looking man seemed to think about it, "No, not at all. But it's the law, Rothery, and the next guy will be a thug or worse. We have the law for a reason. The law is holy, it's pure. It's what assures that the richest and poorest must drive the same speed; that they are held responsible for the same actions. It's not perfect and there are times when we need to amend the law, but it's the one unifying force that keeps us civil despite any cultural, political, race, gender or sexual persuasion differences. Any exception leads to anarchy." Rothery frowned.

"The man will be fine," Dylan assured. "Let me buy you a drink, mate."

"You're not interested at all in the seventh cop? Or who is chasing the American?"

"It's just a bit hard to swallow. Why would anyone care a farthing about this guy? Seriously, if he's some corrupt former CIA agent, it's the life he chose."

"Hmm, your tune has certainly changed since the interrogation room."

"I was playing bad cop. Someone had to, you were much too nice. But unless that guy has a cape under his suit," the young man threw up his hands, "what can I say? Corruption exists, Rothery. What can be corrupt is corrupt. Hell, half the people in that room haven't lost an ounce of sleep over the deaths of five people, they're only thinking how it has impacted their position and how they'll be able to use it for re-election.

"Clever, really…" Dylan briefly paused, "it's actually the only part of the system that truly works, as strange as that may sound. Although extremely slow, the system is based on the inevitability that corrupt men must eventually adhere to the will of the people if they want to maintain power and their standard of living. In contrast, of course, to the zealot who will sell the farm to give money to the poor and consequently cause his children and grandchildren to BE the poor. Therefore," he summarized, "the most dangerous politician is a sincerely good man. You want to have a beer?"

"Thank you, no," Rothery sighed. "I'm going home."

Chapter 50

SITTING AT HIS DESK staring at the computer monitor after having been kicked out of the Pressroom Pub long past closing, Henry typed and deleted the same sentence several times. The fact that he had reported on the foiled terrorist attack prior to police's entry into the restaurant— uncovered the wounded man of mystery and made him a hero then a villain; delivered the only exclusive interview (albeit, completely manufactured from Henry's imagination but authenticated by the date-stamped photo of Micah in a parking lot days after the attack)— had given Henry complete and absolute liberty to say whatever he wanted to. He had revived his career by making fools of Downing Street and Scotland Yard's blundered manhunt. It was imperative to keep the ball rolling.

It had been the kind of opportunity a newsman only dreamed of. Henry's articles had been picked up by Reuters and read internationally, thus forcing extreme political pressure to continue the manhunt— but with no-win kid-gloves. His television interviews on Sky, BBC and a number of local affiliates had all gone viral on YouTube making him the number one followed journalist on Google, Facebook and Twitter. Interviews with Fox, CNN and MSNBC were currently under negotiation and the vigilante's apprehension ensured a callback from each. *Let the bidding begin,* he thought.

Still, it all appeared to be coming to an end far too soon. With Micah's capture Henry would now be forced to take a position, a side. Hero or villain. It was more risk than he wanted to wager. The smart move would be to play the uncommitted journalist, *'Hero or Villain, we'll see how this plays out... back to you, Frank.'* But then again, if he dared the risk and guessed correctly, there would be no other anchor betting on an unknown pony and Henry could find himself uttering the phrase, *'You heard it here first!'* from an anchor desk.

But they'll break him, he thought. *And they'll rip him apart and all of my work will have been for nothing. Wolfe Blitzer got Desert Storm and that gave him the anchor's desk. I should have… but now with this new forum— this twenty-first century warfare… there are no borders to get out in front of. It's a war of mixed words from the anchor's desk to the analyst's column.*

"How could that schmuck do this to me?" Henry complained out loud. "Couple more days would have been enough but he had to go and get himself caught… and with Victoria Adams, no less! A million tourists and he couldn't find a cheap hotel to hold up in?! I offered him to stay with ME, for fuck sake! Wanker owes me an exclusive. And I kept her out of it… I could have been on Entertainment Tonight!

"I've got to find a fag," he grumbled. "Karen's a closet-smoker, I can smell it on her. God, I hate smokers… she'd better have a stash."

Henry went to Karen's desk. *Locked.* He broke-in with a letter opener. "Only thing these are good for anymore is breaking into colleagues' desk drawers… or to visualize stabbing your editor," he mused. Nowadays everything was electronic or came in a perforated envelop. He missed envelops— birthday cards with a five pound note. Though he hadn't received a card for thirty years or better, still some things stuck with you.

"Ugh, menthol!" Henry grimaced, finding the hidden treasure. "You've got to be kidding. Nope, not worth falling off the wagon for." But then reconsidering, "Well, maybe it won't be that bad, it'll likely taste like shit anyway."

He placed the cigarette to his lips. "No lighter? Bloody hell! Can't catch a break! Wait, Phil used to smoke, yeah? He's got to have a lighter in his desk, he hasn't cleaned it out since his wife died ten years ago…"

Rummaging through the desk next to Karen's, "Rusted," he whined. He flicked but only got sparks. "What the hell! It's too late to be torturing myself. Oh… oh…!" he managed a weak flame, dropping the cigarette in surprise.

Careful not to extinguish the lighter, Henry reached down and picked up the cigarette. With the success of an igniting drag, a real sense of accomplishment washed over him (though the taste was absolutely horrid). More than pleased with himself, he made his way back to his own desk now committed to finishing Karen's entire pack. Or at least what was left of it.

"Harry?" a voice called out in the dark.

Henry ignored it. He fell back into his chair closing his eyes in delight.

"Harry?" The voice had become louder. It was still unable to disturb the reporter's moment. "Harry!"

Henry opened his eyes. Wally, the janitor, was leaning over him inches from his face.

"Wally," Henry acknowledged barely opening his eyes.

"Harry…"

"Wally, how long have you worked here?"

"Thirty years."

"And how long have I worked here?"

"I don't know. At least twenty."

"That's right, Wally. My name is Henry."

"Isn't that what I said?"

"No, Wally, you called me Harry."

"No, couldn't have, sir. My son-in-law is named Harry."

"Congratulations, Wally. What can I do for you?"

"You can't smoke here."

"Wally, do me a favor just tonight… forget I smoked."

With a sour grimace, "I don't know, sir. They'll think I was smoking."

"Do you smoke, Wally?"

"No."

"Have you ever smoked, Wally?"

"No."

"Everyone knows that, Wally. They won't think you did it. Tell you what… I'll put out the fags in my plant and leave the butts on my desk. If anyone notices, I'll blame Karen."

"No, not Miss Karen!"

"I'm kidding, Wally. I'll take responsibility."

"Well," the janitor seriously thought about it. "I s'pose that'd be all right," he decided. Wally headed back down the hallway.

"Night, Wally."

"Night, Harry."

Henry was beside himself, quite self-satisfied with the success of his covert mission into Karen's cubicle. Rolled up in a ball like a cat who'd gotten to the cream, he cherry-lit his next cigarette.

Chuckling he blathered to himself, "Harry, huh? More than twenty years every night and I'm not Henry Wilkens, I'm Harry, Wally's son. Harry Wallyson!" he laughed. "Why does that sound so familiar? Too tired to think— oh, I know! Prince Harry of Wales. Ha! Hard to believe that kid's all grown up. Hmm… wonder what the royal family thinks of our terrorist fighter."

Henry hit the mouse waking his computer. Email was up on the second monitor.

"Junk mail, junk mail, hate mail…" delete, delete, delete. Henry came across a recently sent message from source@ymail.uk.co. It was titled, 'You'll want to hear this'. Delete.

For some reason, as soon as that particular email disappeared, he paused. *Hmm.* Struggling for a moment he reluctantly pressed Ctrl Z to undo. The message reappeared at the top of his inbox.

Henry blinked at the subject line for a solid minute. He winked with an exaggerated squint and opened mouth. Then, remembering he could only wink with his left eye naturally, using much concentration and a heavy wince, he managed to also wink his right eye— the effort reminding him how his ex-wife had made fun of him because he couldn't curl his tongue, flare his nostrils, or wiggle his ears. "Circus freaky bitch!" he said so loudly he worried Wally might have heard. Henry liked Wally but Wally actually looked a bit like a sideshow act and would have certainly taken the comment personally. Probably tell on him for smoking.

Once certain Wally hadn't been within earshot, with a huge exhale the reporter roughly sat up in his chair, grabbed his mouse and double clicked on the top email. The reflex movement so quick, it made Henry nauseous and caused him the need to sit still with his eyes closed.

A couple of long nods of almost falling asleep, his head bobbed extra hard causing a kink in his neck. Next, a deep breath through his nose and Henry was awake once more. Insomnia to the point of sleep deprivation (topped with one-too-many at the pub) was more than so cool.

Glancing back at the screen he saw an embedded video in the salvaged email. "Porn?" he thought excitedly. "Who would send me porn?" Henry spent a couple moments attempting to come up with anyone.

The only person who came to mind was his ex-wife's brother. He recalled that the last time he'd seen him they'd both been arrested for disorderly conduct. "Yeah," Henry conceded, "no one would send me porn." He remorsefully hit the play button anyway.

The camera in the video was focused on the floor and a pair of men's dress shoes. "Cheap ones," Henry laughed thinking the SOB couldn't have spent more than 100 pounds on them. "This guy better not pull out his dick," he snickered.

That possibility started Henry on a comical binge imagining he had pissed someone off so badly they'd actually sent him video of their junk. "Oh, God! Oh, please! I'll bloody post it!"

Out of nothing more than morbid curiosity and the sheer pleasure of uncontrollable laughter, "He'd better not be a wanker, I'll lose it!" As much as he thought he should, he couldn't get himself to hit pause. "I should shut this off…" It would be the ultimate, though; some offended reader taking an article so seriously they'd sent him 'junk' mail. "Junk Mail!" The pun literally had Henry falling off of his chair.

Waiting for what he thought was the inevitable, Henry rose back to a seated position and started pounding on his desk. "He's sure taking his time," he said to the screen as it continued to show nothing but the man's shoes.

It really was the last thing Henry wanted to see. *If he touches himself, I'll gag,* Henry thought, *but it'd be bloody well worth it! I wonder if it will be a big one or a little one?* Laughing even harder, he imagined someone sending a video of their tiny dick.

Suddenly, whoever had filmed the video lifted the phone for a quick scan of the room. Henry's laughter instantly silenced, "Holy fuck!" The footage briefly showed the room and its occupants then flashed back down to the floor and the cheap, tasseled shoes.

Pausing the video, Henry was stone-cold sober. He rewound two and then three times to be sure he saw what he thought he saw. It was then that he remembered who had worn tassels on their shoes. "Where are my headphones?!"

* * * * *

The front page of the Register Guard morning paper once again sported a single word title— 'Crucified!' Subtitle, 'Hero of Kensington jailed indefinitely!'

Chapter 51

"CHIEF PROSECUTOR, CHIEF PROSECUTOR! Do you have any comments on this morning's article in the Register Guard implicating you and other high-ranking officials for denying the hero of Oceans Restaurant terrorist attack his civil rights with the intention of holding him indefinitely?"

"My office is looking into the allegations. Due to the fact that I am personally implicated in the accusations I am removing myself from the investigation. In an earnest attempt at full disclosure and transparency, a public review board has been selected to oversee the investigation."

"Is it true that the reason for his extended detention is due to him exercising his right to remain silent?"

"That, too, is a topic of the investigation. Full disclosure to the public and press will be forthcoming."

"In that case, when will the Terrorist Fighter be released?"

"As you know, he is the subject of an investigation. Suspicion of collaboration with terrorists has yet to be ruled out; denying cooperation has only exacerbated suspicion. I can assure you his release is the primary focus of the investigative body."

Standing back in the crowd, reveling in his single-shot that took down nearly every seat of authority in London, "Chief Crown Prosecutor... Chief Crown Prosecutor!" Henry hollered over the crowd.

The Chief Prosecutor looked in Henry's direction, recognized him, and then scanned the crowd to give anyone besides Henry an opportunity to ask a question. "We have time for one more question," the prosecutor prompted expecting to see a barrage of hands.

No one responded. The other reporters, recognizing Henry as well, silenced to watch the inevitable exchange knowing that any discussion between the prosecutor and his now famed accuser would be far more news-worthy than any question they could ask. Half the cameras on the politician, the other half on Henry; Henry stood in the middle of the reporters, hand raised high, a smug look upon his face. The prosecutor grimaced then relented, "Yes, Henry Wilkens... you have a question?"

"Thank you, Chief Crown Prosecutor." Henry dramatically lowered his hand. He took his time knowing he would be the top news story on every channel by noon. With a pensive look, a subtle profound nod, and a gaze to the heavens, *This is my defining moment,* he mused.

"Any time, Henry," the prosecutor said with annoyance.

"Chief Crown Prosecutor (CCP)... may I call you CCP?" asking rhetorically. "Considering the prosecutor (you), the commissioner, the mayor, members of the House, and representatives of the PM's Office were all indicted..." pausing for poetic justice, "tell me then, who dare we trust to select an unbiased tribunal of magistrates and barristers to preside over the fate of our silent Hero of Kensington?"

The prosecutor bowed his head, gritting his teeth in an effort to cover his absolute disdain for Henry. Raising it again he smiled, "As I've said, I have dismissed myself from the proceedings in an attempt at full transparency. However, I assure you details will be released quite soon."

In unison the crowd began chanting, "Nemo Tenetur se ipsum Accusare! Nemo Tenetur se ipsum Accusare!"

Smiling from ear to ear Henry yelled over the enthusiastic gathering, "Do you have a name selected for your Star Chamber Tribunal, sir?"

The Chief Crown Prosecutor just stood there— cameras flashing, video cameras zooming in, crowd still chanting. With a look of complete frustration and contempt for the reporter, he finally motioned to silence the crowd, "Mr. Steinbeck..."

"Who?" Henry yelled.

Glaring, the prosecutor forced another smile, "Our beloved Hero of Kensington is set to be released early this afternoon— as it so happens." The congregated public cheered. "Of course," he added quickly, warding off a new wave of questions, "due to political unrest and for security reasons, the exact time and place of his release is highly classified. Ladies and gentlemen, you must excuse me, we're out of time. Thank you all and good day!"

"Whatever changed your mind?" yelled Henry over the clamoring crowd.

The prosecutor frowned as he fled into the building behind him with his back to the press. Muttering in a gritted whisper to his aid, "I hate that nasty sod!"

Chapter 52

THE ROOM WAS MORE than confining, it was quiet. It was sterile clean without the smell of bleach, ammonia or the penetrating scent of lemon. Good ventilation kept the air fresh. Surprisingly, although the cot was thin, Micah slept well with his back to the door of his cell.

The cell pass window opened. "Get up."

Micah casually spun to a seated position to face the metal door. "You know the drill," the guard said from the other side.

Micah slowly walked up to the pass-through, protruded his arms through for wrist restraints. "Now back up, turn around and kneel on the ground," the man ordered. Micah obeyed.

The officer entered and patted him down— which Micah didn't understand; there was nothing in the room nor was anyone allowed inside. He had to reason the protocol was likely attributed more to discipline than safety. The officer placed leg restraints on Micah's ankles and connected wrist and leg shackles to a belt around his waist.

A second officer entered the cell and the two men lifted Micah to his feet. Trying to sound menacing, "Aren't you interested in where we're taking you?" the second officer jabbed.

Micah thought for a moment. He replied puzzled, "You're releasing me."

The two guards exchanged a perplexed look. Quickly shaking it off, "Come along," the first officer ordered.

The men walked Micah down the hall to a small locker room; removed his restraints. "Your clothing is on the table, it's been washed and pressed. Any other possessions will be given to you after processing."

Shortly after Micah had finished changing into his own clothes, a young suit entered. "Good afternoon, sir. My name is Steven Marsh, I'm with the Chief Prosecutor's office. I will be facilitating your release."

"No more guards?"

"No more guards."

"That's got to be an interesting story."

Steven smiled, "Yes, they couldn't keep those details from you if they tried at this point."

Steven walked Micah down a number of completely empty corridors. "It looks like a ghost town," Micah commented, "something special going on?"

"Yes, you."

Micah lifted a brow in surprise.

"You're going to hear a number of things, sir," Marsh advised, "...much of it is true. But just so you are aware, after your apprehension there were a number of reasons those in charge kept you in custody. The most significant was coming up with a way to release you without exposing you to the many... oppositions."

"There are MANY oppositions?"

"Oh, yes, of course. One of which is a small minority within the immigrant population that would like to make an example of your recent heroics. But equally, there are a number of more powerful entities on your side that might have been sympathetic to your plight had they not been continually portrayed as fools to the public in the media."

"Henry," Micah assumed.

"Yes, your friend at the Guard definitely didn't help. Then of course there are always other potential crazies that would enjoy being forever written in the chronicles of the Hero of Kensington— in whatever manner that would have taken form."

"What's the Hero of Kensington?" Micah asked.

Steven, bewildered, "Uh, quite right. Hmm... you're certain to find out. None the less, safely getting you out of here is priority one. Your 'right' to privacy, shall we say," he paused to emphasize, "added complications to expediting your release."

They proceeded down a service lift to a lower basement floor. They walked another half-mile through the dark subbasement passageways of several buildings, then rode back up another service lift to the small back lobby attached to the loading dock of a water treatment facility.

"Nice smell."

"Right… sorry. But no one will think to look for you here." Steven grinned.

They stepped up to the exit doors. "Here you are, sir. On behalf of the Chief Prosecutor's office, we thank you for your patience with our… how shall I say? …judicial process. Because you've provided us no name or identification of any kind, there will be nothing to sign for your release. You are free to walk out that door."

Micah stood silently staring at the exit. He was overwhelmed, almost in disbelief. He was simply being let go.

Mr. Marsh continued, "There were no credit cards nor currency in your possession so I'm obliged to assist you safely to any location within the United Kingdom— either personally or by some form of public or private transportation. If you'd like, you also may use this wall landline to ring for a ride. It looks prehistoric but it does work." Micah graciously shook his head to decline.

"I assure you no one knows when, where or how you're being released," Marsh added. "Not the police, not my office, not even the investigators who arrested you. It's just you and me. Honestly, sir, no one knows… and truthfully, no one should."

"All surveillance cameras are off?"

"Yes."

Micah looked Steven up and down, "I believe you."

The man nodded with a modest smile, "Please stay alive long enough to get out of my country— however you might accomplish that."

"I intend to."

"So, where to?" Steven asked.

"Well, as I said, I trust you," Micah began, "so Cornhill on the east side of town will be fine. If you could drive me there?"

"I have an unmarked car fifty feet from here. Shall we?"

* * * * *

The commute across town during mid-afternoon traffic was tedious. Steven Marsh didn't say much, attempting to respect Micah's anonymity. Yet he couldn't help but to express his gratitude. "If I may?" Steven began.

Micah nodded.

"It's not enough to merely say 'thank you'..."

"For?"

"You were a godsend, sir. Walking down those stairs, defending the people who were at that restaurant," Steven tributed. "For those who went home that night... well, you were no less than an answer to the many prayers I'm certain went up from that room. I won't forget. And neither will they— or their children."

Humbled, Micah gave a nod. "Can you pull over there?" changing the subject.

"Are you certain? This isn't a particularly pleasant neighborhood."

"Yes, but as with the sewer plant, no one should be looking for me here."

Marsh grinned, "Yes, I suppose you're right."

Micah opened the door and stepped out of the car. Before turning to walk away, he paused. "Thank you for the ride, Mr. Marsh. You're a good man. And I honestly don't say that very often."

"It was truly my honor, sir." Steven's heartfelt sincerity was moving.

Readying to leave, Micah hesitated. "Mr. Marsh?"

"Steven."

Micah held out is hand, "It was a pleasure meeting you, Steven. My name is Micah Graff."

The man smiled, gladly shaking Micah's hand. "I'll tell my children."

Chapter 53

"WHO TOLD YOU HE would come out from the water treatment plant? Even the PM couldn't get that information for me." Dylan was baffled.

Rothery explained. "They were releasing him in secret, correct? There were no scheduled prisoner transfers or provisional relocations in the database... even unscheduled releases follow hours of procedural preparation which could have been easily observed. It was a process of elimination. Logically (although the tunnels under Police Metro are vast) there are only a few which could be cleared of all traffic which also led to destinations with small, unattended arterial roads. So, between the qualifying choices, the dock entrance to the UK Sewage Treatment Plant seemed the least likely place the media would look for him."

"That's quite a gamble, isn't it?"

"Not really. I've had Tilman and Harris watching the other possible locations. Pull over, he's getting out of the car."

Dylan slowed the car to a stop as Micah walked away from a silver BMW. "Why here?" he asked Rothery. "It's a horrid neighborhood. I have a gun and I'm not comfortable."

"That's probably part of his reasoning," the agent answered.

"What's he doing? He's just standing there pacing."

"Are you nervous for him or you?"

"He's got to be waiting for someone," Dylan posed suspiciously.

Rothery paused, studying his partner's anxiety. "Do you mind if I tell you something I've noticed about you?"

"Sure. Anything, mate."

"Well, to be quite honest, I actually didn't notice— oddly. It was something Michael said."

"Who's Michael?"

"That's what I'm calling Steinbeck now."

Dylan, suddenly more intent. "What did he say?"

"Oh, he just mentioned that you could win a staring contest. I didn't understand what he meant at the time, I had assumed it suggested you were a cool-headed investigator or the likes."

"I suppose that's complimentary, yeah?"

"Yes, but it did cause me to realize. You don't blink." Rothery looked directly at Dylan.

Dylan pulled back. "Listen, I told you I was only playing bad cop trying to follow your lead," he defended.

"No, no. I mean your eyelids don't physically shut. Strange. I don't know why I've never noticed."

Dylan blinked hard a couple of times. "Hmm, that is weird."

"I didn't mean it offensively, it's just an observation. You have a firm stare."

"Thank you?"

Rothery returned his attention to Micah standing on the street corner. "Just look at him."

"What?"

"He was so accommodating, humble— almost whimsical in the investigation room, don't you agree?"

"I suppose. He was bright, polite— maybe even a bit passive; not whimsical," Dylan answered.

"Passive, possibly. Happy to be there to cooperate, I would say. Maybe over-inviting. But that's exactly my point. Look at him now. His stance— confident, commanding; the way he is carrying himself has purpose. That is not the same man we had in custody."

"Huh. I'd say you're reaching. Anyone would become submissive and apprehensive under SIS investigation."

"At the time did you get the impression he was in the least bit intimidated or threatened at all? He was being held and interrogated for conspiracy to terrorism leading to the deaths of five people, yet that seemed to be the least of his worries."

"So, are you now agreeing that Mr. Steinbeck is a sociopath, Taylor?"

"Actually, I think you mean psychopath. Psychopaths are fearless because they are missing a moral compass. Sociopaths, on the other hand, are not typically fearless; they have a moral compass it's just greatly skewed. Sociopaths are pathological liars whereas I believe Michael believes what he is saying— whether delusional or not."

"Perhaps, then?"

"If he is a psychopath, he's a brilliant one. There were points in his testimony that were truly moving. I'd have to wonder how someone who felt nothing could inspire others to do so. No, he's no psychopath, Dylan. He's a... a... I don't know, I can't put my finger on it."

Dylan frowned. "I think he's standing that way because he has a pebble in his shoe. The look on his face is because he's probably waiting for Victoria Adams and thinking about shagging her. Now I'm thinking about shagging Victoria Adams... am I emitting testosterone?"

"You're missing the point..." Rothery stopped suddenly, "I believe we've been made."

"Why do you say that?"

"Look," Rothery pointed. Micah had stopped pacing, his stance changed submissive. "I told you. He knows we're following him. Now THAT'S the man we had in custody."

Micah smiled, hopped awkwardly on one leg, took off his shoe and made the gesture of removing a pebble.

"Ah-ha! See? I was right!" Dylan exclaimed.

"Wait a minute... how did he know you thought he had a pebble in his shoe?"

"What? Are you paranoid? He had a pebble in his shoe."

"That's what I'm saying... how did he know?" Rothery questioned.

"How did he know what?"

"That he had a pebble in his shoe," Rothery answered.

"Because he stepped on it? His foot hurt?" Dylan was baffled by Rothery's confusion.

"But how did he know you knew?"

"He didn't. I didn't know, I guessed. He actually had a pebble..."

"Stop, stop, I'm getting confused." Rothery looked up. "Damn all! Where did he go?"

"You weren't watching him?"

The back door of the car suddenly opened startling both men. Micah jumped into the back seat. "Now what's really going to mess with your minds is that I DIDN'T have a pebble in my shoe," Micah taunted. "But you guys do need to give me some space, I'm meeting Victoria and you're really cramping my style."

"See? He did know," Rothery announced with satisfaction. "Hey... wait a moment, how did you know?"

"He didn't know," Dylan scoffed, "he heard you rambling as he got into the car."

"But he took the pebble out of his shoe way over there."

"Yes, of course he took a pebble out of his shoe!" Dylan sounded exasperated.

Micah interrupted, "Gentlemen, as much as I hate to say this, I think you've really gotten off topic."

Rothery was most bewildered by his own confusion. He took a moment then deductively continued speaking directly to Micah, "All right, I'll give you the pebble." Micah nodded in sarcastic appreciation. "But the Ms. Adams comment was made in a closed car from fifty feet away."

That fact did catch Dylan's attention. Micah had been too far out of range to hear their discussion about the actress. *It could be coincidence. He could be meeting her, but why here? And the way he said he was meeting her seemed much too suggestive...* Dylan's thoughts caused him to turn a suspicious stare in Micah's direction.

Micah attempted to laugh it off to break the silence but Dylan's eyes bore into him. "Well, Agent Vasko— or is it Vassiago?" he said instead, his address jarring Dylan's trance. "I hadn't noticed this side of you before."

"Side of you," Dylan repeated.

"And now you're repeating me. Why so surprised, Vassiago? Does this concern you?" Micah probed.

Dylan backed off. He shrugged and turned away, looking out the driver-side window. Micah studied the young man's eyes in the review mirror.

Dylan had the paranoid sense that Micah had specifically chosen this location knowing they would follow. "Why here, Steinbeck?" he interrogated. "What business do you have in Cornhill?"

Micah leaned in to examine Dylan's face in the mirror. "This area of town make you nervous? I'm sure you're both armed. Besides, I'll protect you." Micah placed a comforting hand on Dylan's shoulder.

Micah's gesture caused Dylan a reflex jerk-reaction. With gritted teeth, he stretched away from the man in the backseat.

"Now that I've been exonerated," Micah continued, "I just wanted to find a nice, quiet little spot where we could all talk."

He's reading my mind, Dylan thought, his eyes narrowing. Rothery just smiled.

"Something entertaining you, Agent Taylor?" Micah asked.

"About everything entertains me, Michael. Most of all the fact that everything around you never ceases to surprise me."

"Enlighten us, we've got time. There's nowhere to go, is there, Vassiago?"

While Dylan sneered, Rothery spoke unemotionally, logically. "You were hard to read at the hotel, Michael. I had assumed the military style infiltration— your apprehension, Ms. Adams' clear involvement— would have expectedly put you out of sorts. In detention; the allegations and possible indictment would have accounted for some anxiety, as well. However, there were no signs. And you, as far as I could tell, told the truth. All but your name and who was chasing you. Your heart rate stayed even, pupil dilation…"

"What do you see now, agent?" Micah asked, maintaining a visual on Dylan.

"Well, your heart rate is difficult to gage monitoring your aortic artery from this angle… but the focus of your pupils is unwavering. Your nerves are solid— though there is an apparent unconscious gesture in your right hand which, I admit, is a bit unnerving. It's new. I studied the footage from the restaurant and even facing down three men you showed no nervous ticks nor hesitation… though the angle of the film failed to capture you until you committed to head down the stairs. I speculate now that this tick could be a precursor to 'commitment to the moment'… subconscious anxiety?" Rothery postulated.

Remaining clinical he went on, "Neither of us have pulled our guns. And though these are close quarters with you in the backseat and us in the front (far different than the restaurant environment) I suspect from your build and training, this situation only adds to your advantage. But the intense conviction in your eyes is exhilarating! I could add, as well, although it may just be me, it feels as if the temperature in our vehicle has increased dramatically these past three minutes."

"That's enough!" Dylan yelled.

"Has it been three minutes?" Micah questioned with sarcastic innocence. "I do believe this is the longest conversation you and I have had, Agent Vassiago."

"My name is Vasko! Please, stop calling me that," through clenched teeth.

"You call me Allen, he calls me Michael. Neither seems to transform my disposition."

Vasko's demeanor suddenly succumbed to the provocation; his voice a low, hateful growl, "What is your goal here today?" Holding Micah with an icy stare in the rearview mirror, Dylan briefly darted his eyes toward Rothery then returned his threatening glare back to Micah.

"To tell the truth, of course." Micah answered casually, though the threat was not lost to him. "Aren't you interested? You were quiet fervent in the interrogation room. Is that the way you play it, agent? You won't believe the truth unless it's obtained under duress? It seems you need to have a bit more faith in HUMANITY. Or maybe if you pulled your gun, cocked the trigger, you'd be more interested."

"The truth is obviously relative to you, MR. STEINBECK," Dylan retorted.

"Touché. Alright, I was offering." His eyes still locked with the reflection of Dylan's in the rearview mirror, "How long have we been here, Rothery?"

"Just over four minutes."

Micah put his hand back on the younger man's shoulder. "You think I can't tell by the back of your head? It's seldom by sight, you know."

Dylan spun around, staring Micah down like he was nothing; unworthy of consideration. "Face to face," he spat ferociously.

"Looks like you've been out too long," Micah whispered, "you're assimilated."

Dylan, shocked by the phrase, broke his tough-guy guise. "What are you?" he asked in a surprisingly calm voice.

Rothery interrupted, "Do you two know each other from a previous life? Exhilarating exchange! I'm honestly not certain who wants to kill who. It does leave me with some unanswered questions, however."

"I need to spend a minute." Micah pointed to the historic church on the corner and reached for the door handle.

Dylan watched with disgust as his ex-prisoner got out of the car. Micah pulled his hood over his head for protection from the rain, then ran across the street to the gate of the church.

Rothery picked up the radio hand-piece, "Tilman, he's entering St. Michael's front entrance. Circle around, cover the back."

"Will do. But didn't he just get out of your car?"

"Yes, yes… I still want to see where he goes."

Rothery put down the handset, "What was that all about, Dylan?"

"He was goading me," Vasko answered flatly. "I think he knows more about us than you think."

Chapter 54

ST. MICHAEL'S IN CORNHILL had been in existence since the eleventh century. It had long been a place of interest to prominent architects and the subject of local lore. A mystical feel to the structure itself— even architects in recent years had noted that its walls failed to form right angles indicating that for some mysterious purpose, great effort had been spent during numerous renovations throughout history to maintain the original medieval foundation. Legend from sixteenth century bell-ringers told of shape shifting creatures who had caused men to fall unconscious, only to then awaken to devil claw marks upon the masonry. It was believed that strange forces continued for centuries to besiege the edifice to no avail; that the precision of the structure was imperative to its resilience.

Micah entered the large blue door of St. Michaels. An older priest, well into his eighties, greeted him halfway down the aisle. "How may I help you tonight, my son?"

Micah removed his hood.

The priest laughed, "David! I saw you on the telly! I had a feeling you'd be by for confession."

Micah smiled and nodded, his heart warmed by his old friend, Father Ignacio.

The old priest nodded back with approval, "I'm so glad the fact you're not catholic has never stopped you from confessing to me."

"True, my friend. And the fact that you're not Jewish has never prevented you from collecting mitzvot, either."

Micah laughed but seriousness darkened the sound. Father Ignacio sighed, "I wish you could stay. It's been a long time but I know you... you will stand here until I give you permission to leave. I can see by the look in your eye that you came to see Father Abraham."

"I did."

"David, seven years is too long— even for a dead man. We must compare notes."

Micah saddened, "Father, I've lost..." He wasn't even sure where to start.

"What David? What have you lost? Life is long." The priest paused, "Listen, you can hide all you want, but hold your tongue? It only turns to fire. Let's go see if we can find Father Abraham."

Father Ignacio led Micah to a back chamber where Father Abraham sat reading. Slowly looking up, in a thick New York accent, Abraham skipped the niceties, "Listen, I've already talked to your cohort, I've been expecting you. Time to leave the isle?"

"You need to work on your British accent."

"And you need to work on how to be a tourist." Abraham shook his head disapproving of the mess which seemed to follow Micah wherever he traveled. Still, the older man couldn't help but smile.

"Actually, I need to use the phone, Abraham. Does it still work?"

"Last time I checked. Haven't had need for a few years. Remember how to use it?"

"I'll manage," Micah answered. "Just not sure I remember how to get to it," he added.

Abraham cleared his throat, "Penitent side, close the veil; sit on the shriving stool. Open the penitent lattice screen, lift the testimonial table; kick the leg, kneel. When the martyr's kneeler gives, watch your head."

"Close the veil... open the screen... uh..."

"Sit on the stool, open the screen..."

"Veil, stool, screen, table, leg, kneel. In that order?"

"Yes."

"Okay. Oh, how do I get to the testimonial table from the penitent side?"

"Through the screen. That's the safety lock. Priests don't open the screen and martyrs don't lift the priest's table. So, you're getting out of town?"

"Yes, probably... I..."

"I don't like the sound of that. You're not a spy, David— or whatever you've been playing this week."

"Yeah, well, you're not a priest, either."

"Your friends out front... are they with the bobbies in the back?"

"I suspect."

"They going to come looking for you after you're gone?"

"Probably."

Abraham scowled. Micah shook his head, "No, no they're alright— sort of." However, as Micah headed for the confessional chamber, he turned back, "Just watch the cold one. He won't doing anything with the others around, but still..."

"How COLD?" Abraham questioned, sternly.

Micah nodded slowly, "Stone cold."

Abraham dropped his head to his chest, exasperated. Scolding, he yelled after Micah, "What did I ever do to you, David? You bring this to me? What...? You bring Satan as a parting gift for Father Ignacio?"

*   *   *   *   *

Micah entered the parishioner's side of the old confessional chamber in the former oratory. Five-hundred years ago the room served as the main sanctuary of the historic edifice, but the building had been renovated several times since and the former historical chapel now was the inner chamber of the larger chancel, yet still served as a personal prayer chapel for the priests.

The old confessional chamber was now primarily ceremonial, though some of the younger priests still considered it sacred in their right of holy passage to priesthood. The inner furnishings of the chamber were made of stone; the outer cabinet was finely engraved English oak resembling fifteenth century English stone architecture with arches and steeples— likely built later when anonymity of confession had been added to the act of holy consecration.

As Micah pulled the veil, he sat upon the ancient, stone shriving pew. He then opened the lattice screen and reached into the priest's chamber to lift up the arm table. Kneeling on the stone step, nothing appeared to happen. He went through the steps again in his head. *Oh yeah, kick the leg,* he corrected. Which really didn't seem reasonable— both the bench and kneeler were solid stone and carved into the very large foundation pillar. The pillar (which was at least seven or more feet in diameter) likely dated back centuries to the origins of the building before the first roof had ever been built.

Upon his knees, Micah gave a swift kick out to the hind bench leg. To his surprise, the leg moved with ease, folding into the stone wall and causing the bench to drop. The kneeler slipped into the floor under the weight of his body triggering a mechanical lever that rotated the inner stone contents of the confessional chamber (including Micah) into the huge cylindrical foundation pillar. Just as Micah and all the inner contents of the penitent side of the confessional chamber rotated passed, the heavy oak table slammed down on Micah's head. "Ouch!"

From outside the moving confessional Abraham's muffled voice could be heard, "Told you to watch your head!"

Micah, surprised to be able to hear so well encased in the hollow stone pillar, rubbed the newly forming goose-egg. *He was probably standing right outside just waiting to hear that happen.*

From inside the pillar the floor continued to shift. Giving way, step by step, a spiral staircase leading down was exposed.

*   *   *   *   *

Sergeant Tilman entered the chapel. Father Ignacio graciously met him near the altar in the main sanctuary, "May I help you, officer?"

"What makes you think I'm a policeman?"

"You and your partner have been out back for some time, son. Why don't you invite all three of your friends inside?"

"Three?"

"Those boys in the second car must be getting cold by now, as well. They've shut off their engine."

"You keeping an eye on us, Father?"

"My parish has always reached beyond these four walls."

"Where is he, Father?"

"Father Abraham is in prayer right now."

"And the American that entered the church?"

"Certainly a learned man of Scotland Yard knowingly upholds and defends the Right of Asylum?"

"Right of Asylum?" Tilman was incredulous, "Seriously, Father…"

"Oh, don't jest with me, son. Surely you know a man merely need touch the door-knocker or sit on the frith-stool." Pointing above them, "That cross under which you stand has been an acknowledged sanctuary stone by centuries of Kings of England. Therefore, I am sure you certainly don't expect me to answer questions regarding residents of this church."

"Is that true, Father?"

"In the height of the law there were twenty-two sanctuary churches in surrounding London, including Westminster Abbey. St. Michael's has provided more refuge than any other of royal decree."

"All right, Father. Do you mind if I have a look around?"

"Not at all, make yourself at home. Should I put on some hot tea for your colleagues?"

"That won't be necessary, thank you."

Having taken only a few steps down the staircase, the trapped door sealed behind Micah. The stairs below were lit by the open-air sky in the hollow pillar leading up to the bell tower above. Miniscule cracks in the pillar's outer walls also added to the illumination. Micah stopped suddenly when he heard Father Ignacio and the constable only a few feet beyond the curved stone; he listened breathlessly for any indication that the closure had alerted the sergeant.

Dylan and Rothery's voices came next; Father Abraham's followed. Dylan's voice grew louder, echoing around Micah's position. The young agent was suspiciously close to the pillar. It sounded as if he was purposely speaking for Micah to hear. "Where is he?" Dylan asked Tilman.

"He must be in the building... although the padre has claimed sanctuary—Right of Asylum," the sergeant answered.

Rothery smiled, "Quite nice, Father. Though you must know the church's right of asylum was abolished some time ago... about 400 years?"

"Really? You're quite certain?" Father Ignacio questioned innocently as if unaware of any recent change.

"Quite."

Tilman looked at the clergyman with disappointed shock. Seeing his expression, the priest meekly shrugged.

"You lied, Father?" Tilman seemed almost disheartened.

"Actually officer," Father Ignacio explained, "what I said was that St. Michael's had provided more refuge than any other of royal decree. I didn't say that any royal in this century recognized it. None the less, my obligation as a priest still forbids disclosure of a man's confession. Tea, light snack, anyone?" Tilman managed a wry smile.

Ignoring most of the exchange, Dylan continued to pace around the stone pillar keeping an eye on the priests, watching for a reaction. Micah felt Dylan's proximity, his presence like a sickening in the pit of his stomach. His empty right hand ached a longing like the ghost memory of a held weight of great mass. His wrist strengthened to bare the unseen weight so prominently, he held his hand up to the penetrating light to gaze upon its insistence to grip the illusionary object. *Your hands are smarter than your head will ever be.* It baffled him that his fingers denied his mind's directive to close, refusing to give credence to what his eyes failed to behold.

Dylan held his large palm against the stone, his fingernails in the cracks as if examining the ancient structure. Glancing over his shoulder to Father Ignacio, "I appreciate your loyalty to the tradition of law, Father. Of course, I assume your faithful servitude to the law requires respect for those of us who now uphold it."

Facing back toward the pillar, Agent Vasko appeared intent on Micah's exodus from London. He spoke loudly to the hidden stone chamber as if to make that point clear. "We do not seek your patron in malice, Fathers, we only want to assure that he leaves London safe and IMMEDIATELY." He gave a poignant pause, "It would be regretful should misfortune befall him... *or his friends.*"

Micah was struck with a piercing pain; like a stabbing icepick to the socket of his eye popping both ears and stripping him of his equilibrium. In that instant, his right hand launched instinctively to a defensive position to shield; his knees bent for impact, his back arched, his head cocked to attack. A bright blue light emitted from his eyes. Then as quickly as the pain came, it vanished.

Thrown off guard by the intense power burst emitted through the pillar, Dylan suddenly pushed back from the wall in surprise.

The abrupt, unexpected move and shocked expression on the handsome man's face was enough for Rothery to notice. "Are you all right, Dylan?"

It took a moment for the young agent to respond. "I'm fine."

"Maybe you should leave, gentlemen," Father Abraham suggested, backing a few steps away from Agent Vasko.

Eyes darting to Abraham, contempt crossed Dylan's face. He turned to Rothery, "I'll meet you in the car."

*   *   *   *   *

After hearing the group disband, Micah descended the curving stairwell. Upon reaching the bottom of the staircase, dim motion-sensor bulbs lit the musty passage. He proceeded down a long stone corridor that continued downhill into the depths of London's underground.

The tunnel eventually opened to a dimly lit room; an early 1900's crank telephone mounted on the rough stone wall. Micah picked up the receiver and cranked the phone three rounds, paused a moment, then cranked two more rotations before waiting. Cranking the old phone charged a magneto N°, 6-inch zinc-carbon dry cell which generated all the electricity necessary to ring and signal a switchboard operator across the wire.

Next to the hanging phone on a small hallway desk, an even older telegraph device began receiving a message. ".. _ _ _   _ _   _ _ _   . _ .   ." Dot dot dash dash dash; dash dash; dash dash dash; dot dash dot; dot.

Micah cranked the phone twice again and was instantly met by a voice on the other end of the phone receiver. "Operator."

"Ugarte, please."

"Connecting. Hold, please." The line held for a moment.

A male voice on the line, "Ugarte."

Micah quoted, "Who did you have to bribe for your visa, Renault or yourself?"

"Myself. I found myself much more reasonable," the voice answered.

"How did you answer this phone so quickly, Kip?" Micah asked.

"What? Are you suggesting I've been standing by the phone since they announced your release?"

"Ah, I wouldn't presume."

"I have other clients, you know," Kip defended. "Maybe none as fun or dangerous, but matter of fact, I have a friend of yours upstairs at this very moment."

"Your use of the term 'friend' is a bit too generous for me to guess whom you might mean," Micah retorted. "But considering most of my 'friends' in London are upstairs HERE interrogating Abraham, I'll assume you mean the pretty one."

"Well, I don't know," Kip teased, "the PM's boy is a looker... might give her a run."

"Wouldn't he look nice in a dress?" Micah added sarcastically. "But he's upstairs, too. By the way, the PM job... it's a side gig for him."

"Really? You don't say? Hired help or stakeholder?"

"Oh, he's on the fricken board of directors."

"Hmm," Kip pondered, "didn't strike me as that brilliant."

Micah heaved a frustrated sigh, "How many times have I told you they're not all rocket scientists?"

"So, St. Michaels, huh?" Kip chose to leave the discussion for later. "Do you know your way out?"

"Not in a hurry."

Kip began to explain, "Continue away from St. Michaels. You'll come to a six-way intersection. Take the corridor north... oh wait, how will you know north from underground?"

"Don't worry about it."

Kip chuckled, "Oh, that's right. Forgot who I was talking to. The corridor continues to switch and turn; stay north... I don't remember how many turns. Anyway, about four hundred meters from where you are now, you'll come to a 'T'. Turn left and forty feet up the way..."

"It might be helpful if you kept to just one measurement system."

"You'd have rather I said a quarter mile north, turn west for 1200 centimeters, smartass?"

"My! You get testy on these old party lines."

"Party line? Maybe you'd like your iPhone back? Then Ring Finger, NSA, KGB, SIS and the Mossad could listen to every word!" Kip expounded defensively, "Do you know how many lives, saved by this hundred year-old secure rescue line, you disrespect with that comment? I can connect the Kremlin with Quantico on this phone."

"Are you trying to give up caffeine again?"

"There's nothing wrong with caffeine, Nutria-Sweet is the killer." Kip paused. "Do you want to know what's forty feet off the 'T' or not?"

"I'm all ears," Micah grinned.

"Plummer's overalls and a manhole."

"That doesn't sound pleasant. "

"It's so you can walk out the security door. The key is under the coffee can on the shelf by the door."

"Coffee can," Micah snickered.

"Lay off coffee!" Kip snapped.

"No, no, no, I'm just thinking 'under the coffee can' seems a bit cliché. That would be the first place I would look."

"It's inside the security door. Anyone who gets to the can already has a key anyway. The key is for guests like you that want to get out from BEHIND the security door."

"Oh, okay."

Kip instructed, "Unlock the door, leave the key. The door locks behind you. Then you'll be at Banks tube station. You know your way from there."

Micah squinted, "Um, Central to Oxford Circus; Bakerloo to Charing Cross."

"Yeah, but I'd rather take Northern to Elephant & Castle, then Bakerloo north to Charing Cross." Thinking about it, "Wait… actually if you walk from Bank to Circle or District you can take either to Embankment…" Kip heard a click. Jiggling the receiver holder, "Hello… hello?" Frowning, Kip put down the phone. "Can't believe that ass hung up on me. This phone doesn't disconnect!"

* * * * *

Arriving at the six-way intersection Micah closed his eyes and circled slowly until he was facing south-southeast. From there he adjusted true south, turned a 180 degrees, and took the north corridor.

Chapter 55

THE MOMENT MICAH ENTERED through the back door of Kipley's Appliances, Victoria wrapped her arms around him.

"Where to?" Kip asked Micah.

"Home. Got to feed my dog."

"Glad to hear it," Kip replied jovially. "If you can leave tonight, you'll be out by morning. If not, when was the last time you were in country?"

"About 8 months ago, why?"

"Do you know the exact date?"

"It's in my passport… but I can leave tonight."

"That's better yet. There's a ship leaving in the morning from Dover. From there it goes to Amsterdam before heading south to the channel. Backstory— you've booked passage in Nova Scotia for a piece you're writing. Your passport has been stamped in Nuuk Port, Greenland; Reykjavik, Iceland and Dublin, Ireland. You took sick and stayed aboard in Dover and spent most of your time in the cabin before sailing on to the Netherlands."

"So, it's over?" Victoria looked at Micah sadly and with resignation.

Micah shrugged, unknowing.

"Then we walk away, right?" she asked.

Micah chuckled, "You remind me of my daughter. Victoria, it's not a movie. These guys don't go away. We don't need to seek them out, they find us. We were just in the wrong place at the right time."

"But they are here for a reason, right?"

Micah shrugged, "They always are. But I can't stop terrorism and I'm not here to save Rome." Micah sighed.

"He's right," Kip said. "Micah, your debt has been paid."

My debt. The words echoed in Micah's head. Thoughts of his wife, her untimely death, his first born son. He wanted to say, *I've paid... hasn't it been paid in full?* But he couldn't even finish the thought in his head yet alone speak the words out loud without seeing the richness of his life— his daughter, his son, and the spirit of his wife just to have known her. He smiled to himself, *She was such a pain... she's STILL a pain in my ass!* He chuckled. She was someone he could fight and argue with and it would never effect how passionately they loved one another.

Micah turned away, grabbed a book off the shelf, opened it pretending to read. He mumbled under his breath, "I've paid Lena, haven't I?" He pictured her, heard her voice, *"It's ALL a gift, Kai, you get to take it."*

"So, its home then?" Victoria's voice pulled him back to the present.

Micah shut the book, "If ever in doubt, that's right." Changing the subject, "There's this really cool hotel in Canterbury. It's where, uh... Geoffrey Chaucer wrote his books. I think I may have stayed in his room. Oh, and there's a theatre. I saw '39 Steps' there once upon a time. It's called the..." Micah snapped his fingers trying to remember, "Shakespeare's competitor... you know... um... the Marlow Theatre."

"There's no one like Marlow," Victoria quoted.

"Shakespeare in Love," Kip commented.

"Victoria," Micah continued, "why don't you come with me to Canterbury for the night?"

Victoria was very aware of Canterbury history and had stayed there many times but didn't want to ruin the lightness of the mood and Micah's proposed guided tour of the quaint city.

"Your car is in long-term, Gatwick Airport," Kip mentioned.

"Ugh. That's a journey."

"No problem, take one of mine," Kip offered. "I'll have Felix drive your car in tomorrow."

"Uh, and how will we get your car back to London? Never mind, we're not in a hurry. We'll take a cab to Gatwick and hit M25 east," Micah decided.

"You're going to call me, right?" Kip asked.

"How about you plan a trip to my place?" Micah suggested.

Kip raised an eyebrow.

"Bring Kassandria."

"Who'll mind the store?"

"Better idea… send Kassandria, you mind the store."

"Alright, alright, we'll make it out there," Kip assured.

Chapter 56

THE STREET OUTSIDE KIPLEY'S Appliances was lined with hackney carriages. Just because thirty or more of the 'London Taxis', 'black cabs' or 'hacks' could be seen within a single block didn't mean Micah would necessarily find one unoccupied in a reasonable amount of time; there always seemed to be an equal amount of people attempting to hail one.

When finally one arrived out front, as a gentleman exited, Victoria and Micah jumped in before there could be any question of who was first in the sidewalk queue. "Gatwick Airport," Micah requested.

"Right away, sir," the driver replied.

Fairly unique to London, the typically black, oversized icon of the UK often offered seating on both sides in the back compartment allowing patrons to face each other— half facing the rear and the others to the front. Micah sat in the back facing the driver; Victoria took the seat across from him, smiling. A sense of relief overtook the couple; the week-long Oceans Restaurant adventure was over and there was no question in either's mind of what might be on the Canterbury agenda.

As the driver by-passed the freeway entrance, Micah spoke over the seat, "Excuse me, you missed the motorway entrance."

"The motorway is stop and go all the way around the loop, sir. I can cut through the city faster."

"Really? How's that possible?"

"Tell you what, if I don't get you to your destination in less than an hour, you'll have one less debt to pay."

One less debt to pay, hung in the air. "Excuse me?" Micah leaned forward into Victoria to have a better look at the driver.

The driver glanced at Micah in the rearview mirror and repeated, "I'll get you to Gatwick in less than an hour or the ride is on me."

Victoria chimed in excitedly, "Or, how's this… you get us there in under an hour, I'll double the ride as a tip!"

As Micah attempted to check out the driver's face, Victoria (sitting across from him with her back against the glass partition) grabbed him by the hands and pulled his attention back to her, "It's been an adventure, hasn't it?"

"That sounds so final," Micah grumbled.

"I wonder what a tropical vacation with you would be like… take down a drug cartel?"

Micah scoffed and flopped back into the seat, "Oh, God, I can't compete with myself!" He adjusted himself getting comfortable, "I'm actually a very boring person, Victoria. I wake up every morning, drink my coffee, play my guitar…"

"We can do that. Let's pick up a guitar in Canterbury; sit in the hotel and you can play for me. Do you sing?"

"You haven't heard me sing?"

"No."

Micah thought about it, "Hmm, this really must have been a busy week because I always…"

Just then a loud explosion came crashing through the air. The windows of the car rattled, the seats shook. Cars slammed on their breaks bringing traffic to a complete stand-still as far as Oxford Circus. The city's neon lights on the backdrop of the darkening evening sky, along with the rotating ground-level spotlights in front of the Royal Opera House, made pedestrians into shadow-giants against the towering city skyline.

Looking to see what had happened, for a moment everything seemed to be moving in slow motion. Confetti rained down upon a large crowd, the blast having come from a confetti cannon. A screaming police siren wailed in the distance before Micah could catch up with his senses. The streets, flooded with people, gave this Friday night celebration the feeling of Mardi Gras or Carnival, Rio de Janeiro. Everyone and everything moving appeared staged in a pulsating strobe light.

A skeleton dressed character pounded on the taxicab back window providing a startling bass back-beat to the ominous collage. Victoria, facing the rear, saw the skeleton face, but Micah didn't have to look. The expression on her face was enough. Micah faced front with a view out the windshield; it was surreal. Their driver shouted in Arabic at a parade of costumed pedestrians— his words, though lost in the noise, added to the haunting scene.

The blasts, siren, lights and sounds of people circulated into a perfect storm of deafening silence, no one noise any more distinguishable. It was a party, no more, no less, yet a sense of dread manifested as the siren grew nearer.

Victoria scanned west as Micah scanned east until their eyes met in the middle. Before that moment neither were aware of the other's share in the menacing illusion. Their eyes fixed on each other as if reading minds, both knowing this event was more than a coincidence, more than premonition or accident. *'One more debt to pay,'* rang in Micah's ear.

The siren crept closer and closer. Another cannon blast caused them both to jump drawing Micah's attention out the driver-side window. The parade having passed, now gave way for a police officer carrying a long thin duffle bag to dart around the hackney and cross the street. Though able to see the man for only an instant, Micah recognized him immediately— the mysterious imposter policeman from the Tower Hotel.

The look on Micah's face was enough to tell Victoria that he was seeing far worse than a man in a skeleton costume. His alert disposition collapsed into exhausted sadness, grievous thoughts overwhelming him. She had seen the look before. In the restaurant. Just before rising against the terrorists.

Victoria swiftly turned her attention out the window. Seeing only the back of a policeman carrying a long duffle bag and heading toward the back alley behind the Royal Opera House was enough. A sickening feeling hit the pit of her stomach; she, too, saddened and knew exactly what Micah felt and why. His heart was made for love. Micah's heart— the most passionate man she'd ever known— wanted only to unite, ignite, inspire, and delight. But this was not his world. So much to give but no one to listen; hunted and despised— a deer in the jungle led into unavoidable circumstances.

From across the street they could see dignitaries exiting chauffeur-driven limousines. Given the barrage of reporters and camera flashes, Micah knew someone of prominence was coming or had just arrived. *This, too, is more than coincidence,* he noted.

With a sudden sharp pain to his head, he closed his eyes tight. Images bombarded his mind; blood painted victims, a child screaming for her mother, a woman shaking speechless in empty terror while standing over a faceless loved-one. Visions of horror, disbelieve, and emptiness. Micah couldn't even speak.

A howling substantiated the vision, the premonition. Micah knew (and feared) who might exit the next approaching limousine. *The target, the victim, collateral damage…? It doesn't matter.* One thing was certain; Micah had the strongest impression that something would cause him to leave the cab.

As an older gentleman emerged from a distant limo Micah was almost relieved. It was no one he recognized. Obviously some politician or dignitary of note, but no one he had ever seen before. *Is he a good man? Does that even matter? Is he just a statistic— die today, tomorrow, or the next? Is there a difference? And what does that mean… one less barrister, one less corrupt official?*

Micah shook his head. *How is it my debt is not yet paid? Maybe this is all in my head. Maybe I create my own trouble. Shell-shocked, it makes sense…*

But then Micah saw him. Watching the next chauffeured vehicle as it pulled up in front of the Opera House, "The Crown Chief Prosecutor," he stated.

"What?" Victoria asked.

"The man," Micah continued solemnly, "who will get out of the next limousine across the street must be the Crown Chief Prosecutor."

"Do you know him?"

"No," he answered, emotionally drained, "but the man standing on the curb to meet him is Steven Marsh. I met him today. And that must be his wife and kids standing behind him." Victoria stared at the family waiting on the sidewalk.

Micah took a deep breath and let out a sigh of resignation. "It's cold out tonight, isn't it?"

"Yes, it is," she barely managed.

As Micah reached for the door handle, Victoria didn't have to ask where— or why.

Chapter 57

HENRY CRUSHED OUT HIS cigarette against the wall of the Opera House building as he awaited the approaching Crown Chief Prosecutor. Henry's article (and following interview with the prosecutor) still topped the headlines having played live that morning and then replaying on the evening's early broadcast. *One more victorious recognition from the accused and my fate will be sealed in the minds of UK citizens and political analysts worldwide!*

One more validation and Henry was convinced he would finally join the elite league of trusted journalists; a spokesman for political justice— a voice of reason. He would no longer have to chase the story but make it, influencing political policy for years to come. Pushing off the wall, he headed toward the approaching entourage.

As he worked his way into the tide of excited theater-goers and mulling journalists, an enthusiastic reporter bumped into him causing him to drop his pen. Grumbling, Henry reached down to pick it up just as the crowd briefly parted in the rush. Looking up toward the south of the building through a small hole in the wall of people, Henry spied Micah high-footing it toward an alley behind the Opera House.

"What the hell...?" In bewildered disbelief Henry stared, eyes fixed on Micah.

"Prosecutor! Prosecutor! Has he been acquitted? Can you confirm his release? Will the investigation continue?" Reporters cried out to the passing official.

Homed in on Micah, Henry ignored the crowd and quickly rose to his feet, stepping in the direction of the alley. Moving too rapidly, he happened to run head-on into the Crown Chief Prosecutor.

The two men stopped, the prosecutor not at all surprised to find Henry in the sea of ambitious reporters. Cameras instantly flashed capturing the men face to face. The prosecutor, all too aware of the unavoidable media exposure, posed a friendly face for the cameras. "No questions for me, Mr. Wilkens?" Although Henry was slightly stunned by the run-in, he was more distracted keeping an eye on Micah who was darting almost out of sight.

The momentary pause seem to last indefinitely. Finally Henry smiled. To the shock of the prosecutor and the media blitz, the reporter put a hand upon the prosecutor's shoulder. "Sorry, mate, too busy just now. You go enjoy the show." He rushed away from the crowd and after Micah.

The prosecutor smiled large, turning toward the reporters— apparently redeemed. "Well, ladies and gentleman, you have just witnessed that justice has been served and accusers satisfied! We may not always get it right the first time, but I stand by the honest men and women of the Prosecutor's Office. This was another fine example of hard work, brilliant relationships and tireless perseverance..." the prosecutor went on and on.

Henry left the scene shaking his head in disgust as he shuffled toward the alley. He pulled out his phone, opened his email to source@ymail.uk.co, and pressed REPLY. Using voice dictation as he moved, Henry composed his message, "Our boy is in a hurry to go to the opera. Debt paid!" He clicked SEND.

*　*　*　*　*

By the time Micah had reached the south alley, the questionable officer was nowhere in sight. He checked every side-entrance door; locked. He reached the back loading docks; trucks barricaded the motorway entrance. Finally in his search, Micah found one of the loading dock's sliding metal gates had been left ajar. He pushed back the heavy screen and slowly entered a large warehouse-sized receiving area.

The warehouse was filled with huge sets and stage props the size of houses— matter of fact, many of the sets were finely detailed fronts of buildings. There were crates, electronic hoists, and portions of multi-floor stage risers. And within the web of faux buildings, rows of small offices veered off in each direction. *Too many places for an assailant to hide, searching would be pointless. And besides,*

Micah thought, *an assassin doesn't come to a crowded arena full of prominent dignitaries to hide in the loading dock.* Micah continued to head for the mainstage.

At the far end near the warehouse's primary pathway to the mainstage, distinct fresh blood splatters dripped down a back wall. Two bullet holes were clearly visible— one about waist-high, the second at eye-level. *Close range, low caliber. No sound. Must have been silenced.*

Streaks of blood on the floor led to a nearby broom closet. Micah donned his gloves. *This will be impossible to explain,* he thought, shaking his head. Everything in his mind was telling him to back out of the theater, cover his face, and get out of the country that night.

Micah cracked the closet door and saw a security guard; eyes opened, bullet wounds to the chest and head. Two fingers to the guard's neck revealed no pulse but still warm. This was one time he hoped for surveillance cameras zoomed in and fully focused. On the upside, the killer having moved the body, was now leaving a blood trail thick enough for him to follow.

Out the door to another staging area of near equal size and with an equal number of places for the assassin to ambush, flank or elude him... *Elude me?* Micah pondered the realization that he, once again, was pursuing an armed killer without a weapon. *Just great.*

Weaving through an endless maze of extremely narrow corridors with no clue as to where he was headed, he passed by a series of greenrooms with many people coming and going; last minute rehearsals. A voice over an intercom counted down time to curtain, "Act One to the stage... Act One to the stage. Places, places! Fifteen minutes to curtain," causing Micah an additional sense of urgency and instant flashbacks to his days in college theater.

There were few things as stressful as opening night jitters (not being able to remember a single line at fifteen minutes to curtain) now amplified by the minor fact that he was once again ENGAGING a crafty, armed killer/assassin without even a ticket in his hand for the show. None the less, he knew that whether he failed or succeeded, his only chance was to make up ground and get between the man and his proposed target. *Fifteen minutes to curtain. The killer will likely take his shot before the lights go down in the auditorium.*

Completely lost within the maze of the enormous backstage, Micah was left to his intuition. He stopped, closed his eyes, and oriented himself. His wife used to call him a human compass. Having traveled around the world to new and foreign cities, he had an uncanny sense of direction, up/down, altitude. He'd driven to addresses he'd never been to long before GPS and without looking at a map… or buying a map at a gas station within the final mile, only to find that he was merely a couple blocks away from his final destination or was heading in the correct direction on the correct road (nine dollars and ninety-five cents down.) However, that hadn't stopped his wife from being the most obnoxious backseat driver… even though Micah had never been the cause of them being late to the party.

He couldn't explain how he did it; just attributed it to being raised on the I-5 corridor in the Pacific Northwest with the Cascade mountain range to the east, the Pacific Ocean to the west, and the rain coming in with the Arctic cold fronts to the north. *"Still,"* Lena would refute, *"growing up in the PNW doesn't explain how you found your way home to Navotas from Smokey Mountain through the barrios of Divisoria while we were in the Philippines."*

Through yet another door and thin winding corridor, at the end of the hallway he spied the suspect entering a room. Running to the end, Micah vigilantly opened the door to find a warehouse of costumes and props roughly the size of Macy's.

Making his way through quickly and cautiously, he came to an opening where two women stood making last minute alterations to an elaborate dress. "Did a police officer come through here?"

"No," one woman replied while the other moved toward a back entrance with a handful of clothing, presumably heading toward the dressing rooms. Micah stood puzzled.

As the second woman reached the rear door she looked back at Micah. She gave him a suspicious grin as she exited. *What does that mean?* He considered his option of searching through the department-store-sized mall of costumes, wigs and props, but knew every crevice would be impossible to check. He opted instead to follow the deviously cheerful woman.

Following closely out the back door to another hallway, the woman had already mysteriously vanished. Micah paced the hall of many doors. Back and forth with no inclination of which way to go, he spotted a smudge upon the floor; darkened brown with hints of red. Could be paint, could be mud, could be makeup… could be blood.

"Act One to the stage, ten minutes to curtain. Places, places!"

Micah hit the door without hesitation, then up a few stairs to the stage-right wing of the Royal Opera House mainstage. He could hear running footsteps on the scaffold lattice above causing him to look up. Diverse colored floodlights shined down in his eyes, but Micah knew at a glimpse, the officer was up there.

Mid-stage a temporary ladder led to the scaffold above; the permanent stairs towards the back on the opposite side. Micah hesitated, "Seriously? This is way too cliché." *It doesn't make sense, he'll never escape. Or maybe he's not worried about it… he did disappear from the top floor of the Tower Hotel.*

Micah resigned and scaled the ladder to the upper platform. Along the side then across the bridge in the dark, he saw what looked to be a man kneeling on the catwalk center stage setting a rifle in position. Micah slowed and stopped twenty feet from the assailant.

Looking up the assassin spoke, "You are so predictable." The counterfeit officer smiled and shifted his eyes down to Micah's feet. A military issue Glock 17 9mm pistol with silencer laid on the bridge. "Pick it up. END this!"

Micah remained motionless.

"I'm sure you can reach it before I can raise this rifle," the evil man taunted.

"I don't get it," Micah said cautiously, "this is no assassination attempt."

"Read the papers tomorrow, the story has already been written. All that remains is the title. Best-case it reads, 'Murder/Suicide by Police— Opera House Assassin'. Regardless, you'll be out of the way."

The policeman rose to his feet. Briefly glancing to his peripheral upstage, he raised his hands as if to surrender. He shouted, "Don't do it, mister! Please!" Strangely his voice was female and his sinister grin had morphed into a look of horror. Micah was confused.

Suddenly, the man's face became distorted; his skin changed like forming putty. He shrunk in size; the color of his clothing changing right before Micah's eyes. Micah stared speechless watching the assassin completely transform into a round, timid, female stagehand with STAFF written on the back of her coat.

"Don't do it, Michael!" a voice called out from upstage-left.

The assailant's sinister voice, exhilarated, "Best-case!" then instantly reverted back to the pleading of a young woman, "Please, please don't!"

Micah looked down, the Glock had somehow mysteriously appeared in his hand. He glanced to his left and saw SIS Agent Rothery Wyndham Taylor atop the staircase at the far backstage catwalk. In a startling movement, Rothery drew down on Micah.

Micah immediately dropped the gun and raised both hands— fingers widespread— in Rothery's view. The men locked eyes and the agent began to slowly lower his gun.

Not daring to look away, Micah cautiously moved his arm to point to the assassin. But as he did, again Rothery raised his gun at Micah.

Betwixt, Micah quickly shifted his eyes to find the Glock once more grasped in his hand now raised and pointed at the terrified stagehand. Micah, wide-eyed in disbelief, knew what would inevitably follow.

No sooner had the thought formed than a blood stain unexplainably manifested on the woman's chest quickly growing in diameter. Blood sprayed and spilled down her blouse.

Stepping backward as if recoiling from the impact of an imaginary gunshot wound, the stagehand's foot caught purposefully in the dividing chain. The woman gave a wicked snarl and darkly jeered, "Weave your way out of this one, Micah Graff!"

Her eyes rolled back into her head; her skin already pale as she stepped one more step backward, taking her off the bridge and plummeting her to the floor below.

Micah dropped the gun and threw up his hands stunned. Rothery lowered his weapon in bewilderment. The two men stood speechless, staring.

Horrified screams followed the loud thwack of the woman's body hitting the wooden stage. A chaotic commotion commenced behind the mainstage curtain, spilling over onto the apron and arousing alarm in the seated audience. Stagehands, actors and concerned patrons rushed upon the stage.

Much to Micah's surprise, Rothery did not pursue him but instead turned and headed back down the fixed staircase to the gathering crowd below.

Micah knew he had seconds to get off the scaffold before shouts and pointing would be aimed at him. Running across the bridge would only give away his position sooner, so he decided to quickly and quietly make his way across a beam back to the furthest point upstage-right. The ladder, too far downstage; the stairway, on the left— only cable mounts and ropes holding various curtains against the back wall presented themselves as a way to get down. As the crowd formed toward the front of the stage, Micah took the risk and leaped from the lattice work to the canvas backdrop cable.

Catching the cable with one hand, it only slowed his descent toward the stage floor. He quickly kicked out his foot snagging a diagonal rope and causing him to slow and flip forward in a face-first fall. From there, locking his feet on the rope and releasing his hand from the cable, he had enough momentum to swing toward the closest curtain wing. Hitting the heavy material was enough for him to re-adjust, sliding feet-first to the floor below.

As his feet hit the wooden mainstage in the darkened wing, his knees buckled beneath him into a sideways barrel roll absorbing his landing like a trained paratrooper. Having remained unnoticed amidst the panic of the moment, Micah rushed to the front of the stage.

The girl's neck broken, leg twisted above her shoulders, blood pouring under the curtain onto the apron and towards the front stage stairway— Micah carefully backed away, mingling with the initial onlookers. He then fled inconspicuously into the crowded audience who had yet to fully understand what the commotion was all about.

He turned to make his way to the nearest exit only to run face to face into Steven Marsh, standing in an aisle near the first few rows of seating.

Surprised to see Micah, Steven glanced down at his seven year old daughter who was holding tight to her daddy's coat. "Emily, this is the man daddy told you about today."

Micah calmly crouched down to the child whispering, "*Your* daddy is a hero, Emily." The little girl smiled brightly in agreement.

Micah stood upright and turned back toward Steven, "Get the prosecutor and your family out of the building now. Stay away from any public event tonight."

The color instantly drained from Steven's face. "What? Uh, yes, of course. Are you all right?"

Micah gave a curt nod, "You're going to hear a lot of things about tonight, Mr. Marsh, NONE of which are true. Despite what they'll say, I want you to know you did the right thing this afternoon." Micah gave the man a sorrowful smile then stepped back into the aisle, weaving through the crowd.

"Micah?" Steven called after him, concern on his face.

"Get your family out now. Go home."

* * * * *

Victoria could now see Micah across the growing panic of the crowded auditorium. She began crossing over seats and rows trying to make her way to him. She had managed to get within ten feet of him with as many people in between when he turned and headed away from her toward the main doors of the opera house. She yelled but he couldn't hear her.

Continuing toward the lobby exits leading to the halls and outer doors of the building, a hand reached out and forcibly seized Micah by his arm. Though pumped on adrenaline, Micah stopped, fighting his reflex to strike.

"Mr. Steinbeck, you need to turn around."

"No time for a photo tonight, Henry," Micah replied without looking at the man.

"Don't want a photo, already got one. I just want you to turn around."

"Ah, I can only imagine what that might entail. But come to think of it, wouldn't you rather I escape?"

Henry released Micah and folded his arms, "I suppose that wouldn't hurt the headlines…"

Micah met the reporter's eyes, "Henry, which way out of here?"

"Turn around."

Micah reluctantly turned. His eyes softened as he saw Victoria coming through the crowd; breathtaking in an evening gown fit for the opera, but struggling with the garment in her efforts to catch up with him. She must have changed in the cab.

Henry now instructed, "Head down toward the stage to the left. Don't try to go out the front door— a wall of reporters are waiting out that way. You need to leave now."

"Thank you."

Micah moved toward Victoria, reached for her hand, and pulled her up close against him. As if seeing the two together brought Henry back to his senseless self, the journalist began to backpedal, "Well, maybe just one more photo for Entertainment Tonight...?"

"Sorry, Henry. Thanks again, but you said it— we need to get out of here NOW." The couple quickly started jumping seats, row by row, heading to the floor exit to the left. When no vacant seats were available, Micah grabbed Victoria's hand and pulled her through the mobbing crowd.

As they closed-in on the stage, they could see police entering the auditorium from both the right and left floor exits preventing people from leaving. Having previously traversed the immense basement floor, Micah pulled Victoria down into the orchestra pit, then exited it from an inside doorway leading back up the wing stairs and through the long windy corridors of the route from which he had entered.

Rushing through the costume room, Micah quickly exchanged his coat with one from wardrobe and donned a hat. "Ugh," Victoria pouted, "I just bought that for you. It looked so nice."

Micah stopped in his tracks, took two steps back, grabbed his coat and wrapped it around her shoulders, "Better?" Victoria seemed pleased.

Finally reaching one of the alley exits, as Micah reached out to touch the door handle (the crisp night air awaiting them), a voice from behind him spoke, "Who's hunting you?"

Again, Micah stopped. "Leave it, agent," Micah said attempting to continue out the door.

"I saw him— the seventh policeman," Rothery said. "I saw him. I watched a MAN fall and land a dead WOMAN."

As strange as it sounded, Rothery was no longer confused. No longer questioning, no longer bound to reason. He was merely stating the facts. "I need to know what I'm going to find up there on the scaffold."

"Well, you'll find a gun. A gun that any reasonable man would have hidden, destroyed or taken with him. And although you can see I'm wearing gloves..." Micah held his hands out with spread fingers just as he had on the scaffold, "you'll probably find my prints on it, as well. You'll find all the evidence you need against me, agent."

"Why? Why, Michael?"

Micah shook his head, "Honestly, I really don't know. I truly fear that I'm merely a distraction. I suppose you'll know for sure if tomorrow's top headline ISN'T about the Opera House murders."

"What are you saying?" Rothery was concerned.

"I'm saying, once again, I don't know."

"How will I sleep if I let you walk out that door?"

"I can't help you tonight, agent. I suggest alcohol. But tomorrow when the body of that girl disappears..."

"What?!" Rothery rubbed his forehead then ran his hand down his face. Resigned he flatly replied, "I don't ever want to see you again."

Micah paused briefly, "Believe me, I don't want you to, either." He pushed through the door.

Chapter 58

AVOIDING THE FRONT ENTRANCE of the Opera House, Micah and Victoria made their way back to the cab parked around the corner. "I kept the meter running," Victoria said. "What happened?"

"I'll tell you in the car," Micah answered with reservation.

Climbing back into the cab, the driver looked nervous. "What happened in there? You weren't going to the opera... we stopped, you got out... now floods of people are leaving! The police are blocking the building!"

The man let his head fall to the steering wheel. "Mister, I'm a Muslim. After what happened last week...? I know how this will go and I tell you, I can't have anything to do with this."

Victoria turned to the driver, "Sir, do you know who I am?"

He raised his head, "You look like that movie star."

"That's right. My friend here only stopped to see someone we knew. I think there was just an accident inside, that's all."

Still suspicious, the cabby was only half-heartedly persuaded to drive what he perceived to be the get-away vehicle. He reluctantly flipped on the wipers, put on his blinker, and pulled away from the curb.

Victoria switched sides and sat next to Micah facing forward, "So, now tell me."

"It was a trap." Micah shook his head, "Or more like a distraction. I don't know. It's all coming to a head and I don't know... I don't want to know." He ran his hands through his hair trying to make sense of everything that had happened.

The cabdriver weaved through town passing up major thoroughfares for small alleys and passageways, through gas station parking lots and supermarket roundabouts. Like watching the Dodger in Oliver, if jumping from roof to roof or sliding down the chimney saved even a minute, the taxi driver would do it.

He took a quick right into an industrial area, spun a U-turn and pulled out in front of oncoming traffic to avoid a stoplight just seconds before it turned green. The time saved seem insignificant, but all added up, this cabby was in line for a 100 pound tip.

Micah and Victoria were in awe of the man's ingenuity. He was either running-up the fare or a genius navigator through the streets of London. "I guess the clock on our hour-bet is still running," Victoria commented, forcing a smile.

Passing through a series of speed-bumped alleys, crossing empty intersections, Micah and Victoria were as much in the air as seated on the backseat of the cab. Victoria couldn't help a small giggle. She turned to Micah with a coy smile preparing to say something, when suddenly a horrified look crossed her face. Micah barely uttered the word, "What?"

The impact of a T-bone car crash slammed into Micah's door and lunged him into Victoria. Glass shattered; cold, frigid air rushed in. The cab horn wailed as the taxi tipped over and slid on its side more than thirty yards before coming to a stop against a parked truck, crashing back down on all four tires. The rear passenger door was completely caved in.

* * * * *

The sound of the impact deafened Micah and continued to echo in his ears. The horn blared, the rain blew in the shattered window. On the empty street outside, a single young man stood near a streetlamp clutching a backpack and staring.

Attempting to remain conscious, Micah reached for Victoria's limp body as he looked toward the street for assistance. The man had clearly been startled by the crash yet seemed to have no intention nor concern for the passengers. For mere seconds Micah's eyes' plead sparked humanity on the stranger's face, but just as quickly, it glazed back over to a look of maniacal intent.

The apathy enraged Micah— the man's expression, entranced. He had seen it before. He had seen *him* before— or at least the demon in his eyes. The will of an assassin; determined, bent, twisted.

Glass shards everywhere, rain and wind flew in sideways through every crevice. Micah could barely breathe; his head spinning, fading in and out of consciousness. Unable to move or reach Victoria, he was unsure what prevented him from touching her; not knowing whether he was pinned or paralyzed. He chanced another look out the broken window, but the young man had turned and walked away.

Victoria remained motionless. Micah looked to the driver now who seemed to be conscious, struggling to unbuckle his seat belt.

A muffled voice came running toward the cab. From outside the car, barely understandable, "Are you okay?" asked with monotone melody.

Micah realized he wasn't moving because his body was failing to respond to his mind's commands. He thought he was speaking but his mouth wasn't moving, either. The voice outside growing closer in the evening's dimness; the only control he was confident he had was the movement of his eyes, shifting his blurred vision to the approaching pedestrian.

Fighting to stay awake, Micah watched the shadowed figure approach the driver's door— the sound and movement slow motion. "Are… you… okay?"

The cabby turned toward the person outside his window. Still trying to focus, it looked to Micah as if the driver threw up his hands to shield his face. Then came dream-like screams, "No… no… no…!"

A point-blank gunshot blast rang out echoing through the car and taking what was left of Micah's hearing. The driver's head shot backward spattering blood and brains all over Micah. Micah's senses so sluggish, he didn't even close his eyes when it happened.

Falling into unconsciousness, Micah caught a glimpse of Big Ben towering in the overcast sky just out the window. As the image faded to black, he thought he heard a voice he recognized.

Chapter 59

ROTHERY SAT AT THE back corner table of a bar; a bar he had never visited— and on purpose. He didn't want to be seen or found by anyone. He was not typically a drinker, and definitely not when alone. And certainly not with a new baby at home. But tonight it felt like the thing to do.

He wasn't sure how long to sit there. He wasn't sure what he was looking or waiting for. He supposed it was to get drunk. Or until something made him happy… or at least helped him reckon the events of the night.

It was all new to him. Cops made mistakes and he was no exception, but this felt bigger than that. Was it a mistake? Should he have let the Samaritan go? It was not deducible, calculable. To even try seemed like venturing abstract calculus beyond the grasp of nature. Humans were simple, predictable— find a motive, find your killer. But the events of that evening had proven to be everything but.

Rothery thought of how strange the world turned; how much he knew that amounted to nothing in this moment. What was most strange was that there was no one he wished he could talk to— wished would walk through the door, more than the man he had hunted. The man he had caught. The man he had let slip away. He kept his eye on the door as if it made sense that someone would show.

But no one knew where he was. In fact, he couldn't have given directions even if he had wanted to.

"Rothery?" a familiar voice called out from behind him.

Rothery turned, less surprised than he expected he should be.

"Don't get up," Dylan said as he sat down across from him, pulling a coin from his pocket and knuckle-rolling it between his fingers.

"That's quite dexterous of you," Rothery commented. "You never struck me as an illusionist."

"The best never do."

"So, is this the pledge, the turn, or the prestige?"

Dylan palmed the coin, then with a snap of his fingers, spun it on the table. The sound was loud, increasing and decreasing in decibels not unlike a wet finger on a crystal goblet but lower, more earthy in tone. It was disturbing and soothing at the same time. The spinning coin became a hypnotic hum in the background.

Dylan's eyes never left Rothery's. Though Rothery still pondered Dylan's sudden appearance, he knew it was beyond coincidence and far more than he wanted to consider that night. He hadn't even bothered asking the man what he was doing there. He assumed Dylan wouldn't have sat down unless he intended to tell him, though nothing about their case seemed to follow the norm.

"You've gotten a lot of exposure, agent. Good for you. You've done a brilliant job. Brilliant, should I say, short of..." he sighed, "tonight's one, insignificant little mistake— however drastic the consequences might be."

Dylan leaned back, "And believe me when I tell you, you cannot imagine how insignificant that little man really is. Matter of fact, it's your one flaw, Taylor. If I may give you a piece of constructive criticism?"

"What's that?"

"You give undue respect to him— and your hierarchy of officials. Even Prime Ministers are elected, my friend. Whether knowingly or not, they are all pawns in the bigger scheme of things. On the other hand, there are those who have been here a long time and will stay longer than you can imagine. You can't fight this. You don't even know what this is."

"I suspect there is someone who does."

"Perhaps. Some believe so." Dylan reflected, "Although he's been more of an annoyance than anything else. But next time you see him," he added flippantly, "do me a favor and just shoot first? You and your fucking questions— or is it answers? I honestly don't know which of you is more annoying."

"Somehow I feel complimented by that."

"Oh yes, you're in good company."

The coin continued spinning, not decreasing nor increasing in speed. Rothery glanced down and noticed a groove forming in the old wooden table. He ruminated on the amount of force required, the friction of the wood, the imperfection of the coin. By its speed and size he couldn't tell its denomination though knew it was not British Pound Sterling, US or Euro and too thick be third-world. Most countries, other than the US and Britain, had standardized their currency and certainly their coinage. His best guess was that it was not in current circulation.

Rothery had collected coins with his father and thought himself somewhat knowledgeable on the topic (at least once upon a time.) But in recent history there had been nothing particularly interesting in the field— specifically since the creation of the Euro. History, however, as far as he knew hadn't changed.

All this Rothery considered during the conversation without giving any perceivable clue to his distraction— or at least he thought. "There are no answers for me, are there?"

Dylan, almost regretfully, "No, there are not. Not for you." He considered further, "Not ever." He seemed dismissive about it. He liked Rothery; the man had almost impressed him. But still, it was all a bit beyond the SIS agent. Then reconsidering, the young man smiled, "On the other hand, there is one answer I can give you." He snapped his fingers above the coin, it stopping dead in its tracks and standing straight up on end.

Dylan didn't say a word. Rothery looked at the very old, solid gold coin. Undistinguishable, a language was written on it he didn't recognize.

The well-dressed agent rose from his seat, swallowing the last bit of his drink standing. Rothery glanced up away from the coin and looked his partner in the eyes. "Good bye, Rothery," Dylan said as he prepared to leave. It sounded so permanent. "Keep the coin," he added, turning towards the door.

Rothery glanced down at the table. The coin had vanished. He looked back to Dylan as he walked away.

Dylan's voice trailed over his shoulder, "That, my friend, is the Prestige."

Rothery pushed his drink aside and leaned back in his seat.

Chapter 60

ENTERING HER KITCHEN, A HORRIFYING sight stared Pamela in the face. "Oh, my!" she exclaimed. Her husband stood at the kitchen sink manually doing dishes at six in the morning on a Saturday. She nearly dropped her coffee.

Speechless, Pamela was unsure what more to say about this strange new spin of the universe. The only rational aspect of the enigma was the fact that there was as much water on the counter and floor as in the sink, and that the dish towel still hung dry next to the perfectly functioning dishwasher (an appliance she was sure he didn't know existed.)

She stood there a moment, staring and debating whether to interrupt him or not, when a graver, far more frightening thought hit her mind, *What if he attempts to do the laundry?*

Pamela abruptly cleared her throat, "Rothery, love, what are you thinking about?"

"Nothing."

She laughed.

"Why? What's so funny?"

"You're home, awake, and washing dishes… when MY MUM is staying with us. I'd expect if you were up at this hour at the weekend, it would only be in an attempt to escape unseen. So, my dear, what's on your mind?"

"A coin trick," Rothery sighed.

"Now I'm at quite a loss. A coin trick YOU couldn't figure out?"

"Do you believe in magic?"

"Oh, my Lord, Rothery! Magic…? I'm not certain but perhaps I do suddenly believe in alien abduction." Pamela waited for him to laugh.

Rothery didn't laugh, smile, or scoff. Now Pamela knew something was terribly wrong. "All right, all right." She went to the sink and stopped him from washing. She took his hands and held them still between hers, letting the warm water flow over them for a moment. Then with one hand she grabbed a new shammy from the kitchen towel drawer and shut off the water with the other. She dried off his hands as she walked him over to a kitchen chair and sat him down, leaving the shammy clutched in his grip.

"What do you know about magic tricks, love? Where's the trick?" Pamela coaxed.

Rothery stared off into the distance, rubbing the towel between his fingertips. "It's in the turn," he mumbled.

"And what's 'the turn'?"

Rothery gave her a wry look knowing full well she knew what the turn was. His expression didn't faze her, still patiently waiting for his explanation. He sighed again, "The turn... what is already there. What you assume is there. What you don't consider— what's never presented to you. Hmm..." Having a thought, he asked her, "What's on the back page of the newspaper this morning?"

Pamela, a brand new stay-at-home mom— a scholar turned novelist; gave up a promising, prestigious academic career when she couldn't get over the deductive ingenuity of her former Cambridge lab partner and current husband. Her wedding vow (singular) consisted of reading a Ninja food processor advertisement that ended with the phrase, 'One per household.'

This morning she assumed Rothery was asking about out-of-place or improperly prioritized articles. She too, with a near eidetic memory, also assumed she must list at a rapid pace, summarizing as much as possible.

- "The Crown Chief Prosecutor vindicated in manhunt scandal.
- Six female youths returned to their families after police raid uncovered a human trafficking ring in a Chinese restaurant.
- Lord Starlin indicted for insider-trading.
- The environmental summit's unexpected chair nominee, Merlo Charles (former nuclear physicist) replaced the late Heimlich Phelps.
- Another mass shooting in Iowa.
- In sports, Manchester United..."

Rothery sat up in his chair, "That's enough." He kissed his wife and headed straight to the study.

"Now THAT'S the look I married!" Pamela grinned, happy to see the wheels spinning in his head again.

* * * * *

With intense purpose, Rothery slid the mouse across his home-office desk awakening six, 32-inch flat screen monitors; three on one row and three mounted above on a monitor tree. Using a remote, he turned on a wall-mounted 55-inch flat screen television that automatically flipped through local, national and international news broadcasts. A police scanner played in the background.

The Parliament terrorist attack monopolized headlines and appeared on every channel. "The body of MP Eleanor Aldous was one of the first casualties identified in last night's horrific explosion outside of Parliament near Big Ben…" the BBC blared before Rothery muted the television. The Parliament terrorist attack, having taken place the night before within the same hour as the Opera House murders, left any reference to the Opera House as a tickertape report rolling periodically across the bottom. Rothery found himself remembering Micah's parting comment.

With very few keystrokes, Rothery VPN'd into SIS intranet and began scanning articles from all major news providers stopping only briefly at Henry Wilken's next article. Shaking his head, he quickly moved on to 'alt-tabbing' through a large number of police crime logs, pensively tapping his keyboard to the beat of a nursery rhyme playing for the baby in the other room.

He leaned back in his Ergo-Tek, black mesh office chair with its mounted two-piece ergonomic keyboard; half of the keyboard on the right, the other half on the left armrest. He kicked the adjustment lever under his seat as if it were an extension of his body and put himself into fully reclined, rocking position— he knew he was going to be there a while.

Moving from article to police report to the television and back, his perfectly synchronized screens displayed the information in one fluid circular pattern. Finally, after more than an hour, something eventually caught his attention… or rather, was not quite dismissible.

With another few keystrokes he displayed multiple versions of the report of interest (including photos) then launched an application that gave him SIS access to street-level video throughout London. Once he had found what he was looking for, on a hunch, he initiated Google maps and searched every possible route between two specific locations using the video feed to confirm. Still, he couldn't find the path he presumed was there.

Frustrated, Rothery began talking to himself, "There's no way anyone could have gotten from here to there in that little time! Who the hell was this driver... Mario Andretti?!"

It wasn't working and taking too long, so Rothery donned a head set and began voice command, "Switch to Google Earth," he prompted. A three-dimensional satellite view of the city appeared on screen number one. "Lay over 'Eye in the Sky'," he continued. A red skeleton map of the city lit up over the Google Earth application and displayed the locations of all government controlled cameras within the city. "Now, move maps to screen seven," he commanded.

Rotating his chair to a touch-screen monitor on the credenza behind him, Rothery began to zoom-in and view-out with simply the gesture of his hand. A double-tap and he could watch the video feed of any camera within the city or move a selected feed from one screen to any of the other monitors in his arsenal. With just a swipe, he opened, closed, adjusted and transferred videos from one monitor to the next.

After about ten minutes Rothery turned back to the monitor tree on his desk and pushed play. A few seconds later, a time-synchronized video of six different camera feeds now followed the trail of a specific taxi all the way from the Opera House to the car crash of interest.

"Pamela, love," he called to his wife.

"Yes?" Pamela walked into Rothery's office carrying junior.

"Exactly what time was the terrorist attack at Parliament?"

"Do you mean what time did the bomb go off? Hmm," searching her memory, "20:46."

Rothery watched the final video feed displaying a looped repeat of the taxicab's slide out of view post-crash. A GPS clock running on the menu bar read 20:38. Analyzing the driver's projected route, "Where was it headed?" he considered out loud.

Pamela glanced over her husband's shoulder. Looking at the irrationally woven trail her eye's opened wide, "Due south it seems… towards Big Ben and Parliament."

"The cab was just minutes away… our man would have passed right by!" Rothery's next voice command, "Save, Bluetooth Android. Call Tilman!"

*　*　*　*　*

"Sergeant Nathaniel Tilman, speaking."

"Case number 10720172148."

"I beg your pardon?"

"This is Rothery."

"I know who it is. You finally crossed over to the Matrix and are stuck in the internet?"

"Seriously, Sergeant, case number 107…"

"I'm working on the Parliament terrorist attack now," he objected.

"Pakistani national, nothing interesting there. This is important."

"Right." Tilman released an exasperated groan to the heavens, "Hold on." A minute or so later, "All right, which number?"

"10720172148."

"Uh… yeah, got it. What about it?"

"What do you have on this?" Rothery waited.

"Hmm… hit and run; murder. Location, blah-blah… suspect's name is Moha…"

"You already have a suspect?" Rothery interrupted.

"Yes, the husband of a woman the victim was sleeping with. They'd had a violent domestic the day before."

"What happened to your obsession with innocent until proven guilty? That's wrong."

"Where are you?" Tilman asked.

"Home."

"Did you go to the crime scene?"

"No."

"Did you read the prior disturbance report?"

"No."

"Then what's with the interest?"

Rothery ignored the question, "What side of the car did the truck hit?"

"Passenger-side," Tilman responded.

"Front or back?"

"Hold on. Backdoor," he answered.

"Meet me at the Impound, Sergeant."

"Pfft, I have more important responsibilities, sir."

"Not one that will get you your Inspector's badge."

"You are so full of shit, agent… I need more than that to go on."

"Right." Rothery conceded and explained, "If you wanted to shoot someone, Sergeant, you wouldn't first hit them with your own traceable car, correct? And if you wanted to kill a driver in a car wreck, you wouldn't hit the passenger-side backdoor, would you?"

"All right, makes sense. And your interest?"

"The report on record failed to mention that the car was a taxi," Rothery stated. "Therefore, it stands to reason that the target was not the driver but the passenger— or passengers, I'd wager to say. They have been abducted."

Tilman scoffed, "The report supports no evidence of that, Rothery."

"And THAT, sir, is why we're going to the Impound."

"How soon?" The sergeant tried not to grumble.

"Now."

Tilman lowered his head, "No, no. You've still got to give me more than that."

"The taxi was heading for Parliament!" Rothery exclaimed.

"For Parliament? Last night…? Bloody hell! I'll meet you there."

Rejuvenated, Agent Taylor jumped up, darted into the kitchen where his wife was just beginning to prepare lunch, and kissed her on the cheek. "I've got to go."

"Find what you were looking for?" she asked.

Rothery grabbed his keys off the key-tree by the back door, "More like what I wasn't looking for!"

Chapter 61

"HEY, HENRY. ARE YOU in early today or another all-nighter?"

"I got a couple of hours. How are you doing, Pete?"

"Well, thanks. What are you working on?"

"Phantom of the Opera House."

"Brilliant piece! Thought you sent that to print already?"

"I did. This is a follow-on— personal segment," Henry answered.

"Right," Pete nodded. He crossed his arms. Shifting uncomfortably, he put his hands on his hips in an awkward attempt to appear casual. "Sooo... the Crown Prosecutor story? Got a lot of heat, yeah? You're certain it isn't going to come back and bite us?"

"Yeah, yeah. No, we've got video."

"Well, you sent that first piece out quite quickly. You passed it by legal?"

"Pete, if I had to wait for legal every time I published an article, I'd never have published. My job is to hunt down the story; I trust you to hold off the league of solicitors and barristers."

"Well, that's actually what I came to talk to you about. We need to have a meeting upstairs."

Henry was instantly defensive. "This is bullocks, Pete, and you know it. The story is legit! If it's a question of my source, I'd love to tell you who it was but you know the drill— give up a source, dry up the well."

"That is always a concern, but it's not about that."

"Sure it isn't," Henry doubted. "Let's just say it's as high ranking a source as it goes, shall we? Besides, we got him— got them ALL on video! If it's not that," Henry challenged, "what the hell are we talking about here, Pete?"

"Henry, you know how this works. We do what we can to stay in business. We must dot our 'i's and cross our 't's, especially when the PM is involved. And actually, going after the Chief Prosecutor concerns me more than your usual PM offensive."

Henry shook his head in frustration and attempted an air of authority, "Pete, I have to put this story to bed, we can do this another time."

"No, can't do it, Henry. Got to do this now."

Again Henry objected, "And if I refuse?"

"Listen, you know I respect you. I respect who you were, I respect who you have become. It's even bloody admirable how you plodded through during your rough period. But the decision has already been made on this one. It comes from way above my pay grade."

"Right," Henry sulked, shaking his head.

"Grab your laptop, you're going to need it."

"My laptop? I'm not giving up my source, Pete. I'll format the hard drive before I do that."

Pete chuckled at the idle threat.

"I'm serious! I have a special script; with the click of a key it's gone— BLOODY ALL!"

Pete laughed, "Seriously, mate? We had to stick a big 'ON' sign to your laptop just so you knew how to turn it on and off for the first six months you had one. You kept a manual typewriter until 2009. Fortunately, in those days, you were a valuable reporter."

Henry reluctantly followed Pete out of the bullpen with his laptop in tow. "So, where are we going?" he asked, resigned.

"Eighth floor."

"Eighth floor?" Henry grew concerned. "Will Jacoby be there?"

Pete lifted his hands in affirmation.

"Why?! Jacoby was involved?"

"Afraid so."

Now seriously nervous, Henry walked remorsefully, fidgeting. His voice low, "How high does this go, Pete?"

Pete answered solemnly, "All the way up, Henry."

The reporter rubbed his face. He was no longer obstinate but honestly grieved. "Doesn't have to go as high as Jacoby to fire a veteran," Henry mourned.

"No, it doesn't."

"Is there going to be a lawsuit?"

Pete shrugged.

Henry swallowed hard, "A personal suit?"

The editor, now cautious of his words, "You'll probably end up with at least one of those."

Henry's heart sank. He felt like a man walking the green mile, his hand covering his mouth.

The two men walked down the long corridor of the eighth floor passing the open cubicles of the media crew, the legal team, and marketing. They veered off toward the executive offices at the face of the building.

Henry noticed everyone looking at him as he walked down the corridor. He lowered his head in shame. "They're looking at me, Pete. Do they know?"

"Everyone on this floor knows."

"You told them?"

"We had to, Henry. We couldn't have kept this from them if we'd wanted to."

Henry walked slower trying to turn away.

"Henry, there have been a lot of complaints of late, especially from the bullpen. You've had quite a few of those over your tenure but this obviously goes much higher than that."

"I work nights when no one is down there..." Henry pleaded.

"Yes, but you're there during the day, as well."

"Just getting the story out... hey, what about Frank?"

"Frank was involved, too, he's the anchor— the face of the Guard. His opinion matters," Pete answered.

"What does Frank have to complain about? I'm not after his desk... I fed him exclusives!" Henry put his hand over his face. "Pete..." his voice forlorn, "I've burned all my bridges fighting for this story. No one will hire me out there. I walk with a limp because of shrapnel I took in the gulf covering the story; I can't sleep at night. I've lost two wives over this job. That's why I'm here all the time. I have no reason to go home. You should have fired me last year when I was tired, not now when I'm back in the game!" Tears actually began to form in Henry's eyes.

"You're right, we should have fired you last year— or any of the last five. But we can't have you disturbing the bullpen, now can we? We can't have you working alongside, distracting them downstairs. They put out seventy percent of the content, the bulk of our newspaper."

Pete walked Henry into the far southeast corner office; eighth floor, floor-to-ceiling glass overlooking London. There was a single, mahogany desk in the middle of the office; full-sized couch, matching credenza against the wall. No one was in the room. "Where is everybody?" Henry asked.

"Oh, they'll undoubtedly be coming soon," Pete answered. "As I said, this goes way above my head and you know how management is."

Henry's eyes were wide.

Pete paused dramatically, "So, Henry Wilkens, because we've known each other the longest, I was the one they asked to walk you up here…" taking a deep breath, "…to give you your new office."

"My what?"

"An executive decision was made to have you head up an investigative tiger-team taskforce covering the most important, controversial breaking stories. You will have your own team specialized in various disciplines— politics, economics, foreign affairs. With the recent political unrest, we think it's time for the Guard to make our mark! And as I mentioned, I'd definitely suggest a SUIT— or actually, a number of new suits— to go with your new title."

The editor met the reporter's eyes, adding, "Oh, and by the way, there is one condition. We all ask that you leave your NEXT British Journalism Award as it is… we'll get you a matching case so you can properly display your accomplishment."

For the first time in his life, Henry was speechless.

Chapter 62

"WHAT ARE YOU LOOKING for, Rothery?" Chief Philips asked. "You can't pull my men off their duties."

"Give me Tilman for the day, Chief. I'm a good man to have owing you a favor."

The chief, rubbing his brow, "Then just for today, mind you… the bloody busiest day of the year!" Philips left grumbling all the way out of Scotland Yard's automotive impound.

"Has the car been touched by anyone?" Rothery inquired.

"No, no reason. The shooter was never assumed to be inside the car," Tilman answered.

Prying open one of the mangled car doors, Rothery managed to crawl inside. Examining every crevice, "And there was nothing found in the boot?" he called out.

"No."

"Is that something?" Rothery pointed.

Tilman peered inside from the passenger front window, "Where?"

"Pinned between the wrenched metal and the backseat."

"Uh… can't tell from here."

"Give me your flashlight." Rothery reached out his hand.

Tilman handed him the light. "I still don't understand, agent. Even if this has nothing to do with the driver, what does it have to do with you or the Parliament attack?"

Using his foot and hands, Rothery kicked the dented-in interior and freed a trapped, dark blue handbag. Falling back onto the rear seat, lying with his eyes to the ceiling; between his fingertips, he rubbed the fine material of Victoria's expensive designer purse. He almost grinned. "The Turn."

Rothery felt like himself again. He sat up confidently. "Well, Tilman," he announced, "is murder PLUS the brutal abduction and kidnapping of a famous movie star and a wanted assailant big enough for you?"

Tilman's eyes were wide. "Oh, my God! How did you even know to look?"

"I've already told you, Sergeant… time of day, location, insignificant crime— the TURN." Rothery pondered.

Chapter 63

MICAH AWOKE, SLUMPED IN a folding chair in the middle of an open warehouse of some kind. Two men of extraordinary size stood one on each side of him. He could hear the unusually loud sound of their breathing over his own wheezing, which spoke volumes to their size.

Micah wiggled his toes in his shoes to check for any lasting damage from the car wreck; his fingers moved— albeit, with cramping pain; and he shut both eyes one at a time— mildly blurred. He also suspected his shoulder had been knocked out of place but realized it had been popped back in— likely restored by his hosts.

"You are awake," a voice spoke from across the room. Though the voice was older and raspy, Micah knew instantly it was Agent Vasko.

"Well, you bleed. I wonder if you die," Vasko commented with indifference. "That SUV hit directly into your door and yet you sustained the least amount of injury."

"You're not as polite as you were before, Vassiago."

"Don't bring me to this. I actually liked you, rooted for you. I merely needed you out of the way." Vasko made his way across the room. "So what are you still doing here, Micah?" He shook his head in disappointment. Micah raised a brow.

"Yes, I've known your name for some time now, Mr. Graff," Vasko said as he made his way into Micah's view. "We released you to LEAVE. Why didn't you go and crawl back under the fucking rock from which you came? Was it the woman?" He shook his head, "Do you have any idea how far out of your depth you are?"

Micah's head slumped. He yawned hard to catch his breath and settle the pain in his chest just to breathe. His eyes were almost swollen shut. "So, is this where you have your apes beat me up?" he asked coldly.

"Come now. Do you know nothing? I don't need to hurt you, Micah. Matter of fact, until as of late, you were deemed off limits."

The information caught Micah's attention. "Off limits?" he questioned, glancing up at Vasko.

Micah wasn't completely sure if it was an illusion caused by the injuries he had sustained in the car wreck, but it was now apparent that more than Vasko's voice and demeanor had changed. Staring down at him was a man in his mid-forties, not the young, energetic agent he had met before. Even Vasko's facial features seemed extended, more pronounced; his eyes duller, his voice lower. "Off limits?" Micah repeated. "Are you suggesting I have allies among you? If so, you certainly have a funny way of treating your friends."

"I don't think I would necessarily say allies," Vasko answered. "My colleague— singular— seems to think that you are unbreakable. Perhaps he is right. You are one resilient fuck."

"Your colleague... Ring Finger?"

"Is that what you call him?" Vasko chuckled. "The way he plays with that thing is nearly as annoying as you are. But Furcus thinks too much of you which brings too much upon himself. He thinks you're immortal or a cosmic anomaly; that if killed, some sort of atomic reaction or the likes might detonate." The tall man laughed.

"That's the second time I've heard that this week," Micah commented offhand. Glancing up, he pointed a thumb at the two giants. "So, are they human? You know I can barely hear you over their grunting. They sound like some perverted species of gorilla... your progeny?" he mocked.

"You can't goad me, Micah," Vasko, completely indifferent. "Dylan only appeared frazzled. Roleplay, Mr. Graff; emulating the frailty of YOUR species. Honestly, you overestimate what I think of you. I don't consider you... not at all. I am merely fulfilling an obligation. I honestly have no interest in you, but I am also quite thorough in my job."

Micah closed his eyes and breathed deeply. In his mind he searched for Victoria. He searched for her breath, her heartbeat; almost trying to breathe for her or God FORBID, sense her absence. It took a few moments but soon his breathing cleared and became easier. His heartbeat slightly increased— not rapid, but constant— and he felt her. *She's cold, scared and alone, but ALIVE.*

"Awe, you're thinking about the woman. You know she's alive." Micah's ability interested Vasko. "That is a bit disappointing, though. I was going to taunt you with wondering."

Micah scowled.

"It is interesting… what you did there. What else can you do, Micah Graff?"

"Oh, you may find that I am full of surprises," Micah threatened.

"Hmm," Vasko smiled, "maybe I can muster a bit of interest in you after all. We are going to be spending a considerable amount of time together, you and I. Might I suggest we discover exactly what you are capable of? Would you let me do that?"

"Well, if you're asking my permission, I would prefer not."

"That's too bad," the agent sighed, "unlike my colleagues, I enjoy humanity— their pleasures, their pains, their fears. There is so much for you to be afraid of. You're all so fragile, temporal. It's confounding how your species finds the will to get out of bed in the morning. Can I tell you what I've learned, Micah?"

"It appears to be your dime."

"Thank you for noticing," Vasko nodded sarcastically. "Fear and confidence, pleasure and pain go hand in hand. You have to experience loss to truly know what you've— *got*. To make a hero of the average person… I can't tell you how gratifying it is to give that to someone.

"For instance, take last night. While you were so graciously fulfilling our agenda by participating in the ultimate ruse at the Opera House, a young Pakistani man became an eternal hero to his people— a man who had previously lived an absolutely insignificant life with no opportunities whatsoever."

"Here in London?" Micah asked.

"Yes."

Micah sighed knowing his suspicions had been correct— he had been the distraction.

"Something bothers you?"

Micah met the stare.

Pointing toward the door, "My obligation was fulfilled as of last night," Vasko stated carelessly. "You are free to walk away from this place only slightly detoured… due to your uncanny ability to get in the way. Honestly, had Rothery detained you at the Opera House, Ms. Adam's would be on her way back to fame and glory in Hollywood. But unfortunately you proceeded suspiciously too close to our…" considering the proper term, "end game. However, now that I have you here, I'd like to give you the opportunity to consider an alternative."

"An alternative to?"

"Whether you go to prison (which provides absolutely no benefit to you) or stay here. Either way, we're going to be spending some time together, you and I. I have been assigned to discover the extent of your potential. I believe you've only scratched the surface. And I have some experience with this. Actually, I may be the world's leading expert.

"Societal structure inhibits man's potential, Mr. Graff. Once you take away all the distractions; family, friends, loved-ones, and all meaningless and ignorant pursuits, you can fine-tune an efficient tool. A child finishes high school wanting to be a rock star, gets Diane pregnant in the back seat of his car… well, you know the song. He spends the rest of his life pumping gas for three kids and a wife— a wife's who's pumping someone else. Meaningless. I typically don't even have to meet my subjects. Remove the obstacles, point them in the right direction, dangle a carrot… instant hero.

"But a man of your unique skillset may require more face to face tutorage, I'm afraid. Though we can still use your diversions as focal points as we squeeze them from your grip. How much better, don't you agree, that we could discover AND develop your abilities? Once all your distractions are gone, of course."

Vasko looked to Micah for a response as he continued, "Take the hero from last night's event at UK Parliament. I never had to meet him, I just gave him no better reason to live. Everyone wins. That man reached his pinnacle by strapping C4 to his body and crying out 'Allah Akbar'. I admit he could have been more effective, but twelve dead and over thirty injured and counting; it's as much as he could have possibly hoped for."

Micah lowered his head in grief remembering the young assassin on the street outside of the demolished hackney. "How does everyone win with a terrorist attack that kills twelve people?"

"It's all quite technical, really. A tad above your pay grade."

"Try me," Micah said angrily.

Shaking his head with a feigned groan, "Why not? The boy became a hero; his people are parading his picture in the streets. One fifth of the world's population knows the name of this insignificant, driveling cunt. The US and UK will reassert force in the Middle East because of it. Russia will back off (quite important right now), balance will be restored. Syria's war will soon come to a close. Terrorist organizations will be stifled, subdued."

"You'll never get rid of them. That only spawns more terrorists," Micah rebuked.

"Perhaps. Have them or not, with or without a war, makes no difference to us. It simply changes the means. The US pulled out of Iraq, terror increased, ISIS was formed. It's truly not a considering factor. You think I'm a beast, but in a matter of years nearly a half-million people died in Syria, alone— not to mention the atrocities in Sudan or the number of fatalities in a half-dozen other godforsaken places. You think the deaths of twelve politicians or their families in Parliament is a casualty? a tragedy? or even terrorism? More people than that will die in London today due to some sort of economic violence that will never make the news. One of the richest countries in the world... people killing each other because they're not content with one car and a three-bedroom flat. And is it really a tragedy that London loses a few more so that a hundred-thousand will live another year, eat food, sleep outside of a bomb shelter? Yes, Micah, I am the beast."

"And how do you win?"

"Well, that's the best part of it all. But we'll save that for another chapter, shall we? Maybe that incites you to consider my offer?" He seemed to sincerely want to know.

Vasko raised his hand to listen to something beyond the scope of the room. Though Micah could hear nothing, Vasko frowned. "The police are here and so is Rothery." His voice held dismay.

Micah's eyes widened.

The agent suspiciously grimaced, "Is this your doing? How do you manipulate situations like this? The attack in the restaurant meant to kill you made you a hero; the reporter bent on crucifying you freed you from prison! It's as if you weave your own trouble for your own good. You cannot be that smart."

Now Vasko mocked, "I watched you— your foolish ploy for anonymity in the interrogation room? I wanted to laugh! We already knew your name. The police didn't, but we did. You clearly didn't realize your situation. You didn't even recognize me at first. You think we don't know exactly where your son and daughter are right at this moment? You're not that smart, Micah Graff. Who are you working with?!"

Micah grinned.

"Lock him in a cell! Arm yourselves and take out as many police as you can," Vasko commanded. The two apelike men grabbed Micah and dragged him out of the room.

*   *   *   *   *

Half dragged, half carried, the giants brought Micah down three flights of stairs to the ground floor. Just off the stairwell was a small, 3-foot iron door. It looked like a crawl space to possibly an old boiler, but when the door was completely pulled open, it revealed a drop floor and an open staircase heading downward.

One of the men dawned a flashlight and began the descent. The stairs switchbacked five or six floors beneath the surface with no openings, doorways nor entrances to any other floors along the way. The building's foundation was cement, but after the first couple of flights, the stairwell and walls were made of stone.

Micah ran his hand against the dark stone wall noticing the further they descended, the larger the stones became. *What is this? Some kind of Roman ruin?*

The bottom of the stairway opened to a strange, convex stone floor. In the corner was a hole exposing more stairs continuing downward. It was then that

Micah realized he wasn't standing on an arched floor but rather on the vaulted roof of an ancient edifice buried beneath. He recognized the ancient masonry. *This predates Rome… possibly pre-Celtic, even Neolithic.* But the building itself wasn't rudimentary, the walls curved from cut stone— it was the domed ceiling that was the anomaly. It appeared out of date, possibly added later. Vaulted or arched roofs dated back as far as 2000 BC or further, but structures that old were typically made of unfired mud bricks, whereas this had been built from sophisticatedly cut rock.

The stairs led to a hallway that circled around the circumference of the underground building. The age of the structure explained it being beneath the surface, the depth and size of the stones dated it.

The building itself housed a number of inner chambers, their entrances through large, heavy iron doors accessible from the circular hallway. A huge, 3-foot long deadbolt secured the iron doors from the outside suggesting the rooms were likely a place of involuntary confinement— prison cells of some sort.

The giants threw Micah into an empty cell and locked the door. The sound, the reality of the closing metal followed by the ominous echoing slide of the deadbolt, was more terrifying than any dungeon horror movie he'd ever watched portrayed.

The room was lit only by a shallow oil canal chiseled into the wall and running from corner to corner a dozen feet or so above Micah's head. The sparse lighting revealed nothing more than a small cot in the corner. Ventilation came through circular holes near the apex of the ceiling. He was grateful they had left him light; he couldn't imagine what a long stent of solitude in the utter dark might be like for him, though he was equally certain that during some point in history, the chamber had been used for exactly that purpose.

By the size of the room and the curve of the wall, Micah deduced there were likely six to eight identical chambers within the round leaving possibly a hexagon, heptagon, or octagon shaped room in the center; maybe a meeting room prospectively designed for some ritualistic purpose. He surmised all this by considering the trapezoidal shaped room with its rounded outer wall, the perfectly diagonal, straight-sided walls, and the shorter straight inner wall. Like a pie cut into eight equal-sized pieces, it left an octagon in the center.

Micah squatted down on the stone floor. Marveling at the vaulted ceiling above, he placed his hands on the ancient stones and removed his shoes.

Chapter 64

ROTHERY ARRIVED AT THE back of the warehouse parking lot. He reached for his 9mm in the glove box and strapped the shoulder holster in place.

"Don't shoot yourself, agent," Dylan chided, walking up on Rothery from behind.

"You're one to talk," Rothery replied without missing a beat, "the way you pulled your gun at the hotel, it looked as if you'd never used one before."

"I typically have no need; secret service takes care of me when I'm with the PM."

"Doesn't look like you're carrying one now."

"No."

"Hold on, you can take the shotgun," Rothery offered. "I have it in the boot."

"Good idea... *mate*."

Rothery moved to the back of the car. He opened the trunk and grabbed the shotgun while his partner walked around the other side of the car. Looking down, kicking the gravel Dylan said, "Aren't you at all curious to know how I knew to be here?"

Rothery shut the door of the trunk. "No."

The answer surprised Dylan. He looked up from the gravel to see Rothery holding the shotgun, aimed right at him. "Not at all," Rothery said.

"What are you doing, agent?"

"This is the Prestige," Rothery answered with a scowl.

Vasko folded his arms, shaking his head. His voice grew deep. "Why didn't I see this coming?" He began reading Rothery's mind, step by step everything Rothery had discovered— from the dead taxi driver and Victoria's purse, to accessing the GPS location of Dylan's mobile phone. "My, my, you've been a busy lad. And I really didn't want to kill you. What a shame."

Rothery raised the rifle, "Shan't be a problem— *mate*. I'll save you from that."

Vasko sighed and in less than a split second, the rifle was no longer in Rothery's possession but in Vasko's hands, pointing at Rothery's head. "Now the pistol, agent."

Rothery was stunned, even nauseated by the speed of Dylan's movement. He turned pale.

"Are you going to vomit?" Vasko asked. "You look as if you're going to vomit."

Just then, automatic gunfire came from inside the warehouse. Police calls were heard over the radio, *"Shots fired, shots fired! Suspects on the third floor... at least two."*

Rothery looked at the radio trying to derive how to call for backup from the officers around the front of the building.

"I'll leave it to you," Vasko calmly stated.

"Leave what?" Rothery mustered.

"Whether you radio Tilman and the boys or not. They have enough to deal with right now, by the way, but they may still live. Of course, if you call them, they won't."

Rothery was surprised by his partner's perceptiveness, the fact that he seemed to know what Rothery was thinking. Dylan had never been that smart before. "So, this is what you meant when you said the PM was a puppet..." Rothery deduced, "you don't even consider us."

"Actually, it was Mr. Steinbeck who put it so eloquently."

"Is he alive?" Rothery's breathing was beginning to normalize as he settled into the bizarre situation. Much to his surprise, Dylan seemed to be accommodating by giving him the time to do so. "Give it up, Dylan. The building will be surrounded soon. Looks like you will finally see Sergeant Poe's team in action."

Dylan furrowed a brow in disappointment as more police sirens became prominent in the distance. "We really need to take this inside," he said, motioning Rothery to take lead into the building. "If you don't mind...?"

Hearing gunfire, Rothery hesitated. Careful to open the door slowly to assure it didn't creak, he entered the building cautiously, stepping into the warehouse's receiving-dock area. He glanced quickly behind the door to his right, then rapidly scanned the room to the left. He tiptoed across the warehouse floor.

"Uh, what are you doing?" Dylan asked.

"Being cautious," Rothery whispered.

"That's really not necessary, mate. This is my building."

"Right. Right. Habit, I suppose."

"By the stairwell." Vasko gestured to the small iron door, "Open it."

Rothery obediently began to open the iron door when Dylan all at once stopped him, "Wait," holding up his hand. Standing silently for a moment, the sound of gunfire and bullets had recommenced, riddling the building above. "Over here," Dylan commanded using the pistol to direct Rothery to a small storage closet instead.

Vasko motioned the agent to open the closet then forced him inside, "Now kneel down on the floor and face the wall," he ordered, taking a stance behind him.

Kneeling with his back to the door, Rothery bowed his head and shut his eyes. He could not believe he was going to be executed. THIS was not his job. His position did not include danger for the most part. He was a glorified analyst, not an American cowboy.

He thought about his wife and their new born child; how Pamela would blame herself for drawing him out of his depression that morning and setting him on the path that led to his death. With his eyes closed, he pictured her and his son, Rothery Wyndham Taylor IV. The name of the boy echoing in his head reminded him of the inevitable coincidence that had led to that legacy. Rothery smiled.

"What are you smiling about?" Dylan asked, annoyed.

Head to the floor, Rothery's voice cracked with winsome emotion, "That I named my son ROTHERY WYNDHAM TAYLOR."

Chapter 65

MICAH KNELT ON THE floor near the furthest inner wall. He listened as the iron door down the hall opened and closed with the sound of a dungeon gate. Wind rushed within the hall whistling through every crevice, shrieking like the sound of crying cats or a tortured child screaming for his life; a mother's lamented high-pitched wail.

Approaching footsteps echoed, shaking the very room. The cell door breathed, contracting and retracting with each step as if a beast which could not be contained approached— the hinges creaked and swelled. Fear, isolation and darkness invaded Micah's mind. *This is not real*, he told himself.

But reality gave him no less horror. His own mind began to imagine the worse of human depravity making even the supernatural evil less horrifying. Intense hunger suddenly overtook him; the sensation of starvation spawned visions of eating the flesh off Victoria's dead corpse like an animal fighting to survive. Micah shivered at what Vasko might force upon him to 'free him of the distraction'.

Seconds seemed like minutes as the intruder's entrance loomed. The steel lock-bolt lever released slamming free with incredible force. When Vasko entered the room, Micah's body shook like a fully-charged defibrillator had burst upon his chest. His eyes opened wide.

A strangely warped version of the once young and handsome Dylan carried Victoria's limp body in just one hand. With absolute disregard, he roughly dropped her to the floor like a wet rag. The darkness within Vasko seemed to be accentuating the developing deformity of his face; his likeness, as if seen in a funhouse mirror, revealed the agent was somehow no longer able to maintain a boyish façade. Barely raising his hand, the door closed with the deadbolt locking behind him. The sound echoed throughout the cell and wind from the closing door momentarily extinguished the encircling oil flame. Slow to re-ignite, the light added a haunting strobe effect to Vasko's manifestation.

Micah didn't move. His focus was on Victoria although his eyes never left Vasko. She was hurt, cold— certainly frightened, but alive. What she had gone through and her mental anguish, Micah couldn't imagine and couldn't afford to. He needed to stay calm and in control. Anger would only inhibit reason. If she was unconscious, it was best she remained that way. If she wasn't, hearing his voice in control would serve her best. The less he considered her, the less Vasko might use her against him.

Vasko fixed his gaze upon Micah, his voice accusing, "What have you done to me?! All I've put into play now in jeopardy!"

"Why, Vassiago, you seem frazzled."

"Remove this curse or I will force you to feed upon the woman's flesh while she still breathes!"

"Interesting," Micah replied, "I was just thinking something along those lines… strangely consoling." Vasko, having uttered the words of Micah's horrific thoughts, confirmed they were merely a threatening projection from this enemy.

Condescending, Micah continued, "CURSES? Seriously, you too? How is it you think there are no consequences for your actions? I thought you more reasonable. I am but a mirror, Vassiago, exposing your true image. You break the mirror, stay as you are forever."

"How is that not a curse?"

Micah laughed, "That's funny. I've had vile people steal from me— con-men, self-righteous, self-serving frauds. Instead of cursing them I've merely said, 'May God bless you as you have me.'" Micah chuckled, "And they always instantly get so angry."

Vasko appeared confused, "I don't understand."

"I didn't think you would."

"Hmm." The agent narrowed his eyes, calmed and now intrigued. He continued, "You appear so fragile, so docile cowering over there on the floor— insignificant. But you have chipped and chipped everything away from me… how is it that you do it?

"You would think I would be angry but on the contrary, my interest in you has expanded. Now I need to know what it is that drives you— from where you draw this power. I know it is neither intellect, wisdom, *or earned*. So, I am augmenting my offer, Mr. Graff.

"I can no longer permit you the luxury of prison here in Britain because, thanks to your 'reflection', I, myself, will now likely have to leave. But I also cannot tolerate anyone tainting our project. You have limited my choices, so..." Vasko exhaled, "either agree or die."

Micah scowled.

"You seem less than receptive, Micah. That's disappointing. Of course, I really don't need your permission, you know. Come now, I'm attempting civility here to begin our venture on the right foot. I think you will find I can be very useful... although before you ask," briefly dropping his gaze to Victoria, "I can sense the woman is on your mind. Unfortunately, there really is nothing I can do for her. I'm sure you understand we can't afford the level of exposure which would most certainly be a byproduct of her fame. Besides," he added, "I have no interest in babysitting."

Micah's anger grew.

"As I said, I can rid you of that distraction." Vasko fully believed himself sincere, crossing the room to Victoria.

Victoria had regained consciousness. Seeing Vasko approach, she screamed, scurrying in panic to the furthest corner. Vasko, annoyed, moved with great speed to beat her there. He knelt down, grabbed her by the legs and spread them with such force, she broke backwards like a rag doll. He looked her in the face as she tried to squirm.

His strength was uncanny, restraining her with just a touch to her knee. One finger upon her leg nailed her to the floor like a thousand-pound weight with extraordinary finger dexterity. If she moved even slightly or barely flinched, with the lightest thrust, Vasko was able to force her back against the wall completely immobilizing her. It was thoughtless to him like a man restraining a snail under his thumb. Utterly debilitating to Victoria, he was actually rather gentle.

Vasko began deliberately reaching his hand up her evening dress. "I mean no offense, just curious," he toyed. "I do see the attraction, the world's fascination. But I have always wondered..." slowly running his hand up her thigh, "is man's fantasy justified?" He paused and stared into Victoria's eyes, "It feels good to be out of control, doesn't it?" Looking for a reaction, he smugly turned to taunt Micah.

But Micah had risen to his feet.

Surprised yet disappointed, Vasko scoffed, "You are stubborn… too stubborn." He returned to his feet shaking his head. "Given the anomaly that is you, Micah, I regret I must release you from my offer. It seems you've made your choice… so I will accommodate."

"I appreciate that," Micah retorted, taking a stance.

With a sinister cackle Vasko jeered, "So, you want to make sport? How ambitious of you! Although I would love to tell you the idea exhilarates me, you know I would be lying. But I can exhilarate YOU." He smiled, "I'll tell you what, little man, sports begin with a coin toss."

A thick gold coin suddenly appeared in Vasko's hand. He rolled it over his knuckles then spun it at a great speed upon the top of the worn, wooden bedpost of the cot. "Heads or tails?" he asked. Then added "Ah, don't bother," shifting tone, "you will be dead before the coin comes to its rest."

Micah slowly paced the floor in a semi-circle, eyes fixed on the demented figure.

Though elated by Micah's confidence, Vasko knew it would be over all too soon; humiliation was his game and he intended to play at his best. "Your confidence is entertaining," he chuckled, "I'm going to enjoy this."

Watching Micah's display, the agent gave him his moment. "Oh, what fun we could have had, you and I."

Micah stopped, quiet in the center of the room.

A cocky grin on his face, Vasko motioned to Micah, egging him on. "Ready? I want you at your best so you can quickly see the disparity between us. It will be good for you— though I fear your lesson will not last long." He said the last, sincerely remorseful.

Micah's lips began to move, speaking an ancient language under his breath.

"Rattle your incantations elsewhere, that doesn't work on me. I am not spirit, but flesh."

"That's good. I'm tired of toiling with the spirit of your unholy spawn. Time to dance!"

Micah closed his eyes whispering an ancient proverb; "Gam ki-elekh b'gia tzalmavet … kol harada shamanu pahad v'ayn shalom … anush l'shivrekh nah-lamaka-tekh." He spoke it like a eulogy.

Almost nefariously, Micah stretched forth his hands slowly. He opened and closed them repeatedly making fists as if catching snowflakes. Quietly he spoke again, "La-tzig et atzamekh… show yourself!"

With that Vasko jolted into an arch— his back and neck stretching backwards. His legs grew, his arms reached above his head as if standing for the first time. He transitioned over seven feet in height, three feet in breadth; his back and chest cracked with the strain of his transformation. His jaw wretched side to side revealing hideous fangs. His skin greyed pale giving the appearance of a standing gargoyle. Each eye spread back half the width of his face; only pupil filled the revealed sockets. There were no eyelids nor brows— a nocturnal creature designed for darkness without rest.

Vasko's clothing ripped to reveal a muscular physique with little earthly resemblance. His breath so deep, it filled the room with the stench of sulfur and burnt ash. The air thickened, the room heated. His fingertips grew a sixth and seventh digit upon each hand.

"Ahh," the beast groaned, "so liberating!" He uncurled his massive hands, scrapping the steel blades of his nails along the stone ceiling. "You see? This room was not made for your kind but for MINE— a millennia ago!"

As the beast transformed, Micah's right hand fell to his side with a warmth he had only recently been reminded of. A surge through his body from his core— his soul, his nashama— to the tips of his fingers, the top of his head, the ends of his toes. His eyes glowed piercing blue, so bright it tinted the room.

Vasko looked down expecting to see Micah huddled in a corner in fear; instead he was confronted by indescribable faith.

The fingers of Micah's right hand began to twitch erratically, uncontrollably. Focusing on the sporadic finger movement, with his left hand Micah reached to brace his right wrist. As his hands grew closer together, an arching blue spark jumped from one hand to the other; a power beyond his experience began flowing between them as he cupped his palms together and watched the dance of his nashama. The energy became physical— an almost solid substance having a predestined agenda of its own. With absolute purpose, Micah slowly raised his eyes to his opponent; his stare challenging, assured, unwavering.

Vasko remained disinterested, unruffled; seemingly unaware. Micah tilted his head from side to side to release a kink from his neck and readied his stance.

Determined to fulfill its destiny, Micah's right hand reached across his chest and over his left shoulder. The solid energy cupped within his palm took form— an ethereal blade. He drew it slowly as if it had been sheathed upon his back forever; a faithful friend manifested as a brilliant sword— the gift given him years ago. A blistering sapphire-blue pummel; the grip like contoured gold-laced dolphin skin; a blade made of pure virgin carbon steel so clean, it was near invisible. Only the echo of an elusive reflection was mirrored on its diamond-tipped edge. Double-edged, it captured all light— the reflection spanned to every corner giving the impression that the sword was its source.

Micah wielded the sword with great finesse, rolled the hilt from elbow to fingertips. It spun against his arms like a lover undressed. "There you are, my friend. I hadn't forgotten you," he whispered. "I forsook and banished you, yet still you remain."

Vasko sneered, "What is that you hold in your hand, human?"

"Oh, so you can see it now? Something you couldn't see before?" Micah chided.

"I HAVE seen that before…" Vasko searched his memory.

"My father gave me this years ago… wasn't certain what it was for until today."

"Your father?" The beast's eyes fixed on the immaculate blade.

"That's right," Micah smiled. "I see that concerns you. It's written on your face."

Vasko was unable to release his gaze from the blinding weapon. Visions suddenly flooded his mind— banished memories from long ago now exposed like a lit room. His eyes shifted repeatedly as he speedread the liberated images of the past. "Ah, how illuminating!" he proclaimed.

The veil had been lifted from the creature's sight; layer after layer, year after year to near beginning, hidden from his kind. Banished power without purpose— immortality without reason suddenly made clear. "How could I have not known? How did I not see? So clear, lying all this time in front of me."

Shaking his head as if resurrected, "I toiled in the sewer of mortals. Furcus' unconscious itch… even that was inevitable!" Laughing to himself he turned his attention to Micah. "He drove you to me! I see mortal man— your place. I knew your father and he knew me. Shall I tell you of him?" Vasko, too overwhelmed with his new found purpose to care, "Never mind," he said instead, "let me send you to him! Never fear… you may be remembered after all, human, for what you've brought to me today— the glory of my past… and now, my future, held within that blade." Pointing at the sword with resounding reckoning, "I WILL LEAD!"

Now contemplating the nature of his revelation as memories raced through his mind, "I am he?" There was little question in Vasko's statement. "I must be… I am the one! If not me, who? If not now, when?" he declared.

Micah laughed, "Have an epiphany, did you?"

Vasko shook his head in disregard. "Lay the blade at my feet and I may show mercy. It belongs to me, it is not of this Earth."

"Neither am I!" Micah announced with authority, slowly beginning to raise the blade.

"Ah-ha!" the beast laughed. Then in the blink of an eye, Vasko was in front of Micah, mouth opened, fangs revealed.

Micah didn't even have time to even lift the sword. Like lightening, the creature appeared behind him, pressed up against him with a vile lust, and whispered close to his ear, "You see, it matters not if you'd had a hundred swords; you can neither raise your hand nor see me move."

With Vasko's claw now on his shoulder, Micah was completely restrained, the grip cutting off his circulation. Micah's left arm fell limp to his side.

"It's already over, human," Vasko sneered.

The creature's foot slipped between Micah's legs lifting him off the ground by the scrotum. Vasko stopped and held him there as he listened, "Hmm, can you hear? Atop the stairs Rothery is coming. You must be dead before he gets to the door. Do you see what I mean…? how you rob me of my pleasure? Still, I will remember this moment when I run your children through with the sword of your father!"

The span of Vasko's hand suddenly spread the width of Micah's back. The beast grasped Micah by his entire ribcage, the grip crushing his chest. Rounding his fingertips, Vasko's fingernails grew like stiletto blades and pierced into Micah's body cavity. The air fled Micah's lungs. He gasped but could not fill them.

"Are those your lungs collapsing? I'm told it's really quite painful. Oh, what we could have learned, you and I." The beast slowly bent a knuckle. "And now you will see that I am not without mercy... wait. Do you feel that?"

Twitch, twitch. Micah's heart skipped two beats.

"That is the tip of my finger holding your life by a mere flex. You see how gracious I can be?"

The beast turned his eyes blatantly toward the door. "Is Rothery knocking yet? No, no... not yet. But he will; our time is precious. Find solace in the fact that toying with you lessens Victoria's suffering— I may only have time to break her neck. But then again, as you have now seen, time is quite relative to me." He released Micah and in an instant, knelt before Victoria.

Micah nearly collapsed to the ground, his knees barely holding. His right hand gripping the sword braced him like a cane on the floor. Body convulsing, head bowed, Micah waited for air to return to his lungs. "Father, I failed you. I ran, I hid, I cried, and for that now I die." Oxygen deprived, the room appeared to move. He focused all his attention to not fall.

Vasko grabbed Victoria by her hair, lifting her dangling above the ground. "I thought to give you one last look, woman, I know how much he means to you." He turned her head to face what she feared too much to see.

Smiling wickedly, the beast groaned with mock regret, "Oh, my, my, look at that. I'm so sorry, Victoria, it seems I've already killed him."

Micah, barely standing, faced an empty corner of the room. His eyes glazed over and fluttering, his lips parted and moving involuntarily; a body left with only its final fall.

Vasko shook his head, "That really is sad. It honestly breaks my heart. He had such spirit, such will. To see him like this almost grieves me." He dropped Victoria like a coin to the floor, truly pitying the man he once sought; the unique man he nearly believed.

Through her tears Victoria saw Micah weak and pale, shaking with nothing more than will to stand. His nashama had faded pale blue like the last flicker of an extinguished candle, adding to the image of imminent death. She threw herself upon the cold stone and lowered her eyes in hopelessness. She wished to cry out, to shove the unthinkable into the floor; yet somehow she found no solace, sympathy, nor empathy within her... but most surprisingly, no fear.

No fear? She didn't understand her emotionless experience. She drew a deep breath attempting to muster horror for what she soon would undoubtedly face. But searching her thoughts, even her imagination could not dissuade her fearlessness.

Am I conceding? resigned to die? She questioned but didn't care to answer. She rubbed her hand over the stone floor— not to draw warmth, but cold. *What is this?* She glanced up to the beast who loomed over her... curiously, his victory now appeared lost to her. No matter what she imagined he might do, she had peace.

Closing her eyes she began to rock, sliding both hands across the stones. She considered how many had lain there and died there. *How many centuries? How many millennia?* An overwhelming kinship to the former occupants of the room grew within her as if she had known them; as if they knew her now, as if she could feel them. Her hand found a place on the stone perfectly fitted like a glove, worn by the touch and footsteps of many. Echoes from the past— a thousand prayers— concealed in the ancient single-slate, sarsen stone floor. Visions suddenly poised to enter Victoria's mind like ghosts walking the floor— and she knew.

The revelation forced her eyes open to focus. Blatantly staring at her fitted hand, she found a smile. Though speaking quietly, her voice calmly came through, "Micah, it's time."

"What did you say?" Vasko snarled. "I didn't think I would hear more than a whimpering wail from you." Seeing her face, "What is that expression you wear...? do you taunt me to finish him? put him out of his misery?"

No longer panicked, Victoria chanced another look toward Micah, "Go on," she whispered.

Micah's hand, slow to move, reached as if touching something that wasn't there; his bare feet began shifting on the stone. Her eyes widened and tears flowed. Hope spread across her face— she had seen this all before. She looked back to Vasko with a confident glare of distain.

* * * * *

"I've waited for you. I knew you would come," a voice spoke in the darkness.

"Where am I?" Micah asked.

"You're still in the temple."

"Can you see me?" Micah asked.

"Yes."

"Then touch my face so I will know for sure you are here."

"Open your eyes, Micah."

Micah stood in the middle of the same room sometime long before. An old man dressed in dirty rags squatted on the floor.

"I stayed for you, I could have left here long ago. They're all gone now, but I knew they would return and so would you."

"I've been here before?"

"You'll be here again."

"Am I breathing?"

"Not yet, but it will come."

"He's too fast," Micah wept.

The old man nodded, "But when wasn't he?"

Micah bowed his head, searching within himself, *I should know this.*

The man heard a loud noise, "It's coming, Micah... it is coming."

As the room faded from Micah's view, the man whispered in his thoughts, "Take your TIME, Micah— it is TIME!"

The old man, disappearing into the haze of light, knelt before a young boy. The boy's eyes fearful and astonished, "There is so much to come, grandfather," the child said.

"Yes, yes... but long after we're gone."

Micah's eyes began to ache as if he'd been beaten by a strobe light; day to night, night to day he passed through time— all while standing firmly upon the stones of the chamber. He saw his feet changing in size and shape; narrow, wide; rough, smooth; those of a young boy, then an elderly man and finally his own. The sword shined constant, a light brilliant; he felt its energy flow through his body. His back strengthened, his posture straightened.

He methodically scanned the room over and over again, taking his time as it rapidly changed lest the speed of the journey devour his mind. He wanted to close his eyes, but having seen utter darkness with his eyes wide open, he cherished bathing in the light.

Suddenly Micah felt the coolness of a slight breeze passing over his tongue to the back of his throat and slipping slowly downward. With a prayer he threw back his head in hopes that his lungs might receive and fill.

*   *   *   *   *

"I can endure this no longer," Vasko uttered, "how quickly it all ended! How fragile. I was merely toying with him." The beast motioned to step towards Micah.

Micah's disposition changed. Although still moving extremely slowly— body violently shaking— he began turning toward Vasko. "What is this?" the beast said. "What am I seeing? Man reanimated? Is that your strength, Micah... what Furcus meant when he said that you refused to die?!"

Vasko glanced at Victoria still huddled in the corner, her arms held closed around her knees, but her eyes bearing hope and fixed on Micah.

"Are you seeing something I am not? Pfft, even if he awakes at ten-times strength, it will not matter! I will... AHH! Ahh... ahhh!" Vasko cried out.

Shifting his eyes to his leg Vasko screamed, "AHHHH!" Blood poured down to his knee. A gash over an inch deep crept slowly down his thigh; two, five, then nine inches in length. The beast howled. A great sound of anguish shook the room and filled the halls with thunderous tribulation. Grabbing his leg with both hands, he could not hold back the blood. It sprayed as if the wound had hit a primary artery, or that the newfound experience raced his heart intensifying the blood loss. He looked up at Micah.

Micah stood upright, left arm to his side, legs strengthened shoulder-width apart; right arm bent across his chest holding the immaculate sword dripping from the tip with blood.

"AHHH!" The beast groaned, growling with gritted teeth.

"First time for pain? A first time for everything," Micah said. "Oh, how you mock what you don't know. You are already dead, Vassiago, you just don't know it yet. But it's coming." Micah paced the floor deliberately, searching for his place, his footing upon the stone.

Hearing the cries of anguish, Rothery rushed to the outer cell door pounding to get in. Grabbing the bolt-latch, he pulled with all his weight to release the ancient 3-foot bar. But Vasko, aware of the pending intrusion, waved his hand and mystically caused the outside deadbolt to forcibly slam back into place.

Micah's right foot fell into place, his left followed. His eyes flickered. Vasko, bewildered, moved one step towards Micah and instantly felt another slash— this one growing across his abdomen and deeply breaking the surface of his skin. If it weren't for his lightning speed and reflex to stop, Vasko knew the sword would most certainly have impaled him.

Vasko howled a horrific roar, fell to his knees upon the floor; one hand gripping his thigh, the other his stomach. Fear that his insides might spill to the outside overtook him.

Micah circled Vasko, "You were right, there is so much you can learn! I CAN teach you. But I'm afraid we've only just scratched the surface of YOUR potential. What you are experiencing now is FEAR. For an immortal who has never felt anything before, in only moments you find your hand's feeble attempt to prevent your stomach from spilling out upon the floor. I think we've made a lot of progress today, don't you agree?" Micah laughed, proud.

"You arrogant fuck!" Vasko spat, "You think I don't learn? You think I don't see? My mind works as fast as my body! You need to find your place on the stones… and lightning will strike you before you move again!"

"You really don't understand, do you?" Micah's voice was commanding, "I was ALREADY THERE!"

Vasko's face suddenly paled; he realized Micah had been striking him willfully from the past— in the past moving through time. Now he feared the next inevitable gash. Had it already happened as Micah had declared?

Vasko questioned for the first time if it would be his last. He was suddenly frightened to move, afraid his speed and strength would be used against him. He recognized that what was once impossible— his own invulnerability— was now his weakness. As strong and fast and impenetrable as he was, that which had already happened in the past was far faster than the speed of light— and inevitable.

Unable to comprehend everything the new sensations implied, in a frantic, unbridled move, Vasko struck at Micah sending him sailing into the stone wall. Cautiously, the beast stalked after the soaring body uncertain what his next action should be.

But using the momentum and force of his opponent, Micah hit the wall climbing. One step, two steps up the wall; a back-flip over the beast. The sword, trailing the motion of his body like the tail of a comet, completely encircled Vasko's throat causing the beast to freeze. Micah landed on his feet near the center of the room facing the creature from the back.

Vasko turned to face Micah mere inches away, a sinister smile upon his face. But opening his mouth to speak, he found no words came out. He tried again and again. Nothing. It took a moment before he realized air was neither coming in nor going out. He opened his jaws wide attempting to inhale, but even the muscles to breathe failed him.

Bewildered, Vasko had no former experience to draw from, no sympathy nor empathy for pain, panic, nor mortality. Having never thought his existence could be in question (might end), he was void of thought. Minutes passed before his eyes widened and the room began to fade.

Micah stood still within an arm's reach of the creature. Waiting, watching, he held the sword tight, absorbing its energy and regaining his own strength while observing how quickly his adversary weakened.

"I should probably explain," Micah started. "So much I could have taught you. The gap. What was the word you used...? the disparity between us? You can't even fathom. Really, we're having to begin with such PRIMAL basics like dealing with pain and breathing... I fear all our quality time is going to such waste given the minor predicament that you're not going to be around to utilize it. On the other hand, as my mother-in-law always says, no education is wasted education, don't you agree? She received her law degree at my age."

Vasko fell to his knees. Unable to breathe, he dug his fingers into his throat trying to muster air.

"But now look at all we have learned... once we removed those meaningless obstructions, that is. Wait, that's not the word you used. Hmm, I believe the term was 'distractions', wasn't it? Like immortality... control. You are becoming more and more HUMAN, Vassiago. So, while I have your attention… it's my dime now." Vasko raised his eyes, glaring.

"Thank you for noticing," Micah nodded. "Maybe this gives you a slight understanding of human emotion though you've never cared for anything… in the past. Now, I suppose, you at least have a bit of understanding about desire, yearning, need. In your case, it's the desire to breathe, live, to stop bleeding. Maybe, had we had more time, you may have even discovered the joy of needing someone."

Vasko's eyes widened. "Don't look so shocked, I'll elaborate. For instance, imagine how elated you might be to see Ring Finger right now; if he walked into the room how much joy that would give you… as if your life depended on it (which it does.) You might have even begun to understand love because right at this moment you might have said (if you were able to talk), 'So nice to see you, Furcus. I've missed you, Furcus.' Given enough time you may have even developed empathy for another— wishing them well because they added meaning to your life or, (as in your case) because they could actually have extended it."

Shaking his head, Micah continued, "Oh, but the pupil… you have been so stubborn! Well, if it gives any consolation, I will be going to see your friends." Micah glanced obnoxiously at his watch, "It's amazing how long you can survive without oxygen. You really are a resilient fuck."

Panic set in. Vasko's body convulsed.

Seeing Victoria rise to her feet, "Honey, do you mind stepping over to the corner," Micah requested, "this might get a little messy."

The creature began pounding the floor.

Looking back toward Vasko, "I'm sorry, Vassiago, I forgot you were there. As I was saying, I was retired. I tried to stay out of everyone's hair. But you just couldn't let it be, could you? I've never chased you, I've never sought to get in the way. I've tried to live a quiet life! You must be thinking now… oh, wait a minute, of course you're not. You never did much of that, did you? But I'll tell you anyway. How you underestimated me…? You are not alone. The whole world underestimates the power of a spark— what a flicker of light can expose in the dark."

The coin spun slowly to its final resting place upon the bed post. "Well, I think we've tried Rothery's patience long enough, don't you?" Micah said, glancing at the coin. Then, stepping up to the beast, he placed his blade under Vasko's chin using it to raise the bowed head to look him in the eye. The sound of shredding flesh, the gasping for breath— new blood splashing upon the stone floor as he tilted Vasko's line of sight. "I'm sorry my friend, it's HEADS!" Micah dropped the creature's chin and turned away.

In a last strike effort, Vasko reached for Micah, grasping for his leg. Micah wheeled about with the sword 360 degrees— and decapitated the beast with a single blow.

The room shook and filled with vile smoke and ash. The corpse of Agent Vasko disintegrated, disappearing into nothingness (along with the sword) all before the beast's body had time to hit the floor. At that same moment, the lock-bolt slammed opened and the door released. Its ancient hinges broken, the iron door crashed to the floor.

Micah fell back to a seated position on the bed, now feeling the pain in his chest, his legs. He was completely exhausted. Victoria hobbled to his side, still nursing her own injuries from the car wreck. She sat down upon the bed next to him.

Rothery broke through the entrance. Smoke lifted like steam, trailing out of the room and down the hallway. Rothery called on his radio, "Get someone down here! We need medical aid!"

After quickly scanning the room, Rothery approached the bed. "Michael, can you hear me?"

Micah, dazed, stared oblivious.

"Are you okay?" Victoria worried.

Micah didn't respond.

"Where's Dylan?" Rothery questioned.

Micah still didn't respond.

"Where's Vasko?" he asked again.

"He's gone." Victoria's voice, empty.

"I know he was in this room... was he in this room?"

Micah, still struggling to breathe, took a deep breath, "You're a smart guy, Rothery. What do you think happened?"

Police officers slowly began to enter the room. "We've called for an ambulance, sir."

Rothery nodded. "Michael," sounding relieved, "are you all right?"

"I will be."

"I thought I told you I never wanted to see you again."

Rising to his feet, Micah managed a half-grin, "I had no intention of you seeing me the first time, agent."

With Rothery's aid, he and Victoria managed their way out of the room and up the staircase to the parking lot.

* * * * *

By the time they exited the building the ambulance had just arrived. Seeing the growing number of policemen and EMTs, the SIS agent pulled Micah aside. "You really need to leave, Michael. Your fingerprints were on the gun at the Opera House."

"I told you."

Rothery gave a knowing frown. He motioned to Victoria. "We'll take care of her," he assured.

Micah gratefully nodded and hobbled to where the EMTs were attending her. He stepped up close and bowed his head into her chest. She folded her arms, both hands across the back of his neck. She laid her head upon his. "You need to go with them," he whispered.

Victoria began to cry.

"Take care of yourself, Victoria. Get healthy."

"Okay," she whispered. With tears streaming down her face, "It's been an adventure, hasn't it? You sure know how to show a girl a good time."

"Shopping... what's a girl to do?" Micah smiled. "And everyone thought this was going to be a chick-flick."

"It's not a movie, Micah."

"Well, I have a feeling that if you have anything to do with it..."

"You know, we never did get to... you know." She gave a shy grin.

"Double digits? Yeah, I'm aware."

The actress smiled, "I don't even know what time it is."

Micah held her face in his hands. Neither of them were the people they had met on the plane; he wasn't looking through her anymore and she wasn't looking up at him, either. Face to face they gazed into each other's eyes. Neither realized they had been kissing.

"Michael, it's time to go," Rothery nudged quietly.

Micah slowly stood. He turned to face Rothery holding out his hand. "Agent? Rothery?"

Seeing Micah's outstretched hand, without hesitation Rothery shook it.

"I'm Micah Graff."

"MICAH," Rothery exclaimed, "I was so close."

"Take care, Sherlock."

Chapter 66

MICAH WALKED UP TO the bar at the Rumpus Room Mondrian, London. "Give me a double of your Jura 21 Limited. Are those Cubans?" he asked.

"Of course."

"I'll take a Churchill Cohiba and a Monte Cristo number two."

"Cuban or Dominicans?"

"Havana."

The bartender nodded, "Brilliant choice, sir. Out of the box or…"

"No, in the aluminum round."

The bartender handed Micah the scotch and cigars. "Run a tab?"

"Sure."

"Cutter?"

Micah nodded. The bartender threw him the cigar cutter.

The man Micah sought sat at a corner table with his back to the bar. Walking up behind him, Micah held the Churchill aluminum container to the patron's head like the barrel of a pistol.

Cocky, Micah brushed a piece of lint off the man's shoulder and put the Cohiba in his front jacket pocket. Micah circled the table and boldly took the seat across from him.

Ring Finger glanced down at the Cohiba. "A 30 pound cigar, how generous. Let me buy you a drink."

"I already have one, but thank you."

"What's the occasion?"

"I'm celebrating, Furcus. Although from the look on your face, you don't seem eager to join me."

"Celebrating? I'm still seeing your face on the television. I'm not certain your celebrity status warrants such luxuriousness."

Micah had ignored the comment seeming to have his own agenda. "You and I have known each other for some time, it seems. Longer for you than for me, I suspect."

Ring Finger raised a brow suspecting Micah knew more than before or had somehow confirmed at least one of his crazy conspiracy theories. Smiling smugly, "Think you know something new? Interesting."

"Not new… VERY old," Micah answered. "How long have you been stalking me?"

"The truth?" Furcus paused but continued, "Before you were born."

The man in front of him appeared years younger than Micah; either Ring Finger was aware he'd been exposed or was now prepared to do just that. "Actually I take that back," Furcus decided after a moment, pointing at Micah, "you were stalking me."

"Before I was born?" Micah challenged.

"That's right. And now, seeing you sitting here, I suspect far longer than that." Although Ring Finger seemed to be confessing like a man on death row, Micah was cautious. He had come to know (all too well) his adversary's power of deception, manipulation, and even telepathic persuasion.

But at that moment Micah felt a familiar feeling— an ingenuous spirit of conviction. Conviction often manifested as an intense presence filling a room preventing lies or malice intent— even evil yearned to confess. "Hmm, do share," Micah offered.

"Saint Joseph's."

"Saint Joseph," Micah laughed, "husband of the blessed mother, Mary?"

The large man looked annoyed, "St. Joseph's hospital, more than four decades ago... almost five now."

Micah, suddenly shocked, "Asheville, North Carolina? July?"

"That's right. Young governor— what was his name? Was it Sanford? No, never mind that..."

Ring Finger's voice began to change as he told the story. He fell into a thick southern drawl, his voice and appearance transforming. His hair shrunk into his head; a flat top mysteriously greased back. His shirt turned white and his tie and nose broadened. He aged twenty years in seconds. Micah could only imagine Furcus was taking the form of the man he had been on that day in the past.

Ring Finger continued, "Governor was causin' all kinds o'trouble. He believed it was time to put away all prejudice of the American Negro, a hundred years after Lincoln's emancipation. Mr. Sanford thought the job hadn't been done quite properly... well, that'd be *FINE* in the north, but comin' from the Carolinas? There were interested parties that liked the national tension as it was— keep the status quo, so to speak.

"There was a new wing at that there hospital— pediatrics. We'd done some work there and Governor Sanford was set to cut the ribbon. But ya see, we thought the hospital needed to be *completely* remodeled; renovated up to modern standards for the good people of North Carolina. In fact, the donation had already been made...

"The unfortunate thing was that the remodel would require the demolition of the new wing, too (along with Mr. Terry Sanford, hisself, did I mention?) It's simple, son... you see a snake in the grass and you have a machete, you hack away. You don't worry about the slug, the worm; the mouse or rat in its belly."

"I'm not quite understanding how I fit in," Micah said.

"Well, I didn't neither at the time; mere coincidence I reckoned. But on that day, for the first time in nearly a century, a chain reaction of events prevented the demolition of that there hospital— and of Mr. Sanford. I didn't start figurin' the possibility of a single point of obstruction until Seattle a couple years later."

"Seattle, huh?"

Now Furcus dropped the accent and turned stern, "That's right," Ring Finger affirmed. "First, there was Seattle, but I didn't put a name and face to the

impediment until August ten years later when my sweet Julie killed herself...
over a drunken car wreck that took place in Oregon. She was the passenger
when I hit two young boys on a dirt bike while crossing the Cascade
Mountains."

Micah remained silent as the man seated across from him casually dismissed
his brief emotion. Recomposed and without feeling he continued. "Julie never
got over it. But the bitch of it all was that the boy walked away without a
scratch. Sixty-five miles an hour... he flew fifty, sixty feet in the air and walked
away without a scratch. The other boy, a cousin I believe, in traction and a coma
for over a month... and he still came out just fine, too. As you can see, YOU
have been stalking me, Mr. Graff."

Micah bit his lip.

"On the other hand, I suppose that's not completely true. I did need to see
exactly what you could do. So, years later in San Antonio..."

"Oh, my God! That's enough!" Micah commanded.

"That doesn't sit well with you? Knowing you were a part of something..."
Ring Finger's eyes swelled with excitement, "MASSIVE!"

Micah sorrowed at the thought of so many dead and lives ruined because of
him. So many people affected just so this creature might test Micah's unknown
abilities over the years. *How many more were there?* He couldn't begin to
fathom. Somberly, Micah had to ask, "Why haven't you just killed me then?"

"Would it be that easy? Seriously? If I stood up, walked over there, could I
break your neck? Would it even be possible? Oh, I've killed plenty with my bare
hands; no resistance, no hesitation. And you're just sitting there. Should be a
'snap', you would think?"

That thought— that possibility— made Micah's enemy's eyes glaze over.
Slowly tilting his head in a barely conscious state of euphoria, Furcus was clearly
more than imagining it. He was living the possibility in his mind, high at that
moment on the thought of taking Micah's life.

Angered and intense, Micah snapped his fingers loudly rousing Furcus from
his daze, "What are you doing in town?"

"What are you doing alive?"

Micah flopped back in his seat, "Maybe you should ask Vasko when you see
him."

Ring Finger was bewildered by the innuendo. He gave a condescending chuckle, "Your arrogance— that's new for you. I'm not sure what all you think you know. I really don't care. As I've told you, you're not my problem anymore."

"Ah, Vassiago."

"Know a little more today, hmm?" Furcus gave a sincere nod of approval. "What it must be like to be you," he admired sarcastically. "The gap between the known and unknown must be exhilarating; sitting there so confident in the Mondrian, of all places. It's downright admirable. Walk proud!" Ring Finger pushed out his chest, mocking, "Yet you have no idea... you could be hit by a bus this afternoon."

"Likewise for you," Micah responded with equal distain. "To be so certain. No blind spot, then?" Micah questioned.

Furcus confidently shrugged off the possibility.

"Nowhere you can't be? Nothing you can't see? Nothing you can't hear? Have you ever even considered, 'what if?'"

"What if, WHAT?" Ring Finger narrowed his eyes.

"What if there was something you couldn't see, something you couldn't hear. What if your arrogance was the device of your demise?" Micah stared at Furcus— the creature with the gold ring— directly in the eye, challenging. Ring Finger returned his stare, unwavering.

Micah slowly sat back in his seat and announced, "Vassiago couldn't see, Furcus... not until the very end." He threw Vasko's gold coin on the table.

Furcus sat up almost startled, staring at the coin. "That's impossible, he'd never give you that coin."

"Well," Micah shrugged, "he's not around to keep it."

Ring Finger leapt to his feet and scanned the room 360 degrees. He wasn't looking at the room they were in, he was looking beyond it in all directions as if he could see through the walls to the ends of the city. Then he scanned the floor. It took Micah a moment to realize Ring Finger was scanning the entire EARTH.

"Lose something? Can I help you find it?" Micah taunted.

Furcus sat back down in his seat perplexed. In disbelief, "I warned him," he said solemnly.

"He mentioned."

The comment caught Ring Finger's attention.

"Hmm? There's something new," Micah observed, pointing at Furcus' chest. "That feeling you're experiencing? It's called grief. It appears to be your first time— I don't suspect you've ever known it. I also don't suspect you'll actually miss HIM, but I do know that there IS something you don't know... how he DIED and how YOU will, too!"

Furcus paled.

"Blind spot. Blind spot. Something you didn't know, after all. Though if it's any consolation to you, there was something Vassiago knew... he remembered."

Ring Finger's eyes widened, "Remembered?"

"Yes, everything. Who you are... or more appropriately, WHAT you are."

With an impetuous spin of the ring around his finger, the doubt was apparent in his voice, "You think you know."

"I know YOU don't," Micah countered. "It's so entertaining when a predator suddenly discovers he's not at the top of the food chain. What if I were to tell you we had it planned all along?"

No longer able to uphold his cool demeanor, Ring Finger felt suddenly confronted with why Micah had haunted him so. In an emerging ancient accent, "Talking, talking, talking..." gesturing, waving his hand, "your words— like a mosquito buzzing." His own undeniable lack only intensified his rage.

"Need I speak slower so you might understand?"

Infuriated, Furcus grew silent.

Micah settled a bit, "I understand this is a lot to absorb in one night. Why don't you take seven days to consider it?"

"You're not so untouchable, my friend. What of your children? Your son!" Furcus threatened.

Micah deliberately failed to hold back deep, sincere laughter. Then abruptly stopping, he glared at Furcus. "You think you're threatening me?" His amusement was genuine. "Let me give you some advice, Furcus; stick to what you know where you stand a fleeting chance."

Ring Finger scoffed, "Our reports show that neither of your children have shown any aptitude to follow in the FAMILY BUSINESS."

Micah smiled, "Your KIND may have well owned the past, but you really have a blind spot for the future."

"You're abandoned, you're an anomaly. You're a prehistoric relic," Furcus proclaimed.

"You may be right, you may be right. But I was raised by a single mother who didn't know what she believed. I slept with the lights on until I was eighteen years old; wet my bed as a child at every nightmare. And still, look at how you struggle with me! My children were not raised to toil the sewers like their father. They were raised to rebuild from your ruins. You should keep your focus on me. Stick to the minor league, my friend, you couldn't handle their game; THEY don't even consider YOU."

Ring Finger's face went cold at the thought. He, the only one of his kind to scarcely understand the threat Micah posed, recognized the blinded arrogance of his colleagues. Although still not enough to dissuade him, it was enough to make him briefly consider Micah's warning.

"You all have that same look about you," Micah noted. "You think you're hidden, but you're more and more obvious. You are all psychopaths by definition; immortality is your curse. How can you love the temporal? What if natural is the supernatural to you; something you can never obtain? What if Terra Firma is beyond your grasp? How empty that must be for you. To touch but not feel; eat but not taste; to live but not love. Well, I have your cure now, Furcus. I cured Vasko! Come get your medicine, you spawn of the abyss."

"That's a good offer," Ring Finger retorted. "It's tempting, it really is. It nearly seduces me. Still, I have the brotherhood who depend on me. You are right, though, they are shallow in thinking. They are overconfident. They have no vision for the future. They can't even hear the words you speak, it's jumbled like static. It hurts their ears like noise."

"I was retired. I tried to live a quiet life but you refused to let me. I tried to leave and Vasko— by your ORDER, threatened me, squeezed me, forced me, drove me back. You think you had a lot on your hands before?" Micah rose to his feet.

Furcus stood as well, aggravated by his inability to intimidate Micah; something he had never experienced. The large man's heart began to pound. He didn't understand what he was experiencing— it enraged him and caused him to curse. "I could crush your skull! I could rip your arteries from your throat, your heart from your chest before you felt the prick of my fingernails!" His nails began to grow.

Micah stepped boldly into him, "The anxiety you're experiencing…? Perspiration, trembling? That's called FEAR!"

"That's absurd." Furcus paused to analyze his newfound emotion.

"It's like the cold… do you even know cold?"

Ring Finger stepped toward his prey, threatening. Micah didn't flinch and looked away unafraid, disinterested. "You bore me. What is it with your kind? You can appear so sophisticated, elegant and intelligent until tempted, then you instantly turn primordially stupid… like the smell of blood to a starving, bloodthirsty pack of hyenas."

Ring Finger composed and sat back down in his chair.

"I'm done with you for now, Furcus. But know this… I'm coming back for MY RING." Micah turned his back and walked out of the room.

*   *   *   *   *

Furcus leaned back in his seat watching Micah leave. He spoke to the decorative curtains, "How much did you hear?"

"Enough," Europe said revealing himself from behind the curtain and taking a seat at the table.

"He's not running anymore."

"I see that. The Collective believed you thought too much of him, Furcus; clearly, we didn't consider him enough. And Vasko…" Europe remorsefully shook his head, "this changes the game. Do you think our comrade actually remembered everything?"

Ring Finger shrugged.

"Do you think Micah knows?"

Furcus contemplated, "Well if not, he has played a brilliant bluff. We can't afford to kill him now."

Europe agreed, "He has created more questions than answers."

The reflection of the waning sunset bounced off Furcus' ring. He slowly slid the broadened crown of the heirloom signet ring back and forth to cause the light to dance. *Coming back for his ring,* Furcus pondered, combing his goatee with his fingertips. "HIS ring!" he whispered, eyes wide. He abruptly removed the gold band. He set it on the table and backed away.

Europe eyed the ring and began to reach. Seeing his colleague's intention, Furcus quickly snatched it up. "It's probably not in your best interest, my friend," Ring Finger warned.

Europe furrowed his brow. Letting it go he changed the subject, "The Syrian soil samples were positive."

An elated expression brightened Furcus' face. "With the Parliament attack we will soon have cart blanch access over the region. The summit meeting was equally successful," he stated. "In the end, I suppose Mr. Graff only made it more interesting. Hmm... didn't realize how much I'd missed him."

"Still," Europe finished, "I think it's time you told me about the 'other'."

Chapter 67

ROTHERY SAT IN HIS living room lounge chair holding Rothery Wyndham Taylor the IV. His mobile phone rang on the kitchen table.

"Are you getting that, love?" his wife called from the back of their flat. Rothery didn't move.

Pamela scurried into the kitchen as the phone continued to ring, "Are you getting that?"

"Sorry, holding the baby. Just put it on silent."

The phone stopped ringing just as Pamela picked it up. As she placed it back on the table, the flat's landline, her mobile, and Rothery's mobile again, all began ringing simultaneously. "Rothery," she called out, "that must be your office calling."

Rothery sighed, slowly rising from the lounge chair. Under his breath he began to rant, "I'm not going, I'm not going! Nothing will get me to leave this house." He made his way to his phone answering abruptly, "On paternity leave!"

"He was spotted at Heathrow Airport."

"Don't care."

"They're sending everyone out; declared him armed and dangerous… don't try to apprehend alone, and all. They've said everything but 'shoot first'— no one will ask questions later."

Tilman got nothing but silence from the other end of the phone. "Rothery? Rothery? They have no intention of questioning him…"

Still silence.

"Rothery? Agent Taylor, did you hear me?"

Heavy sigh, "I heard you." More pause, "Keep me updated along the way, I'm forty-five minutes out. Heading out the door now."

Rothery kissed his wife and son goodbye and jumped into his car, the radio tuned to BBC Radio London. "A massive manhunt is under way for the man once called the Kensington Hero— now known as the Phantom Opera House Killer. He's being pursued in link to the murder of Sharon Applebee, backstage assistant, and Johnathan Nikelbaum, theater security officer, in what appears to have been a failed assassination attempt at the Royal Opera House a few nights ago. Forensic evidence and eyewitness reports put the Kensington Hero at the scene of the crime…"

Rothery shut off the radio and turned on his police scanner. The private scanner channel crackled, *"How did he get past security? Do they have an eye on him now?"* Rothery listened.

"Negative, he was lost in the crowd. We're checking every plane manifest now according to departure time."

"Cover every departure."

"Heathrow is too large."

"Which terminal?"

"He was last seen in Terminal 2."

Rothery picked up his phone and speed-dialed Tilman. "Sergeant, it's Rothery. If he's in Terminal 2, he's likely heading to Ireland or switching terminals beyond the passenger-only zone."

"Not certain what you mean…"

"He was spotted in Terminal 2 but he might take the internal terminal bus to another terminal."

"They have those covered, sir."

"You have to get to him first, Tilman. I was there. He's not a killer. If he's beyond security, he doesn't have a weapon."

After ten minutes or better, another report came over the scanner. *"Surveillance cameras spotted him boarding the express train at the Terminal 2-3 station heading to Terminal 5."*

"Stay with him."

"We can't. He was identified on surveillance camera just after the train doors shut."

"And no police are on the train?"

"The policemen had just arrived to Terminal 2. Terminal 5 was the first terminal we shut down."

Over the phone Rothery told Tilman, "Why would he leave the passenger zone to have to go back through security? How did he get past immigration?"

"What do you mean?"

"He could have taken the internal terminal bus, why didn't he? The train is on the other side of security... he'll have to go back through a security checkpoint."

"Maybe he saw all the security and bolted?" Tilman suggested.

"He's risking too much. He could have taken the express back to London in fifteen minutes; going to Terminal 5 is definite capture."

Rubbing his brow, Tilman finally responded, "The police have barricaded the express station at 5. It'll be over before you get here, agent."

Over the scanner, *"Have security cover offloading of the train upon its arrival to Terminal 5."*

"It's just arrived. We're checking now— every passenger."

Rothery drummed his fingers atop the steering wheel, checking his watch impatiently.

Ten minutes passed before voices recommenced. *"He's not here, we've checked every passenger, every car."*

"Did the train stop in route? Could he have jumped?"

"Driver says the train slows down but there's nowhere to maneuver if he had jumped."

"Send a team into the tunnel."

Twenty minutes later Rothery was pulling into passenger pick-up at Heathrow Airport Terminal 5.

* * * * *

Just as Agent Taylor was turning off his car, another report came over the scanner. *"He's changed clothes but we've got him."*

Rothery stopped to listen, opening his door but staying seated in his car. *"I'm zooming in on him now. Yes, it's definitely our boy. He's in 'World of Whisky' talking to the salesclerk. He's wearing jeans, a black sports pullover, white tennis shoes."*

"What is he doing?"

"He's bloody taking shots! Looks like Glenmorangie Signet."

"You're certain it's our boy?"

"Yes, it's definitely him."

"Is he carrying anything?"

"No. No bags, hands free. Nothing but a whiskey goblet in his right hand."

"How far out?"

"Three minutes."

"Come in from both directions, we don't want him getting away."

Tilman spoke over the phone to Rothery, "Well, that should make it a peaceful capture."

Over the scanner, *"Keep an eye on him."*

"I got him… wait… hold on. A tourist group just got in the way. I'm certain he's still there."

Rothery grabbed his radio, climbed out of the car and started to head toward the terminal entrance.

"Excuse me, sir?" An airport bus line attendant pointed at Rothery's car. "You can't park there."

Rothery waved him on without slowing down.

"SIR!" in a stern, menacing voice, "This is a BUS zone. That's the bus coming, you can't park there."

Rothery stopped.

The bus line attendant (now addressing Rothery's back) loudly warned again, "You will not only be fined, sir, but I will personally make certain your car is towed IMMEDIATELY and lost in the system."

Rothery eyed the waiting tow-truck parked at the curb a hundred yards down the pick-up lane. Reluctantly he turned around and started to pull his badge from his pocket.

Barely reaching into his jacket, the attendant shook his head, "Don't bother, mate, I don't care. Don't care if you're MI-fucking 6."

"Actually I am," Rothery frowned, showing his badge to the attendant. "You tow this car and I'll…"

"You'll what?"

Rothery, at a loss for words, "Uh… your wife will disappear."

"That's a threat? I'll give you the keys to MY car if you can make my wife disappear. But your car is moving RIGHT NOW." A bus pulled up behind Rothery's car and began honking.

"For the love of God, please! Have you not noticed there's a police manhunt taking place?"

"What I have noticed is the thirty passengers behind you that need to get to Gatwick Airport, sir, and your car is standing in their way."

"You tow my car and I'll… I'll…"

"You'll what?" the attendant glared.

"Bloody hell, keep the car!" Unwilling to waste time on the distraction, Rothery threw the man his keys.

Turning back toward the entrance in frustration, the agent ran smack into the relief bus driver heading toward the now waiting Gatwick express bus. "Excuse me," the driver said impatiently with a hand on his cap. His head bowed as he quickly shuffled his way past Rothery.

"Unbelievable," Rothery muttered, running a hand over his face as he headed into the terminal.

The bus line attendant greeted the relief driver saying apologetically, "Sorry about that, mate. Are you going to be able to get around this wanker's car?"

"I'll manage. Thanks Felix, that was close." The driver chuckled as he went to relieve the driver exiting the Gatwick bus.

Felix called after him, "Hey, it's nice to see you… stop by and see ME next time you're in town!"

"Will do, Felix!" The relief driver waved as he jumped onto the waiting bus then greeted the departing driver, "Hey Charlie, have a good break."

Charlie handed off his official bus driver's cap, "Take care of her, it's my job on the line if she gets a scratch."

* * * * *

As Rothery walked into the terminal, over the police radio he heard, *"He's gone. He's not here."*

"Did you cover both entrances?"

"Yes, we couldn't have missed him."

"Aren't there two World of Whiskeys in Terminal 5?"

"Yes, I believe there is a small store near the B gates."

"Where is the tourist group now?"

"They must have left the store right before we got here."

Rothery picked up the radio and chimed in, "What did their hats say?"

"What hats?"

"The tourists. I assume they were all wearing matching hats or you wouldn't have called them a tourist group."

"I don't know."

"Where's the video screening room, I want to see the footage," Rothery demanded.

"Please keep this channel free…"

"Where's the bloody booth?!" Rothery yelled into the radio.

Just then Tilman caught up with Rothery in the departure hall, "I'll show you, sir."

Radio continuing, *"Keep checking every departure."*

Rothery was pacing pensively— not running to the screening booth, not heading to the gate, not going anywhere.

"You don't want to get to the gates, agent?" Tilman ventured.

Rothery stood there tapping his foot, looking to the ceiling, breathing heavily. He was clearly agitated. The two men didn't move for almost ten minutes.

Rothery contemplated; biting his lip, squinting, winking, blowing out his cheeks. He finally folded his arms and sat down on a bench seat in the huge check-in hall. Still tapping his foot he was now nodding his head back and forth to the beat of an unheard nursery rhyme.

Tilman grew more and more anxious to get back in the game. He scanned every passerby as if hoping for a machine generated lottery ticket to actually pay off. He got up many times, started to walk away; but he knew far too well that staying with Agent Taylor was his best bet for a win.

Finally sitting down next to Rothery, Tilman joined in the foot tapping. He kept his legs bent, feet underneath him, tapping with the heels of his feet against the support bar beneath the bench. He, too, had his arms crossed but kept his head still, only moving his eyes right to left then left to right to the beat of the rhyme. He inspected everyone.

Finally Rothery stopped. He raised a brow, dawned a silly look, exhaled. He lifted his finger and finally spoke, "Any minute now they are going to spot him at Terminal 4."

"Why, where's he headed?" Tilman asked.

Rothery folded his arms and returned to tapping his feet.

No more than a minute later over the radio, *"I've got him. He just entered a restroom in Terminal 3."*

Rothery slowly picked up the radio transceiver, "Do you have eyes or surveillance camera on him?" he asked.

"Camera. We don't have surveillance in the restroom but I'll pick him back up when he comes out."

Rothery jumped to his feet, "Let's go." He started to head to the door.

"Wait," said Tilman pointing, "we can catch the internal bus to Terminal 3 over there. It's faster."

"We're not going to Terminal 3."

"We're not?"

"No. He's not here. He's flying out of Gatwick Airport."

*   *   *   *   *

Micah screeched the bus to an abrupt stop with both feet on the hydraulic brake, grinded the gears attempting to put it into neutral. At last killing the engine with a jerk, it did everything but a backfire. Chuckling, Micah announced over the bus intercom in a British accent, "Last stop, Gatwick International Airport. Please be sure to take all of your belongings with you when you depart."

Micah got off the bus and threw his cap to an approaching driver. "Hey again, Charlie. Get a couple of smokes in on the way?"

"You, my friend, are a TERRIBLE driver. Scared the holy hell out of me! I thought you were going to lose it on the M4 exchange." Charlie shook his head, "I'll always remember what you did for me, Micah, but from now on, we are even."

"Charlie, seriously… it was fun this way, wasn't it? Don't be upset."

Charlie gave Micah a menacing frown which relented into a smile. "You take care of yourself, old friend."

"Thanks, Charlie. Come and visit some time."

"God willing."

Micah walked into Gatwick Airport and headed straight to the restroom. Carelessly knocking the swinging door into another man coming out, Micah barely slowed down.

"You in a hurry, fella?" the other man said.

"Sorry, didn't mean to inconvenience you."

"That's what you always say." The stranger shook his head and tucked something in Micah's outer coat pocket.

Micah smiled and quickly entered a stall. Minutes later, he headed to the security line.

∗   ∗   ∗   ∗   ∗

The stranger walked out the main international terminal door of Gatwick Airport. Walking down a ways, he took a seat on a bench next to a tall gentleman working on a laptop.

The man on the bench nodded, "Dale."

"Kip. Was that Charlie?"

"Yep."

"Still drives bus?"

"Yep."

Dale nodded. "You know, the way you say my name sounds funny."

"Yep."

"Hmm."

"He get out?" Kip asked.

"Well, he has my phone, passport, wallet and credit cards. Either you'll be getting a text from him shortly or the police will be dragging his ass out that front door fairly soon. He's got fifteen minutes to make it to the gate but he'll be able to fast-track. By the way, nice of you to set that up for me, Kip."

"Wasn't for you, Dale."

Dale frowned and changed the subject, "You got any games on that computer?"

Kip laughed, "Oh yeah, I've been playing one all morning."

Dale leaned over Kip's shoulder. There were multiple live video feeds running across the laptop screen. Dale squinted, "Is that Heathrow?"

"Yep. Watch this... count of three as soon as that guy moves... and... switch!" the screen displayed a new version of the same location.

Dale laughed, "When did you film that?"

"It's footage I pulled from eight months ago, the last time he was in country—actually, the last two times he was here. Now listen to the scanner. Wait, it takes them a couple seconds to see him."

Over the scanner was heard, *"I got him... he's in terminal 4, women's lingerie. Probably buying something for Ms. Adams."*

"How are you hearing Heathrow Airport security over your scanner?"

"I had Felix put a long-range repeater on the roof of the bus line booth."

"You should publish that game, you'd make a fortune."

Kip chuckled, "So, Dale, how are you getting out?"

"Don't know."

Kip sighed. He reluctantly offered, "I could probably get you out next Tuesday. You can stay in the room."

Dale scoffed, "With you? No thanks."

Kip bit his lip. Mumbling under his breath, "Hate that guy."

A voice suddenly came from behind the two men. "Mr. Holland."

Kip shut his laptop and turned around. He squinted a long ponder then questioned a guess, "Agent?"

"Nice of you to remember."

"Well, it's not every day I get a double-aught spy in my store."

"Double-aught, huh? I had someone else call me that this very same week."

"It's a common phrase."

"Is it?"

Kip's phone dinged with a received text message. "Beg your pardon, agent. If you don't mind, I need to take this." Kip read the message and took his time responding. When he was done, he casually returned his attention back to Rothery. "You were saying, agent?"

"Oh, please," Rothery offered, "don't mind me. Go ahead with your call."

"It was a text message."

"Of course. Everything get out alright?"

Kip's phone sounded again. He held up a finger, "Another moment, officer?" Rothery nodded.

Finished with the second message, Kip tucked the phone into his pocket. "Right. So sorry. You were saying?"

Rothery spoke slowly, "Did everything get out alright?"

"Oh, just fine, agent," Kip smiled. "Everything is just *fine*."

"I'm glad to hear it. Do you come to the airport often, Mr. Holland?"

"I like watching the planes."

With a sense of peace, Rothery absently ran his hand across the rough surface of the bench. "I don't even notice them anymore."

Kip smiled big. Pointing to a plane taking off, "See, agent? There's one leaving now."

Rothery didn't even bother looking up.

THE END

Character Endorsements

"It reads like a movie... too bad Harrison Ford is too old to play lead."
— *William Cleese*

"A character driven story... the dialog is as good as it gets."
— *Carol Cummings, Sky News Morning Edition*

"It has everything including my kitchen sink."
— *Pamela Taylor, author*

"I can neither confirm nor deny the events in question."
— *George Morison, Deputy Liaison to the US Ambassador to the UK*

"Dekanu has a vivid imagination. We'll be keeping a close eye on him ... and his children."
— *RF Furcus, entrepreneur and political lobbyist*

"I wonder if Victoria will play herself in the movie."
— *Joan Perpedex, nurse / actress*

"The attention to historical British accuracy made for an intelligent read. Though I prefer Suntory 18 over Jura 21."
— *Nigel T. Butler*

"Dekanu should stick to Comical Suspense Thrillers, the poetry atop of Chapter 43 was cheesy."
— *Frank, the Register Guard anchor*

"I liked the poetry..."
— *Kevin, the Guard cameraman*

"You would."
— *Henry Wilkins*

"Can I say something here?"
— *Pete, publishing editor for the Register Guard*

"No!"
— *the Entire Guard Staff*

"The artistically woven political savvy of Inevitable Coincidence is a credit to the rightly elected and honorable hard working civil servants of Her Majesty's government. We may not always get it right the first time, but ..."
— *CCP Evans, Chief Crown Prosecutor*

"Bloody Hell . . ."

— *Henry Wilkins*

"I can neither confirm nor deny..."

— *George Morison*

"We heard it the first time, George."

— *Lawrence Philips, Chief Superintendent Scotland Yard*

"He's only attempting accuracy. Clear communication requires concise, accurate and fully descriptive sentences, don't you agree, Lawrence?"

— *Helen Goff, Scotland Yard Medical Examiner*

"But George didn't even make the uncut version of the book."

— *Chief Philips*

"How did I not make the cut but Denise did?"

— *George Morison*

"That's D'neese, and that should tell you something."

— *Denise, Avis Lead Sales Associate*

"Manners, people."

— *Mrs. Goff*

"Yes, Mrs. Goff."

— *Everyone*

"I disagree with Henry Wilkins on about everything. Inevitable Coincidence has more than five brilliant characters."

— *Sara Jennings, Producer/Reporter from the Guard*

"Thank you, dear."

— *Mrs. Goff*

"You're welcome."

— *Sara Jennings*

"I was never in London."

— *Ariel Shachar (a.k.a. Allen Steinbeck)*

Made in the USA
San Bernardino, CA
03 March 2019